Saving the Magic Kingdom

SAVING THE Magic Kingdom

A Novel

JEFF DIXON

Magic PRESS
AN IMPRINT OF MORGAN JAMES PUBLISHING

NEW YORK

LONDON • NASHVILLE • MELBOURNE • VANCOUVER

Saving the Magic Kingdom

A Novel

Published in New York, New York, Magic Press, an imprint of Morgan James Publishing. Morgan James is a trademark of Morgan James, LLC. www.MorganJamesPublishing.com

Proudly distributed by Publishers Group West®

ISBN 9781636984957 paperback
ISBN 9781636984964 ebook
Library of Congress Control Number: 2024936697

Cover & Design by:
Christopher Kirk
www.GFSstudio.com

What Would Walt Disney do?

That question is one that has been asked by people from all walks of life with various degrees of connection to the Disney Company. Fans have used the question through the years as the evaluation standard of a Walt Disney Picture, whether a live action feature or an animated film. Inevitability in judging it, the question whether or not Walt Disney would have done it in some particular way is asked. Is it a motion picture that Walt Disney would have greenlighted? Would Walt Disney approved of the soundtrack? Would Walt Disney have added additional sight gags? Would Walt Disney have created more emotion in the finale? What Would Walt Do or WWWD becomes the standard in evaluating a film.

The same criteria is used in any of the Disney named destinations across the globe. Guests of theme park resorts ask the same question. In every expansion or opening of a new attraction, the WWWD standard is applied. In other words, the criteria for judging the value of the attraction is always done with thought to whether or not the new thing is worthy of carrying the Disney name and brand. The same standard is applied with greater intensity when a familiar or long operating attraction is closed and removed in a themed resort. The WWWD question gets emotional for people when a loved and revered classic attraction is changed or permanently disappears. More often than not, the answer is an emphatic, *Walt would not like it...* and that conclusion is followed by an exclamation point and a lament that somehow Walt Disney would never have changed a beloved part of the theme park's history.

Inevitably the question or standard also shows up in the conversations that swirl around the corporate side of the Disney Company. This usually manifests itself in some type of concern on the direction of the company. There will always be pundits making commentary and scrutinizing the messaging done in the Disney brand and product. The inevitable discussions about company leadership, decisions, and vision for the future emerge. Never too far removed from the business questions is how well the stock prices are doing and how the quarterly and annual report will impact the bottom line for the stockholders and the Board of Directors.

Of course, the answer to the WWWD question is impossible, but it is not improbable to ponder. The history of the company since the passing of Walt and his brother Roy is one that is well documented. Like any iconic corporation the ups and downs have been discussed, recorded, and analyzed. If nothing else, the Walt Disney Company is a model that is often studied, researched, and explored. As stated a few sentences ago, the WWWD question is impossible to answer but it can be pondered because we have such a rich history of the life and times of Walter Elias Disney available for our research.

In just a few moments we are going to take a fictional journey into the world of Disney but before we do let's anchor our fiction to some facts and see what conclusions we can find that will launch us into our story. To accomplish this we need to go back into history and see a moment in the life of Walt Disney.

The Moment

In an interview with Pete Martin for a series of articles originally given for *The Saturday Evening Post* in 1956, Walt Disney offered up this account.

"I feel sympathetic toward Roy because he has to sit with the bankers. He has to sit with the stockbrokers who come in and harass you and say, 'I haven't turned any Disney stock in six months now. Do something so I can turn it and make a profit.'

"I used to tell Roy, 'You've got to get away from those guys. They'll beat you down.'

"He always wants me to come to the annual stockholder's meeting. There's nothing I can do there. It's a formality. We give 'em a report, tell 'em what we've got, and that's it. Who's sitting out there? Just representatives of brokerage houses and financial reporters. And maybe some little character who likes to attend stockholders' meetings like some people go to funerals. My real stockholders aren't out there."

That summarized the attitude that Walt had toward meetings with stockholders, boards, and others who bogged down in the bottom line of running a company. One particular year, when the company's fortune, finances, and future seemed particularly low, Roy urged, nudged, and convinced Walt to attend the meeting.

Walt addressed the meeting, "I don't know how many of you out there are stockholders. I've got a letter I want to read to you. It's from a lady in Florida. She writes: 'Dear Mr. Disney. I'm a Disney stockholder and I'm very happy to be one. I don't care if you ever pay any dividends. I just hope you go on doing the fine work you've been doing.'"

Walt dramatically folded up the letter. Put it away, securing it into a place firmly hidden in his pocket, and said: "Now that's the kind of stockholder I like. It's been very nice to appear before you. Now if you don't mind, I'd like to go back and try to get this company on its feet."

Walt summarized his brief speech and encounter with those at the meeting by describing the room when he was done. "They were all dead pan. Don't ever try for a laugh at a stockholder's meeting."

As Walt laughed as he shared that story, it should be noted that a copy of that letter was never found. It is not a part of the official Walt Disney Archives and is not on display at the Walt Disney Family Museum. There will be some that question whether or not that letter really did exist, but it ensured that Roy Disney would never insist on his brother making appearances at any stockholder's meeting in the future.

Walt was emphatic about the waste of time those meetings were for him. He had no desire to sit for hours discussing or digesting financial reports. He truly believed his time was best spent doing other things. As threats would rise from time to time as stock prices dipped, and the prices did dip and there were usually threats of lawsuits from stockholders, Walt would face those with the same tough determination that he brought into the studio. He would invite anyone who wanted to sue him to do so with the promise that he was doing what he thought he should do. It was his name on the company and the decisions being made were in the best interests of the company, not for any individual stockholder.

Walt Disney firmly believed in doing the right thing for the right reasons.

And that may be the answer to the question – what would Walt do?

There was a right way to do things and there were reasons to do things the right way. That mattered to Walt and that is what he wanted to get right. Walt believed that his guests would respect the effort and when they did things well, it would create a friend that would want to come back and experience it over and over again. And Walt also believed that people paid attention to detail and that doing things with excellence was always the best plan. That commitment to quality was driven by the desire to make sure his name, the Disney name, the Disney brand would always be thought of as being the best. The attitude of Walt Disney that we see in those three moments are the same values that have allowed moments experienced by those who love Disney to become memories that will last a lifetime. Walt Disney has become a part of the fabric and fiber of family memories and holds an important place in the hearts and minds of many. The commitment to quality has added value to the lives of others.

This novel is best known as "faction" or factual fiction. The novel itself is an adventure that hopefully will take the reader on a thrilling romp through the amazing world that Walt Disney created, and that world will serve as the backdrop. The places and things mentioned in this story are real. The reader can go and find many of them for themselves and enjoy them on any visit to Central Florida and the Walt Disney World Resort. And the reader is enthusiastically encouraged to do so.

This story was originally dreamed up in a global pandemic. Those days have been dark days for people worldwide. Lives have been lost, people have grown ill, businesses have been decimated, and the lives of people have been radically altered. Over the course of the pandemic, The Disney Company shut down theme parks across the planet and have reemerged in a post pandemic environment. The Walt Disney World Resort is different now. In the early days of reopening the parks, guest service and the high quality guest experience delivered by cast members had been replaced with the constant badgering of guests to wear masks properly, followed by the threats of security removing the guests if they didn't. "Have a magical day" was replaced with "cover your face." Masks were worn in every WDW location, although Florida did not have a mask mandate.

As the largest employer in the State of Florida, Disney began massive furloughs and then layoffs as the COVID-19 coronavirus blasted its way across the landscape. Disney worldwide has downsized, people have lost jobs, and the once full Disney properties have become much less glamorous, with Walt Disney World in Orlando, Florida being the only one that is showing signs of its previous glory days. As career cast members were let loose from their jobs with either a definitive termination or a vague furlough, not knowing when they would return, the highest level Disney executives also took pay cuts. Some took deep cuts in the annual salaries and many did not receive bonuses as has been the pattern in years past. Although criticized by many for compensation packages that were awarded, the numbers were less than they had been previous years and reflected an attempt to respond to the serious cuts that were being made company wide.

The numbers for the company are staggering. Whether it is the number of tourists who did not make their trek to Walt Disney World, whether it is the numbers used to determine park capacity, whether it is the number of people whose jobs have forever disappeared, whether it is the number of people whose future still remains in limbo, whether it is the economic impact of the Disney struggle on the Central Florida region, each whether has become another factor in the storm the company is attempting to weather. Slowly there is a new normal settling across the Disney Empire, heavily influenced by culture and trying to find the best ways to move forward.

As always, the inevitable WWWD question has emerged in articles, among fans, in social media outlets, and news organizations. The question has no answer, because there has never been a global pandemic that any individual or company has had to endure like the COVID-19 virus. But before we simply shrug our shoulders and give everyone a fast pass, which is not to be confused with a Disney FastPass+, which is another element of the company that disappeared in the post pandemic world, we can go back and remember what Walt Disney reflected as being important as a leader. Walt would do things with quality. There was a right way to do things and there were reasons to do things the right way. The pandemic would have been a challenge but he would have wanted to get it right. Walt would have aggressively been thinking about and working to do things that would get the resorts ready for the time when his guests could return. Walt also believed that people paid attention to detail and that doing things with excellence was always the best plan. That would have equated to doing things that would associate his name, the Disney name, into the conversation on how to be a leader in keeping the company moving and bringing the company back from the pandemic. We can know that based on his track record and the moments we have in history of how he led, even in the midst of a crisis. History will reveal how well or how poorly the current leadership of the company has done during these interesting days. Many are not satisfied and there is a high level of disappointment from those who expected or at least hoped that Disney would emerge as a leader. No matter what the rebound in the days ahead will look like and I believe it will come, it is safe to say that Disney has not been a leader it has simply been a reactor to the circumstances that have surrounded it. They have simply had to ride out the storm. Many had hoped they would leverage their brand, influence, and power to lead through it, it has not been easy for them, just like it has been difficult for so many others.

In leadership conversations, I often get to encourage leaders to be thermostats, not thermometers. A thermometer can give you an accurate temperature of the environment you are currently in and that is tremendously useful. But a thermostat can change the climate of the environment and impact the temperature that will affect all around you. It is not easy to lead on any given day. It is even more difficult to lead in a crisis. So, in this work of fiction, I have the very easy luxury of creating the world in which I can be the thermostat. I will control the environment, the events, the characters, and the flow of the action. In doing so, I have done my best to create a world where the fictional characters will faithfully attempt to answer the WWWD question with an outlook toward the future.

It is against that backdrop that this book, Saving the Magic Kingdom is written. It is easy to be a thermostat when you are the author of a fictional work, but let me remind you, this is a work of faction. One where fact and fiction will blend together and when we are done, you might wonder which is which. What I do hope is that you will have a great time on this adventure. I also hope that in the days ahead people will flock back to not only Walt Disney World but all of the Disney properties across the globe. I have great hope that they will truly save the Magic Kingdom and rediscover the art of storytelling (and how to effectively manage the company.) Some of the best news ever will be to hear, there are no rooms available at the Walt Disney World Resort and there is no more room because theme parks have reached their capacity. A capacity that occurs because there are people in every room and the resort if filled to the brim. That will be a great day indeed.

This work if fiction is built upon the backdrop and the facts stated in the paragraphs preceding it – enjoy the adventure.

Wrapped inside each moment there is unimaginable potential. I suppose that is what makes each moment so mysterious. Within that mystery you can forever make history. A moment can be small enough to be ignored but the very same moment might be big enough to change your life forever. You have to choose to unwrap the moment or choose to let the miracle in the moment remain hidden. The choice of what to do with (and in) the moment are yours.

What will you choose?

–Jeff Dixon

Facts can be annoying and easily forgotten

In 1947, Admiral Richard E. Byrd, aboard the command ship ice-breaker Northwind, led 4,000 military troops from the US, Britain and Australia in an invasion of Antarctica called Operation Highjump. Operation Highjump was rumored to be a covert US military operation to conquer secret underground Nazi facilities in Antarctica. This has always been denied by the US Military.

As Germany was defeated at the end of World War II, a select group of military personnel and scientists executed a plan as Allied troops swept across Europe. This plan found the Germans mounting submarine expeditions to Antarctica, shipping important objects and important people to secure the future of the Fourth German Reich after the failure of the Third German Reich. These secret bases established on the frozen continent provided storehouses for secret research materials, stolen artwork, precious treasures, research, and items of value that Hitler began to hide when faced with the failure of the Third Reich.

Heinrich Himmler, was obsessed with the occult and the power it might possess to help Germany accomplish its darkest goals. His commitment and zeal to the effort rivaled that of Adolph Hitler. Himmler was known to make replicas of some of the priceless treasures and as the Reich began to collapse began an intricate plan to smuggle original objects of value to secret bases in Antarctica. Included in the inventory of items was potentially the most powerful relic in their possession, one so important to Himmler that he kept one of the replicas in his own personal office, known as the Spear of Destiny.

Antarctica at that time was largely unexplored, difficult to get to, and even more difficult to survive in. As a location, it was thought to be the perfect place to wait and relaunch an attempt at global domination. A *New York Times* article from July of 1945 mentions and documents a secret Nazi Antarctic haven in the frozen region along with reports of crew members of German vessels depositing valuable treasures in the secret installation. Discovering and securing this base was one of the officially denied objectives of Admiral Bird's Northwind.

The Spear of Destiny was the artifact that if successfully smuggled into Antarctica, might be the key to launch a Fourth Reich. Hidden away aboard a U-boat that traveled down the Eastern coast of the United States, this spear along with other precious treasures was bound for its deep freeze holding home in Antarctica. However, the U-boat never reached its intended destination. It was sunk off the coast of Florida, where the bulk of the submarine still rests at the bottom of the Atlantic Ocean to this day.

Despite reports of the Spear of Destiny being located in the Vatican or in Vienna, it is believed that these are actually replicas that were commissioned by none other than Heinrich Himmler. According to legend- *He who holds the Spear of Destiny is invincible. He who loses the spear loses his life.* Somewhere in the depths off the coast of Central Florida, the Spear of Destiny was lost into a watery graveyard of twisted metal.

Buttered Popcorn

Chapter One

Day One-Early Morning

Shadows flickered on the floor of the Royal Anandapur Forest as the last streaks of sunlight fought their way through branches of the trees that reached upward to brush the evening sky. Some days' time flew. On other days it crawled at a snail's pace. This was a crawling day, thought Elliot Drayton, or perhaps a sloth's pace might be more fitting. Elliot pushed back a strand of spider web that clung to his face, then shook his hand violently trying to get the wispy strand of web to dislodge. He was tired, and had hoped his day was almost over, but when he had counted, there was still one missing. So here he was, hiking through the jungle toward the ruins of the royal hunting lodge.

Elliot looked at the crumbling structure in front of him and smiled knowing it was not really crumbling at all. He knew the story by heart. The rajahs of Anandapur had once hunted tigers in the forest. King Bhima Disampati had by decree designated the forest as a preserve with only the royal family and their invited guests allowed to be there. That had happened in 1544, the same year he commissioned the construction of the Royal Hunting Lodge in the forest. In an elaborately designed work of architecture, he enclosed a portion of the forest within the walls of the lodge. Then luring tigers inside, they could easily be captured and killed.

Elliot rolled his shoulders back repulsed by the thought. According to lore, the king's clever plan to trap tigers had proved to be a fatal mistake when he was killed during a tiger hunt. In the years after his death, the king's successors had worked to protect wildlife before eventually leaving the lodge abandoned. In 1948, the British at the end of their rule, gave the Royal Forest back to the people of Anandapur. Following in the footsteps of those that had followed King Bhima Disampati, the people turned the ruins and surrounding areas into a nature preserve dedicated to protecting the tigers and other wildlife that remained.

It was a rich history and one that Elliot had repeated more times than he could remember to guests along the Maharajah Jungle Trek in Walt Disney's Animal Kingdom. The elaborate backstory had been created along with one of the most detailed backdrops that theme park explorers could see every day. As tourists walked along the trek, they could gaze through glass openings in the ruins and look out into tiger enclosures where they could see the tigers move about freely. Three different tiger habitats can be seen with one that allows guests to cross over a bridge past the ruins of the Tomb of Anantah, the first ruler and founder of Adandapur. The Red Temple which was built by one of Bhima's successors became the final resting place of Anantah when his sarcophagus was placed there.

Elliot always enjoyed regaling the guests with the legend of Anantah, who cut down the sacred tree and upset the balance of nature. After a devastating season of natural disasters, he had to learn to replant, preserve, and live in balance with nature. Elliot would always stress the importance of learning that lesson and reminding guests that we should never worship nature but instead learn to be good caretakers of it. His role as a cast member at Walt Disney World had started nearly twenty years ago, but he got great fulfillment in his role as an animal keeper at Animal Kingdom, specifically because he got to work with such a wide variety of creatures in one of the most unique animal observatories in the world.

As much as he liked his job, today had just been a long day and now here he was moving through the Anandapur Forest looking for a tiger that had decided to disappear. Elliot reached down to his waist and loosely gripped the container of spray that he would use to repel the tiger if he needed to do so. The special blend of pepper spray would not hurt the animal but might cause the tiger to not be so eager if was inclined to attack him. On the other hip was the tranquilizer weapon, a cross between a pistol and short hunting firearm, especially designed to use in extreme emergencies. In his hand he carried what he always described as a cross between a walking stick and a ski pole, usually just enough gentle humane persuasion to convince an animal to move if they had the initial desire not to do so. Most people never realized that many zoos, in order to get accreditation, have to train emergency personnel on how to handle dangerous animal situations. This bit of information was never included in the brochures and managed to hide deep within the offerings of search engines. Elliot knew when you worked in the area of preservation and protection of wildlife, there would always be tension when you had to take extreme measures to protect those who cared for the protected. It was complicated and some people never could justify why it was needed, but he was a member, albeit an unwilling member of the Disney DART team. The Dangerous Animal Response Team that spent most of their time trying to distract and redirect animals that experienced some type of difficulty in getting along with others in their environments.

The animals in Animal Kingdom responded to audible calls that prompted them to return to their enclosures where they were fed and cared for each night, only to be released into much more expansive enclosures, especially created for guests to experience and interact with them during the daylight hours. The guests were gone and when the Sumatran tigers were called to their enclosures for the evening, there was one who had not come back.

Elliot thought about this male tiger, Saber, who admittedly had not been exhibiting his usual healthy tiger behavior as of late. As he slowly moved into an area of the Red Temple that Saber liked to relax in, he remembered that a month ago there had been some concern when Saber had experienced an unexpected and unusual thickening of his nose and foot pads. The tiger had been examined, watched, and there had seemed to be nothing else out of the ordinary, so Saber had been allowed to roam the Royal Anandapur Forest habitat. This was the first time that Saber had not returned at the end of the day when called and Elliot was concerned and had made the decision to enter the habitat and look for him.

Standard protocol would have had another cast member, more than likely two cast members with him, but since the pandemic and the recovery from it, there had been some things that they as a cast had done differently. There had been extended months where the normal routine had been changed because there had been no guests allowed in the theme parks. Reese Bolin had been on the schedule to work alongside him today, but Reese had taken a sick day, apparently he was not feeling well. No surprise, Resse had been missing a lot of shifts as of late and was rumored to be next on the furlough parade.

Elliot pursed his lips, paused and listened for any sound near him. As he cautiously moved next to the edge of the temple ruins, he grew more concerned than he had been when he entered the forest because he had anticipated finding Saber quickly and coaxing him back to his nighttime enclosure. Elliot knew he was now nowhere close to the entrance of the enclosure and he was moving through the heart of the tiger habitat.

The scent of buttered popcorn drifted past Elliot's nose. He strained to process the smell. Over five million bags of popcorn are popped every year at the Walt Disney World Resort. A cast member who worked as a popcorn vendor in the Magic Kingdom had once described it as three hundred and forty-five thousand pounds of buttery goodness, or over a thousand pounds of popcorn a day being popped at Walt Disney World. But there should not have been any popcorn here, near the temple ruins.

Elliot froze and felt his teeth bite down slightly into his bottom lip. His finger slowly crept down toward the canister on his hip. The member of the Disney DART team rescued some snippet of information from his mental storage bin that now screamed at him to act. Deciding to forgo the spray can he made the choice to reach toward the weapon instead. To do so, he released the walking stick and it clanged against the rocky stone flooring of the temple. Until this very moment, he had always thought it was an interesting fact and something that most didn't know about tigers. The smell that emits from tiger's urine smells like buttered popcorn, which is a warning sign to any intruder that you were now very close to a carnivore. Elliot reached for the weapon as he turned his head and looked directly into the face of a snarling Saber.

The Tiger King

CHAPTER TWO

Day One – Early Morning

Juliette Keaton's brain was hammering through the tally list of all the things that could have gone wrong. The dark thoughts of dread blocked out the appreciation of the beautiful dawning of a new day in Disney's Animal Kingdom. When Jillian Batterson had called her at five forty-five this morning, she knew something had to have been wrong. Jillian had greeted her with the words, "You need to get to the Maharajah Jungle Trek in the zoo," Juliette had snapped into full consciousness. Trying not to wake her husband Tim, she allowed her two children and the love of her life to enjoy those last few hours of sleep that had suddenly been snatched from her. Scurrying about to get ready, Juliette knew that the call meant something was not just wrong, but something was catastrophically wrong. Jillian's clipped one sentence summons had been more than enough to put her on high alert.

It hadn't taken long for the Chairman of the Theme Park Division, her official title, to arrive at Animal Kingdom. Jillian Batterson was the Head of Security for the entire Disney Company, although her primary duties kept her very close to where the Chief Creative Officer of the Disney Company was at any given time. One of the things that Juliette liked best about Batterson is that she did not come to work for Disney as a fan. Even after a few years of leaving her job at Homeland Security for a life at Disney, she still did not always get the terminology correct and most of the time didn't even try. But when she called the theme park a zoo, Juliette had known exactly where she meant.

In the early days of Disney's Animal Kingdom the promotion department had been meticulous about differentiating DAK from a zoo. So intent were they on this that, Michael Eisner, then chairman of the company, had them create a marketing plan using the phrase – *notazoo*. Although their catch phrase has been '*notazoo*' Disney's Animal Kingdom is a leading member of the Association of Zoos and Aquariums or the AZA. The park itself is actually a theme park zoological center. As a member of AZA, the resort takes pride in caring for the animals and prides itself on being recognized as one of the best places in the world for people to see and interact with animals.

Having skipped the usual process of preparing for her day, Juliette had bypassed the usual work attire of professional dress suit, heels, and styling her hair. Instead she had settled on a jogging suit over her slender frame, running shoes, blond hair pulled back in a ponytail, and poked through the back of a running cap. Walking briskly through the foliage lined Animal Kingdom pathways, she came to the building which served as the entry of the Maharajah Jungle Trek. Glancing up she saw the newspapers stuffed into the ceiling of the building, these were there not by accident but very much on purpose, in keeping with the theme and backstory of the area, they served as an inexpensive form of insulation as one might expect to see in the geographical region the attraction was based upon. Her eyes searched until she found the newspaper that most guests would never notice, it was the front page of the *Orlando Sentinel*, the Central Florida newspaper, which commemorated the day it was discovered that Walt Disney was bringing his latest dream to Florida. As land was being acquired at an unprecedented rate there was much speculation on who the purchaser was. October 24, 1965 the paper ran the headline "We Say: Mystery Industry is Disney" announcing to the world that Florida was about to become the new home of Walt Disney and company. The paper goes unnoticed by the guests that march through the entrance building but usually gave her reason to pause and smile. However the morning paper on this day did not accomplish that, instead she was already building strategies as how to best manage whatever complication she was about to walk into. She was convinced that the morning news this day was not good news at all. Reminding herself to relax, she calmed herself by allowing her surroundings to immerse her into the world she had now entered.

Making her way deeper into the jungle trek she rolled her shoulders attempting to loosen her neck muscles. Juliette felt them growing tighter as she moved past the murals that told the stories of the maharajahs who once lived there. The powerful storytelling was a cautionary tale. Her stride quickened as she went past the first of a prince who felt it was his place to control the natural world. Next to him there was a prince who cared only for the material world. As the balance between man and nature broke down, a third prince attempted to regain some sort of order, as the fourth prince allowed nature to take over as he left the palace to live in the surroundings. One of the difficulties for her as the head of the theme park division was to find ways to balance how to best care for nature and still provide the parameters for the corporate side of the equation to work. Usually, if something went wrong, it was because something had gotten out of balance. The jungle trek has completely taken over the ruins of the hunting palace and she now crested the bridge giving her the first look at what was going on.

Looking out into the animal habitat, she could see a swarm of people moving about the area. It appeared the edge of the temple ruins was the center of their attention. There was something there, on the ground, but what it was she could not yet see. Juliette felt the throb of her heartbeat in her tight neck as she caught a glimpse of Jillian standing next to the team of people. Jillian looked up and caught her eye, shook her head grimly side to side, and waved for Juliette to step off the pathway and join them.

The cast member door, well camouflaged was slightly ajar, meaning that there were no animals currently released into the area. She knew this was the tiger exhibit and normally guests would line the walkways and view the tigers roaming about through Plexiglas or from an elevated bridge. Just as she was about to move through the doorway another body banged into hers coming from the other side. Both retreated a step backward and both had emerged from the collision unharmed.

"I'm so sorry." The cast member, dressed in safari uniform, said with concern. "I didn't know anyone was on the other side of the door."

"Not a problem." Juliette glanced at the cast member finding the name badge. "Kevin, I didn't know you were coming through the door either."

Kevin tilted his head and recognition washed across his face. Smiling ear to ear, he held out his hand to shake Juliette's.

"I didn't recognize you." Kevin spoke quickly. "You are Juliette Keaton. Normally you are dressed, er... well, a bit..."

"Differently? More put together? Professionally?" Juliette filled in the missing words as she smiled.

Rarely did cast members get to see her when she was not at work in the resort. Baseball cap and a sweat suit was definitely not the norm.

"That's not what I mean." Kevin stammered slightly.

"I'm Juliette," she said grasping his extended hand and greeting him with a handshake. "Juliette Keaton. I am the…"

"You are the head of our theme park division. I know." Kevin said, releasing the grip. "I'm Kevin Grey, I work here." He gestured to the area surrounding them. "And I am so sorry to have to meet you like this. I'm a big fan, really I am. And what you did for us all during the virus days, well… I can't thank you enough."

"It has been a tough time. I'm glad our team was able to help, but there are a lot of people who have worked hard to keep things going. Thank you for hanging in there." Juliette stepped to the side to move away.

Nodding, Kevin's momentary enthusiasm at meeting her seemed to fade. Looking back toward the doorway, he bowed his head slightly.

"It is too bad, I have no words." Kevin said softly.

Juliette could see the sadness etched in the corner of his eyes.

"If you will excuse me, I need to go." Juliette said politely.

Kevin stepped back and pushed the door giving her room to pass. Sliding through the opening, she now stepped off into a backstage area that she knew would allow her to wind her way to where the activity was taking place. Picking up her pace she made her way down the pathway. She stopped abruptly as Jillian had worked her way toward the backstage area to meet her.

"Thanks for getting her so fast." Jillian said without any emotion.

"Of course." Juliette inhaled deeply, her walk was more rushed than she realized. "What's happened?"

"It's not good." Jillian reached out and placed a hand on Juliette's arm, pulling her to the side of the path.

Emergency medical professionals rushed past carrying a body board and cases of equipment.

"They are going to have to walk him out." Jillian said as they watched them move. "He is as stable as the first responders could get him, but they have to walk him out because they can't roll a stretcher back there."

Juliette immediately began making her way to follow the medical team that had just passed. "Who is it?" She said over her shoulder.

Jillian fell into step next to her and matched her stride for stride.

"A cast member named Elliot Drayton. He is an animal keeper."

Rounding the corner of the temple, Juliette slowed as her eyes raced over the terrifying sight that presented itself in front of her. There was a man, covered in blood, she assumed he had been attacked by a tiger since they were in the tiger habitat, being hoisted to a body board with an assortment of tubes, wires, and temporary bandages. The emergency medical team consisted of at least ten people, many of them now being pressed into service to carry a case, monitor, or some type of drip back. Four of the team began to move toward them with the body on the gurney. Both she and Jillian stepped back out of the way to let them pass.

"So Elliot is not dead?" Juliette's voice ended with a slightly higher pitch at the end of the sentence.

"No, he is unconscious. He has lost a lot of blood. I don't think I've ever seen that much blood lost by one person before." Jillian cleared her throat, "It doesn't look good."

"An animal attack?" Juliette asked looking back to the group of people still at the edge of the temple ruins. There was something else there that they were huddled around. "A tiger?"

"Yes, but there is something else..." Jillian's words trailed off as Juliette now had gotten close enough to see what the others were looking at.

Her mouth opened slightly as she absorbed what she now saw in front of her. Stretched out on the ground, not moving, was a full grown tiger. It was massive, or at least it looked that way because she realized she had never been that close to a tiger that wasn't behind a cage. Unmoving and being looked at by the remaining group of people, she stopped, not wanting to get closer and spoke again, not turning her gaze away from the activity in front of her.

"Has the tiger been tranquilized?" Juliette asked.

"No."

The response caused Juliette to turn to look at Jillian who had moved up beside her.

"It's dead?"

"Apparently so. At least that is what the animal keepers have assured us of." Jillian seemed content to allow the extra distance to remain between them and the big cat on the ground in front of them.

"Is that the tiger that attacked...?"

"Elliot," Jillian filled in the name allowing her to process what she was seeing.

"Yes, Elliot." Juliette looked back toward the tiger and the attendants surrounding it. "And Elliot killed the tiger?"

She watched as one of the cast members stood up and backed away from the tiger on the ground. Looking up toward them, she began to make her way up toward the pair. Juliette noticed that Jillian had not answered her question about Elliot killing the tiger. Facing her she was surprised as Jillian shrugged her shoulders slightly, indicating that she didn't know.

"This is Katie Rose." Jillian said stretching out a hand toward the approaching cast member. "She is the head of the large cat team here in the zoo and was the one who found Elliot and the cat."

"Saber," Katie extended her hand. "Saber is the name of the tiger. Been with us for years." She turned toward Jillian and completed the thought. "The tiger has a name, Saber."

"Got it." Jillian sighed deeply. "Have you figured out yet why the tiger is dead?"

"Not yet." Katie turned to look back to the animal on the ground. "It doesn't make any sense really. There seems to be no indication that Elliot did anything to Saber. If Saber attacked, then Elliot didn't fight back or even have a chance to fight back." She paused and swallowed hard. "I've never seen an animal attack that vicious before. I don't know how Elliot survived it."

"You were the one that found them?" Juliette asked.

"I did." Katie replied. "When I got here this morning I saw that Saber wasn't in the cage and then I saw the gate was unlocked into the habitat."

"Did you just walk into the area looking?" Juliette said in disbelief.

"No, no, no.... I called security, got our DART team in place...."

"DART team?" Juliette interrupted.

"Dangerous Animal Response Team," Jillian injected. "Most zoo attractions have them if an animal goes rogue or something bad happens."

"OK, and then?" Juliette looked back to Katie to finish.

"Then we moved in, ready for anything." She paused and thought for a moment. "I really just thought that someone messed up and didn't get Saber back in last night. It's never happened before but there is always a first time for everything." Another pause before she continued. "We made our way down here and saw Elliot, covered in blood and Saber next to him. We immediately called in all emergency services and we couldn't figure out why Saber wasn't moving. We were afraid to get too close to Elliot because we couldn't tell what was happening. But we realized as we got closer that Elliot was still breathing and we couldn't tell if Saber was or not, so we got ready to take care of Saber so we could get to Elliot."

"But then they discovered that the cat was dead." Jillian again entered the story.

"Yes," Katie said sadly. "Saber was dead. So we could get in to help Elliot."

"Like I said, there is no sign that anything happened to Saber or that Elliot had done anything trying to defend himself. But we are just now getting a chance to look closer, we tried to stay out of the way to get Elliot help. I want you to know that whatever happened, it is just some type of strange thing."

"Meaning?" Jillian tilted her head.

"Saber has never done anything that would hint that this could happen. And Elliot is the best, he is great with animals, and especially with tigers. We used to call him the Tiger King until that insane documentary about those crazies showed on television."

"Thanks, Katie." Juliette nodded. "Let us know when you figure out what happened to Saber."

"I will." She turned and moved away from the two women who were now watching the sheriff's department crime scene team work the area. Pictures, notes, and lots of questions were being asked of the Disney animal keepers as they tried to piece together what had happened.

"I thought you needed to get here and see this." Jillian said as neither broke off their watching the activity in front of them.

"I did." Juliette looked away from the tiger. "I'll delay the opening of the park until we can get things squared away here. We also will close the Maharajah Jungle Trek until we have some idea what happened and how it happened."

"I am planning on staying here until we get things worked out." Jillian gestured toward law enforcement and the crew of animal keepers.

Juliette turned to leave and then came up short. Turned back and took in the scene one more time. Looking back toward Jillian she said, "So we have an animal keeper that entered the tiger habitat, he gets attacked and nearly killed, the tiger ends up dead, but there is no sign of injury to the animal?"

"Right." Jillian finished the narrative. "And when they were found this morning, Elliot is unconscious bleeding out and the cat is laying there right next to him."

Silence settled between them as they both surveyed the nightmare situation before them.

"What happened here?" Juliette absently rubbed her arm.

"Don't know." Jillian began making her way toward the tiger. Stopping and turning abruptly she came back to where Juliette now stood. "But we will figure it out. There is an explanation, we'll find it."

Juliette nodded slightly in agreement. "Yes, of course. I know you will. Thanks."

Waiting on a Bell

CHAPTER THREE

Day One - Morning

The Black Bell 525 helicopter, also known as the Relentless, banked and turned in the clear Florida morning. The sleek and distinctive exterior, along with the custom paint job left no doubt what company owned and who was aboard the chopper. The two men in the car watched from a distance, hidden from ground level eyesight, and not concerned because of the distance between them and the helicopter traveling overhead.

"They say the inside cabin of that copter is a high end board room. It has oversized plush seats and is like a luxury apartment." The dark haired man, eyes hidden behind black sunglasses said.

"Great," huffed the man in the passenger seat. "That is how the other half lives."

The dark haired man glanced over at the man who had just spoken, then turned back to look skyward.

"I'd like to see it." The dark haired man continued. "I'll bet it is amazing."

The man in the passenger seat looked older than the driver. His hair a dusty brown, eyes hidden behind the same style of shades, and his weathered face sported a two inch scar down the side of his cheek. He gave off the persona of man who you would not want to mess with, at least, that is what the driver believed.

"Maybe when this is all over, you can buy it." He spoke, his voice sounded like gravel rattling in a plastic cup.

The Black Bell 525, emblazoned with the famous Disney signature logo, now slowed and hovered for a moment before descending out of the sight line of the two men behind the windshield of their vehicle.

The gravel voiced man touched the screen of his cell phone and then tapped the blue tooth device in his ear.

"Is everything ready?" The man said, still looking toward where the helicopter had been moments before.

Nodding his approval, he reached toward the gear shift and put the automobile back into drive. Tapping the gas pedal the call smoothly rolled forward. Rolling across the parking lot toward the roadway, the dark haired man studied the wooded area outside of the passenger side window.

"Do you think this will work?"

"Of course," the driver said confidently. "Today is a day that will change the future, it has to work."

Hand over hand, turning the wheel to the right, the car made the turn and then straightened out on the pavement stretching out before them. The pair fell silent in the car before the driver continued.

"It is just a matter of time and the time is now."

"And timing is everything? Right?" The passenger asked.

The driver, reached up and ran his finger along the scar on his cheek as he nodded agreement. The vehicle continued to pick up speed away from the parking lot where they had been waiting.

Welcome Home

CHAPTER FOUR

Day One - Morning

The Disney Company owned luxury helicopter, the Relentless Bell 525, had been named The Flying Mouse by the team that operated and maintained it. It was used to transport company executives in and around the state, or in this case as a shuttle back from a short trip across the state. As sleek and distinctive as the exterior of the craft was, the interior had a generous amount of space and amusing amenities. The Bell 525 has a Garmin G5000H avionic touchscreen, uses a fly-by-wire control system, and has a range of 926 km. Engineered for safety, there is space on board for fifteen passengers in the rear cabin. The cabin itself would have been described by some as a high end board room, complete with stylish interior and plush seating. On this trip there was only one man sitting alone in the rear cabin. His hands were gripping the arm rests on the leather chair tighter than he intended.

Banking sharply and putting the entire aircraft into a tilt, the passenger on board leaned to compensate and stole a glance outside the window. The aerial view of the Walt Disney World Resort was spectacular, as it always was, at least in the opinion of the one who gazed through the window. The rays of the sun stretching out across the blend of natural Florida woodlands and the amazing surprises of the Walt Disney World Resort was beautiful to behold. The aircraft came to a hover and began to make it's descent to the landing pad below. There was no doubt about it, the passenger did not like to fly. Although it was a necessary part of his job, he still tried to avoid it whenever possible. Speaking through an intercom that was linked to the pilot's headset in the cockpit, he spoke as the air ship rotated slightly giving him a view of Cinderella Castle in the distance as they began to slowly lower from the sky.

"You know Cap, these things don't really fly." Grayson Hawkes exhaled as he felt the helicopter drop.

"Of course they fly sir." Captain Vince Kirkus answered back. "We're flying now aren't we?"

Hawk, as those who knew him best called him, smiled to himself. Vince Kirkus had been the pilot of this helicopter for the company for at least two years. He always had a great attitude and was always willing to travel in a moment's notice, which in his role as a cast member was essential.

"No, this is not flying." Hawk answered back. "The helicopter is beating the air into submission."

"Whatever it takes, right?" Kirkus replied. "At least we're in the air."

Many times, Hawk had sat in the co-pilot's seat during trips. In doing so, Vince Kirkus had taught him to fly the bird, and on a few occasions had actually dosed off and taken a nap as Hawk took the controls. Hawk smiled as he thought about that, because he knew that in reality, the captain was just feigning sleep to encourage the Chief Creative Architect of the Disney Company, in his attempt to pilot a helicopter. Those trips were always fun but more often than not, Hawk had to work in the flying office space of the Relentless Flying Mouse, and this had been one of those trips.

"Cap, I was thinking that this helicopter is actually a very expensive, loose collection of parts all moving in close formation." Hawk looked toward the cockpit for a reaction. "We're always on the verge of falling out of the sky, you just don't slow down long enough for it to happen."

Kirkus looked over his shoulder toward Hawk. "Never underestimate the power of momentum, sir."

The helicopter floated from the sky and touched down on the old abandoned airport on Walt Disney World property. The Lake Buena Vista STOLport was located just to the east of the Magic Kingdom Parking area. Opened in 1971 to serve as an airfield for Walt Disney World guests and employees, a STOL airfield is an airport designed with "short take off and landing" operations in mind. In the late 60s, STOLports were envisioned as a way to transport people across towns and eliminate car and bus traffic congestion. At one time, the airport had scheduled passenger airline service to Orlando International Airport and Tampa International Airport, provided by

Shawnee Airlines. In his original dream for the Florida property, Walt Disney himself had seen an airport with four runways as a part of Epcot. The scaled back version next to the Magic Kingdom parking lot was as close as the resort had ever gotten to that part of Walt's dream. Today, although it had plenty of room to serve as a helipad, it was lined with maintenance buildings and was often used for a storage area to stage larger items needed in the never ending changes that happened at the resort.

Hawk had a helipad landing space put into the area when he found himself having to spend more time than he liked needing a way to travel quickly and get in and out of the resort without having to navigate the burgeoning Central Florida traffic patterns. Vince Kirkus had landed the Bell helicopter perfectly, as he always did, and cut off the rotors. As the whirling air beaters slowed, he had jumped out and tried to get to the door of the cabin to open it for Hawk, but was too late. Hawk had bounded out of the aircraft and was already waiting for him on the landing pad.

"You got out too quick." Kirkus said. "I was going to open the door for you."

"Not necessary. I can get the door myself, thanks." Hawk shook his hand, thanking him for the safe flight. "You need a ride?"

"No, sir." Kirkus gestured toward The Flying Mouse. "I have a few things to do to wrap up here. I have to make sure I keep all the loose parts ready to move at the same time when you need to go somewhere."

"Great!" Hawk laughed and waved as he began to walk across the pavement toward the ride that was waiting for him.

The vintage red Mustang sat in the parking area on the edge of the old abandoned runway. Opening the door and climbing into the vehicle, Hawk caught himself smiling because he was going to do something that he always tried to do when he was on the old airstrip. The runway at the STOL airport had a surprise for guests who would travel there. When landing, the grooves on the runway, similar to those you would find on the side of a highway, made noise inside the vehicle as the tires rolled over them. If you could find just the right speed, somewhere between 35 and 40 miles per hour, you would hear the song, "*When you Wish upon a Star*" serenading you as you drive.

The musical airstrip had been an idea the Imagineering Department had included as the Magic Kingdom was first opened in the early 1970s. Most people never knew there was a musical airstrip and through the years it had fallen into disrepair. Once the STOL airport was closed permanently, some of the grooves and the elaborate design had been dismantled as the area was repurposed. Hawk had found out about the original design of the runway from his old friend and mentor, Imagineer Farren Rales.

Although it was different today than it was originally built, Hawk had commissioned some work to be done to restore it as much as possible to the original state. He always felt a twinge of guilt about creating this hidden gem that most people would never get to experience. It was a perk, he realized, but he hoped it would be something that one day others would remember fondly and get to use from time to time.

Putting the car in gear, Hawk hit the gas and the automobile jumped out of the parking space and began to increase speed along the abandoned air strip. Allowing his eyes to check the speedometer, Hawk eased off the gas pedal and found the perfect speed, as the rubber of the tires met the asphalt of the runway, the notes of the song began to sound off the pavement as he rolled across it.

"One of my favorite songs." Hawk said to himself, enjoying the sweet spot of music, before he cut the wheel to the right moving onto the roadway.

Accelerating through the turn onto World Drive, the Mustang picked up speed as Hawk pondered whether he should stop by his office in the Bay Lake Towers before he headed to his home on Main Street USA. Rifling through the things he was already aware of he knew it would be best to head to the office. But it was tempting to head home and find something else to distract him before he got back to work. Moving along the road with the guest parking area of the Magic Kingdom to his left, something on the right side of the roadway caught his eye. The heavily wooded area on the opposite side of the roadway was the home to a variety of wildlife, most of the animals had grown accustomed to traffic and guests moving about their home. Something in motion along the tree line is what he had seen and as he focused in on where the movement was at, he blinked in disbelief. A bear, or what appeared to be a bear was dragging a deer next to the trees. The cinnamon colored creature had unusually lengthy hair for a bear, or so Hawk thought, and there were streaks of maple syrup colored strands of hair giving definition to the creature. Slowing the car and looking back over his shoulder, Hawk tapped the brakes to slow down the galloping Mustang from a trot to a walk before coming to a stop in the middle of World Drive. As Hawk watched with curiosity, the creature suddenly stood upright, the movement causing Hawk to squint to get a better view at what he was seeing.

Rising up to its full height, Hawk could not be sure but he guessed it was at least seven feet tall, and as it stood, the animal saw the car stopped on the road. The longer Hawk looked the more he began to doubt his original conclusion. This did not look like a bear, it was built differently, more humanlike in stature and appearance. Hawk turned the wheel on the car and pumped the gas to pull the car off the road on Timberline Trail, the road that served as the entrance to Disney's Wilderness Lodge.

Driving beneath the concrete monorail tracks, he kept his head on a swivel between the road and the woods, so as not lose sight of the big brown shape. Bringing the car to a halt, he opened the door and stepped out, looking across the roof of the Mustang toward the creature in the woods. Rubbing his eyes in an attempt to somehow make him see with more clarity, Hawk realized he had no idea what kind of creature he was looking at. It was just a big, tall, hairy creature dragging the body of a deer along the tree line.

Instinctively, Hawk walked slowly toward the front of the car and saw the creature let loose of the leg of the deer. Crouching forward slightly, the creature seemed to be studying Hawk just as much as the Chief Creative Architect was studying it. Hawk moved away from the car and took a step toward the woods. In reaction to his step toward the woods, the creature turned and stepped back into the forest, quickly disappearing from sight due to the color of his hair. Hawk broke into a sprint and raced across the grass between Timberline Trail and the woods, slowing as he neared the edge of the tree line. This was the first moment that he slowed down long enough to wonder what he was going to do if he caught the creature. Even worse, what would happen if the big bearlike animal decided to attack him? Breaking out of the jog and coming to a stop, he stood a few feet away from where the deer lay on the ground. The deer was not alive, he was certain, and it was bigger than it had looked from the road. But the big creature had seemed to drag it without much effort and Hawk took a step back and peered closely into the dense trees trying to see if the creature, whatever it was, might still be there. He could see nothing.

The breeze blew threw his mop of hair as he thought about what to do next. The snap of a limb, by the sound of it a large limb, jerked his attention to a spot deeper in the forest. It was then that he saw movement, a mass of brown hair bolted out of his sight line. Impulsively, he chose an opening and raced into the trees in pursuit. Pinecones and acorns crunched under his shoes as he tried to follow a rough pathway that wound in and out of trees and thicket. Moss dripped from the tree branches as he frequently would duck under one and then begin sprinting again. Deeper and deeper he raced forward into the trees as undergrowth reached out to grab his pants leg slowing him down as if trying to hold him back.

As the path disappeared, he pulled up and once again stopped. He had no idea how deep in the woods he had gone, how far he had run, and really what direction he had traveled. As he did so often in his life, his direction was always one way, forward. More often than not, it had worked for him, but running into the woods chasing an unknown creature, he realized may not have been his best course of action.

What are you going to do if you catch it? Hawk thought to himself. He answered his own thought with another. *You should have thought about that before you chased it into the forest.*

Sweat trailed down his back as he stood quietly, listening for any sound that seemed like it did not belong. He was deep enough in the woods now where the morning sunlight was being blocked, as if it had faded, where the shadows cast by the trees created dark vacuums of space, where anything might be hiding. The wind rustled through the trees and he heard more branches crashing to the ground. The sound came from his left, so once again he ignored his sane self that was reminding him – *You don't even know what you are chasing* – and began heading toward the source of the noise. His legs slowed allowing him to high step through the thickening undergrowth. Hawk's mind began to calculate where he might be. Natural undeveloped land was plentiful throughout the Walt Disney World Resort, which is exactly what Walt Disney had been looking for when he chose the location. Most people never realized the massive size of the entire resort. It had once been described to him as being the size of two Manhattans, it was actually a bit bigger than that. It measured over 40 square miles, and to say it was huge was an understatement. The dense wooded area he was in now was flanked by two different themed resort areas. Disney's Wilderness Lodge on one side and the expansive Fort Wilderness Campground on the other. Although they were connected by some carefully hidden roadways and service drives, for the most part, there was enough of the natural wilderness still in place for someone to get lost and turned around.

Suddenly the world smashed in from behind him. A thundering blow struck Hawk as he ducked once again to move under some tree branches. The force of the impact drove him face forward into the spongy decomposing leaves on the ground in front of him. This dirt carpet bed of forest floor met his chin, mouth and nose and he inhaled the sweet earthy smell of leaves and took in a mouthful of Florida forest. Turning to his side, he quickly inventoried what had happened and knew he wasn't hurt. The creature he was chasing however had been smart enough to circle back and catch him from behind. The surprise attack made him even more curious as to what was lurking in the woods. Rising to his knees he once again surveyed the dense mass of trees, branches, and thicket around him. Pain crackled in fine lines across his shoulders and back, he was going to be sore tomorrow. Having no idea which way the creature had gone, and not seeing any sign of it, he knew that his chase was over.

Getting back to his feet, he sighed deeply and began to orient himself to retrace his steps and get back to the car. Walking back in what he hoped was the right direction, he looked down and in a wet spot of soil on the forest floor he saw it. Blinking and shifting his body to make sure he was not casting a shadow on what he was seeing, he crouched down and with his finger traced the imprint on the ground. It was a footprint, not of a shoe, but an imprint of something that was foot-like, but it was only a partial print. The partial print that was there was massive. Longer and wider than a human foot, but distinctly different from what a bear paw might look like. Hawk reached into his pocket to use his cell phone to take a photo, but much to his surprise his phone wasn't there. Looking over his shoulder, covering the ground he had just walked over with his eyes, he didn't see it anywhere on the ground. Memory reminded him that he hadn't had his phone out of his pocket since he had begun this woodland expedition, so it probably hadn't fallen to the ground. The last time he had seen it had been on board The Flying Mouse. The phone had been sitting on the conference room table inside the helicopter and he didn't remember retrieving it when he exited the craft. Satisfied with his conclusion, he must have left it on the chopper.

Once again, he was aware of a trickle of sweat creeping down his back, he poked his tongue into his jaw and wondered what in the world he had been chasing. Whatever it was, the creature had managed to out maneuver him in the woods and attack him from behind. It was big, smart, and aggressive enough to make sure it was not going to be followed. Hawk rose to his feet and continued in the direction he had hoped would get him back to the Mustang, as he did he knew that this, whatever it was, was going to be a problem. The quicker he could figure it out and take care of it, the better for everyone.

Deep Scars

Chapter Five

Day One - Afternoon

The glistening offices of the Global News Network, or GNN, as most people knew it filled up an entire building on Broadway in New York City. Some of the sets they used for various news programming featured magnificent views of the lights, motion, and excitement of New York, although the city had been through some hard times and was finally starting to show some signs of bouncing back. People were slowly making their way into the oversized conference room for the daily production meeting. The conference room featured an exterior wall that was made of glass that gave those meeting an amazing view of the city as it stretched out below them. Flanked on both ends of the room by massive mahogany covered walls, the meeting space was prime real estate in the heart of Manhattan. Shadows moved along the wall opposite the expansive view of the city behind another wall of glass, different from the parallel counterpart as it was made of thick frosted sound-proof material. With massive video screens visible from anywhere in the room, this was the space that was used for production meetings like the one that was scheduled for this morning.

Allie Crossman, a senior producer for GNN, sent a quick text message to the reporter that she now worked exclusively with at the network, David Walker.

"Where r u?"

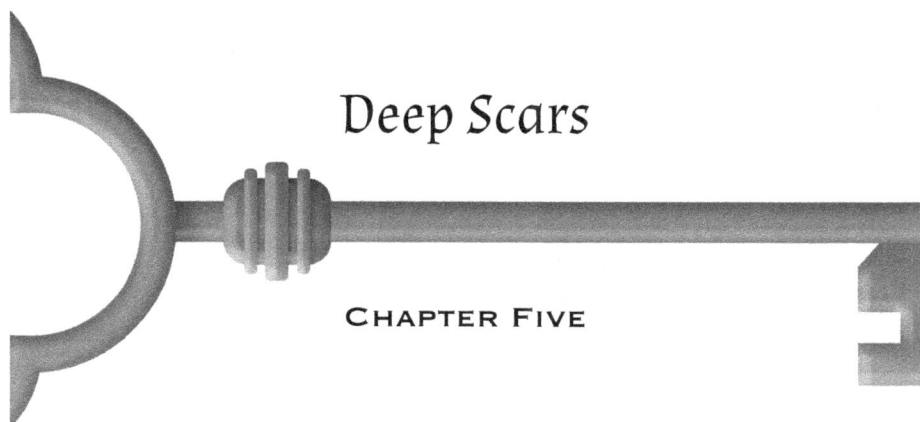

She pressed send as someone across the room greeted her. She smiled and returned the morning pleasantry without using the person's name. Allie caught herself trying to remember the name of the voice who had spoken to her, they were new to the network she believed. They had met a few times, his name was Mitch, or so she thought, but she was not confident enough in having it correct to turn the greeting into a conversation. As more people streamed into the room, the empty chair next to her seemed more noticeable now as other spaces were filling up. She glanced at her phone as it vibrated in her hand notifying her of a text message being received.

"Sorry-running late, be there soon." It was from David.

Allie's career had been everything that she had ever dreamed it would be. Her pleasant smile and likable demeanor had helped her navigate the sometimes phony facades that accompanied the cable news network industry. Originally she had arrived at GNN after spending a few years working alongside the late news journalist Kate Young on a show called *Total Access*. The contacts she had made, her relationship to and the ongoing respect that many in the industry had for Kate, along with some additional media contacts, had propelled her through the ranks as a producer where she now enjoyed seniority and prestige among her peers. It was a good place to be and she had a great feeling of satisfaction and accomplishment in where she was in this stage of her life and career. The one glaring distraction for her had been her inability to stop being angry about Kate's death. There was an accountability for that senseless death that had never really been fulfilled. It was a constant, always burning somewhere inside her mind.

Harrison Banks burst through the door and immediately took his place at the head of the oversized thick sunburnt wooden table. The table complemented the wooden walls perfectly, Allie had always assumed that some interior design company had laid out every square inch of the GNN World Headquarters. Plopping down his iPad, a notebook, and turning his attention to an open laptop screen placed strategically next to where he was seated, he spoke as he used his finger to wake up the device by running it over the mouse screen.

"Good morning." Harrison said, without looking up.

As a smattering of good mornings were offered back the room slowly fell into silence as they waited for the man at the head of the table to begin their day. Harrison Banks had been a very popular morning anchor at GNN and had one of the highest rated morning news programs in the world for a number of years. Occasionally he would remind you in a conversation that he was number one for seven years in a row. That had changed during the global pandemic that raced across the United States and the rest of the world during 2020. After a rapid spread from a lab leak in Wuhan, China, the first US case of the 2019 novel coronavirus, which caused a disease known as COVID-19, showed up in the state of Washington. The virus that would rage into a pandemic was first reported in China on December 31, 2019. Halfway across the world a month later, a man who had returned home to Snohomish County, Washington near Seattle on January 15, after traveling to Wuhan, checked into an urgent care clinic after seeing reports about the outbreak as a passing news story.

Experiencing all the signs of a severe version of the flu, the Centers for Disease Control announced on January 21 that the 35-year-old had tested positive for COVID-19. He was hospitalized, where his condition grew worse and he developed pneumonia. His symptoms abated ten days later. That had been the beginning. In the months that followed Seattle became the epicenter of an early US outbreak. 39 residents of Life Care Center, a nursing home, died from complications from the virus in one four-week span. According to the CDC, 14 US coronavirus cases were recorded by public health agencies between January 21 and February 23, 2020; all of the patients had traveled to China. The first non-travel case was confirmed in California on February 26, and the first US death was reported on February 29.

That has been the beginning of a virus that rapidly marched across the country. Businesses, schools and social gatherings were largely shut down, while, by May, unemployment rates reached some of their highest levels since the Great Depression. The virus spread to nearly every country and brought with it a scrambling of medical resources and research to meet the crisis. As was to be expected, it was complicated by misinformation, politics, people who were suddenly thrust into the public eye and seemed to relish their new found positions of power, conflicted news reporting and after a year of lockdowns, mask wearing, and vaccinations had finally subsided and life was slowly trying to discover a new normal.

Allie had concluded early on in the pandemic that there seemed to be no one prepared or confident to lead through the pandemic. As a result, distrust, unrest, and strife had clawed at the fiber and unity of the country. Harrison Banks' extended post as the news anchor for the number one morning news show had come to an end during COVID-19. He had contracted the disease, he had been gravely ill and it was feared he would not recover. He did, thankfully, and after seven months of battling back the after effects of the disease, returned to the network, tired and damaged, or so it seemed to Allie. But to his credit, he came back ready to work. Harrison was named as the Head Strategist of the News Division, a new role that occasionally found him on the air, but more often than not, he worked behind the scenes and gave guidance to the direction of how the news was to be covered, reported, and made assignments.

Allie knew his role was more than just strategic in title. The pandemic had disrupted the world and the everyday lives of people were turned upside down. The trust or mistrust of news organizations was at an all-time high and had become the most joked about and ridiculed subset of American culture, with the exception of the United States Congress. Allie rolled her eyes as she thought that and was so glad that David Walker was no longer covering the Washington Beltway and specifically the White House. There had been a few years that she had to admit, it was exciting to be a part of that environment of power at the hub of every piece of news that seemed most important. What she had realized is that what happened in Washington, although impactful, really was not as important as she had always believed. David Walker had been the one to show her that real news, real people and the real world was always more important than a bunch of shrill, silly, shysters who loved to hear themselves speak and would do almost anything to hang onto the drug of power that seemed to addict them all. It was cynical, she knew that, but sadly far more truthful than she had ever realized.

Now, just as it seemed that the life was going to find a new normal and begin to improve, the first reports of what might become another pandemic were beginning to emerge. Allie believed that is what this meeting was specifically called to address. It worried her, not that she would get sick or die, she had survived COVID-19 and adapted as she had needed to. Instead it was the rest of the world she was worried about. The echo chamber of people who had seemingly unbridled global access to information combined with social fragmentation and conflicting world views had nearly destroyed people before, the culture had not changed, nor had it had time to recover from the pandemic that just had been. It certainly was not ready to face a new one.

Harrison cleared his throat. "Thanks for being here." His remained fixed on his computer screen as he began.

The door swung open and everyone in the room turned toward it as David Walker entered. Smiling apologetically and dressed in a stylish suit, he quickly glanced across the room, caught eyes with Allie and made his way to the chair she had saved for him.

"Thanks for coming in David." Harrison said as Walker sat down into the seat.

"Sorry I'm late." David mouthed silently to Allie.

"Where have you been?" She whispered back.

A louder than normal clearing of the throat from the other end of the table caused her to abandon any answer that might be coming from her question.

"It goes without saying that this has been a rough few years, so what we are going to talk about today is important." Harrison now scanned the faces in the room as he spoke. "You have been seeing some of the same news reports I've been seeing. We have been very selective in what to put on the air and what to hold back on, for obvious reasons." He sighed. "But let me catch you up on what we're beginning to hear and then we'll strategize what to do with it."

"Is there another pandemic?" Vickie Wallace, Harrison's former co-anchor, who still sat at the morning news desk came right out and asked her friend.

"Perhaps." Harrison's reply was sharp and short.

An audible gasp battled the sighs as staff members reacted.

Harrison Banks held up a hand motioning for the room to grow quiet. He gently sat his hand down on the table and spoke in a tone that he had often used to reassure viewers through the years.

"There have been three deaths reported among the membership of the South Chattanooga Christian Church in Chattanooga, Tennessee. Two of the church members had been on a mission trip to Singapore providing disaster relief. The third was the father of a church member, whose daughter had been on the same mission trip. The daughter had some mild flu-like symptoms but her father had a much more virulent illness. The Tennessee Public Health officials got the Center for Disease Control and Prevention involved where it was determined that none of the three deaths have been from influenza."

Harrison paused letting everyone absorb what he was saying then pressed on. "Research has determined the emergence of a novel coronavirus in Southeast Asia and it has been determined by the United States CDC that all three of these patients had been infected with a novel coronavirus. It has been named South Chattanooga Acute Respiratory Syndrome Coronavirus or SCARS."

"How does it spread, Harrison?" David asked.

"It spreads by droplets."

"So it is happening again?" The person who might be named Mitch asked.

"Perhaps, but that is still not for certain. We have been through a coronavirus pandemic, so we are very familiar with the drill. We also know how important it is to report this accurately and at the same time, give people the information they need without the hype and hysteria. Our rival network has just scrolled a headline across the bottom of the screen that SCARS is feared to be the latest pandemic to attack the world. We don't know that yet and hopefully it will not happen."

Allie watched as the expressions of the team in the room fall as they realized that the experience of COVID-19 that had left them so weary might be lurking out there again.

"At this point, the CDC believes that this is something that can be contained and is more than likely going to be just like the majority of the coronaviruses that emerge far more often than most ever realize. But with all we have been through, there is a fear not just of a virus but of public response." Harrison again paused giving everyone in the room a chance to breathe. "So let's begin to strategize how we want to investigate, cover, and project this to our viewers."

The room was quiet but those next to each other murmured and spoke in muffled tones. Allie glanced over at David who had pursed his lips, which is what he did when he was in thought and getting ready to speak. What was he about to say?

"Harrison," David was not going to make her wait for her answer. "None of us in this room are ready to live through another protracted pandemic, much less report on it." He gestured with a wave of his hand across the occupants gathered in the room. "We are worn out after going through COVID-19 and what most people don't understand is that we have influenza outbreaks, airborne illnesses, and as you mentioned coronaviruses that happen all the time. Most of them never become a pandemic and usually, outside of the medical community and some hyper-interested news junkies, never know they are happening." He pursed his lips again, hesitated, then continued. "My suggestion is that we report what is happening. We do our best to keep it informative and stick with the known facts. But we don't start marching out our resident prophets of gloom and doom, and for goodness sakes, don't interview anyone who was a controversial authority during the pandemic."

Some heads nodded as they listened. Allie knew that David was wise and unlike many news journalists of the era. He was old school in many ways but he really did think that the truth mattered, whether people liked it or not, and whether it fit into the predetermined talking points that news agencies always used to make information fit into their own agenda. That is why she liked working with him so much. He had swagger and clout. Due to longevity and substance he was regarded as one of the most trusted news voices in the world. He had proven that a few years ago during a national crisis when the President of the United States and the First Family had been kidnapped during a vacation trip to Florida. Those dark days and the aftermath had forever solidified his reputation as a journalist and hers as a producer.

"I agree." Harrison smiled for the first time. "As always David, you are thinking clearly. So, let's take a few minutes to start mapping out the way we present this today."

Allie immediately swiped her finger across the screen of her tablet to call up her notes. As she did, she became aware of someone looking in her direction. A quick glance across the table gave her chance to see that Harrison Banks was looking directly at her and David. While everyone else was preparing to map out strategy, Harrison had paused to look in their direction. David noticed it as well, looked toward Allie and then joined her in looking toward Harrison.

"David and Allie, when we are done here. I have something that I want you to do. It will probably make more sense once we are done with this meeting, but go ahead and clear your schedules, you are getting ready to do some traveling." Harrison said and then turned his attention to the rest of the room.

Allie raised her eyebrows and once again looked over at David. His quick shake of the head indicated that he had no better idea than she did about what was coming next. Whatever it was, she thought, was going to be an adventure. Whether it was a good one or bad one was yet to be determined. But she had no doubt it would be an adventure.

Man in the Woods

CHAPTER SIX

Day One - Afternoon

Shep Albert ran his fingers through his unkempt, wiry hair. Slightly graying, always tousled, he knew after using his hand comb the hairdo would look no better than it had when he decided he needed to fix it. He was damp with sweat as he moved through the woods that connected The Wilderness Lodge and the Fort Wilderness Resort. Glancing through the trees on either side of him, he could see other members of the Disney Security team moving through the woods searching. Twisting his husky frame sideways to slide between two trees he scoured the foliage near him looking for some sign of the creature that his boss, Grayson Hawkes had seen less than an hour before.

"I've got nothing over here." The voice of Morgan Blanca cracked over the radio.

"Nothing on this side." Bart Wheeler responded.

"Keep looking." Shep answered the two security cast members who were accompanying him on the mission. "There has to be something out here. Some sign of the...."

Shep was searching for the right word to describe what Hawk had seen, or claimed to have seen in the woods. The call had come from Hawk's office explaining that the Chief Creative Architect had seen a large creature, dragging an animal, and then chased the creature into the woods. It had ambushed his boss and then fled. Hawk's office had explained that if there was a creature that could do harm to some guest on the property that it had to be found, caught, and removed. Instantly Shep had pushed back on the assignment suggesting it was a task best suited to their animal control division, but as he was given more details he began to understand that there really was some mysterious creature out in the woods that had attacked Hawk. At least, something had attacked Hawk and manage to surprise him so badly, he had no idea what kind of animal it was.

Shaking his head, he knew that his title of Security – Special Assignments had been a gift and a promotion from his boss and friend, Grayson Hawkes. They had been very close for years, until he had made some boneheaded choices that he realized Hawk could never forgive him for. Surprisingly, Hawk had forgiven him and continued a friendship, although it was strained and tense from time to time. This role in Security had been completely unexpected but allowed him a level of leadership and at the same time kept him connected to his friend. Shep now answered directly to Jillian Batterson, who was the Head of Security for the entire Disney Company. His relationship with her was a bit stressful as well, she was very protective of Hawk and Shep was working hard to earn her trust. He wasn't real clear if this walk in the woods he was on had come as an assignment from her or from Hawk himself. The call had been from Heather, who ran Hawk's working office in the company, Shep assumed it was from the man himself.

"Some sign of the Bigfoot?" Blana's voice cracked again, snapping Shep back to the reason he was here.

"Or maybe a Yeti escaped from the Forbidden Mountain." Wheeler blasted back, clearly referring to the attraction Expedition Everest in Disney's Animal Kingdom.

"I'm not sure what we're looking for." Shep tried to sound assertive. "But if it is as big as Hawk reported, you will know it you see it."

Shep had some doubts when he had heard what Hawk had reported. A creature that sure sounded a lot like a Sasquatch was not the usual kind of wildlife here at the resort. Shep didn't think that Bigfoot really existed, so he assumed Hawk must have been mistaken. But a big hairy creature that is willing to attack can't be left to roam about. A snap of limbs ahead of him brought Shep into high alert. Pressing the talk switch on his radio headpiece he whispered.

"Did you hear that?"

"Roger that." Came the whispered reply from Wheeler.

Crouching slightly and slowly creeping forward, Shep squinted into the trees trying to see what was in front of him. Another rustling sound and this time Shep's heart skipped a beat as he froze in place. The underbrush seemed to come alive as he watched in relief as a deer bounded across the line of trees in front of him. They had startled the jumpy deer and the deer had startled him right back.

"Bambi is on the run." Blanca had seen the same thing Shep had seen."That is because man is in the woods." Wheeler almost laughed as he said it.

Shep didn't answer, he was breathing hard from being startled. His adrenaline had spiked and he was more afraid than he wanted to be. The forest area in the resort was much denser than he had remembered or realized. This assignment was not turning out to be a mere walk in the woods.

"Do we keep moving?" Wheeler inquired over the radio.

Shep had been strategizing as what the best way to search might be. He had decided to do this initial search by moving through the woods from where Hawk had seen the creature and keep pushing deeper until they emerged into the Fort Wilderness Resort area. It would take time, but again he knew they were covering a lot of ground.

"We keep going all the way through to Fort Wilderness." Shep answered after a moment.

"Can we get more people?" Blanca requested. "That is a lot of ground to cover."

"It is just us for now." Shep said in a clipped response back.

If there really was a Bigfoot, Yeti, or Sasquatch in these woods that was something that they would like to keep contained. If there wasn't and Hawk was wrong about what he had seen, then it would minimize the damage control that might occur if word ever got out that the Chief Creative Architect at Disney had been attacked by a creature out of the pages of cryptozoology. Shep sighed and thought to himself, this really was a special assignment.

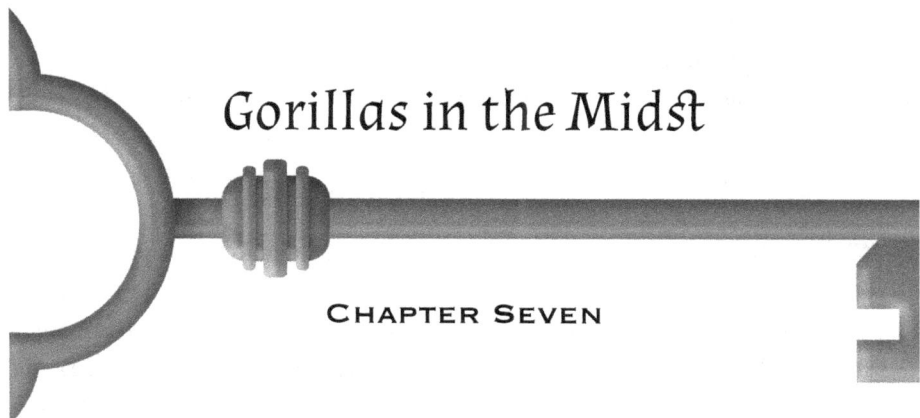

Gorillas in the Midst

CHAPTER SEVEN

Day One - Afternoon

Aaron Bailey and his daughter Charlene, walked side by side over the uneven slabs of the cracked walkway along the Gorilla Falls Exploration Trail. Their day together had been perfect in Disney's Animal Kingdom. Although both had been disappointed when they had been informed that the Maharajah Jungle Trek was shut down for the day, but those feelings were long forgotten after a laughter filled ride on the Kilimanjaro Safaris had led them to an excursion into the Gorilla Falls Exploration Trails attraction. Aaron listened intently as the cast member, who identified himself as a research student at Pangani Forest Conservation School and Wildlife Sanctuary, under the direct supervision of Dr. Kulunda, who was supposed to someone important to be sure. This cast member or research student had a name tag that identified his name as Patryck featuring a translation of what the name meant, "a nobleman" below it. The nobleman Patryck informed the group within earshot that Pangani means "place of enchantment" in Swahili.

"Isn't that enchanting?" Charlene whispered to her father with a giggle.

Aaron smiled and as the group began to wander along the trail as Patryck's presentation came to an end, he and Charlene turned their attention back to the Wilderness Explorers game they were both participating in. This was a free interactive game where guests could explore and earn stickers that were available from cast members throughout Animal Kingdom. On the Gorilla Falls Exploration Trail there was a jackpot of five possible badges or stickers waiting to be discovered. They were strategizing to find the Ham Radio Badge, which is earned by listening to a radio and recording requested information into the Wilderness Explorers Handbook. The Hiking Badge is earned by recording requested information along the trail into the Wilderness Explorers Handbook. The Birding Badge is earned by viewing the birds in the trail's aviary, the Tracking Badge is earned by identifying footprints and scratch marks of animals. Then last but not least, the Gorilla Badge was earned by walking the trail and imitating a gorilla's behavior to a research student. It was silly but added to the experience of just walking down a trail, looking at animals.

Charlene's eyes were wide with wonder as she took it all in. Aaron kept reminding himself to slow down, which he rarely did, and enjoy this with his daughter. After all, they were there celebrating her ninth birthday. He had asked her to be his tour guide and she was taking her role very seriously. She had read the signs, looked closely and faithfully pointed out an abandoned termite mound, Colobus monkeys, small antelope, and Stanley Cranes. There had been a giraffe relative, the okapi, spiny-tailed lizards, pancake tortoises, and mice. Mole-rats and African Hedgehogs had given them a chance to sit for a moment and take a water break. Then Charlene was back on the job as a tour guide leading her dad into an aviary with birds. Then came the hippopotamuses, gerenuks, meerkats, and now they were making their way toward the gorillas.

One of the better designs of this area in Aaron's opinion was the way that Disney had used suspension bridges to cover areas and break up the walkway so guest could observe and see the wildlife all around them. After moving out of the Gorilla outpost, they began making their way along the path, moving through the gorilla sanctuary area, when Aaron stopped short, reached out and quickly took a firm grip of Charlene's hand. Startled by the sudden stop and sensing that something was wrong, she looked up into her dad's face and then followed his gaze out toward the suspension bridge in front of them. Her mouth dropped open slightly as she looked back toward her dad and softly said.

"Daddy, why is there a gorilla sitting on the bridge?"

A silverback gorilla was crouched right in the middle of the bridge. Fiddling with something he was eating. Aaron knew it was a silverback because the guides at the Gorilla Station had explained there was a number of male silverbacks all trying to discover who would be the next leader of the family unit. Their rambunctious roughhousing for supremacy provided entertainment for guests on any given day.

"Daddy?" Charlene's voice again asked the question without saying it again.

"I don't know, baby." Aaron said as he took his first step backward.

Charlene did the same and he could feel her grip tighten as they both stared toward the gorilla on the guest pathway, the swinging bridge in front of them. Aaron momentarily tried to come up with a rationale or reason that the silverback might be on the path. Could it have been a new feature of the exhibit? Was there something that he had missed to explain this? But with each step backward, he carefully moved his daughter back down the path from the direction they had come from.

The gorilla jerked his head toward them as if noticing them for the first time. A sneer crossed his face and he turned his massive frame toward the pair who were facing him but walking away. Aaron's heart was pumping wildly. His eyes locked eyes with the gorilla and instantly he thought of some obscure animal fact that when you stare a gorilla in the eyes it is a challenge for supremacy. He had no idea if that was true, but he had done it, and he was not about to look away.

The silverback began knuckle walking toward them. Aaron heard Charlene let out a soft gasp of fear. The gorilla lumbered, then galumphed across the bridge, coming toward them, omitting a quiet growl. Aaron caught his foot on a crack in the concrete and instantly turned toward Charlene, jerked her arm as he did, and pulled her forward.

"Charlene, run!"

Aaron and his daughter began to run. Once again, he searched his brain for the way to behave around a charging gorilla. He knew you should never run, which of course they were doing now. A quick glance over his shoulder let him know that the gorilla was now running after them. His brain was telling him that he needed to make themselves less intimidating to the gorilla. He vaguely remembered the tour guide saying if you are ever chased by a gorilla to make yourself small and less threatening. Turn your back to the animal and crouch down low, revealing that you are no threat. Another glance over his shoulder let him know that he and his daughter were not going to be able to outrun the gorilla, so he began to scour the path ahead to see what he could do next.

Finding a spot and a clump of rocks to the right side of the path at the next curve, he panted instructions to Charlene.

"We'll jump behind the rocks and then crouch down. Get as small as you can, make yourself into a little ball and sit on the ground with your back to the gorilla. It will leave us alone."

"OK, Dad." She answered back in a voice trying to catch her next breath.

The father daughter tandem veered around the next corner and leapt behind the rocks along the side of the pathway. They balled up into the smallest, most unintimidating form they could muster as the gorilla was now right behind them. The animal growled as he ran next to the pair, reached out and slapped Aaron knocking him to the side on top of Charlene.

In the distance Aaron heard screams as other people had noticed the gorilla. The silverback snorted and looked away from Charlene and Aaron to the other people on the path. Daring to steal a peek, Aaron watched as the gorilla left them and charged toward the now fleeing group of guests, doing the same thing he and his daughter had done. Relieved that the gorilla had moved away, Aaron made sure his daughter was not harmed when he became aware of movement close to them. To his horror he turned as another silverback was drawing near to them and Aaron instinctively dove on top of his daughter covering her to protect her.

In the distance he could hear the screams of guests as more and more of them became aware that the gorillas were no longer contained in their enclosures. But the screams faded into the background as he heard the footfalls of the heavy monster closing in on them. He felt the warm breath of the creature as it leaned in over top of him and Charlene.

Meeting Kong

CHAPTER EIGHT

Day One - Afternoon

Jillian was leaving the Asia section of Animal Kingdom, leaning underneath the barricade and then straightening up, she glanced at her watch to see what time it was. Almost three p.m., she had been in the Majarajah Jungle Trek since early this morning and they were still working the area like a crime scene. A badly injured man and dead tiger didn't constitute that a crime had taken place, but it was strange and unusual. She didn't like it when things didn't make sense and there was nothing about the situation that was making her feel any better. The Florida sun was running full throttle and made the walkways through Animal Kingdom steamy. The mixture of senselessness and now sweat, had her momentarily distracted. According to Hawk, her foremost Disney authority, the foliage and greenery that made the park so beautiful also prevented the cooling breezes that might blow through away because they were blocked. As a result, you would sweat more, which is what was happening now. The crowds were light in this area because the entire section had been closed off all day, but she had been at Walt Disney World long enough to know that the park was nearing capacity. Having a section of the theme park closed meant less space for people to spread out and it made every other section of the park and the rides much more jammed. More people would have added to the sweat, so she was thankful for the extra space.

Her earpiece blurted the alert with the phrase signal 96E. Jillian was on the operation channel for Animal Kingdom, which meant that only Security, Managers, and Animal Science staff were on the same channel. Normally she would have been connected on the channel reserved for first responders, but the morning had been so busy, there had been so much noise as the emergency teams had moved in, that it had been more helpful for her to be in contact with the Animal Science cast as they tried to unravel what had happened. She was still on that channel as again the alert was sounded, signal 96E!

Jillian rotated her stiff neck from all of the tension of the morning as she tried to remember what a signal 96E was. Not used to being on this radio channel, she had not memorized all of the codes that were specific to this team in Animal Kingdom. Her brain stopped trying to figure out the code as she heard what sounded like screams in the distance. Turning toward the sound, she slowly broke into a jog, which increased into a trot, then became a dash as the sound of screaming grew louder and seemed to be coming toward her.

Once again the earpiece notified her of signal 96E but this time the person calling it added the explanation of the code-Escaped Animal! As those words filtered their way through her brain she was now in a full tilt sprint. Legs churning, feet pounding out a steady rhythm on the path, she zeroed in on the direction the screams were coming from. Harambe, the section of the park that featured the Kilimanjaro Safari ride, where she assumed the noise was coming from. Rounding the corner through the tree lined guest walkway, she knew she was correct. A wall of people, on a dead run, screaming, out of control, and panicked were charging directly toward her. Swallowing hard and bracing for the worst, she continued her sprint and tried to choose a small opening between the bodies of running guests. Immediately her progress began to slow as she was fighting her way through the throng like a fish swimming against a strong tide. Moving side so side, no longer able to run, she used her arms to push past people and gently bumped past them trying to battle against the sea of humanity that seemed to be pouring down the path in a relentless push of power. The streets of Harambe were a mass of people all going in the opposite direction.

As quickly as she had thrown herself into the masses, she found herself breaking free, having successfully navigated the screaming frightened guests that were moving away behind her. It was then she could finally see why they were running and she knew what the signal 96E code had meant. Surreally, the village of Harambe was now nearly empty, evacuated and deserted with the exception of a very small group. In front of her were two full grown gorillas. One was standing on his back legs, beating his chest, and roaring as he watched the approaching Animal Science cast members. The second gorilla was moving into the restaurant to her right, which was an opened air structure, with no real interior to speak of. Gorilla number two, flipped tables and chairs as he made his way across the empty patio. The creature paused, inspected some food left on a table, and began to help itself to the snack freshly discovered.

The first gorilla now lept toward her, teeth barred, looking ferocious. Jillian squared herself and set her feet in a stance that she hoped would give her a fighting chance against a gorilla. She locked eyes with the animal as it moved toward her, again raising up on two legs.

"Don't look him in the eyes." A voice came from her left. "The gorilla thinks you are challenging him to a fight."

"I'm not challenging him, he is the one doing the challenging." Jillian screamed back toward the source of the less than helpful instruction.

The gorilla collided with Jillian and grabbed her with a powerful arm and flung her across the path into the trees. Suddenly sailing like a rag doll launched from a cannon, she twisted in the air trying to make her landing less painful. It didn't work. Colliding with the nearest tree, the thud of her body hitting it snapped branches and sent waves of pain coursing through her. Rising up to a knee, she tried to shake her head and clear out the cobwebs. She once again locked eyes with the gorilla, who had momentarily was distracted by a cast member who had tried to get the attention of the beast. But the gorilla seemed to sense that Jillian was still close and the dark haired creature turned to face her once again.

Willing herself to her feet, she reached behind her toward the small of her back, where she often holstered her handgun. Her fingers found nothing but empty space as she remembered she was unarmed. More often than not, she did not wear her weapon unless there was a clear cut security reason to do so. She would have to rethink that, if she survived to get the chance to do so. The gorilla now moved toward her and began to pick up speed. Jillian heard voices yelling, trying to distract the animal, who now pounced toward her with a loud roar.

I'm getting attacked by King Kong, she thought as her frame buckled under the weight of the massive beast. Drawing her arms up instinctively in front of her, trying to protect her face while drawing her knees up to create some space between her and the gorilla above her, she felt a sudden shift in the weight of the animal. Instead of strength and muscle it had become a heavy mass of bulky hair and it fell to her side. Gasping and catching her breath, she rolled away from the animal and once again rolled to her knees before jumping back up to her feet.

A cast member carrying a weapon stepped into her line of sight and she realized what had happened. She had been rescued and the gorilla had been tranquilized. Turing her head back in the direction of the restaurant, she could see that the second gorilla was also unconscious, draped over a table, where she assumed it had been eating leftovers. The adrenaline subsiding, she felt her knees grow week, her fight or die reaction began to wane, and she fell forward catching herself with her knees forward on the ground. The cast member raced over to her and placed a reassuring hand on her back.

"Are you hurt? Did the gorilla bite you?" The concerned questioner inquired.

"No, I don't think so." Jillian hadn't had enough time to do an examination, in the heat of a battle you don't usually have the time.

Taking inventory, she quickly ran through a mental checklist of her what was in pain, moving her limbs to see if anything might be broken, and she was surprised and pleased to find that there was no serious damage done. The dull pain she was feeling, was going to get worse because she had collided with a hairy freight train.

"I'm sure I will be sore in the morning." She responded. Now there were more cast members arriving in the area. Their reactions ranged from stunned disbelief to morbid fascination. Jillian realized that she was still in charge and with that awareness she had a situation that by now had impacted the rest of the theme park as people had run in terror from gorillas on the loose. She reached for the call button on her radio only to find that her radio was gone. She felt for her earpiece and it was also missing. Glancing over and examining the ground with her eyes she tried to find it but knew there was an easier way.

Reaching over and taking the radio from the cast member assisting her, she pushed the call button. "This is Batterson, we have a 10-18 and 10-11. Clear AK of all guests. The park is closed."

Immediately, once she had identified herself as being on the channel, reports starting coming back quickly in rapid fire. There were injured guests, that had gotten hurt in the trampling herd of people. There were people trying to get back into the Harambe area and the bridge was being closed by security. Cast members were dealing with waves of people who had fled in terror now jumbled in confusion at the front entrance to the park. Confusion was an understatement. The cast member next to her gently tapped her on the arm. Jillian looked up at them only to see them pointing toward two people staggering, as if in a stupor, from the pathways near the entrance of the safari ride.

Jillian got to her feet, with a little assistance from the cast member, tried to straighten her clothes and was struck with just how quickly she had gotten stiff and how much it hurt to move. Ignoring the pain, she walked over to the pair. It was a man, holding hands with a little girl, both looked as if they had been crying.

As they came face to face with Jillian, the little girl looked up at her and spoke.

"My name is Charlene." Jillian nodded for her to continue. "We were chased by a gorilla."

The man holding her hand, nodded confirmation of what she was saying.

"I know." Jillian tried to smile and stepped back pointing toward the gorilla on the ground next to where he had attacked her. "Did the gorilla look like that one?"

"I haven't seen enough gorillas to be able to identify one from another." The dad said. "But if I were to guess." He nodded once again.

Jillian held her hand up and motioned for the pair to walk with her. There were now first responders, medical techs, and more and more security and Animal Science cast members moving into the area. She realized that just like she had done, they had made the short trip over from where they had been working all morning, only to find another crisis. She could also see the animal trainers and cast members working to make sure the gorillas were safe but also unable to move if they woke up unexpectedly. She passed off the father and daughter to a medical tech who began to examine them.

Something that she had heard somewhere popped into her head causing her to smile. "When you are wrestling a gorilla, you don't get to quit when you are tired. You quit when the gorilla gets tired." Or in this case, goes to sleep, with a little help from a tranquilizer. She stopped smiling as quickly as she had started because it hurt to smile. She was going to feel terrible tomorrow she reminded herself mentally once again.

"Did you really try to fight with a gorilla?" The female voice got her attention.

Squinting to make out who it was with the sun behind them, she recognized Katie Rose from the tiger habitat earlier.

"No," Jillian said. "I just got caught in the wrong place at the wrong time."

"I'll say, you OK?" Her voice gave the sense that she was impressed she had survived.

"Yes, I think so." Jillian shook her head and began heading toward the Gorilla Falls Exploration Trail. It made sense, if there were gorillas loose in the theme park, they had to have come from somewhere and that is where they kept the gorillas. "Thanks for asking."

Gorillas loose in the park. A tiger attacks a handler and after mauling him, suddenly dies. Both unbelievable and unprecedented events. Jillian knew there was a connection and there was no way they were random. What in the world was going on? What was going to happen next?

Eyes Wide Open

Chapter Nine

Day One - Afternoon

"James Cameron said, "it's like dreaming with your eyes open." Laurie Terrill said to her son, just before the wall in front of them vanished.

Instantly, amazingly they were in flight aboard a banshee. Avatar Flight of Passage had been the one attraction that Laurie's son, Bailey had insisted that they must ride on during their vacation. The ride vehicles resembled motorcycles. Guests rode them in a way similar to how they might have climbed aboard a motorcycle in a video game. In the story line you were climbing onto your link chair, where you would be linked to a banshee which had been selected based upon your scan in the queue line. Straddling the seat, with a leg on either side, the guest then leaned forward with their chest resting on a support, hands on a rail that ran along both sides of the vehicle. Laurie felt a bit claustrophobic when a brace flipped up and came to rest on her back, securing her in place. In her head she knew it was like the safety bar of a roller coaster, only reversed. But still, she fought back the discomfort of feeling like she was trapped and being pressed into the link chair with the pressure on the small of her back.

Glancing again toward Bailey, she quickly forgot about her discomfort as he was grinning ear to ear in anticipation of getting started. Each ride vehicle is individual, but groups are seated together alongside one another. The feeling of togetherness is short lived as soon as the attraction begins. In a very convincing transition, the wall in front of you vanishes, and you are suddenly in flight aboard a banshee. Laurie smiled as she could feel the banshee breathing beneath her on the link chair. She had been a bit disappointed that like the Na'vi River Journey, there was no mission or story set up to the actual ride sequence. The bigger idea of being immersed in the world of Pandora surrounded you, but there wasn't the often successfully used classic Disney "Something has gone wrong" storyline. This was an attraction that was heavy on giving guests physical and visual sensations.

The flight is so immersive that you forget you are in a simulator. The experience allows the rider to feel the sensational joy of being in flight. The 3D imagery is in and of itself a work of art, there is no distortion, no glitches in the film in front of you, and you are immersed in a world that has come alive all around you. Feeling the wind, smelling the scents and the coolness of the water effects bring the experience to life physically. Laurie gasped as a crosswind blew across her, rocking her gently during the simulation. The visuals are what struck her the most. She had ridden simulator rides in other places, but the team that put together this attraction, in the world of Pandora, tucked inside Disney's Animal Kingdom had managed to create an experience that was unlike any she had ever been a part of before.

The music she heard added to the beauty and the emotion of the ride. She had told Bailey that it had been recorded for the attraction by the London Symphony Orchestra. The wait to get in had been long and in her mind she had expected crowds, but they seemed even greater than she had anticipated. Laurie had been asking a cast member about this and they explained that the Asia section of the theme park had been temporarily closed so that might explain the number of people she was seeing. As the ride came to the conclusion, she could feel the shifting of the link chair and the soundtrack begin to wrap up. She guessed the entire ride must have been over four minutes, certainly worth the wait, and she was not disappointed. The Avatar Flight of the Banshee was a not to be missed attraction.

Suddenly the ride came to an end, but then the unexpected happened. The back support bar locking her in place leaning forward did not release. There was a momentary look of confusion on her face as she looked to Bailey, who also had not been able to sit back up straight yet, his back support was still in place. Then the ride sequence suddenly started again. She felt the banshee breath beneath her and the ride had begun again without letting them off. This time, there was no disappearing screen, no film surrounding them, just a blank screen and each guest holding on to a link car that was pitching and moving as if the attraction were unfolding around them. Not only was there no film, there also was no majestic sound track, only the movement of the ride vehicles.

"Mom?" Bailey turned to his mother. His eyes were wide. "Why didn't it let us off?"

"I don't know, son." Laurie smiled at him. "I guess we get to ride again." Then with a desire to alleviate her son's anxiety said, "this will be an experience that most guests don't get."

"Kind of like riding Space Mountain with the lights on?" Bailey strained to smile.

"Exactly, just lean forward and enjoy the ride." Laurie wiggled trying to create a little extra breathing room to relieve the feeling of being trapped and pushed forward.

Behind her she could see Disney cast members moving about, attempting to decide how or if they should stop this second unexpected ride for the guests. She tilted her head as she thought she heard a voice behind her say "it won't respond." But the words trailed off as she tightened her grip as the banshee-less link chair tilted forward, jerking her headlong on the ride car.

"Hold on Bailey." Laurie said, trying to sound calmer than she felt. "Something has gone wrong."

Laurie realized that although she had wondered what the attraction might be like behind the scenes, she now was certain she did not want to experience it for real.

Finding Nothing

Chapter Ten

Day One - Late Afternoon

The grass swished in the breeze as Hawk made his way across the lush green of nature's carpet. Looking ahead of him, he saw Shep Albert, moving along the edge of the tree line where he had seen the creature earlier in the day. Shep had been Hawk's friend for a long time. Back in the days before their lives were intertwined with the legacy of Walt Disney, Shep had served alongside Hawk at a church in Celebration, Florida. The shift into running an entertainment empire had proved to be difficult for Shep and he had inevitably done the wrong things for what he believed were the right reasons. The result had been disastrous and their relationship was carefully being rebuilt after a number of years. He had decided to return, to see how the search was going. Hawk wanted to know what he had met when he was here earlier. The honk of a car horn interrupted his thought and he turned his attention to the vehicle driving into the entrance of The Wilderness Lodge. The family in the vehicle was waving with smiles, perhaps recognizing him. Hawk stopped, turned toward the road, and returned the wave. Instantly the wave was answered with a quick burst of horn blasts from the car as they made their way toward the guard house at the resort entrance.

The aroma of warm earth and sunlight made this a beautiful place to take a walk, although very few people did, because when people were at the resort they were far too busy moving about to experience the magic of Disney instead of exploring nature. The only exception to this rule were those campers at Fort Wilderness, many of the glampers, a more glamorous form of camper, would enjoy the Disney version of nature. It was wilderness to be sure, Hawk knew that, but it was also carefully maintained and cared for. Safety and comfort of guests made them vigilant to remove any creature that might harm a guest or create a hazard. Fortunately there was more than enough space to relocate any such problem. That is why he had Shep and his team out looking, trying to solve the mystery of what he had seen in the woods earlier.

Shep waved as he saw Hawk approach. Returning the wave, the Chief Creative Architect asked, "Have you found anything?"

"Not *yeti*." Shep smiled with satisfaction at his Sasquatch abominable snowman reference.

Hawk appreciated it but feigned disappointment, which caused Shep to continue.

"See what I did there, boss?" Shep shrugged as he continued to smile satisfied. "Not *yeti* – you get it right?"

Rolling his eyes slightly, Hawk answered. "I get it, but it is not as funny as you think."

"Sorry," Shep pointed toward the ground beside them. "I haven't found anything that would give us a clue as to what was in the woods with you."

"Well," Hawk did not glance up from staring at the ground as he spoke. "If you do it will be quite a *feat*."

Silence hung between them for a minute, then Hawk followed the same track of conversation Shep had moments ago. "See what I did there? Quite a *feat* – like a foot print? Funny, right?"

Shep now did the same thing to his boss as his boss had done to him. Not cracking a smile he responded. "I see what you were talking about, just not that funny."

They both laughed out loud, no longer able to contain their amusement at their very bad puns.

"Seriously?" Hawk moved back to why he was here. "You have found nothing?"

"No sir, nothing." Shep said and motioned for Hawk to follow him.

Together they walked along the edge of the wood line. Both quietly looked to the ground and then Shep held out his hand.

"Is this where you say you saw the big creature dragging something?" Shep queried.

"Yes, it would have been right here." Hawk oriented himself by glancing from the tree line to where he had stopped his car earlier.

"As you can see...." Shep pointed toward the ground. "There is some smashed down grass and some type of marks that look like something has been dragged through here. But there is nothing here. No animal remains, no carcass, no injured animal, nothing."

"But I know what I saw." Hawk scratched his head slowly, thinking and remembering.

"Like I said, something was pulled through here, but it is nowhere to be found."

"And the big footprint?" Hawk asked looking over to where he had spotted the print earlier.

"No footprint." Shep sighed. "Lots of wet dirt, mud, obviously something has been moving around out here. But that was you, the creature, animals, and my guys moving around. But we have been over the area multiple times, there is no footprint."

"It was there, really it was." Hawk said sharper than he intended.

"I believe you." Shep stepped back slightly. "After all the things we have been through, seen and done together, I believe you. I'm just saying, it's not there. At least we haven't found it yet."

Hawk inhaled and tried to relive what had happened earlier. Glancing around, he asked Shep, "Where is the rest of your team?"

"We are doing a slow crawl through the woods from here to Fort Wilderness. Trying to find any sign of what you saw and hopefully find it before it messes with someone else." Shep shook his head side to side. "But for right now, there is no evidence of what you saw out here anywhere to be found."

Shep looked right toward Hawk and narrowed his eyes.

"What? What is it?" Hawk tilted his head slightly.

"Why are you here?" Shep asked. Wrinkling his forehead as he asked the question.

"I wanted to see how your search was going."

Hawk saw Shep take a step backward and rub the back of his neck before speaking again.

"No, there is more than that, Hawk."

Hawk shrugged. "No, there isn't."

"You're upset and bothered because this creature got the drop on you." Shep tapped his finger against his lip. "And you never saw it coming. It rattled you."

Hawk felt a twinge of heat race through his body.

"It didn't rattle me and it didn't hurt me." Hawk exhaled deeply. "But it did surprise me. And to be honest, it seems as if I was attacked by a creature that I don't really believe exists. I would like an explanation as to what it is, I want it found, and I can't have it wandering about the resort where guests might run across it."

Shep held up his hands. "Whoa, whoa, sorry boss. Didn't mean to upset you. I just knew there was a reason you came back out here to see what we were doing."

Hawk smiled, relaxed, and then said. "Yes, it did get the drop on me and I want it, no strike that, I need whatever it is found."

"I'm on it. I'll let you know as soon as we find anything." Shep reassured him. Jerking his head at an angle, he looked like he just had another thought. "Why aren't you there?"

"Where?" Hawk now studied Shep's face for some type of clue as to what he was talking about.

"Animal Kingdom." Shep said, "I figured you would be at Animal Kingdom."

"Why would I be there?"

"Because it is insane over there. They didn't call you?"

"Who would have called?" Hawk's mind began to whirl. "I don't have my phone, so I haven't been able to talk to anyone."

Shep gravely looked at his boss. "Oh, Hawk, you need to get over there."

"What is going on?" Hawk was already backing away and moving toward his car.

Shep fell in lockstep with him, keeping pace, trying to fill him in.

"You have an animal attack or two happening." Shep said.

Hawk broke into a run. "An attack or two?"

"Yes" said Shep. "And an attraction that has malfunctioned."

"With guests on board?"

"Yes."

"Are Jillian and Juliette there?" Hawk asked as he slid behind the wheel of the Mustang.

Shep's drew his eyebrows together. "You should get there fast."

Hawk put the car into gear. "How did you hear what was going on?"

"Chatter on the radio." Shep slapped the car loud enough to get Hawk's attention before he drove away. "It's bad, when I say it is insane over there, I mean things have gone crazy."

Hawk cut the wheel and punched the accelerator to the floor as the car whined and responded at the sudden change in direction. Shep jumped backward to get away for the Mustang as it swung around. Tires spinning, slightly squealing, the rubber clawed at the road and rocketed the automobile forward. His mental GPS mapped out the quickest route to the Animal Kingdom, which was the largest theme park on property. He was about as far away as he could be right now, but he wasn't exactly sure where he was headed. In his panic, he had forgotten to ask Shep for any more details. It didn't matter, he would be there in a few moments and see for himself what kind of insanity Shep had convinced him was happening there.

Tensely gripping the steering wheel, he found himself running through an endless stream of worst case scenarios at Animal Kingdom. Cutting in front of the Ticket and Transportation Center of the Magic Kingdom along Seven Seas Drive, Hawk forced himself to take a deep breath and tried to relax. He felt the car shudder slightly as he made the left onto Floridian Way because he was driving too fast. Aware he nearly hadn't made it successfully through the previous turn, he reasoned that the next part of the journey, as he merged onto World Drive, was a straight shot so he confidently pressed the gas pedal to the floor.

Pushed back into his seat as the car responded with speed, he began to weave in and out of the cars traveling along the main highway on Disney property. Nearing the intersection of Buena Vista Drive, Hawk strategically decided to miss turning there as a way to avoid traffic signals and slower moving traffic. Instead he headed for the Osceola Parkway, calculating it was the best way to get to Animal Kingdom. A glance to his left he could see sneak peeks of Disney's Hollywood Studios rising above the tree line. The landmarks confirmed he was on the right track and he believed his choice had been correct. Slowing down, cautious not to make the same mistake again, he steered the Mustang into the curve that would put him on the parkway and headed for Animal Kingdom. This time, the turn was perfect. The car hugged the road and smoothly rolled through the turn.

Traffic was heavy on the other side of the median. Hawk knew that was traffic leaving Disney's Animal Kingdom. The volume led him to believe that if people had time to get in the cars and get away, things must be far worse than he had previously imagined. Taking the left lane the Mustang shot past the toll booth of the resort and headed toward Disney's Animal Kingdom Lodge. Hawk knew that he would continue along the service road that wrapped and snaked its way around and behind the Animal Kingdom. As planned, he turned right and again pushed the accelerator hard moving down the service entrance into a backstage cast member area.

Pumping the brakes he pulled up to the security booth where the person working it recognized Grayson Hawkes behind the wheel of the Mustang. Rolling down his window, Hawk watched as the man waved him through. Hawk read the tension in the lines of the man's face and waved back slightly as he drove through. It was then a thought hit and he slammed on the brakes. Opening the door, he shoved the car into park, and trotted back to the security checkpoint.

"Do you have an extra radio?" Hawk asked as he arrived at the booth.

"Just this one." Nolte was the security guard according to his name badge.

"Nolte, can you let me borrow it?"

Hesitating, Nolte thought about it but quickly answered. "It's all yours, Hawk."

"Do you know what's going on in there?" Hawk gestured back over his shoulder as he began to back away toward his car.

"I know what I hear. It's bad, sir." Nolte shook his head. "There are some animal problems and some of the attractions have malfunctioned. I'll bet the folks in there will be glad to see you."

"The animal attacks…where did they happen?"

"One in the tiger exhibit and one in Harambe." Nolte confirmed.

"What attractions have malfunctioned?" Hawk now began to run back toward the car before waiting for an answer.

"Pandora" Nolte yelled from behind him as the Mustang once again accelerated toward the parking area for service vehicles. Sliding to a stop, Hawk jumped out of the vehicle and turned the radio to what he believed to be the Animal Kingdom emergency channel.

"Security this is Hawk, has anyone seen Jillian Batterson?" Hawk asked.

Hawk made the assumption that somewhere Jillian had to be on-site. Knowing her, he also calculated that she would be cleaning up the most pressing or recent crisis. The radio crackled with interference, but there was no response to his question. Hearing no answer was strange and Hawk now running behind the show building for Legend of the Lion King. He knew if he used the cast member only pathways, he could eventually end up in the off stage area of Pandora, since that is where Nolte had said there was a broken down attraction, he would head there. Running along the emergency exits of the theater, he pushed his way through a service gate, allowing him to stay out of the public section of the park and move backstage toward Pandora.

"Hawk, come to Harambe." The female voice spoke over the radio.

Hawk stopped in his tracks recognizing the voice. It didn't belong to Jillian but instead was Juliette Keaton.

"Juliette, what's going on? Is Jillian with you?" Hawk now changed directions and retraced his steps so he could quickly get to the area of the park near the safari attraction.

"Harambe, come to Harambe." Juliette repeated.

He picked up his pace and raced toward the Harambe village.

Something Wrong

CHAPTER ELEVEN

Day One – Late Afternoon

The entrance into Africa, at least in Disney's Animal Kingdom is through the friendly, welcoming village of Harambe. Harambe is Swahili for "come together." As the Imagineers built this area, they created a gathering place for a combination of places that were discovered as they researched how to build the theme park. The memories of this unique place come together into a brilliantly themed area that looks authentic, or at least the facades appear authentic, creating the faux setting for Disney magic to happen. There was a fortress found in Zanzibar and a crumbling old building and private home that had been discovered in Kenya that had been placed in this area. The thatched huts found throughout this community were constructed by thirteen Zulu craftspeople from South Africa. The quaint village area was designed to resemble an East African port that caters to tourists prior to their safari excursions. If a guest would take the time to look, they would find a hotel, restaurants, an outdoor bar and the marketplace.

Juliette walked beneath the archway that read Harambe Market 1980 and listened intently to the voice speaking to her through her cell phone. Cast Members dressed in colorful, authentic African costumes to add to the illusion that had now been shattered by uniformed paramedics and law enforcement officers moving about the now tourist free area. Raising her head she saw Grayson Hawkes jogging into the village. Thanking the person on the other end of the phone, she ended the call, waved at him and after catching his attention, moved toward him in the street.

Hawk slowed as he noticed for the first time cast members huddled over a massive creature lying on the pavement. His face registered confusion and his mouth opened slightly at the sight of the gorilla being moved onto a cart to be taken away. Breaking his distraction at the sight, he looked back toward her and rushed over to where she was waiting.

"What happened?" Hawk asked. "Why is there a gorilla on the streets of Harambe?" He turned his head looking at the movement of people. "And where is Jillian?"

Juliette placed her hand on his arm drawing his attention back to her.

"Jillian was attacked by that gorilla back there." She could see him tense at the news. "Like I said, she is alright. A little shaken up but she is tough. She did not back down from the gorilla." Juliette smiled. "At least that is what the witnesses said."

Hawk sucked in a quick breath at what she had just said. "And why was a gorilla in Harambe?"

"Hawk, listen. Like I said, Jillian is fine. But before you get to her you need to know a few other things."

"Things?" His eyes narrowed as he studied her.

"Yes, things have gone horribly wrong here today. We have had a tiger attack and badly injure one of our trainers. The tiger is dead and we don't know why. We had gorillas escape the exploration trail and make it into Harambe. The Avatar Flight of Passage malfunctioned trapping guests on the banshee." She watched his face as he scratched his jaw thinking about what she had told him. "All of the automatic doors in every attraction in Animal Kingdom have malfunctioned. They either won't open or won't close depending on the door. And I just got a call that the Dinosaur attraction is not stopping, it is running on an endless loop, with guests stuck on board."

Hawk frowned and began moving away from her, in the direction of Discovery Island, the shortest route to the Dinosaur attraction. "Did we get the guests out of Flight of Passage?" He yelled at her as he picked up his pace.

"Finally." She yelled loud enough for him to hear her.

"Did anyone get hurt?"

"Don't know yet." Juliette's voice choked back some emotion. The day had been filled with one crisis after another, she was worried and weary. Hawk stopped at her answer, and turned and took a couple of steps back toward her as she continued. "This is all happening real time. But early reports are that no one is badly injured, including Jillian."

His jaw was set and it was a look she had seen before. It gritty and was determined, as if he was getting ready for a fight. Perhaps they were in one and she just didn't realize it yet. There had been so many thing that had gone wrong all at once without any real explanation. But they would find one, she knew they would.

"I'm on it." Hawk turned and now broke into a run. "I'll be at the Dinosaur attraction."

Juliette watched as he quickly disappeared from sight. If things were falling apart all around you, the one person that you wanted in the middle of it to make it right was Grayson Hawkes. She had seen him at his best and at his worst, but when the pressure was on, he was never better.

Mass Exodus

Chapter Twelve

Day One – Early Evening

Parked among the endless line of Disney Security cars, the two men watched the mass of people trying to get out of the Disney Animal Kingdom parking lot. The first guests had moved through the gates and were the start of a rush of humanity as people kept pouring through the exit turnstiles. Security and cast members kept people moving along. Trams wound through the parking lot like caterpillars carrying guests back toward their cars. The sudden rush of people had been so great that most decided not to tarry for the tram, instead they walked across the massive parking lot toward their designated parking areas to find their vehicles. The foot traffic created problems for the trams trying to shuttle people as well as for guests who had managed to get into the cars and were trying to leave. Horns honked, people yelled, and it was a disheveled mess and the dusty haired man, still with his eyes hidden behind dark sunglasses, smiled at the sight.

"What a mess." Exclaimed the dark haired man in the driver's seat.

"Yes, it is a glorious mess." Came the gravely response.

The driver watched as the man next to him once again punched a number on a cell phone and without uttering a word of greeting, seemed to be hearing information offered by the person on the other end of the call. Nodding absently as he listened, never taking his eyes off of the movement of the people in front of him, he ran his finger over the scar on the side of his face. Then he spoke to the unseen person he was connected with.

"Agreed, I think that is enough for the day." The sandy haired man ended the call.

"So this is it?" The man behind the wheel tried to understand what was happening.

It was difficult because he was only given small bits and pieces of what he was doing. He had been told he would be rewarded and compensated handsomely. But for that payoff he had to be willing to not ask too many questions and be compliant with the demands that would be made of him. He had agreed, but he was still curious. Each question he asked was calculated and carefully placed.

"Yes, this is it." The sandy haired passenger said, motioning for the driver to pull out so they could leave. "At least for now."

The driver put the car into gear and slowly pulled out of the line of security vehicles. He waved at a couple of the cast members who stopped oncoming traffic for them to cross and drive and turn toward the exit. He wanted to know more, but didn't ask. He was surprised when his passenger offered something else.

"I think we have done enough to get their attention. What happens next really is up to them, not us." The man brushed sandy hair off of his brow.

The car made its way through the parking lanes toward the exit. The driver hesitated but needed to ask another question. "Did anyone get hurt today?"

The man in the passenger seat continued to look out the front window. His lips tightened almost unnoticeably and he slowly turned his head toward the driver before he answered.

"Does it matter?"

The driver felt a small bead of sweat run down his neck. He did not look back at the passenger as he spoke. "I guess it doesn't. But if we are trying to get their attention, we should be able to do that without anyone getting hurt." He paused and added. "Right?"

"That's not our concern. We did what we needed to do. And for now, for today, we are done." The man still was looking at him, he could feel the cold stare coming from behind the dark glasses. "You and I did our part. Is there a problem?"

"No, no problem." The driver turned the wheel as they increased their speed moving past the traffic around them. "I was just wondering."

Back in Time

Chapter Thirteen

Day One - Evening

Hawk's feet pounded across the hot asphalt on the deserted pathways of Animal Kingdom. The now tourist free theme park made each step as he ran toward DinoLand U.S.A. sound hollow in the empty spaces around him. His mind was firing through thought after thought that seemed to come quicker and quicker with each step. Processing the information Juliette had given him was proving to be impossible, he could find no logical or rational explanation for all that was going wrong. He desperately wanted to check on Jillian, but trusted that she was fine and he knew she would be busy. But still, the lingering unthinkable reality that she had been attacked by a gorilla had no place in his rational thinking. Exhaling and trying to calm himself as he raced past the Tree of Life, he rounded the bend into DinoLand, and allowed his mind to become distracted by where he was going.

DinoLand U.S.A had a backstory that suggested it began as a small highway town where an amateur fossil-hunter found some dinosaur bones in the late 1940s. A team of scientists and enthusiasts combined their money and put together enough to purchase the dig site. Since then, scientists, volunteers, and grad students have been living there trying to find answers about dinosaurs. It was a commune for dinosaur hunters. The Dino Institute was founded and opened the site as a "fossil discovery park." An old fishing lodge located on the property became the Restaurantosaurus.

Eventually, the Dino Institute and their partners at a research facility called Chrono-Tech discovered how to send vehicles through time and this then added a new layer to the research and allowed them to conduct time travel tours aimed at tourists to generate income for their work.

Now striding beneath the bridge in the Boneyard, Hawk picked up the pace as he closed in on the Dinosaur attraction. The attraction placed guests on board ride vehicles called Time Rovers and are taken on a turbulent journey through the Cretaceous period, loaded up with prehistoric scenes populated with audio-animatronic dinosaurs. If what Juliette had told Hawk was still taking place, there were guests stuck on the ride which would be tossing them back and forth as it was truly designed to be an exhilarating rough ride. It was thrilling to ride it once, but to ride it over and over again on an endless loop would be less than thrilling and much too frightening to imagine.

Blasting through the doorway of the Dino Institute, a state of the art paleontological research facility, Hawk recalled two Hidden Mickeys that he had often showed to others on tours or to impress them with details that most might not see. The massive murals as you enter the attraction were works of art. On the far left of the mural to the right there is a tree that hides a Hidden Mickey mouse head where a branch connects to the trunk. Across the lobby there is another classic three circle Hidden Mickey hidden among the chaos of an explosion that capture the volatile changes in the age of dinosaurs. Jumping over a turnstile and moving into the guest queue area, Hawk could hear screams coming from the ride portion of the attraction. Cast members lined the entry area where normally guests would be loaded into the Time Rover vehicles.

Sliding over a rail, Hawk glanced upward and noticed red, yellow, and white pipes running across the roof line. Each featured a chemical compound that meant nothing to the guests as they waited, but in reality reflected the whimsical talent of the Imagineers who created the attraction. The three compounds on the appropriately colored pipes were the formulas for ketchup, mustard, and mayonnaise. Now descending a set of stairs and arriving in the loading area, a cast member recognized the Disney Chief Creative Architect and quickly debriefed what was happening.

"We lost control of the ride vehicles." The young cast member named C.J. yelled. "The attraction is looping, when it is supposed to end, it just sent the vehicles through again."

"Why didn't you cut the main power?" Hawk scanned the area and realized the screams were now getting louder as a vehicle must be approaching.

"We did, sir. It didn't work." C.J. responded, noticing what Hawk sensed about a vehicle headed their way. "We tried to manually shut down each individual vehicle and we did, except one, it will not shut down."

C.J. gestured toward a tunnel where Hawk realized that at any moment a Time Rover would emerge.

"Is anyone hurt?"

"Not too badly, just shaken up best we can tell. Once we got the power cut to the other vehicles we got them off the track. The one coming is the last one, it still has guests on board, and we have no idea how they are doing." C.J.'s eyes widened as he continued. "One passenger jumped off, they somehow got out of the safety restraint. They have a twisted ankle."

"How many times has the ride car looped through the attraction?" Hawk now stepped to the edge of the loading area.

"We've lost count." C.J. shook his head and turned to watch the vehicle that was headed their way.

The tan colored Time Rover burst through the opening into the loading area. Wide eyed terror was etched across the face of the riders. Shoving C.J. out of the way, Hawk raced down the loading ramp directly toward the vehicle racing toward him. Leaping into the air, he sailed toward the oncoming time machine. With a sickening thud, his feet landed on the hood of the peanut butter brown vehicle that didn't slow down one bit as it zipped past the area where normally it should have stopped so guests could get on board.

"It's OK." Hawk crouched down trying to steady himself. "I'll get it stopped."

A few of the passengers nodded at him, some had their cell phones out, and others simply had their heads down looking exhausted. The ride ran smoothly and evenly through the loading area, but Hawk knew that in a matter of seconds, the ride would begin to pitch forward and backward, lean and jerk from side to side, change speeds, and simulate an out of control race through time to find a dinosaur before meteors struck the planet.

The Time Rover veered around a corner and into a time tunnel. The turn caused Hawk to momentarily lose his balance before righting himself. Lights flashed around the vehicle, then the lights went out and a field of stars appeared around them before a prehistoric jungle scene faded into view. Hawk was now on his knees crawling toward the front of the ride vehicle. He could not imagine why the attraction would not power down, but at least they had managed to manually shut down the vehicles and get guests out, except for this one. The main power control for the vehicle was accessible through a panel on the front of the vehicle. Stretching out flat and sliding forward he moved toward the front edge of the time traveling machine.

The Time Rover jerked through the jungles looking for an Iguanodon. Each time the vehicle jolted, Hawk slid in the same direction. A Styracosaurus near a volcanic vent leaned against a tree, pushing it dangerously close to the vehicle. Hawk glanced to the side toward an Alioramus eating a Brachychampsa, whose legs and tail wiggled in the grasp of the dinosaur's jaws. Pretty graphic stuff and definitely not for young kids, Hawk thought as he continued inching closer to his goal. Stretching his arm over the front edge of the vehicle he found the handle and turned it releasing the protective door to the mechanics of the car.

The Time Rover twisted once again and as Hawk opened the panel he slipped across the hood of the vehicle, nearly sliding off the side. Catching himself by gripping a vent on the hood, he pulled himself back toward where he had just been. A mother Parasaurolophus watched over her child as a Velociraptor stands on a ledge in search of prey. Suddenly the vehicle sped up rocking sideways before leaning backward, again Hawk battled a slide that threatened to throw him off the vehicle. Still using the vent as his handhold, once again he crawled back toward the front as the Time Rover rapidly moved through the faux jungle. The guests were staring at him as he stretched his arm down toward the shut off switch on the front of the vehicle. A quick flip of the switch and the vehicle suddenly came to a stop in front of an extremely dangerous Carnotaurus. Hawk was thrown off the front of the vehicle and landing in front of it with his hand still on the power switch, the vehicle was still.

Hawk's momentary elation at stopping the vehicle evaporated like the prehistoric mist as he realized this was a scheduled stop in the attraction sequence, the sudden stop was in front of a dangerous dinosaur and the ride was now programed to speed away. Leaping back toward the Time Rover, he grabbed the edges of the panel opening he had used to find the switch. Both feet planted against the front of the vehicle, hands locked on either side of the opening, he tried to muscle his way back into a better position to keep from being thrown from the vehicle. The Time Rover sped away frantically, jerking left and right, the tires screeching, and then come to a stop near a peaceful herbivore, Saltasaurus who had lowered its head to see what was below it. This new programmed stop drove Hawk forward into the front of the vehicle, but he kicked off the front upward allowing him once again to land on the hood before the vehicle began to move.

The Time Rover raced forward into a clearing in the jungle where a thunderstorm raged behind the trees and where two baby Cearadactylus are perched. Hawk now headed toward the rear of the vehicle. If the power switch in the front would not work, he would disconnect the power supply located at the back. Stepping between guests and over the seats, he lost his balance as the vehicle went down a steep drop just in time to avoid a collision with a larger, flying Cearadactylus. He was now airborne, momentarily suspended above the ride vehicle, above the passengers, with an arm outstretched reaching for something to take hold of. Time seemed to stand still as his body floated above the car, but the seconds caught up with him as his body met the next twist of the Time Rover. Falling with a thud, he worked to regain his footing, once again stepping across seats as a small, leaping Compsognathus passed over his head. Reaching the last seat and moving out to the rear of the vehicle the Time Rover was plunged into complete darkness and the audio track spoke of a loss of traction. Hawk knew what was coming next. Suddenly, after a few movements through the dark, strobe lights flashed to reveal the Carnotaurus. Crawling over the support bar on the back of the ride car, he glanced toward the dinosaur that was now walking toward the vehicle and braced himself for the next sudden movement as the ride would attempt to escape the predator. Accelerating at a bone chilling speed, the car made a series of left and rights turns, only to meet up with the dinosaur again. This time the Carnotaurus raised itself to its full height and roared loudly as bright lights flash around it like lightning. Hawk reached down and took a firm grip on a cable that had a connection point in the center of what was best described as a rear bumper section of the vehicle.

The Time Rover rocketed down a path where large trees tipped toward it. The computer announces to the ride vehicle there are only a few seconds to spare before the meteor impact. Hawk gave the cable a tug, nothing happening as it did not give. Inhaling deeply and tightening his grip on the cable he pulled again and this time it released. The power instantly shut down and the vehicle wearily rolled to a stop. The boom of the meteor resounded through the jungle and a flash of light illuminated the Carnotaurus lunging toward where the vehicle was supposed to have been, but was not, because the Time Rover was still, it had been disabled. The sound of footsteps running past the dinosaur echoed from the future as cast members ran to help the guests. Hawk slid off the back of the vehicle and landed on the cool concrete behind it. He reached across the control panel to his left, threw a switch and the safety bar released with a clunk, just as the cast members arrived to help the guests exit the ride.

Hawk slumped back against the Time Rover and smiled at his success. He became aware of someone looking at him and looked to his right to see a teenaged girl.

"Thank you." She said as a tear rolled down her face.

"You are welcome." He managed to answer as he closed his eyes and once again smiled.

He felt a set of hands on his shoulders and looked up as C.J. was kneeling in front of him with a firm grip on him.

"Are you hurt, Hawk?' He said, with concern.

"Uh," Hawk muttered and then looked around at himself. "I don't know, I don't think so."

"That was incredible." C.J. let him loose with relief. "How did you do that?"

"I just pulled out the cable." Hawk offered. "The kill switch on the front of the vehicle didn't work."

"Yes, we could see. We saw the whole ride on the monitor. Did you know when you were going over the back of the vehicle you were in the photo area? We have a great action shot of you mid-air flying over the back of the vehicle. It is incredible!"

Hawk again closed his eyes. "Incredible is not the word I would pick, but I like your take on it." He smiled and continued. "But feel free to tell your friends how incredible I was."

C.J. laughed. "But how did you know what to do?"

"I just remembered the design of the vehicle. So when the one switch didn't work, I was hoping I was going to be right."

"Can I help you up?" C.J. asked.

Hawk opened one eye and wanted to say no, he really wanted to simply stay where he was for a few more minutes and rest. But knowing what he had just been through and knowing some of what had been happening in the park, he knew the best choice was to get up and face whatever was next. After traveling through time on the Time Rover he moved into the future with a growing concern as he tried to understand what was happening in Disney's Animal Kingdom.

The Command Center

Chapter Fourteen

Day One - Evening

"What were you thinking?" Jillian had both of her hands balled up into fists, firmly planted on the conference room table. She leaned forward, her dark hair falling off her shoulders and surrounding her face like the mane of a lion. Realizing that she probably was growling like a lion, she straightened up, felt a twinge of pain from the gorilla attack earlier in the day, and decided to take a softer approach.

"Why didn't you call for help?" Jillian looked to the other side of the table, where Grayson Hawkes was seated. He was seated with his back to an enormous picture window with the nighttime lights of the Magic Kingdom glowing in the background, framing him as if in a portrait. His eyes were studying her and she felt the back of her neck tingle as a bit of sweat began to emerge.

Hawk didn't answer, so she turned and looked toward the head of the table where Juliette Keaton was seated. Juliette caught her glancing over and merely shrugged. Hawk had the ability to frustrate both of them, Juliette had more experience in dealing with him, but apparently she had nothing to offer in the moment.

"You could have been killed, Hawk." Jillian bit at her lip momentarily, then caught herself waiting for him to say something.

Hawk smiled, or actually it was more like a smirk. There were times that he did that she found it very cute and disarming. But there were other times when it drove her over the edge in frustration, this was clearly one of those moments she had told the edge goodbye.

"Oh, you think this is funny?" Jillian went back to her lion lean on the table.

Juliette looked as if she was trying to suppress a smile at the exchange, which really wasn't an exchange at all, because all Hawk had managed to do so far was infuriatingly smirk at her.

"Well," Hawk shifted forward in his chair, placing his elbows on the table and intertwining his fingers. "It is kind of funny coming from a woman who decided to get into a fight with a gorilla."

Jillian straightened back up as she saw a smile cross his face. He had moved from smirking to being smug, again at times she found it endearing, this was not that day.

"Look, I was doing my job. I am in charge of security and something had to be done." Jillian hated that she was sounding so defensive. "So I did my job."

Juliette shook her head side to side trying to catch Hawk's attention, but he did not notice.

Still smiling, Hawk replied. "Yes, you did your job. But don't you find it odd that you are yelling at me for stopping an attraction while you were wrestling with a gorilla in the streets of Harambe?"

Jillian replayed the moment of contact with the gorilla and eased her posture slightly.

"You could have been killed." Hawk stopped smiling as he tilted his head. "Or you could have hurt my gorilla."

Juliette could no longer suppress her smile and now struggled to push back a laugh. The result was sounding like a tire deflating on the side of sizzling hot roadway.

Jillian turned to her and smiled at the sound. "And you think this is funny as well?"

"No, I think you are both kind of funny." Juliette glanced at one then the other. "And you are both rather blessed that you are here to argue about who was more reckless."

Jillian watched as Juliette reached into a folder and took out an 8'x10' picture and slid it into the middle of the table for them both to see. Reaching down and spinning the picture toward her, she was taken back by what she saw. It was a ride picture, taken on the Dinosaur attraction from earlier in the day. In the glossy photo, there was Hawk stretched out airborne, with guests beneath him looking upward in awe or horror. It was hard to tell which it was. He was in a super hero flying pose, almost as if he had planned it for the camera, and his gaze was focused on the back of the ride vehicle. She wanted to admit that it looked pretty spectacular, but she refused, instead she spun it around for Hawk to see.

Hawk didn't look at the picture at all, instead he was staring directly at Jillian and locked his eyes on hers. "I told C.J. at the attraction, to tell his friends I was incredible, I guess he took me seriously."

Juliette cleared her throat. "I'll say he did. He posted this picture online and there were guests on board that were taking video of you. It has blown up and gone viral. I have calls from every major news network wanting some kind of official statement about what you were doing on Dinosaur today."

"What have you told them?" Hawk leaned back in his chair.

"Nothing yet." Juliette pointed to the picture on the table. "That is only one of our problems. We had to empty out a theme park today. We had every attraction in Animal Kingdom malfunction, we had not only a gorilla attack, but we had a tiger attack with a cast member in the hospital and the tiger that attacked him...."

"Saber." Jillian injected. "I have been told the cat's name was Saber."

"Yes." Juliette quickly remembering earlier in the day. "Saber, the tiger is dead."

"How is Elliot?" Hawk asked. "That is the cast member's name isn't it? Elliot Drayton?"

"He is in ICU, he is hanging between life and death." Juliette glanced down, then back up and continued. "He is seriously hurt but we have no idea what happened yet."

Jillian interrupted and picked up the story. "I have been told that we are supposed to have some preliminary results on what happened to the tiger in the morning. That might help us understand what took place."

"We have a truckload of what we don't know that is going to get dumped if we can't find some answers." Hawk now rocked forward toward the table again. "How did we lose control of an entire theme park? How did Animal Kingdom fall apart all at once?"

"Don't have answers yet." Jillian pursed her lips for a moment. "But you're right, we lost control of an entire theme park."

"We have guests that were slightly injured. Nothing too serious." Juliette reported.

"Good." Hawk commented.

"We seem to have everything working again. But I would like to keep the park closed for the rest of the night and maybe tomorrow to make sure we really are back in control." Juliette continued.

"I don't think we can open it again until we figure out what happened." Jillian now slid into a chair at the table. "You just can't lose control of an entire theme park.

Animals were out of their pens, every single automatic door in the park was opened, and every attraction malfunctioned in some shape or form." She tapped her fingers on the table and then paused as if remembering something.

The silence floated between them and descended upon the table only to be broken as Hawk spoke.

"What?"

"And you." Jillian pointed a finger tipped with a manicured nail toward him. "You were attacked by a Sasquatch."

Hawk grimaced and folder his arms across his chest. "Shep ratted me out."

"He didn't rat you out. He had security out looking for a beast in the woods that attacked you."

"He was supposed to keep it on the down low." Hawk muttered.

"You can't keep that on the down low." Jillian could feel her face redden. "So it wasn't enough to get attacked by a mythical creature of some sort today. Then you had to jump on board an attraction and fly over the guests to save them. You somehow thought I wouldn't hear about it?"

"You've got to admit, Hawk," Juliette stared at him. "A Sasquatch and dinosaurs all in one day is a bit much, even for you."

"Shep told you too?" Hawk looked at Juliette in disbelief.

"Yes, he told me too." She replied.

"Shep needs to learn to keep his mouth shut." Hawk remained defiant with his arms crossed.

"And you need to open yours." Jillian scolded. "You should have told us. We have to figure out what happened. If you haven't noticed we have a bit of a crisis happening here."

"And we don't know why." Juliette added, then looked toward Jillian and then raised an eyebrow as she looked back toward Hawk. "We don't know why, do we…? Hawk?"

Hawk flinched at the question and then sneered slightly. "Of course not."

Both women now had him in their sights and he glanced back and forth at them. They were waiting for more.

"I have no idea what attacked me in the woods. I was going to tell you, but in fairness - I haven't had the chance." Hawk slid his chair back as he spoke. "I was trying to figure out what it was that came after me, then I find out that we have tigers and gorillas on the loose." He pointed at Jillian. "I find out that you were in a wrestling match with King Kong, which could have killed you by the way. Then I find out that we have guests trapped on attractions and we had to evacuate the theme park like we had been attacked…" Hawk paused. He slowly closed his eyes lost in thought. The looking back at them continued. "We were attacked. Everything that happened today was an attack."

The room grew still and the sound of the clock ticking on the wall was much louder than it seemed moments ago.

"Attacked by who?" Juliette asked.

"Or what?" Jillian added.

"I don't know." Hawk swiveled his chair and looked out into the night at the lights of the Magic Kingdom.

"Not to overstate the obvious." Juliette brought them both back to the immediate needs of the moment. "We have a themed resort that we had to evacuate and shut down. That means we have tons of videos that are being shared worldwide and some of them," she opened her eyes widely as she looked at Hawk, "we are going to have to explain."

Jillian picked up the story. "There are photos of you flying. We have animal attacks and a seriously injured cast member."

"As you can imagine, every news outlet in the country is sending someone here if they are not here already. They all want to hear something and they want to hear from you." Juliette sighed, then continued. "We also have had a request from GNN for an exclusive interview with you. David Walker and Allie Crossman are here."

"Why would I give them an exclusive interview about what happened today?" Hawk shrugged.

"They aren't here about what happened today. David and Allie are our friends and they came because GNN wanted to do a feature piece on how you ran the company through the global pandemic. There are rumors that there is another one on the horizon, so your approach is something they want to feature."

Jillian watched as Hawk's expression darkened. They had just lived through one of the most frightening and confusing eras in history. The pandemic had stretched everyone and the way Hawk had navigated it as a leader had been part inspirational, slightly controversial, but personally exhausting. The thought of another one was almost paralyzing. She shook her head and told herself to focus on the present and their current situation.

"Where have you staged the media with so many of them here?" Jillian asked.

Juliette looked down at the table, looked back at them, and with a slight nod answered. "They are located in the Magic Kingdom parking lot, where we usually keep the extra trams parked and stored at night."

"But that is near the woods where I was attacked." Hawk stated urgently.

"By a Sasquatch." Jillian was puzzled as to why the media had been put in that location.

Realistically by now, there would be a sea of temporary tents and trucks set up with the best background shots available to the media. She had already dispatched a full staff of Disney Security cast members to the area and had called in reserves from the Orange County Sheriff's Department. But she made a mental note to check it out because she might need more.

"I didn't know you had been attacked by a Bigfoot in the area when I had them all move in there. Do you want me to tell them to get out because we have some unknown creature creeping about in the forest waiting to pounce on them?" Juliette placed her hands on her hips.

"No, I think they will be fine. But imagine if they could capture the creature on film, all of them at the same time." Hawk smiled at the thought of the discovery and the reaction.

"That is not funny." Jillian snapped to get his attention. "We have a serious problem here. There are answers that we don't have to questions that we haven't even thought of yet."

"Then I suggest we come up with the right questions." Hawk again looked out the window, this time he tried to gaze back to the parking area where he could see the glow of the media lights against their tents.

"Any suggestion as to what we want to say at this point?" Juliette asked.

Jillian knew that in a crisis, time and time again, Juliette Keaton was the face of the Disney Company that navigated media, interviews and much of the press during difficulties. She and her family were some of Hawk's oldest and closest friends, and they were some of the people he trusted when things were bad.

"Tell them as little as possible." Hawk said flatly.

Juliette huffed. "That will only hold them off for a little while."

"But it will buy us some time to figure out the questions we have and the answers we need." Jillian offered.

"What about you? When will you have something to say to the media?" Juliette waited for Hawk to think about his answer.

Hawk didn't answer, he just kept looking out the window toward the glow coming from the media section of the parking lot. It was the Cruella section of the Villains parking area.

"You're better at this than I am." Hawk raised his hands in surrender. "I don't have anything to say to them. You talk with them. We need you to reassure them everything is going to be all right."

Jillian took a deep breath and then unleashed in stilted speech, "But you are the head of the largest entertainment empire in the world. Juliette is telling you what you already know, people will want to hear from you, they need to hear from you."

"I'm not so sure." Hawk broke off his glancing in the distance and turned to the pair across the table from him.

"Not so sure about what?" Jillian shook her head, dark hair bounced with the motion. "Not sure that people want to hear from you or that they will need to hear from you?"

"Nah, that doesn't matter." Hawk waved off the question. "I'm not so sure I am the head of the largest entertainment empire in the world."

Jillian looked toward Juliette who looked as baffled as she was.

"What are you talking about?" Juliette asked before Jillian could say anything.

"I am certainly not in charge of what has happened today because I have no clue what is going on." Hawk inhaled deeply and then loudly exhaled before continuing. "And as far as being the head of the largest entertainment empire in the world, well, there is some doubt about that in the mind of some."

"Huh?" Jillian tilted her head.

"I have been summoned." Hawk replied.

"Oh no, not today." Juliette's mouth opened in disbelief.

"What are you two talking about?" Uncertainty laced Jillian's question.

"I knew things could get worse, but I never would have seen this one coming." Juliette's eyes narrowed as she thought about what Hawk said. "Are they here?"

"Clue me in, what are we talking about? Who summoned you and has enough clout to get you to respond?" Jillian stared at Hawk waiting for an answer.

The answer didn't come from Hawk, instead it was Juliette who provided the information. "The executive committee of the Disney Board of Directors."

Jillian still didn't understand what that meant and how that was a problem. Juliette continued and explained.

"The Walt Disney Company is a publically traded company with stockholders. As a result, although Hawk has complete creative control he also is accountable to the Board of Directors. The executive committee is nervous and upset at how the company has been run during the pandemic and they are less than pleased with Hawk's style and way of doing things." Juliette continued. "Of all the days for them to be here, this is the worst possible time."

"Then don't meet with them." Jillian defiantly offered. "If they are gunning for you, we are busy, tell them to take a hike."

"It is tempting, but they are already here." Hawk offered. "We are meeting tonight."

"When?" Juliette wondered.

"About a half hour ago." Hawk glanced at his Mickey Mouse watch.

"This committee who is angry at you has been waiting for you and you are a half hour late?" Jillian was stunned and also a bit impressed that Hawk was not willing to give them what they wanted. "If you are in trouble, I am going with you." After all, she straightened up and stood tall. "I have to protect you, I am head of Disney Security."

Hawk smiled, his grin let her know he wasn't going to argue with her about going. But he surprised her when he said. "If you are going with me, you have to change clothes. I hate to tell you but you look like you have been in a fight with an ape."

Jillian ran her hands over her jacket and tried to push away the wrinkles. "I look OK."

"You look great." Hawk laughed. "But you still have to dress up, we are going to a fancy place. By now they are already eating dinner, they didn't wait on me to start and to be honest I didn't want to eat with them anyway." Hawk stood up. "Go get changed into something more dressy."

Jillian curled her lip. "More dressy?"

"Sure, what is the word I'm looking for?" Hawk looked toward Juliette for assistance.

"Don't look at me, you're on your own here, cowboy." She grinned, his discomfort was a welcomed respite in a very bad day.

"This place is a formal place, there is a dress code." Hawk was flustered. "Just wash the ape smell off your jacket. We leave in fifteen minutes."

Jillian was already backing her way out of the room. "Fifteen minutes? I will only need five. And don't worry, I will get 'dressy' so I don't embarrass you." She feigned being upset as she teased him. "As a matter of fact, I will look so good that this committee will be wondering how someone who looks like you gets to be next to someone like me." Pausing, she glanced over her shoulder before disappearing in the doorway. "Where are we going?"

"Back to Harambe." Hawk smiled.

"What?" Jillian was confused.

"Club 33." Hawk widened his eyes. "We leave in fourteen minutes. See you in the lobby."

"I only need five." Jillian picked up her pace as she headed for the door. Pushing it open she heard Juliette say to Hawk in the background.

"I'm so sorry Hawk, don't worry, I'll handle the press for now. Take care of business with the committee."

Something Going On

CHAPTER FIFTEEN

Day One - Evening

The brown leather overstuffed rocking chairs were the comfiest place in the Walt Disney World Resort, or so Allie Crossman thought, as she rocked back and forth, so gently she was about to doze off. The Carolwood Pacific Room, affectionately known as the Iron Spike Room by Disney insiders, is often referred to as simply The Train Room. Almost hidden away in the Boulder Ridge Villas of Disney's Wilderness Lodge the room holds one of the most revered artifacts of Walt Disney, two railroad cars from the Lilly Belle, the one-eighths scale backyard train owned and operated by the one and only Walt Disney. Capturing the feel of a Northwestern train lodge of the 1860s, the beautiful room is easily missed by most guests as the hustle to cram in vacation memories during their stay at Disney World. While the train cars are the centerpiece, the room is loaded with tributes to Walt and his well documented love of trains. Allie smiled as she continued to rock, staring at the oversized fireplace with the warm cozy fire blazing in front of her. She was barely aware of David Walker, who was scrolling on his cell phone, until he jarred her out of her Disney induced doze as he said.

"She's here."

Juliette Keaton rounded the corner and breezed into the room greeting David and herself with a hug and light pat on the back. Allie had known Juliette for a number of years and they had become friends. David had met Juliette a few years earlier covering President Tyler Pride and his family when they were kidnapped at the Walt Disney World Resort. Juliette was always professional and had great integrity, but at the same time was willing to be open and candid with people she trusted off the record. Motioning for them to retake their seats, she took an unoccupied leather rocking chair, glanced across the deserted room, and with a sigh smiled at them.

"Welcome to Walt Disney World." Juliette said.

"Thanks," David responded. "We didn't expect it to be so crazy when we got here."

"Well, as you have experienced before, when something happens here it does make the news." Juliette rocked back slightly in the chair.

"But we had no idea that you had reassembled a camp for the press corps on property." Allie injected.

David leaned forward. "We were on our way here for a totally different assignment. We didn't find out about all of the other things that have been going on around here until we were in the air flying down here."

Juliette offered a slight shake of her head in bewilderment. "Yes, your message said you were here to do a piece on the pandemic."

"Believe it or not, we were actually coming down here to do a positive outlook piece on how the Disney Company navigated COVID-19." Allie said feeling a heaviness as she continued. "Because there are early reports of another coronavirus emerging."

Juliette flinched as she heard the words.

"Everyone is still so pandemic weary, we were hoping to do a piece that might offer some hope if… and I need to repeat, if there is another pandemic on the way." David tried to reassure her.

"What is this next pandemic?" Juliette looked from one to the other.

"It is called SCARS, which stands for South Chattanooga Acute Repertory Syndrome. It is similar to COVID-19, but as of yet there is just a lot of waiting, watching, and hoping that it is something that will not become anything like the previous pandemic." David stated as calmly as he could.

"When?" Juliette evenly asked.

"When what?" Allie wondered.

"When is this outbreak supposed to happen?"

"We're not sure there is going to be one. GNN wanted to get a piece ready to remind folks that even if it arrives, there will is a way to face it, and there were some successes during the previous one."

"So it is kind of like watching for a hurricane to see if it develops?" Juliette summarized.

"Something like that." David said.

Allie watched as Juliette nodded her understanding. For just a moment, she thought she could see the strain of the news, coupled with whatever else was going on as Juliette briefly closed her eyes and thought for a moment.

"Well," Juliette made a valiant attempt to brighten her tone. "We will be happy to give you what you need for a good news piece if another pandemic is about to break loose."

"Thanks," David smiled. "But right now, we are interested in what is going on around here. Apparently we have arrived in the middle of something pretty big."

Quiet fell between the three as Juliette glanced toward the fire. Pausing before she spoke again, her eyes came back and looked from Allie toward David.

"Is this on or off the record?" Juliette asked, waiting for an answer that didn't come as quickly as Allie thought it would be offered by her coworker.

"There is some viral footage of Grayson Hawkes flying through the air rescuing passengers on a runaway Dinosaur ride. There are other reports of attractions malfunctioning, animals escaping, and you have had to evacuate a theme park, and that is just the things that we have already heard." David cleared his throat. "As of yet, you have officially said nothing or given no statements to the press."

"And nothing is about to change now." Juliette got up to leave. "It is good to see you. I promise I will have an official statement soon and I will personally make sure you get it first to break the news."

David got to his feet quickly and waved a hand. "Wait, wait, wait… if there is nothing official, that's OK."

"Juliette, we are your friends." Allie got to her feet as well.

"I know." Juliette smiled at them. "But I don't have anything for you yet."

"Fair enough." David put his phone away in his pocket. "So how about friend to friend with nothing being recorded for broadcast? What is going on?"

Juliette's shoulders slumped. Allie stepped up beside her and wrapped an arm around her. Juliette's head lowered and she said softly.

"It has been a very bad day here at Walt Disney World."

Going Out

Chapter Sixteen

Day One - Night

Underneath the gleaming entrance of the Bay Lake Towers, Hawk released the collar of his white dress shirt allowing it to be seen above the rim of the black suit coat he had slid into. He fumbled with the third button down of his shirt, sliding it into place, and pushing open the lapels he wondered if he should have taken the time to put on a tie. Turning back toward the glass doors of the tower, he saw Jillian step through them making her way toward him. She was wearing a snuggly fitting back dress, not too long and no too short, and a pair of dress heels. The outfit was accented subtly with short white pearl necklace that he recognized as a gift he had given her the previous Christmas. Clutching a small black purse, which perfectly matched the outfit, he once again was stunned by just how beautiful she was.

"You're staring." Jillian smiled as her eyes caught him looking at her.

"You clean up real good." Hawk grinned as she slid her arm into his.

"I told you." She said softly. "I make you look good."

Hawk laughed as they started across the parking lot. "No doubt about it."

Jillian suddenly pulled up short causing Hawk to twist at the sudden tug on his arm. He glanced over at her and read the expression of disbelief as she flinched.

"You're kidding, right?" She said.

"What?" Hawk turned to follow her gaze into the parking lot.

It was then he realized what she was reacting to. He hadn't thought about it but he was heading to his motorcycle, parked where he usually parked it, in a reserved slot toward the far side of the parking area.

"You want me to ride on the bike dressed like this?" She now was looking at him, head slightly cocked, waiting for an answer.

"Gawrsh..." Hawk now offered his best Goofy imitation. "I thought you could do anything. But if it is too tough for you."

Jillian released his arm and pushed her hands down across her dress as if getting ready to figure out how to get on the motorcycle gracefully. Shooting him a look to let him know she was up to the challenge, she quickened her pace as she moved toward the bike. She slowed, turned her head noticing that he was no longer walking with her, and spun back toward him raising both palms.

"What are you doing? We are going to be late." She then put her hands on her hips. "I can do this."

Hawk again laughed. "I have no doubt you can. But fortunately for you, I would not ask you to." He gestured to the Mustang that was parked in a private slot between a security fence and a hedge line. "We can take the Mustang."

"No," she said defiantly. "The motorcycle is fine."

"Yes, the cycle is fine." He grinned. "But not as fine as you. We will take the car."

"Wow, good line." She playfully cooed at him. "Do you use that with all the girls or just me?"

"Just the ones I am trying to keep away from my motorcycle." He gallantly swung open the car door waiting for her to walk over. "Your chariot awaits, princess."

He knew the last word he used would get a reaction. It always did and that is why he used it. Hawk watched as she lowered herself to get into the car and glanced away as she slid her legs inside.

"I am not one of your Disney Princesses, Disney Nerd." She shook her head. "And don't you ever forget it."

"Yes ma'am." He carefully shut the door and saw her smiling through the window.

She didn't like being called princess. He only used it when he wanted to irritate her and he appreciated her willingness to always react to it when he picked on her. Stepping around the front of the car, which had been backed into the parking space, he slid into the driver's seat, tapped the ignition switch and fired the engine to life. Effortlessly putting the car into gear, he eased it forward and began navigating through the parking area toward the exit to The Contemporary Resort. As the security bar went up allowing them to move past the guard stand he turned the car to the left at the light and began to head toward Disney's Animal Kingdom.

He could feel her looking at him as he drove and glanced to see her gazing at him with curiosity.

"So tell me about this Club 33." She licked her lips slightly. "It sounds fancy and I've never heard you mention it before. And you have never taken me there before. You should explain that to me."

"Club 33 has an interesting history." Hawk began.

"Everything around here has an interesting history." Jillian interrupted with a satisfied smile. She waited for him to continue.

"Back when Walt Disney was building Disneyland, it was unlike anything that had ever been built before. It was going to be expensive and the way Walt wanted to build it was going to require extensive funding so investors were solicited from a number of major corporations." Hawk said as he steered his car through the darkened roadway.

"And the investors would have the opportunity to advertise within the park, sponsor attractions and promote their products." Jillian filled in the next bit of information. "That makes sense."

"You're right and that is what Walt did." Hawk used the turn signal and waited for oncoming traffic to pass. "Walt needed a place to dine and entertain important guests and associates."

"Didn't you tell me one time that Walt was a fairly conservative Midwestern guy who was not overwhelmed with the glamour and glitz of being all Hollywood?" She asked.

"I did and he was." Hawk agreed. "But he also knew how to do business and realized that many dignitaries would be visiting the park. While he was satisfied with chili and crackers or grabbing a dish of ice cream, he understood that a controlled, secure and elegant environment would be highly beneficial. So, he and Roy agreed that a small club style restaurant needed to be built. But it was going to have to be private and for exclusive use only. Walt passed away before it was done."

The Mustang came to a stop at a traffic signal. Hawk looked over at Jillian and thought again how beautiful she looked. He was glad she had insisted on coming with him.

"Where did the name come from, Club 33?" Jillian reached over and placed her hand on his arm.

"That is a good question. No one is really sure." Hawk glanced down at her hand and felt her grip tighten forcefully on his arm.

"What?" Jillian feigned shock. "There is some Disney fact or trivia information that Grayson Hawkes does not know?" She eased her grip but left her hand on his arm, resting on the console of the car. She gestured toward the light which had now turned green. Hawk decided to drive with one hand so he could leave his other arm in place with her hand on it.

"Some think the number is the original address of the club in Disneyland. According to the State of California Alcoholic Beverage Control rules and regulations, any establishment serving liquor, wine, beer, or spirits of any type must obtain a license for such. The law says that the license has to be issued to an exact address which will fall under the guidelines established by ABC rules. Since the club was the only establishment within the park to sell wine and alcohol, they had to have an address. So 33 Rue Royale Street or 33 Royal Street was created and Club 33 was the name because of the address."

"Fair enough, makes sense." Jillian shared her thoughts. "But you said you weren't sure, so there has to be other theories about the name."

"Right you are." Hawk smiled slightly. "Walt Disney's premature and unexpected death happened while the construction was still going on. Like most things in the aftermath of losing Walt the future of the club and a lot of the ideas about it were in jeopardy. According to the legend, it is told that forty-seven of the main investors of the park were consulted about the club's name and how it would function. Thirty-three members voted to continue with the construction, trying to keep alive Walt's vision. The construction was finished and private memberships where open for application." Hawk saw the back entrance to Animal Kingdom ahead. "Another theory is that when you counted the park sponsors of 1966 and 1967, there were thirty-three."

"But wait." Jillian laughed as Hawk continued. "I already can tell you aren't done yet, there is more… right?"

"Another popular belief is based upon the shape of the numeral "3." If you take a "3" and lay it sideways with the open side on the bottom, the numerals suddenly appear to become mouse ears."

"So, specifically the "33" represents Mickey Mouse." Jillian waited. "So what is the right answer, o' keeper of Disney knowledge?"

"To be truthful, I am not sure." Hawk thought out loud. "The most plausible is the one where they created an address inside of Disneyland to sell alcohol and get their license in California."

The Mustang pulled into the parking lot behind Disney's Animal Kingdom backstage area. Hawk had been here already earlier in the day. As he turned off the engine,

Hawk hesitated and didn't get out of the car. Jillian waited him for to continue but he didn't offer any more information. So she filled the silence. Hawk knew that she would. One of the things that he loved about her was also one of the things that frustrated him about her. If she was in pursuit of something, whether it was a person, a case, or information, she was relentless until she found what she was looking for and was satisfied. He knew he had just primed the pump and she was wanting the information to flow more freely.

"So," she started. "This thirty-three thing was started at Disneyland for the high dollar investors."

"Yes."

"But now you have them here at Walt Disney World?" Jillian continued.

"Yes."

"And this is a place for special elite guests?" Pausing she was piling up her thoughts as she spoke. "Why haven't I ever heard of it before? You would think that this would be something that security should know about."

"They haven't been here that long." Hawk sighed. "And you called it, they are designed for the special and the elite guests."

Hawk continued to walk but for the second time on this outing, he realized Jillian was no longer walking beside him. Slowing to a stop and turning, she eyed him warily.

"How many of these clubs are there at Walt Disney World?"

"There is one in Disney's Hollywood Studios on the 4th floor of The Brown Derby. There is one in Epcot on the upper floor of The American Adventure." He saw her tilt her head slightly listening as he continued. "There is another in the Magic Kingdom in the Adventureland Veranda. And one here, inside Disney's Animal Kingdom."

"Four?"

"Four."

"There are four private exclusive clubs at the resort. One in each theme park. These are private meeting and dining places for special guests and your Head of Security doesn't know anything about them?"

"Yes."

"That's your answer? Yes." Jillian's neck bent forward ever so slightly. "I find that interesting."

Alone in the Wilderness

Chapter Seventeen

Day One - Night

Shep inhaled a lung full of the pine scented nighttime air that wafted around him as he came to the edge of the tree line in Disney's Fort Wilderness Resort. Glancing over at a tree stump that sat barstool high in the clearing, he unclipped his radio, allowed himself to seat himself heavily and then punched the call button.

"Let's call it, team." Shep thoughtfully paused, never releasing the call switch. "Good job. I'm not sure what was out here but I know it did not get past us. It's still here somewhere, but we have done all we can do tonight. I don't think there is any reason for concern."

He doubted the last part of his transmission but he could not think of any reason his team had found to be concerned. Shep knew something had attacked Hawk and that there was something wrong, but whatever it was they just hadn't found. That either meant that it was no longer a threat or it didn't want to be found, at least not yet.

"We have called in added security to patrol all night here at the campground and at the lodge. We'll keep it safe. Let you know if anything unusual happens." The unseen voice came across the radio.

"Roger that." Shep replaced the radio on his hip and wiped his brow with his forearm.

He had deployed a team that had been looking through the woods for the bulk of the day. Now in the dark, they were more likely to scare and frighten guests who might see orbs of flashlight beams bouncing through the trees in the darkness, than there was to be an attack by an elusive and by description, a mythical creature.

Hawk was creative and imaginative, but he wasn't prone to overreacting and Shep had never known him to be untruthful in any way. If he said he was attacked and that the creature had resembled what he believed a Sasquatch would look like, then he had been attacked by a Sasquatch. But sadly, Shep was a skeptic and didn't believe in Bigfoot, even at Walt Disney World.

It had been a long day and he felt a yawn coming on. Alone and seated on the stump, his foot dragged across a layer of spongy moss encircling his makeshift seat. Stretching, he tried to think about what to do next. There is no way he was going to stop looking. Giving the rest of the team the greenlight to shut down for the night was the only decision he could make. They had been at it the bulk of the day, they were trying to find something that didn't want to be found. He could put a unit back on the hunt tomorrow. But for him, he wasn't ready to quit yet.

Replaying Hawk's story of what happened, he decided to go back once again to where the encounter had started. He would head back to The Wilderness Lodge and retrace the steps and places he had already looked, this time he would do it alone. There would be no team backing him up in the woods and he hesitantly allowed himself to think that if there was something out there, that didn't want to be found, he was more likely to find it on his own.

"You are crazy." Shep whispered to himself as he stood to make his way back to the lodge.

As he moved back toward the roadway, his intention was to catch a bus, go back to the entrance of Fort Wilderness, then shuttle back to The Wilderness Lodge and start all over again. This was a challenge and although he had summarized it as crazy, he remembered something that Hawk had once told him. It was something about most new things, most different things, most breakthroughs in life seem a little bit crazy, right up until the day they are discovered. The next day they aren't crazy anymore, they are brilliant. Maybe he wasn't really crazy to be headed back into the woods alone at night, maybe he was being brilliant. In this case, brilliant sure felt like crazy.

The Leader of the Club

Chapter Eighteen

Day One - Night

"Thelathini na tatu" Jillian spoke slowly as she read the words painted on the side of the Harambe House inside Disney's Animal Kingdom.

"It means thirty-three in Swahili." Hawk said softly.

"As in Club 33." She concluded.

"Exactly." Hawk turned her toward him and spoke in a hushed tone. "I'm sorry you don't know about these places. There are now seven of them across the Disney properties worldwide. The resort with the most is here in Florida with four." Hawk glanced toward the side of the building before looking back at her. "These places exist because someone believed it was good for business."

"And you don't?" She tried to read his thoughts as his eyes closed while he was thinking about what to say next.

"No, I don't. I am not a fan of catering to the elite only in our theme parks." Hawk reopened his eyes.

Jillian was aware of his dislike for the inconvenience of VIPs in the resort. The most glaring example had been when the President of the United States had brought his family to visit. That trip had turned into a national nightmare and the First Family had been kidnapped. As uncomfortable as Hawk had been about hosting dignitaries and celebrities prior to that, his displeasure had only been heightened by that experience.

Hawk continued, "To be a member of Club 33 you have to be screened and interviewed by someone at the company before you are accepted and allowed in. The cost of getting in to the Club 33 membership here at Walt Disney World was $33,000 for your initial membership. Once you are in the club your annual dues are at least $15,000 per year."

"Every single year?" Jillian smiled tentatively.

"Every single year." Hawk rolled his eyes slightly. "There are dress codes, you get plenty of perks, the service is great, and there is a secretive nature to being a member. If you are on the outside you always wonder what is going on in the inside."

"Secrets are something that you are good at." Jillian playfully poked him in the ribs. "Sounds like this place should be right up your alley." Then stepping a half step back from him and meeting his gaze continued. "But you don't like it."

"No, I don't like it. I think they are a bad idea and I think it is a way to create something that the biggest Disney fans will never be able to access or attain."

"Then why did you build them?" She asked before she thought about how the question would sound.

"I didn't." Hawk narrowed his eyes. "I gave in to the Board of Directors because they were pushing for them to be expanded into the parks beyond Disneyland. It was good for the bottom line and it provides a guest experience with perks beyond belief. They pushed for it and I decided not to go against it."

"Why not?"

"Because Walt had seen the need for having spaces like this."

He turned and pointed to the walkway that would carry them toward the entrance. As they walked, she slid her arm inside of his. Glancing to her left she saw some words written in Swahili on the wall with the translation inscribed beneath – *He who lives sees much, He who travels sees more*, the signage read. A metal gate stopped them from going any further. It kept them out of a small courtyard area, where just a few feet away a brown wooden door with the word "Private" was imprinted on a sign. On the wall, next the gate was a golden round sensor emblazoned with some sort of logo and the number 33 in the center. It looked like the same type of sensor used for guests to enter and exit rooms, doors, and attractions using their electronic Magic Bands. As if on cue, Hawk stretched out his arm and placed his own personal Magic Band against the logo. Instantly it began to glow and the speaker above the sensor offered a greeting.

"Welcome, how may I assist you?"

"I'm here for a meeting." Hawk said expressionlessly.

"I'll be right there." The voice pleasantly bounced back.

They stood in silence for a moment when she spun him to face her.

"Walt might have been wrong and you might have been right." She pulled in a deep breath. "Your instincts about not needing this type of place may have been correct. Walt is not here anymore, this is your world to manage. If you don't see the need, then they probably aren't necessary."

Hawk slowly smiled at her. "Thanks for saying that."

"Just because Walt Disney wanted to have a Club 33 doesn't mean that you need one." She turned back toward the gate as the private door opened. "You're not Walt Disney, but he entrusted you to take care of his business."

She felt Hawk stand just a little taller next to her. "Indeed he did."

"So let's go take care of business." She said as the cast member, dressed in a tuxedo opened the gate for them to enter. As they moved toward the now opened door, she whispered. "Exactly what are walking into?"

"You ask me that now?" He laughed and whispered back to her. "It will be OK, just let me handle it, the board can be rather persnickety."

Following their guide they moved through a massive meet and greet lounge. Ornately decorated, yet carefully fitting into the area theming, the building was a gathering place for wealthy explorers. This would be the place they would relive and retell their adventures after going on safari. Three men were having an after dinner drink, their rumpled napkins the only remaining reminder of the dinner that Hawk had managed to miss, she thought to herself. They all stood as she and Hawk entered the room. Their reaction to her signaled that the three had expected Hawk to be there alone.

"Hawk, so great to see you." The first man came around the table, followed by the other two and extended his hand.

Hawk shook hands with him and then moved to shake the hands of the other two. He then said, "Gentlemen, I would like for you to meet…"

"Jillian Batterson, our Head of Security." The first man said as he shook her hand.

Hawk continued the introductions. "Jillian this is our President Mark Gross, our Vice President, Edward Altman, and our Treasurer, Jess Marley. These are three executive officers of the Walt Disney Company Board of Directors. They represent the other board members as trustees of the company when the board in not in official session."

"It is nice to meet you in person, it is like meeting royalty." The Treasurer sheepishly said as he shook her hand.

What an odd thing to say, Jillian thought and with a flurry of hand gestures everyone was directed to seats and took their place at the table. Since Jillian had not been expected, an additional chair had been brought in by the tux wearing greeter. He had quickly slid the chair into place and exited during the introductions. They all settled into their seats. She kept a pleasant, albeit forced smile on her face as she waited for the conversation to start. Hawk had told her to let him handle it, whatever it was going to be. Her mouth was dry and she was thirsty. She could feel her anxiety level raise just a bit.

"Hawk, so sorry you couldn't join us for dinner." Gross said. "It was excellent like always and we would have enjoyed your company."

"It has been a busy day around here." Hawk shrugged. "I got here as quick as I could."

Edward Altman snorted slightly at this. "More accurately you waited as long as you could to get here."

Hawk smiled and nodded toward him. Jillian noticed that Hawk did not correct his statement or offer any other excuses for his missing dinner. Mark Gross gave Altman a disapproving look as he spoke, but quickly turned back toward Hawk and allowed a smile to creep onto his face.

"You might be wondering why it was so important to us to speak with you." Altman offered.

"No, not at all." Hawk slightly shook his head as he said it. Almost unnoticed, Jillian saw him glance toward her, then back toward the three board members before he continued. "As a matter of fact I was expecting to hear from you eventually. I am guessing there are some things that are bothering you with the way I am running the Disney Company. You feel it is your duty to talk with me about those concerns."

Altman snorted once again as he pointed a finger toward Hawk. He shook it as he spoke. "I told you he wasn't dumb and he wouldn't be surprised. No need to sugar coat what we want to talk about, let's get to it."

Hawk shrugged slightly, placed his hands on the table palms up before closing them into lightly gripped fists. "I'm ready – let's dance."

"Now, now, now...." Jess Marley spoke. His voice quivered slightly, Jillian thought he sounded nervous or even afraid. "There is no reason we can't keep this civil and have a friendly conversation."

"Exactly, this is merely a friendly conversation." Gross jumped onto what Marley said.

An awkward silence settled around the table. Jillian watched the three board members and noticed that Marley was sweating slightly. Altman was a tad bit flushed, clearly he had some anger built up that he had been wanting to vent at this meeting.

Gross was the one of the three who seemed to be the smoothest and under control. With the ease of a salesman selling snake oil, his face radiated openness and friendliness to both Hawk and herself.

"As you have already surmised we are concerned about the direction and state of the company." Gross opened. "We realize that the past few years have been extremely difficult, and honestly, unprecedented in history. Who could have ever anticipated a global pandemic shutting down every one of our resorts, stopping the release of motion pictures, stifling the sales of products, shutting down all live sporting events, and putting people all over the world at risk?"

"I share your concerns over the direction and the state of the company. As a matter of fact, it has been all consuming for me, but you didn't have to invite me here to thank me for how I have chosen to lead. You could have just sent me a note." Hawk smiled.

Altman almost bounced up out of his seat and once again used his finger as an accusatory emphasis maker. "Thank you, you have almost destroyed this company. We are going to fire you!" His face grew even redder, although Jillian had not thought it was possible. "You are irreverent, politically incorrect, and you are out of touch with the world around you."

She could feel Hawk tense up, she saw his arm tighten through his sport jacket ever so slightly. Searching his face, he was masking what she believed to be rage amazingly well. He looked like what he just heard had not bothered him at all.

"I could ask you what you were unhappy about, but I think I have that all figured out." Hawk leaned back as he spoke. Pausing he slowly allowed his eyes to move to each man seating across from them. Still smiling he plowed forward. "When you say I am out of touch with the world, you are suggesting that I should cower and cave to the cultural trends of the day. I do not. Political correctness is for cowards and we at Disney need to be fearless. Weak, whiny, and woke is no way to live life, much less lead a company." Hawk took a moment and looked into the face of all three men before continuing. "You have seen the financial losses we have taken over the last two years. I know that Mr. Marley here has been giving us constant updates."

Marley cleared his throat. "Our profits are way down, dangerously declining and our stock prices have been steadily dropping."

Raising a hand to silence Marley, Gross added. "Much of that is understandable since we faced a worldwide health crisis. But we have some concerns with the way you have chosen to lead the company through it."

"As you three have communicated." Hawk's chin jutted forward as he spoke. "What exactly has you, how did you put it? Concerned."

"I'll start." Altman jumped at the opportunity. "You kept all of our staff on the payroll while the company was shut down. Do you know how much that cost the company to do that?" Altman looked toward Marley for support.

Marley nodded.

Hawk spoke before Marley got the chance. "Yes, I did. I kept our staff, actually we call them cast members, as you should know, on the payroll. We scaled back their hours since we were closed in all of our theme parks, but how else were they going to survive? So we let them work from home or brought them on our properties using certain safety protocols. We did the best we could in a tough situation, but no one missed a meal and everyone was paid."

"But there was no money coming in." Marely's voice quivered.

"I know, but we have plenty of money." Hawk now leaned forward again. His voice grew slightly more intense as his gaze locked on Altman. "We are a company that cares about our cast members, they are part of the Disney family, and they help make us great. Outstanding guest experiences can only be created by outstanding cast members. I didn't want any of them to go without during the pandemic and I wanted to preserve their jobs. Other companies laid people off left and right, we kept everyone on the payroll."

"It cost us a fortune." Marley injected.

"Money well spent." Hawk replied sharply. "They are our cast members."

"You also exposed us to liability when you reopened the resorts as quickly as you did. The rest of the planet was on lockdown, but at the Disney Resorts you had us out there advertising and almost begging people to come and visit with reduced rates to entice them." Altman picked back up.

Jillian sensed he had a long list of things he wanted to say.

"True." Hawk nodded in agreement. "I opened up and tried to get people back on all of our properties as soon as we could figure out how to operate in the guidelines of each municipality, state, and country. It wasn't easy."

The room grew unexpectedly quiet. Jillian was impressed at how cool and collected Hawk was as he dealt with these three.

"The liability of doing things that way was huge." Gross said. "The rest of the world was still shut down and yet Disney was out there acting like nothing was wrong. That is because of you."

Hawk bristled a bit as Gross spoke, but maintained a peaceful expression on his face. "Not true. Everything was wrong and people knew it. Just like everyone else, we had to make decisions and figure things out real time. But I did what the government kept telling us to do, they said trust the science, so I trusted the science."

"You did not trust the science." Altman nearly exploded.

"I did. I may not have followed the guidelines or political science that seemed to keep changing, but I did follow the real science." Hawk now slapped his palm on the table. "I trusted the science, I trusted our cast members and most importantly I trusted our guests to know what the most responsible thing to do for themselves would be. No one had to come. No one had to visit. No one was forced to do anything. But let me clarify since obviously the board disagrees." Hawk's voiced raised with a razor sharpness. "I chose to lead and not become a mindless lemming. We are the most powerful storytellers in the world. We have the greatest brand of any company in the history of the world. People expect us not to be afraid, hunker down and hide. They expect us to lead. That is what I did, without your help and without your support."

Hawk crossed his arms and forcefully jammed his back into the chair as he waited for whatever might come next. Jillian felt her neck stiffen and the muscles in her back tense up as she kept her gaze locked on the three across the table from them. She felt the rush of adrenaline that always showed up just before she was in a fight. Her arm muscles twitched and her fingers balled into loosely held fists.

Hawk was not done. "And you seem so concerned with me lowering prices so we can entice more guests. I used the global pandemic to do some soul searching and I realized that one of the great gifts we as a company give to the world is joy and relief from the pressures of life, even if it is only for a brief moment or two. Families should not have to mortgage their homes to take a vacation to one of our resorts. We can charge that much money and people will probably still visit." He paused and once again studied the men across the table. "But if you were a Board of Directors that really cared about the people that we provide a service for, then you would understand the importance of making sure they could get in and afford to come see us. You are more concerned with creating exclusive clubs for the wealthy and isolating yourself from the people who we provide experiences for."

Gross was expressionless and his voice trailed off as he spoke. "And what about today?"

"Today?" Hawk almost cut off the president of the company's sentence.

"Yes." Gross tilted his head back and allowed his gaze to drift up toward the ceiling. "Today, Hawk. There are animal attacks. We have people hurt. Animal Kingdom was evacuated. You were involved in some incident as we lost control of some of our rides."

"Attractions." Jillian felt herself speak to correct him before she could stop herself.

She felt Hawk look at her as she said it. Turning quickly toward him, she was relieved to see him smiling as if he was amused that she had gotten a Disney term correct.

Gross leveled his glance at Jillian. "Attraction."

Hawk had managed to see Gross turn his gaze toward her and then she saw Hawk do something that he had never done before. He held out his arm and snapped loudly and angrily at Gross to snap his attention back toward Hawk. Gross seemed surprised but looked at Hawk a bit taken back.

"Did you just snap at me?" Gross flushed.

"Yep." Hawk snapped again. "Just like that. If you have something to say, you say it to me Gross, not her."

"Fine. And on top of everything else, you had some kind of strange creature that attacked you today." Gross gathered himself. "Didn't you?"

Hawk's face registered the coolness of a riverboat poker player. He gave away nothing. Jillian was impressed, she had to admit.

"Well, for someone who got attacked, I seem to be just fine. So perhaps you should check your sources for better information." Hawk was bluffing, again like a riverboat gamler and she knew it.

"Here is what we want, Hawk. We want you to resign." Altman sneered and seemed to fight the urge to point this time. "I have waited for years for this moment but I officially am telling you that you are done. It is time for you to leave Disney."

Jillian could not believe it. A knot formed in her stomach as she heard what the Vice President had instructed Hawk to do. She sucked in her next breath slowly trying to anticipate what would happen next.

"And if I don't?" Hawk asked.

Gross slowly stood. "I will formally gather the board for a special called meeting and we will vote you out. We have been doing a survey of our stockholders and we believe that we have enough support and more than enough shareholders to remove you. It is up to you – do you want to resign and leave quietly with all the perks we can give you? Or would you rather force us to remove you, embarrass you, and have to have a very public ugly vote that will damage all of our reputations?"

For the first time Jillian noticed the ticking of the massive clock on the wall. How had she missed it before? It sounded like thunder claps as the room fell silent. Hawk slowly stood to his feet and slightly cocked his head. He pursed his lips as if he was thinking carefully how to respond. He surely wasn't thinking about resigning, was he? Before she could chase those questions he answered.

"If you want a battle for Disney, then I will give you one." Hawk leaned forward and placed both fists on the table. He spoke softly, slowly and looked at each man as he spoke. "Walt Disney hated dealing with his Board of Directors. They were always getting in the way of trying to choose profit instead of trusting in the quality of what he did."

"You are not Walt Disney." Altman spewed.

Hawk looked at him, then glanced toward Jillian. Her heart sank wishing now that she hadn't said the same thing earlier. When she had said it she was trying to give him a compliment, but the same words, said in a different way sounded cruel and critical.

Hawk smiled. "So I hear and you are right. I'm not Walt Disney. But I do think I know how Walt would want things done. If you want control of Disney, then you are going to have to take it from me. Bring- it- on!"

Hawk straightened up, turned toward Jillian and offered her his arm. She took it and then moved toward the exit. The tuxedoed attendant met them in the oversized lobby and held the door open for them. Jillian pulled up, Hawk turned toward her perplexed, and she released his arm and excused herself hastily retreating back toward the dining room.

Entering the room she saw the surprised look of the three board members who were now busily talking among themselves. Altman had his cell phone out and all three of them stopped and stared at her as she entered the room. Returning to the space they had just been standing in she narrowed her eyes.

"I don't know who you think you are. I didn't know you existed until tonight. But here is something that you need to understand and I just wanted to make sure you knew it before I left. You have picked a battle with the wrong man. If you want to have your Disney war, then so be it, that is up to you. But you have chosen a fight that you just can't win. Grayson Hawkes never loses and he is even better when his back is up against the wall. You have made a terrible mistake. My advice would be to back off before it is too late."

Jillian did not wait for a response, she spun on her heel and headed back into the lobby to find Hawk and leave. As she strode forcefully into the lobby, she saw Hawk waiting for her at the door standing next to the cast member in the tuxedo. In the hands of their host she saw a napkin with a Club 33 logo emblazoned on it, right below the logo she saw the unmistakable scrawled signature that she instantly recognized, "Hawk." The cast member had asked Hawk for an autograph. Allowing her gaze to move from the napkin back to Hawk she noticed a slight smirk on his face.

"What was that all about?" Hawk asked in a voice loaded with curiosity. "Why did you go back in there?"

"I wanted them to scare them just a little bit." She said as they moved through the open doorway. "I told them if they wanted to do battle with you they would have to deal with me."

Hawk laughed. "Thanks, how'd that go?"

Jillian scrunched her nose briefly, paused, then smiled with satisfaction. "I think I scared them."

"I'll bet you did." Hawk pulled her closer as they walked away.

A Doctors Appointment

Chapter Nineteen

Day One – Late Night

A soft white glow of moonlight defied the shadows and drizzled specs of light along the pathway between Pizzafari and Pandora. Juliette became aware of her shoulders slouching from the exhaustion of the day, which was not even close to being over yet, and immediately corrected her posture in an attempt to convince her body to stay alert. Allowing herself an extra roll of the shoulders seemed to rejuvenate herself as she moved through the streets of the Animal Kingdom to the entrance of Tiffins.

Tiffins is named for the metal, multileveled container that most referred to as a tiffin-box, used by travelers and working people in India to carry a light meal. Hawk had explained to her that tiffin referred to the contents of the container, but over time the word had become associated with the Indian lunch box itself. The original idea of this restaurant inside Animal Kingdom had been born out of some conversations between Hawk and the creative development team. She recalled seeing the tiffin-box on his desk as he explained each layer of the container was used to separate wet items, like pickles or yogurt, from other dry items like bread to keep it all from becoming an inedible sloppy mess. Each locking layer could be used as a bowl and the entire contraption would seal together with a handle to create a portable meal holder.

Although he had downplayed his input, she knew the restaurant, even though it is not actually an attraction, was an immersive storytelling experience that celebrated the research and development that went into the Animal Kingdom. The canopy over the door of Tifffins displays a yak carving with big curly horns and red tassels hang from the yak's ears. This seemed odd to her, until the always informative Hawk had explained that to a Tibetan yak herder it would not be strange at all. Domesticated yaks in Tibet have pierced ears and tassel earrings hung from them as decoration. Important to remember she thought if she ever needed to purchase a gift for a yak in Tibet.

Grasping the carved wooden doors, she took note again of the carvings adorning them. A hidden tiger, perhaps more appropriate for this day than she had first considered, hidden among high grass. Moving within the foyer always felt like walking into a museum. Inside the foyer, behind the check in desk is a large stunning wooden carving featuring a map of the world. The detail in it reflects the places the Imagineers visited in creating Disney's Animal Kingdom. The ceiling glowed warm and golden in color, and the lighting radiated from small tiffin carrier boxes converted into fixtures.

There are four areas inside of Tiffins. Three dining rooms and the Nomad's Lounge. The Grand Gallery and the Safari Gallery were to the right of the check in desk. The Grand Gallery is considered the main dining room, with both tables and booths for dining guests, and comfortable seating at all locations. The Safari Gallery is adjacent to the Grand Gallery and is dedicated to the research and designing of the African portions of the theme park. Veering to her left, she made her way into the Nomad's Lounge. This separate but attached bar area has its own bar and lounge feel with transparent drapes covering the windows to the outside patio area, and cool lighting and air conditioning to offer a respite from the sometimes overwhelming outside temperatures. The focal point and hard to miss feature of the Nomad's Lounge are the large number of tags hanging on the ceiling above the bar, and on the neighboring wall. People who choose to contribute to Disney's Conservation Fund are encouraged to write about their most adventurous travels on these tags, which are then displayed in the lounge. This collection of oversized gift tags always made her smile. It was a whimsical addition to an elegantly designed room, a powerful reminder that in the world of Disney fun and adventure were easily intertwined into creating experiences. The bar inside Nomad's was her destination and she assumed the person she was there to meet was already seated and waiting for her.

Furrowing her eyebrows and then quickly releasing them, she forced a smile and spoke to the person sitting there who had not yet heard or acknowledged her approach.

"Doctor Antonio Redfield," she said brightly as she extended her hand. "I am Juliette Keaton."

"Ah, yes." The man spryly turned to greet her. "Juliette Keaton, the chairperson of the theme park division for the Walt Disney Company." With a nod he continued. "I am flattered that you would be the one to come and meet with me."

"Flattered?" The pitch in her voice rose ever so slightly.

"Yes, flattered." Dr. Redfield explained. "I have found that in situations like this, I rarely get to speak to the people who are actually in charge. They rarely have the..." He hesitated, cleared his throat, and continued. "Rarely have the courage to meet with me face to face. They usually have other people who do that and then carry information back to the decision makers."

Juliette pondered this quickly before answering. "Glad for the opportunity to flatter you then."

"I just love Tiffins." Redfield gestured in a sweeping motion with his hand. "I especially am fond of the square box covered in electrical wires, circuit boxes, and photographs in the Safari Gallery up front."

"I'm familiar with it." Juliette slid onto the bar stool next to his. "I've seen it many times."

"You've seen it, but have you seen it?" The doctor's eyes looked past her and then returned to peer at her intensely.

Juliette didn't answer, she simply waited, sensing there was more to follow.

"That display, that square box honors the ingenuity of the citizens who reside in the small villages in Africa. They have to be creative with their resources. It is not odd to see homemade tents along the roadside offering services or wires that seem random, but strung from a meager home to the nearest power grid point." He leaned forward just a bit. "That ingenuity is important because sometimes, in all areas of life, you have to do what needs to be done to make things work and get things done."

Juliette raised an eyebrow and responded. "That display is the Tiffins tribute to the way a community will cobble together and share electrical hookups. In essence share resources, figure out how to make things work and survive."

"Exactly." Redfield broke into a laugh and a smile crossed his aged face. "Perhaps I made a bad assumption a moment ago. I apologize. You have really seen it, you know what it means and you appreciate it."

"An apology is not necessary, Dr. Redfield." Juliette folded her hands into her lap. "As you can imagine it has been quite a day for all of us. I believe you have some findings to share with me."

"Indeed." Redfield pulled in and slowly released his breath. Speaking softly, he continued. "Indeed I do have some findings to share with you."

Stop the Press

Chapter Twenty

Day Two - Morning

Fire-fighting enthusiasts always enjoy wandering past Engine Co. 71 in Walt Disney World's Magic Kingdom. Sitting in a prominent location right next to City Hall, the Firehouse maintains its roots, with decor that sports props and details telling the story of an early-1900s fire department. The company number "71" pays homage to the year the Magic Kingdom opened. For most, the most moving and impressive part of the decor is the tribute to the brave men and women of firehouses from across the country. Located behind multiple glass cases, any guest can view hundreds of local Firehouse patches that have been donated to Disney from fire departments across America. Tucked away inside the Firehouse is a pole that disappears into the roof, up into the living quarters that historically would have been included in old fire departments. Engine Co. 71 is not your typical historical fire station. The upper story of this building is affectionately known by cast members as 'The Hawk's Nest' and is the Magic Kingdom home of Grayson Hawkes.

Over the years, guests have often stopped to look toward the upper windows of the fire station, toward the living area windows, hoping to catch a glimpse of the Chief Creative Architect of the Disney Company. The unmarked metal staircase climbs up the side of the station to a door that enters the apartment. There is a Disney

Security cast member assigned to keep an eye on the stairwell from an unseen location, just across the street at The Emporium. If an unwanted visitor decides to take an unexpected trip up the stairs, there is always a team of people that are immediately visible to stop their progress.

This morning it was early enough that no security was yet on duty. The Magic Kingdom would not be open for a few hours, the sun was just beginning to rise at Walt Disney World, and Juliette was moving briskly across Town Square toward the Fire Station.

"Hey, hold up."

Juliette paused just before reaching the staircase to see Jillian coming down the street past the City Hall.

"I would ask how things went last night with the board, but apparently I don't need to." Juliette reached out and gripped the handrail and turned toward Jillian. She noticed Jillian looked tired, circles under her eyes, and she was not wearing her usual crisp suit that she wore when working. Juliette realized that she had raced to get to the apartment just like she had.

"You've seen it?" Jillian asked as she followed Juliette up the steps.

Ascending the steps quickly the women arrived on the landing and Juliette paused to knock on the door. Jillian reached past her and turned the doorknob and the door instantly opened. With a roll of her eyes, she made a sweeping gesture for Juliette to enter.

"He never locks it." Jillian huffed disapprovingly.

The apartment was much more spacious than it appeared from the outside looking up toward it. There had been a number of remodeling projects and a number of expansions that had created a massive living space, although it was crafted in such a way that the illusion of the original Main Street Fire Station looked unchanged.

"Hawk!" Jillian called out as she moved through the living room toward the television.

"Are you awake?" Juliette added as she moved toward the sofa facing the screen where Jillian was fiddling with the remote.

A sleepy eyed Hawk came out of the kitchen carrying a cup of coffee. He had obviously not been awake too long. Dressed in sweat pants and t-shirt, he looked like he had just rolled out of bed.

"Why are you both here so early?" Hawk paused and took a sip of his coffee. "Have I done something wrong?"

"No, not yet." Juliette almost laughed at his statement. "But it is still early."

"You need to see this." Jillian was looking for a news station.

"What is this?" Hawk took another sip.

"It is on every station this morning." Jillian continued without really answering his question.

"It can wait." Hawk sat down his coffee cup on the counter behind him. "Let me get dressed first." He turned and moved toward his bedroom, hoisting his t-shirt over his head as he went.

Slightly surprised that he didn't seemed overly curious about the two of them being there, Juliette glanced toward Jillian, who had obviously thought the same thing. Exchanging a puzzled glance they looked back toward Hawk as he disappeared behind the bedroom door. As he slid from view, Juliette noticed the scars on his back that were remnants of his being shot by an assassin not too long ago as he protected the President of the United States. She suddenly remembered how close he had come to dying. Immediately she looked back toward Jillian who once again, appeared to be having the same thoughts.

"I sometimes forget how close we were to losing him." Jillian said, rubbing her eyes quickly. "It hasn't been that long ago."

"No, it hasn't." Juliette reached out and patted Jillian on the knee and then motioned back toward the television screen.

The channel she chose was GNN and the anchor was hosting the early morning talk show. He teased that right after the commercial break they would be reporting a shake up in the entertainment world. The set where the anchor was seated blinked out and the telecast went to an advertisement, ironically it was for the Walt Disney World Resort.

"We should all go and visit there." Hawk returned, now wearing a pair of jeans and a stylish button down dress shirt, which he was just finishing with the buttoning process. "What are you going to show me? What do I need to see?" He moved back to the counter and recaptured his coffee mug.

"There is big news breaking here at Walt Disney World." Juliette pointed toward the screen of the television. "It seems that you and Jillian had quite a board meeting last night."

"I had nothing to do with it." Jillian quickly defended. "What a bunch of jerks those three were."

Juliette smiled and nodded knowingly. "Yes, jerk is a good word for them."

"What did they do?" Hawk now moved around the couch and sat down between them as the report began to play.

On the screen, the camera zoomed in uncomfortably close to the face of Mark Gross. Below his chin, the banner gave his name and official title – Mark Gross, President of the Executive Board of the Walt Disney Company.

Hawk turned away from the screen toward Juliette. "When did they film this?"

"Last night, apparently." Juliette heard the strain in her own voice. "I didn't realize they had a press conference. From what security told me, they marched out there, informed everyone who they were and started talking."

Hawk nodded and turned back to the screen. She watched as he leaned in and then became very still as he listened to what Mark Gross was saying to the press.

"We have had a very productive meeting with our Chief Creative Office, a man you all know and respect… as we do." Gross said.

"Liar." Jillian sneered riveted to the screen just like Hawk.

Juliette turned at the same time Hawk did to look at Jillian. Raising her eyebrows, Juliette watched Hawk smile catching her look and then turned back to the screen again.

"It is our belief that the pandemic has peeled back the layers of some issues that we as Board of Directors feel compelled to deal with. As a board we have left the control of the company to Grayson Hawkes and have failed to consistently deal with some issues that are facing our company. Out of respect to the needs of our shareholders, in light of the current financial difficulties and cultural issues that all companies are facing, and because we feel we need to have a management team that can take this great company into the future, we are publically calling out asking for the resignation of Grayson Hawkes. We appreciate his leadership in the past but we feel that he is not the leader to carry us into the future."

There were a few flashes that spilled onto the screen from unseen cameras along with shadows that danced across the outlines of reporters who had hastily assembled for this impromptu press conference. Hawk again turned toward Juliette.

"I assume this has been picked up by most of the networks." He said dryly.

"It has." She exhaled loudly.

"And they are wanting a statement?"

"That hasn't changed." Juliette smiled with a tight lipped smile before continuing. "They wanted one yesterday if you will remember about the problems we had here at the resort. But they have some additional questions to ask now I would imagine."

"So you have officially asked for Hawk to resign?" A reporter off camera asked Gross.

Gross turned his head to face the direction from which the question had come. "We have."

"And has he given you an answer?" Came another question.

"He will be letting us know soon." Gross then turned expecting more questions.

"This guy is scum." Jillian offered her commentary once again.

"I agree." Juliette affirmed.

Another question from an unseen reporter could be heard. "Is the executive board prepared to take action if Hawk refuses to resign?"

Gross again turned toward the question. "We are." He frowned and with a hint of sadness added. "But we don't believe it will come to that point. We fully expect that Grayson Hawkes will resign in the next few days once he has the chance to prepare to do so."

"What exactly does that mean?" Juliette wondered out loud as they watched.

Gross continued his statements. "There really is no other course of action available to him. We have the votes of the shareholders to force him out if necessary, but after all he has done for the good of Disney, we would not want it to come to that."

Hawk grabbed the remote and hit the mute button. Gross disappeared and a news anchor then must have offered more on the subject. In the silence, they kept their eyes on the screen as the scrolling information streamed across the bottom of the network news feed....

Grayson Hawkes has been asked to resign by the Executive Board of the Disney Company.... President of Executive Board Mark Gross delivered the news last night to the press.... Disney stock expected to fall today when the markets open... The Walt Disney Company has experienced the same financial hardship as many others during the pandemic virus era... Hawkes received both praise and criticism for the way he handled the company during the pandemic....

Finally, he seemingly had read all he could stand and Hawk turned off the television. Standing up and moving toward the window to look out over Main Street USA, he hesitated before speaking.

"Are we getting calls from stockholders yet?"

"They have been coming in all night long according to your office." Juliette informed him.

Hawk looked down toward the street. "How is Elliot Drayton this morning?"

Juliette felt a slight rush of adrenaline at the question. "No change, still in critical condition." But she realized that Hawk had just shifted from hearing about the problem to solving the problem. His concern for the tiger attack victim was his pivot back into action.

"Do we know what happened yet?" Hawk now looked directly at her.

"We know more than we did yesterday."

"Then we need to call our own press conference." Hawk now was moving back across the living room and headed toward the bedroom.

Jillian was watching him, slightly puzzled at what was happening, and then finally voiced what she must have been thinking. "What are we doing?"

"We're getting ready to have a press conference and tell people as much as we can about what happened yesterday." Hawk offered back from the bedroom, his voice carried although he was out of sight.

"What did happen?" Jillian shrugged. "We don't have enough information to share yet."

Hawk peered out from the doorframe of the bedroom. "Sure we do. We have enough to change the news cycle for a few minutes and that will give us a little time to figure out the rest."

Jillian now stood, placed her hands on her hips and countered. "You mean you are going to go out there and tell the press what?"

"Don't know. Juliette is going to have to tell us." Hawk now disappeared again into the bedroom.

Jillian now looked to Juliette who was smiling. "Can you explain to me what is happening right now?"

"Yes." Juliette reached over and took Jillian's hand and gently guided her back onto the couch to sit. She sat next to her. "Hawk has some sort of plan he is getting ready to unleash. He is going to tell part of the story to the press to distract them and get them looking one way and he is going to be doing something else."

"And do you know his plan?" Jillian asked.

"No, Hawk doesn't even know his plan yet." Juliette shook her head. "He is going to make it up as he goes… again."

Wowzee-Yikes

Chapter Twenty-One

Day Two – Late Morning

The massive machine whined to life and the noise became louder. The vibration moved up through the floor and then rolled through the seat where he looked out the window. The vibrations continued until the concrete rejected the Bell 525 Relentless helicopter as it shot straight up into the air. The fluttering in Hawk's stomach lasted just a moment as Cap quickly banked and turned the bird north.

"Hold on, Cap." Hawk spoke through the headpiece as he sat in the co-pilot seat.

"What's up?" Cap responded as he quickly checked the gauges.

"Take a slow loop around the woods between The Wilderness Lodge and the campground, please."

"Roger that."

Hawk felt the lift stop and once again the helicopter banked, this time it tilted so he could look directly out his window down into the dense trees below. Searching into the green trees below as they reached upward toward the sky, he studied a ravine that cut between a line of trees and then saw the paths jutting away from it that disappeared out of his sight below the branches.

Cap interrupted his study of the topography below. "What are we looking for?"

Hawk glanced his way, then back to the landscape stretching out below him through the window of the whirlybird.

"That." Hawk pointed and touched the glass with his finger.

Inadvertently sliding forward in his seat, he struggled to position himself for a better view of what he had seen below. A creature, moving upright on two legs, was moving between the trees down a dirt path. Hawk shoved himself against the window and door as if it would somehow help him get closer to what he was seeing.

"Wowzee-yikes!" Cap exclaimed. "What in the Disney World is that?"

The creature slowed, at the sound of the helicopter and attempted to hide under the trees.

"I'm not sure. But I don't think it belongs here."

The Bell Relentless banked once again and this time descended directly toward the tops of the trees below. Leveling out the flying bird, Cap then skirted across the upward reaching limbs of the trees back toward where they had seen the creature.

Hawk felt the thrill of the chase send streams of adrenaline coursing through him. A mixture of amazement at what he was seeing and terrified as to what it might mean caused a lightness in his chest as he strained to catch a glimpse of it again.

"Did you get a good look at it?" Cap asked as he got as close to the trees as he could.

"I've seen it." Hawk said dryly. "Up-close"

Cap glanced at him quickly but kept his attention on the low flying he was now doing. By the time the helicopter banked and turned, both the pilot and co-pilot had lost sight of the creature. Back and forth, in an unrelenting search pattern, the Relentless covered the wooded scenery between the resorts. They were hunting the creature from the air but could not catch a glimpse of it. Finally, Hawk realized that they were not going to see it again. Somehow it had managed to hide and disappear.

Waving his hand, he signaled for Cap to break off the search and instantly the airborne eggbeater slowed and began to lift back into the air.

"You might think I'm crazy, because I've never really seen one before." Cap spoke into the microphone which Hawk heard through his headset. "But that thing looked like a Sasquatch."

Hawk didn't respond, he continued to look back over his shoulder to the woods as the helicopter cut across the parking lot of the Magic Kingdom. The wooded undeveloped area became a landscape of asphalt. Hawk saw the crowd of news media gathered in the corner of the lot and noticed that they seemed to be clumped together in front of what appeared to be a stage with the monorail track as a backdrop. His eyes moved and noticed that a monorail had been pulled up along the track and was now parked on the highway in the sky, giving the media a background that would appear in whatever camera angles they might be using.

"Hawk." Cap once again drew his attention away from the window. "There is no such thing as a Sasquatch. Right?"

Hawk smiled a wavering smile and an hmmm noise came from his throat.

"Of course not." He hoped he sound confident as he fidgeted back into his co-pilot seat.

"Why don't I believe you?" Cap smiled as they increased their speed, leaving the Walt Disney World Resort behind them.

The Known at This Time

CHAPTER TWENTY-TWO

Day Two – Late Morning

"At this point we can say definitively that the reason for the tiger attack and the ultimately the death of the tiger known as Saber, was caused by a virus - canine distemper." Dr. Antonio Redfield stated calmly. "This virus, which by its name you have deduced is usually common to the canine family. It is not unheard of for this type of virus to jump species and it is more than capable of infecting big cats, as was the case here at Disney's Animal Kingdom."

David Walker glanced around the sea of cameras and journalists that had claimed their position and were even now broadcasting and streaming live feeds back to their representative networks. However, GNN was not doing that. Allie had decided that she wanted the extra time to film the entire press briefing and then edit it down into a number of slick, clean, and more succinct packages that they could place on air during all of their news shows. The same clips plus even more of the background material that GNN had been creating throughout the day, could also provide footage for the evening news and entertainment shows if their pundit hosts desired to put this into their rotation that evening. Allie explained to David that the extra time would pay off, they would be less than a half an hour later than others in breaking their first news package, but it would be so much better and so much more memorable.

David agreed and even if he didn't, they would have gone with Allie's plan. She had great instincts as a producer and had a fantastic mentor in Kate Young years ago. So for now, all he had to do was watch and not add his commentary until later in the editing process and the live feeds with the anchors of their programming.

"Although you rarely hear of a virus like this, they are more common than you might think. If I remember correctly, the Tanzania Serengeti National Park had an outbreak of this particular strain of the disease in 1994. It infected nearly 3,000 of their lions and tigers. It was fatal for one-third of them." Redfield removed his glasses and rubbed his eyes.

That simple motion, that almost undetectable movement looked strangely familiar to David. The entire time Redfield had been speaking, wrapped around his listening to the content, his mind had been playing games trying to figure out why the doctor looked so familiar. When he removed his glasses and rubbed his eyes before continuing, David knew that he was right. He had run across the doctor at some point in his career, but where?

Redfield was seated next to Juliette Keaton, who started off the conference with the usual greetings. An extremely grim update on the injured Disney cast member, now identified as Elliot Drayton, and then she turned the briefing over to Dr. Redfield. The press conference was interrupted as a low flying helicopter nearly buzzed the crowd in the parking lot. Instantly everyone looked up in startled fear or disbelief that there was a helicopter that low to the ground. David recognized it as The Flying Mouse, the unofficial name the company had given it, and knew a high level Disney executive was on board. Retracing the flight of the chopper, he saw that it must have come from the nearby landing area close to the wilderness area between resorts.

Why would they have been flying through here now with a press conference going on? David wondered to himself. Turning, he looked back toward the podium and saw Juliette Keaton's face as the helicopter went past. She grimaced, ever so slightly, and he knew that she was not pleased with the distraction. Disney, historically was better produced than that. Even a press briefing at the Walt Disney World Resort had a certain level of showmanship and polish.

"The virus can progress from respiratory and digestive issues to neurological problems. That is what we believe happened in Saber." Redfield sat back in his seat as he concluded his portion of the presentation.

On the opposite side of Juliette Keaton was another woman they had introduced as Katie Rose, an animal trainer and large animal expert according to her introduction at Disney's Animal Kingdom. David took note that she looked extremely tired and upset. He understood that this must have been a very long season of events for their staff and people who were passionate about animals got just as emotional about their health as humans.

"As Dr. Redfield explained, canine distemper may also cause brain inflammation and neurological symptoms, which will often present like rabies. Neurological symptoms of canine distemper include, fever, nasal discharge, eye discharge, lethargy, loss of appetite, the thickening of nose and foot pads, along with pain. Saber had recently had some of these symptoms but they had subsided and there was no reason to think they were anything more than a brief or passing illness." Katie cleared her throat and continued. "Although there are vaccines for dogs, studies have shown the dog vaccine isn't safe for big cats. There has also been a vaccine developed for canine distemper for ferrets, but there is no evidence the ferret vaccine is effective in big cats either. Since Saber was exhibiting no serious symptoms, we would not have even considered any type of vaccine."

"It takes some time for the neurological symptoms to come to the surface." Redfield interrupted. "That appears to be the case in this large cat."

David heard what they were saying but his mind was still rifling through years of experiences, interviews, news events, breaking stories, crisis, and human interest trying to remember where he had come across the Head Investigative Researcher for the International Institute of Health, Antonio Redfield. Why did he seem so familiar? Shaking off those thoughts for a moment, he now realigned his attention to the change in briefing as they were now taking questions from the press.

Juliette pointed to a man seated on the front row of the chairs closest to the stage.

"There are additional reports of a gorilla attack that occurred in Animal Kingdom yesterday. Can you confirm that and was it related to this animal canine virus?" The reporter asked.

"There was an incident with one of our gorillas yesterday, that is true." Juliette said. She glanced toward Dr. Redfield, who once again removed his glasses, rubbed his eyes, and returned them to his face.

"We are not really prepared with a report on that incident, but we have no reason to believe that canine distemper would be involved." Redfield stated quickly.

David Walker smiled ever so slightly.

"What are you looking so smug about?" Allie Crossman whispered to him.

"That Redfield doctor." David nodded toward him, the smile disappearing. "I have seen him before, heard him before, and covered something related to him before."

"What?" Allie turned and looked back toward the stage.

"I can't remember… yet." David looked toward Allie. "But that thing he does, he takes off his glasses and rubs his eyes. It's a tell."

"A tail?" Allie was confused.

"A tell, T-E-L-L," David whispered louder. "It is what I remember for some reason. When he does that move it is a giveaway, he is not telling us the complete truth."

Allie now watched the stage with a renewed sense of urgency.

Another question came from the press corps seated to the left of the stage. "Last night the Disney Board of Directors called for the resignation of Grayson Hawkes as the Chief Creative Architect of the Company. Has he tendered that resignation and is he going to make a comment?"

"This briefing is to update you on the events at Animal Kingdom yesterday." Juliette deflected the question. Her posture became a bit more rigid than it had been. "Any more questions?"

Instantly a couple of more questions came sailing her way all at once, all of them in one way or another had to do with the announcement from the previous evening from Mark Gross. Hesitating slightly, then forcing a smile, Juliette leaned back up into the microphone.

"I know there is a lot going on and we appreciate you covering the news here so fairly. I can tell you in no uncertain terms that Dr. Grayson Hawkes is still the Chief Creative Architect of the Walt Disney Company. If he has any intention of tendering his resignation he has not indicated that to me. I believe Mr. Gross made his position very clear last evening although I do not believe that his opinions are reflective of the culture of our company. If anything changes or there is an update, we will certainly let you know."

"Will there be a statement from Hawkes?" The question flew over the crowd from the rear of the reporter herd.

"I am sure there will be an official statement or response at some point." Juliette pushed her chair back and spoke as she turned to leave the stage. "Thank you for coming."

David watched the event wrap up. Allie stood next to him before summarizing.

"Dr. Redfield didn't take his glasses off or rub his eyes again." Allie correctly stated.

"That's because he doesn't know anything about what is going on with Hawk and the Board of Directors."

"Or maybe he didn't rub his eyes because they didn't itch." Allie elbowed David gently in the rib cage.

He feigned pain and then said. "Trust me, he doesn't have an itchy eye problem, he has a problem telling the truth." David watched as Redfield left the stage. "I know it and I will remember why I know it, just give me time."

Paying Attention to History

CHAPTER TWENTY-THREE

Day Two - Noon

The Flying Mouse traveled in the air above the congested Orlando traffic on Interstate 4. Their destination was a community on the outskirts of the downtown Orlando area known as College Park. College Park is a rarity in a big city because of how it has maintained a sense of local pride and self-containment. The community boasts a lively main street, Edgewater Drive, loaded with shops, restaurants, unusual art displays, and community street parties. It is an eclectic mix of people and activity. Some of the original neighborhood homes remain to this day. These unique 1900s bungalow homes are surrounded by numerous lakes and parks, and are worth a great deal of money in the Orlando real estate market.

College Park has the reputation of being a fantastic place to raise a family and has had some celebrities that have chosen to call College Park home. Astronaut John Young lived on West Princeton Street as a child. The bulk of the streets in College Park are named after colleges, hence the naming of the community. Young spent forty-two years with NASA, the longest career of any astronaut. He was the ninth person to walk on the moon as the Commander of Apollo 16 and he also was aboard a space shuttle. College Park proudly claimed him as one of their own.

Writer Jack Kerouac lived on Clouser Avenue during the publishing of his masterpiece *On The Road*. He also wrote his follow-up novel *The Dharma Bums* at the same home. Kerouac's home now houses a non-profit called The Kerouac Project, a haven for up-and-coming writers. Four writers are selected each year to stay in the home for three months. During their stay, they work on a writing project which is presented at the end of their residency.

The most recent and current celebrity resident of College Park was a former Disney Imagineer named Farren Rales. Chosen by Walt Disney himself, Farren knew the Disney brothers very well. In some ways it had been his responsibility to carry on their legacy when they passed away. That is how he eventually met or chose Hawk. It has been Rales that had paved the way for Hawk to become the head of Disney and it had cost both of them dearly. Now completely retired, Rales never ventured onto Disney property, and if Hawk visited with him it always involved going to wherever Farren wanted to meet, as was this meeting today.

When Rales had asked Hawk how he would be coming to visit, Hawk had casually blurted out that he would be flying. Normally he would drive and spend some extended time with his aging friend. But the events of the previous day and the quickness with which Farren had responded to his flying comment, now found Hawk aboard the helicopter, headed for the coordinates that Farren had texted to him.

The chopper traveled above the street the local high school had been named after, Edgewater. Banking once again they turned and hovered over the high school football stadium. Hawk looked out the window and saw the words on the side of the stadium. Edgewater High School, home of the Fighting Eagles. Twisting ever so slightly, Cap lined up the helicopter to land on the fifty yard line of the football field below. Slowly descending, Hawk could see that all of the activity in the stadium, which seemed to be athletes running on the track below had come to a halt with their approach. Cap set the chopper down softly on the ground below and cut the motor and instantly the rotors began to slow. Not waiting for them to stop, Hawk bound out of the flying vehicle and trotted across the green grass of the football field. Looking up in the stands, he saw Farren Rales, seated on the bottom row, smiling ear to ear, and waving.

Returning the wave, Hawk made his way through the fence gate and climbed the aluminum steps that carried him to where his friend and in many ways, his mentor, was seated.

"Real subtle entrance there, Hawk." Rales said as he stood to embrace his friend.

"Well, I wanted to impress you." Hawk said gripped in his hug.

As they were seated, Rales muttered. "I'm too old and seen too much to be impressed. But good try."

Hawk loved the way Rales face lit up when he smiled. This old Imagineer was a great storyteller and had been involved in the groundbreaking work of the Disney

Studios back when Walt and Roy were still living. Walt had entrusted to Rales the responsibility of passing his most precious and dangerous secrets on to someone that could be trusted, to protect and use them in the years beyond Walt's life. Rales had selected Hawk, and the changes had been almost indescribable, if not unbelievable.

"You're here because you are in trouble, right?" Rales said.

Small talk was never one of the habits Rales engaged in,

Exhaling loudly, Hawk replied. "You could say that."

"I saw that buffoon, Mark Gross, grousing how you were going to resign as CCO of the Company." Rales glanced at Hawk. "You quittin' and forget to tell me?"

"No, I'm not quitting. But they want the company."

"Who wants the company?" Rales allowed his gaze to turn toward some hurdlers working out on the track in front of them.

"The Board of Directors it seems." Hawk turned to watch what Farren was watching. "They don't like the way I led through the pandemic."

"No one had ever led through a plague, so how could you screw that up?"

Hawk smiled. "They don't like the way I handled the cast members."

"You tried not to fire anyone and you figured out how to pay people with no money coming into the parks." Rales countered.

"They don't like my politics."

Rales raised an eyebrow at that statement. "Well, I don't necessarily like your politics either and I'm not real sure about your good friend, the former president of the United States. He nearly got you killed once." He cleared his throat. "But you have tried to steer the company clear of politics and away from the cultural activists that always want to be in charge. I bet they don't like that at all, but you don't care, do you?"

Hawk thought for a moment before answering. "No, I can handle that kind of pressure."

"Anything else?"

"The board doesn't like the stock prices being down and the way I have managed the company during the virus days."

"Bingo!" Rales pointed a finger at nothing in front of him. "That is the real problem. They think you have cost them money and they don't like it. They also don't like it that you have the power to cost them money. It is always about money and power."

"I know," Hawk leaned back and stretched his arms out to rest on the row of bleacher seats behind him. "But this time they have threatened me. They have made it public. It seems as if they want more."

Rales remained quiet after Hawk said this. He was engrossed in watching the hurdlers run over the top of the barriers in the fifth lane of the track. As one hurdler hit the crossbar with his trail leg, the sound of the hurdle falling and resetting itself with a clank, echoed hollowly across the running surface toward them. Rales winced at the impact in sympathy for the hurdler, who now stood beside the hurdle, straightening it and rubbing his knee.

"Here at Edgewater High School, back in 1979 they had one of the best high school track teams ever in the state of Florida. In every event they were a threat. They had a good hurdler, he was undefeated, broke records, and was the state champion. The team was the runner up in the state that year, they would have won it they had been in the fast heat of the 4 x 100 meter relay."

Hawk furrowed his brow. "Didn't know you were a track and field fan."

"I'm not, I'm an Edgewater High School fan and that was one of the best teams ever. I've lived here since 1971 and I have been a part of this community." Rales said thoughtfully. "I know what that team did and I haven't forgotten. I can compare it to other teams because I pay attention to history. You know, that is the trouble for most, they don't pay attention to history and they sure don't know how to learn from it and preserve it."

Ah, thought Hawk. There was a point to the story, there always was a point to the story when Rales told one.

"I moved to College Park because of an old friend of mine, a diver named Hal. He was a famous scuba instructor and the founder of the Professional Scuba Association." Rales motioned with his hand as if giving directions as he continued to speak. "Right around the corner, hidden in College Park's Biltmore Shores neighborhood is an infamous sink hole, called the Mystery Sink, near Fairbanks Avenue."

Hawk had no idea where this story was going, but he always knew that Rales used the art of storytelling to communicate things that always left him stunned, so he focused on Rales' words and kept listening.

"The Mystery Sink was also called Emerald Springs, but locals called it "the sink" and "the bottomless pit" - The US Department of Interior performed a geological study of the sink and the US Navy sonar research department did a study. Documented as the deepest known body of water in the state of Florida, it has been estimated the depths reach 500 feet and beyond." Rales turned toward Hawk and paused the story. "Did you know that the deepest known body of water in the state of Florida is right around the corner from here?"

"No, I didn't." Hawk admitted.

Rales playfully slapped him on the arm. "Don't worry about it, most of the locals here don't either, because they don't pay attention to history." Rales then laughed. "You probably are wondering what that has to do with your problem and why you are here."

"Well, I was beginning to think you might be slipping and were going to tell me that I was sinking the Disney Company into a bottomless pit." Hawk placed an arm on Rales shoulder.

"You seem to be." Rales offered no encouragement. "But you need me to rescue you again, don't you."

"Actually…" Hawk hesitated. "Yes."

Rales laughed. "At one time, the sink was promoted as a roadside attraction, but today it sits on private property. In 1970, just before I moved here, the hole was closed to the public after some tragic deaths. My friend, Hal leased the sink to use for training divers and instructors. In August of 1970, Hal and a young man named Fred, a certified diver, dove into the Mystery Sink to recover an expensive diving jacket that had been left during a previous dive. Hal resurfaced but Fred never did. Two recovery divers descended to 375 feet but were unable to find the body. Underwater cameras were sent down but revealed nothing. Two days later, Hal went back in along with three other divers, attempting to find Fred, but tragedy struck once more when a man named Bud lost his life to the sink too."

"That's awful."

"Neither body was ever recovered. Hal's attempt to save Bud nearly cost him his life as well when he developed the bends, decompression sickness, from ascending too quickly; he was taken to NASA Space Center at Cape Canaveral to undergo decompression treatment. Jacques-Yves Cousteau once said, "From birth, man carries the weight of gravity on his shoulders. He is bolted to earth. But man has only to sink beneath the surface and he is free and diving, though dangerous, allows those brave enough a chance to be free in a mysterious sink, revealing the underworld on which we live every day." Rales looked down, interlaced the fingers on his hands, and sighed. "The Mystery Sink is right around the corner and no one knows it is there, because they don't pay attention to the past and learn from it."

"As a matter of fact, not far from the Mystery Sink, Lake Fairview once had its own mystery that brought visitors to gawk at what they thought was a natural wonder. The Lake Fairview "spouting well" first appeared in the early years of the 20th century at the Davis-McNeill farm on the lake's south side, where a geyser began to erupt about every six minutes and reached heights of 75 to 100 feet."

"It's not there anymore?" Hawk asked.

Shaking his head, Rales story continued, "From my research, an article in Scientific American magazine back in 1911, revealed Orlando officials had faced problems because the city's lakes often overflowed. It was a real problem for old farmers around here who found their fields flooded." Rales grinned, "The remedy was to drive pipes hundreds of feet into the ground in search of underground passageways into which to drain the excess water. At Lake Fairview, around the corner." Rales pointed in the distance. "The top of one such pipe near the lake's edge sat only five inches below the water's surface. The so-called geyser resulted when air pressure built up in a natural underground chamber, reached a critical point, and rushed up out of the pipe. It shot water into the air like a fountain, eventually the city capped the pipe and the geyser disappeared."

Rales stood up in the stands to stretch his legs. "I went looking for that pipe in the lake one day. I was going to take the cap off just to give people an unexpected surprise. I think it would be fun to see it."

Motioning for Hawk to walk with him, the pair made their way out of the stands and onto the running track. The moved in silence for a few moments before Hawk broke it by saying out loud what he knew his friend was waiting to hear. It was the question.

"So what does your diver friend Hal have to do with my problem at Walt Disney World?" Hawk asked.

"I just knew you were going to ask me that." Rales almost giggled. "Hal and I did not meet by chance, Hal found something that you need to find and figure out how to use it."

"Hal was friends with Walt Disney?"

"No, I didn't say that. But Hal found something for Walt Disney because of a mutual acquaintance, a Wernher von Braun."

Hawk stopped in his tracks. The father of modern rocketry had been a friend of Walt Disney. He had appeared in a series of television shows for Walt, but also had entrusted Walt with some secrets. These secrets were kept in Walt's very personal diaries and contained page after page of notes that had been given to Walt by Wernher von Braun. These secrets over the years had become a target for those that knew the connection between Walt and von Braun.

"Hawk, so much in life is about timing. The global pandemic, the disruption of the coronavirus, the upheaval in culture, the global turmoil-the timing is right and there are always people who want to take advantage of what is happening. As I said, it is always about power and money."

"But help me, because I am not tracking with you. There is something that Hal found that somebody wants?"

"Yes, exactly, because they have paid attention to a bit of history that everyone else seems to have forgotten." Rales eyes danced as he helped Hawk put together the narrative.

"And you know what they are looking for?"

"I think I do." Rales nodded.

"And you know where it is?"

Rales shook his head. "No, but I know you can find it and I can help you."

"But you don't know where it is?"

"No and that is on purpose." Rale stopped and turned toward Hawk. "I can point you in the right direction, you will have to find it on your own."

"Can you tell me what I am looking for?"

"Have you ever heard of the Spear of Destiny?" Rales' voice trailed off to a whisper.

"No." Hawk whispered back. "But it sounds like something out of an Indiana Jones movie."

"Good thing Disney owns the rights to those now."

"Seriously?" Hawk shrugged. "The Spear of Destiny?"

"Yes."

"And your friend, Hal found it?"

"Yes, for Walt Disney." Rales seemed to be enjoying himself, which was bit frustrating to Hawk in this current moment. "And you have to find it. I made arrangements for it to be placed somewhere in the resort. But since you know the history and pay attention to it – you can find it and now you need to do so. Because I fear that someone out there believes you know where it is or they think they know where it is. And they want it, badly."

Hawk felt a tremor race across his chest, a mixture of fear and intrigue at what he was about to hear. He was not prepared for what he would hear next.

A Cage in the Steam

CHAPTER TWENTY-FOUR

Day Two - Afternoon

Steam billowed out the door to the bathroom as the man slowly pushed it open. The wave of the warm cloud momentarily stopped him in his tracks. He was jumpy and the feel of warm air racing across his leathery skin caused a tremble to race up one arm and down the other, all the way down to his fist, which was tightly wrapped around the handle of the heavy cage he carried with him.

The initial fog lifted slightly and he heard Jillian Batterson humming as she showered. How hot did she have the water?, he thought to himself as he felt a line of wetness along his collar. Sweat or steam induced, he wasn't sure. But it didn't matter and it would not distract him from the task at hand. Placing the cage on the ground, he was careful not to let it make a sound against the tile floor. Looking toward the shower stall, he could see the outline of Jillian's figure moving behind the frosted glass of the shower door. Puffs of steam climbed out of the opening at the top of the door like a steam engine getting ready to take off down the tracks.

Moving as quietly as possible, he was confident that between the cascading water of the shower, the song that Jillian was humming, and his slow deliberate movements, he was not going to be detected. Getting his bearings in the bathroom, he glanced toward the mirror above the sink. Coated in a misty fog from the heat of the shower, the large expansive counter around the sink held a variety of personal items and he saw the one he was looking for. Crouching down, stepping over the cage, he reached the counter and picked up Jillian's phone. It was playing a Disney tune that she was listening to as she showered. Since the screen was unlocked, this would make what he was about to do easier and accomplish more damage than he might have hoped for.

It had been easy to gain access to her townhouse styled home in Bay Lake Towers. He simply borrowed a maintenance cast member's uniform, walked down the hall with his kit, and turned the handle of the door. When it opened, he smiled with satisfaction because at this moment, every single automated lock in the entire Walt Disney World Resort was unlocked. The system had been hacked, deactivated, and once again a statement was being made about who had the ability to control the happenings in the resort.

The humming now became a song, A Dream is a Wish Your Heart Makes – hardly the song he expected. He didn't know why, he just didn't think Jillian was a singer of Disney princess songs, but who was he to judge.

Reaching down, he carefully slid open the door to the cage and tilted it away from him. His legs began to hurt but at this delicate moment of his task, he would endure a little discomfort for his own personal safety. He didn't have to wait long as the head, the body, and tail slithered out of the confinement that had kept him safe. The black tiger snake is an indigenous snake species of Australia. They were very rare to find in the United States and could only be found in zoological centers. The snake exhibits variance in color mostly banded like those visible on a tiger. Appropriate, he mused to himself, tigers and tiger snakes creating havoc in the land of the Mouse.

Although he was not an expert, he knew a little bit about this type of snake and the little bit he knew terrified him. Once the snake had cleared the cage, it slid across the tiled bathroom floor. Tiger snakes are at their most aggressive in warm temperatures, the bathroom was definitely warm. The seven foot length was scary but fully mature, tiger snakes reached lengths of ten feet. The snake's venom causes adverse effects in humans such as breathing difficulties, numbness, tingling sweating, and paralysis. Each year, usually in Australia, tiger snakes are responsible for multiple human's either being killed or injured.

The snake slid next to the small step into the shower, where the shower door remained closed. Confident now that there was enough distance between them, the man carefully closed up the cage and gingerly set it outside the bathroom door for a hasty retreat. Turning his attention back to the snake and the shower stall, he punched the camera app on Jillian's phone to activate it, then carefully aligned the frosted steamy door of the shower in the box setting up the photograph. He pushed the red button and sucked in his breath when he heard an unexpected "click." The phone was not set on silent and the click was loud enough to be heard, echoing just a bit through the bathroom causing the song to suddenly come to a halt.

The only noises now in the bathroom was the water still running, hitting the shower floor, and splashing against the wall and door. As if on cue, the music track was fading into quietness. Quickly and carefully, he placed the phone back on the counter where he had picked it up. As he did, he allowed his eyes to shift between the snake at the base of the shower door and the now still shadow behind the opaque damp door.

"Hello?" Jillian called out.

Once again, quiet filled the space and it became even more deafening when she abruptly cut the water off. Once again steam billowed through the room, but quickly dissipated through the open bathroom door. The man watched the tiger snake flatten its body and raise its head into an aggressive attack position. He had run out of time and this was his signal to get out now.

No matter what happened next, he had accomplished his task and it went much smoother and easier than he first thought it might go. Closing the door behind him as he exited, he heard the sound of the shower door open. Grabbing the case, he was already at the front door when he thought he heard a shriek or perhaps a scream. He was not sure. Curiosity caused him to hesitate just a half a step, but realized he needed to make his getaway. Whatever happened, he had once again done his part, done enough to get their attention. The events that would happen next were out of his hands.

Doctor in the House

CHAPTER TWENTY-FIVE

Day Two – Late Afternoon

David was jarred from the screen of his laptop as Allie entered the Iron Spike Room from around the corner. He had retreated here and been here for hours, tapping into every research data base he had access to. In the midst of the search, he had lost track of time. But it had been worth it, or at least he thought so.

"I wondered where you had disappeared to." Allie's voice was bright and cheerful.

"I came over here because it is quiet, away from all of our media friends, and as Hawk always tells us, this place is a hide away in the middle of a world of activity."

Allie grabbed the chair nearest to the one he was in, but it was too big to drag. She adeptly stepped behind it, leaned into it and it scraped across the floor until it rested next to his.

"I could have helped you with that." David suggested.

"You could have but you didn't offer."

"You didn't really give me an opportunity."

"Oh no, you are the big news star, I can't have you moving furniture for the lowly producer." She was trying to suppress a smile.

"Since you put it that way," David scrunched up his nose. "You're right. I can't be helping the hired help."

Allie responded to this with a playful slap on the backside of his head. Settling into the chair, she slid toward the arm rest closest to him so she could get an angle on seeing the screen.

"If you're going to be a jerk, at least I hope you are being a productive jerk."

"Always…" David smirked then stopped. "Always productive not always a jerk. I just save that for my special friends."

"I'm so honored." She shook her head from side to side, once again focusing on the screen.

"I told you that Redfield looked familiar to me. That I had seen him before, I had heard of him, that I had run into him. But I couldn't put my finger on it."

"You also said his tell was that thing he does when he removes his glasses and rubs his eyes." Allie turned to face him.

"That was the habit or the mannerism that got me thinking."

"So what have you found?" Allie leaned in closer to the screen to see better.

"This…" David punched a couple of keys and then the screen filled with a document. He pointed at the date on it and began to explain. "In 1951, a woman named Henrietta Lacks visited John Hopkins Hospital complaining of bleeding. Doctors discovered a large, malignant tumor on her cervix."

"Oh no, that's terrible." Allie kept her eyes transfixed on the screen

"Agreed - Lacks began undergoing radium treatment for cervical cancer and later underwent a biopsy to determine the progress of the treatment. What was strange was that doctors were shocked to find that Lacks' cells were unlike any others they had ever seen."

David waited for her to process what he had just said. Then he continued. "Other cells that they used for research would die, Lacks' cells doubled every 20-24 hours."

"That's impossible." Allie's mouth fell slightly open.

"It was, you're right.' David nodded. "But all of that changed with Henrietta. Today, these cells, nicknamed "HeLa" cells, are replicated worldwide and have been used to study the human genome; the effects of toxins, drugs, hormones, and viruses on the growth of cancer cells; and it played a crucial role in the development of polio vaccines and most recently COVID-19 vaccines."

"You're kidding."

"No, I'm not. According to what I am finding, Lacks' cells were the first immortalized human cell line and one of the most important cells in the history of medical research."

"That is amazing and I am impressed." Allie scratched her chin looking toward David. "And that is important to us and Dr. Antonio Redfield, how?"

David's fingers went back to work on the keys and found another article that he had bookmarked in his research.

"Look at this, I found a story about how cell biologist Otto Guy, took one cell from Henrietta Lack's sample, allowed that cell to divide, and found the culture survived indefinitely if given nutrients and a suitable environment. Since then, the work started by Otto has continued and those original cells continued to mutate. Now, there are many strains of HeLa, all derived from the same single cell."

"I'm not seeing the connection to Redfield yet." Allie was trying to follow along. David knew when he was doggedly tracking down information, he sometimes didn't slow down enough to explain it. He had learned to postpone that until he was summarizing for his news reports.

"Researchers believe the reason HeLa cells don't suffer programmed death is because they maintain a version of the enzyme telomerase that prevents gradual shortening of the telomeres of chromosomes. Whatever that is..."

"Again, that is all impressive but the connection?"

David again went to work on the keyboard and then turned the screen so Allie could see clearly without having to contend with any glare from the angle.

"I found this picture of Otto Guy, look close, add a whole bunch of years and who does it look like?"

Allie smiled. "None other than Dr. Antonio Redfield."

"Exactly, but wait there is more..."

David again went to work on the keyboard as Allie thought and then finally asked. "But why did Otto Guy change his name or identity to Antonio Redfield?"

"Don't know, but I have a guess."

"Which is?" Allie tapped her finger on the chair impatiently.

"Look at this." David turned the screen and hit the space bar. The video on the screen started playing a video from years ago, taken at some sort of press conference, set in a lab.

The video showed Redfield or Guy sitting behind a workstation answering questions. The man on the video spoke... "Based on this latest research, we believe that because of these discoveries about the telomerase enzyme that it is possible to replicate cells at a rate where regeneration is a possibility."

The video sound was not clear, but a reporter from off screen asked. "The regeneration of what is a possibility."

Redfield smiled and said simply, "Anything."

Again a voice from off screen asked another question. "Is that ethical? Isn't there a moment where you are worried about playing God or Creator?"

Redfield took off his glasses and wearily rubbed his eyes. Allie jabbed a finger at the screen. There it is, that thing he does, his tell.

David laughed and then watched the screen as the doctor replaced his glasses and then shook his head dismissively before answering. Redfield answered the question he had been asked. "Of course it is ethical, it is science."

"Hmmm… that is a strange answer." Allie noted.

"Yes, apparently if it is in the name of science then it must be ethical." David sighed and pushed the screen away from them both. "And that may have been the problem with our researcher Otto Guy. He seemed to have been running afoul of the ethics boards of some of the research companies that were paying him. He simply disappeared, dropped off the radar."

"And his research?" Allie sat back in her chair.

"It disappeared with him." David blinked looking toward the fireplace. "Whatever he was working on disappeared with him and what happened is unknown. Then some twenty-five years later, a doctor with almost no information available about his past suddenly emerges and is hired as one of the top research experts by a number of health and government institutes. His most recent gig is as the Head Investigative Researcher of the International Institute of Health."

"And if that is Redfield, who used to be Otto Guy, then he never stopped his research but now as the head of the IIH, he is here at Walt Disney World?"

"He is a hired specialist. Apparently there is a reason for him to be here at Disney. But I am convinced that is really Otto Guy and Redfield is just an assumed name."

"But why?"

"Ah, that is the question isn't it? Why is the doctor in the house of mouse?"

The *SEA* Will Tell

CHAPTER TWENTY-SIX

Day Two – Late Afternoon

Leaning against the cool Plexiglas of the window, Hawk twirled the challenge coin between his fingers. Each flip of the coin allowed him a clear view of what was on either side. The heavy metal was gold and one side featured the picture of a painting called, "Walt's Magical Barn." As he stopped flipping the coin, he brought the picture closer to his face. It reminded him that a humble barn can become a magical place. In this case, the magic was creativity where Walt nurtured his ideas into reality. For Walt Disney his quaint red barn served as the hub of operations for his large scale Carolwood Pacific Railroad. The painting captures a fine spring day, he is tinkering on his steam locomotive, which he named Lilly Belle for his wife, Lillian.

The helicopter took an unexpected bump across some turbulence and Hawk allowed the story on this inch and a half painting play out in front of him. Stepping into Walt's view is a boy appearing alongside his older brother, Roy. In the distance puffs an old steamer on its thundering run through Marceline, Missouri. Walt notices the boy looks strangely familiar. It is a young Walt Disney, a memory or perhaps his own inner child calling for him to come outside and wave to the engineer of this train from his own memories past. The engineer was Walt's Uncle Mike.

Tilting the coin and allowing the light to dance across the image, Hawk noticed that the wristwatch on Walt Disney's arm had no hands. When the artist who created the painting, Bob Byerley created it, he told people who noticed that detail that it was very much on purpose. His meaning suggested that as Walt remembers his past, enjoys the present, and anticipates the future, he can and will, above all, remain timeless – as long as his memory is kept alive.

It was a powerful painting and one of Hawk's personal favorites of Walt. He would often look at it in the Iron Spike Room at Disney's Wilderness Lodge. The opposite side of the coin contained the words in all capital letters – SOCIETY OF EXPLORERS AND ADVENTURERS – DREAM IT – DO IT. He once again went back to flipping it in his hand, letting it move over, under, and across his fingers like a magician might manipulate a coin for a trick. Farren had given it to him as he had walked him back to The Flying Mouse. The old Imagineer had placed it in Hawk's hand as they were saying goodbye and gave him some instructions.

"Follow the advice, *go left next to the monkey.*" Rales was smiling as he said it.

Hawk felt his stomach flip slightly as he realized he was about to begin another one of Farren Rales secret adventures. The payoff was always huge and each treasure hunt offered surprises and so much more than Hawk had ever dreamed. But still, he thought those days were done, another treasure hunt, but why? Wouldn't it be easier just to tell him where to go? Before he could say that out loud, Farren had answered the question for him.

"The reason you have to find it is because it so valuable and must remain safe and hidden."

"So this will take me to or help me find the Spear of Destiny?" Hawk looked back at his friend once he was seated inside the chopper.

Farren leaned in and with a glint in his eye said, "Eventually, if you can figure it out. And what you will find, if you can find it, will save Disney."

Farren started to turn away, then suddenly stopped and with an almost theatrical groan said. "Wait a minute. I almost forgot." He came back to the chopper. "You need this also."

Hawk reached out and felt Farren slip the small object into his hand. Nodding to let him know he really did have the object, the Imagineer released his grip on it. As Hawk glanced down he was it was an official WDW Pin - Florida Project - Building One Story at a Time - 20,000 Leagues Under the Sea. It was made to resemble a file folder. This was something that many collectors loved in the Disney theme parks, collectible pins and it seemed to Hawk that their marketing and merchandise teams made an endless number of pins. Although not an official collector of pins, he did have an assortment of very special ones. Turning the pin over, he could see it was a limited edition pin and had a hinge on it. Flipping it open with his thumb, the picture inside shows Goofy receiving a wrench from the squid at the 20,000 Leagues Under The Sea attraction. The hard hat icon on the blue folder's front is included as a pin-on-pin element. The tab on the file reads "Big Squid."

"A collector's pin?" Hawk questioned not what it was but why he had it.

"Yep, it is special." Rales smiled then added. "It will make sense later, I hope."

Hawk shoved the pin into his pocket.

"Hawk, you need to be careful. Once others believe you have the Spear of Destiny, they will stop at nothing to get it. They will kill you. That is how valuable it is."

"Great, someone else who wants to kill me." Hawk winked at his friend. "I appreciate you giving me this job that is always so dangerous."

"No thanking me necessary." Farren stepped away. "You deserve it, no I mean... you've earned it." Then he snapped and laughed out loud. With a wave he had said, "You know what I mean." Hawk pulled back toward the door as Farren reached out one more time taking him by the wrist. "If you find the Spear of Destiny, who knows, you might just save the Magic Kingdom."

Hawk didn't know how to respond, he simply nodded.

"Good luck." Farren said as he released him to move into the helicopter.

"I don't believe in luck." Hawk smiled closing the door behind him as The Flying Mouse lifted off into the air.

"So I hear." He could read his friends lips through the window.

Now he was trying to gather his thoughts and boot up his mental computer that contained his uncanny knowledge of the world of Walt Disney. He was familiar with the Society of Explorers and Adventurers, also known as S.E.A. The Society is a fictional organization in various attractions at the Disney theme parks. The society and its members add a special extra layer of theming without getting in the way of casual tourists. What Hawk liked best about it and probably explained why he had so often green lighted another part of the story is because the way the characters were created helped to weave an intricate and fun way to tie the Disney resorts together. He had always told himself that Walt Disney would have liked it also. Since its inception, Hawk realized that he had allowed the Imagineers to create storylines and connections that he was not as familiar with, but he did know the connections in the Walt Disney World Resort in Florida.

The S.E.A. mission statement was something along the lines of, "Collect, conserve, and curate valuable cultural and artistic artifacts from around the world and make them available to the public in an artistically pleasing and sensitive manner."

Perhaps something like the Spear of Destiny? Is it possible that this fictional club had somehow crossed the line into the factual world and someone had used it as the inspiration to find the spear? Hawk knew that that S.E.A. was a popular topic among hardcore Disney fans, with many taking a liking to the intricate backstory and park-original concept.

The first of the Walt Disney World attractions to be linked to the S.E.A. is the classic Big Thunder Mountain Railroad. The Thunder Mountain attraction tells the tale of the Big Thunder Mining Company owned by Barnabas T. Bullion, a member of the S.E.A. The queue for the ride has letters exchanged between Mr. Bullion and Jason Chandler urging him to end the mining at Big Thunder Mountain due to the supernatural activity at the location. Hawk wondered if there was something, somewhere in the Big Thunder Mountain Railroad that might hold some type of clue.

Another obvious S.E.A. connection was the Skipper Canteen. The Skipper Canteen was used as a meeting place for the S.E.A. In fact, there is an S.E.A. meeting room that guests can eat in. The meeting room has walls with bookshelves that are filled with books written by S.E.A. members. Located in the Magic Kingdom, with ties to the Disney classic attraction, the Jungle Cruise, Hawk realized that there was a lot of detail in this restaurant that he was not familiar with. Typhoon Lagoon had debuted Miss Adventure Falls. This attraction is telling the tale of Captain Mary Oceaneer, a prominent member of the S.E.A., and her parrot. The two are on a treasure hunt when a massive storm comes and strands them on Typhoon Lagoon.

Epcot's United Kingdom Pavilion has the Library of the Royal Adventurer's Society in the Kids' Station. This library showcases the book "Society of Explorers and Adventurers Handbook" as well as other books referencing the S.E.A. and artwork either by S.E.A. members or obtained by S.E.A. members. The AbracadaBar at Disney's Boardwalk Inn Resort has S.E.A. references. The story behind the bar is that it hosted magicians until 1940 when on a Friday the 13th every magician disappeared. One of the props left behind by a magician is a fez with the S.E.A. symbol on it.

These would be all possible starting places for Hawk to figure out what Farren had hidden out there to find. Whatever it was, it could save the park and with a soft laugh he knew it would change his destiny.

"We've got a problem, Hawk." The captain's voice echoed over the intercom in the back of the Bell helicopter.

"What is it?" Hawk tore his mind away from trying to see and start unraveling some type of elaborate puzzle into the present.

"It's a... um..." Vince Kirkus uncharacteristically seemed hesitant to speak.

"Cap? What's up?"

"It is Jillian, sir." Kirkus said calmly. "There's been an accident."

Instantly palming the coin and shoving it into his pocket alongside the collector pin, Hawk moved to pull his seatbelt a little tighter. As if anticipating what was going to be said next, Hawk felt the helicopter bank slightly and the speed increase, driving him back deeper into his seat.

"Get me to her." Hawk's voice sounded strained to himself as he said it.

Message Sent

CHAPTER TWENTY-SEVEN

Day Two - Evening

At the end of the long pale hallway, the doors burst opened and Grayson Hawkes covered the distance between them with long, powerful strides. His eyes instantly locked on them as a pair of orderlies scampered to get out of the way of the incoming man on a mission. Juliette glanced toward Jonathan Carlson, the Chairman of the Entertainment Division of Disney, who was another one of Hawk's longtime friends. Jon had known Hawk as long Juliette and Shep. Their initial move into the world of Disney had nearly gotten them all killed. Sally, Jon's wife had been thrilled when her husband had taken on the role in the Entertainment Division because it kept them on the road and traveling the world. More importantly, it had kept Jon away from Hawk, who in Sally's mind always managed to put her husband in some sort of danger. Jonathan usually laughed it off and reminded her that everyone needed to have a friend worth risking their life for.

"We need to slow him down and catch him up." Jonathan said in his usual even paced style.

"Hawk," Jonathan stepped in front of his freight train of a friend and gently grabbed him by both shoulders. Juliette saw Hawk tense and then focus his attention on Jon. "Don't worry, she is going to be OK. She got here in time."

Juliette stepped next to them and saw Hawk relax ever so slightly at Jon's news.

"She got her in time from what?" Hawk looked from Jonathan to Juliette. "What happened?"

"A snake bite." Came the voice from behind Juliette.

She turned to see Dr. Antonio Redfield, who had come up behind the three of them in the middle of the hallway. Stepping back she made the official introduction.

"Hawk, this is Dr. Antonio Redfield, Disney currently has him on loan from…"

"The International Institute of Health." Hawk finished the sentence for her. "Why is the head investigative researcher of the IIH here, in Celebration Hospital, telling me about Jillian?"

"Dr. Redfield is doing some work at the Animal Kingdom, right now." Juliette offered.

"No, I've got that." Hawk said flatly. "Why are you here?"

"I called him." Juliette offered the explanation.

"Jillian was bitten by a snake. When we got the call, the reports were sketchy and by the time we got her into an ambulance and on her way, we weren't sure if she was going to make it." Jonathan shared. "Juliette knew that Redfield was an expert in vaccines, anti-venom, and exotic animals, so she called."

Hawk was puzzled and trying to take it all in. Juliette placed a reassuring hand on his wrist. "She is going to be OK, Hawk. She is going to be just fine."

"Actually, she will be better than ever." Redfield beamed. "Once I was able to know the kind of snake that bit her, I was able to isolate the correct venom. Now her body will be able to resist and fight back in case she is ever bitten by the same snake again."

"So it was lethal?" Hawk was now focused on the doctor.

"Very." Redfield confirmed. "It was a tiger snake, very deadly and if you don't treat it quickly can cause death rapidly and if you were to survive there will be long term damage."

"But Jillian?"

"Is going to be just fine. No long term damage." Redfield said with a smile and patting Hawk on the shoulder said, "I'm just glad they called me. Glad I was here at Animal Kingdom, glad to have helped. You can go see her. She is going to be just fine. We got the anti-venom in her so fast that they will be kicking her out of here soon."

"Uh," Hawk hesitated and then forced a slight smile. "Thank you doctor, for coming so quickly when Juliette called."

"Think nothing of it. I'm glad she called, glad I could help."

Redfield nodded at them all and made his way down the hall, in the direction that Hawk had come from. The news had calmed Hawk down enough where he was watching the doctor leave in silence along with Jon and Juliette. As he disappeared through the double doors, Hawk turned back to his friends.

"Fill me in. What happened?"

Juliette turned and began moving the trio down the hall toward the elevator.

"Jillian was in her apartment, taking a shower and when she stepped out, she stepped on the snake and it bit her on the leg." Jillian said.

"How does that happen?" Hawk looked at her.

"You already know." Jon injected. "Somebody placed it there and let it loose." He pulled out a phone that he had hidden in his pocket. "We found her phone on the vanity in the bathroom and it was unlocked. Juliette scrolled through the pictures and found this."

He placed the phone in Hawk's hand and then used two fingers to zoom in slightly. The picture was of a steam filled room, a frosted shower door, Jillian's shadow behind it, and there on the floor in front of the door was a snake, rising up as if to strike. Hawk swallowed hard, furrowed his brow and without looking at them asked.

"Who took the picture?"

"We don't know." Juliette said. "We assume it has to be whoever put the snake in the bathroom."

"And they decided to take a picture." Jon said. "It is weird for sure," he didn't really want to know why they did it. "But they took a picture with her phone and then left it there for us to find."

"It is not weird, it is scary." Hawk looked very concerned. "They wanted us to find it. They wanted to send us a message."

"What message?" Juliette queried.

"That they can get close to us. As close as they want. And close enough to kill us." Hawk said as he pushed the button on the elevator door.

"Who is they?" Jon asked.

"I don't know, yet. But they nearly killed our Head of Security and they want us to know that they have that kind of power," Hawk answered.

Juliette felt a slight tremble as she spoke. "What is going on?"

"I'm not sure." Hawk said as the doors opened with a ding.

"But something is happening?" Juliette continued.

"Yes, something. But I didn't expect this." Hawk said. "Not yet."

Jon waved the pair into the elevator. "You had better tell us what's going on."

"I will." Hawk said as he waited for Juliette to hit the right button for their destination. "What happened to the snake?"

"Jillian shot it and killed it." Juliette answered.

Hawk's head jerked back slightly and his eyes widened. "She shot it?"

"Dead, one shot." Juliette cracked a smile as the doors closed.

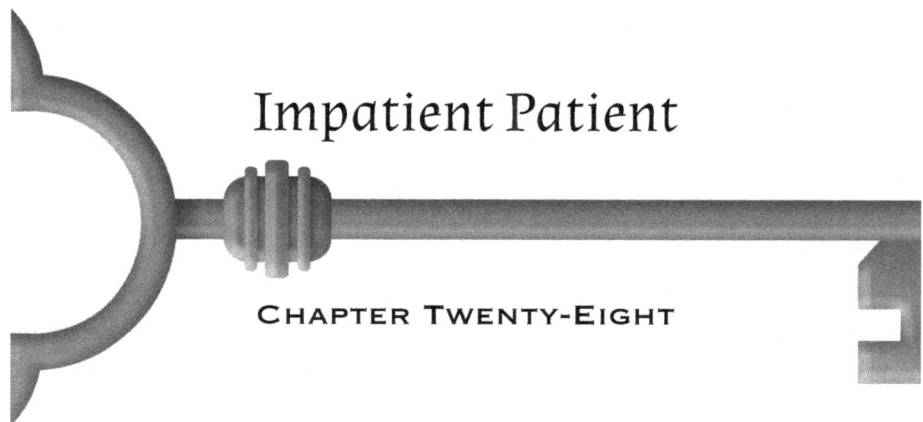

Impatient Patient

CHAPTER TWENTY-EIGHT

Day Two - Night

A nurse deposited a pair of blue gloves into the trash can below the observation station positioned outside the window of the hospital room. She nodded as Hawk pushed his way through the door into the room, closely followed by Juliette and Jonathan. Both of them paused and waited by the small sink located just inside the doorway of the rather spacious hospital room. Hawk glanced toward the white dry erase board on the wall, it read – Jillian Batterson, snake bite, and then contained information on attending doctor, nurse on duty, and under special instructions were the words – Tiger Snake Bite, lethal, anti-venom treatment.

"Where have you been?" Came the sleepy words from the woman in the bed under the covers.

Hawk stopped and took in the sight of Jillian lying in the adjustable bed, guarded by metal rails on each side and hooked to a monitor that kept a running total of her vitals. His eyes burned slightly and he was taken by how small she looked, as if gobbled up and caught in the grip of the hospital bed. Taking in a short quick breath, he moved to the bedside, reached in and grabbed her hand. He felt her squeeze his fingers, her grip was weak and tired, which was to be expected.

"I said, where have you been?" Jillian smiled and looked toward Jonathan and Juliette. "If it hadn't been for Jules and Jon, I might not have made it. Good thing I wasn't counting on you to help." She smiled bigger at that.

"What? I can't leave you alone for an hour without you getting attacked by some other animal?" Hawk smiled back and felt his eyes glisten with tears. They were tears of relief to be sure, he was calmer now that Jillian was poking fun at him. "I'm not your babysitter – after all, you are supposed to be protecting me."

"I know." She slowly turned her head on the pillow as if stretching her neck before looking back at him. "Tell the doctors to get me out of here, so I can keep an eye on you before you do something dumb."

"What are you talking about?"

"Don't think I don't know where you were." The less than strong voice came from the bed. "You went to see Farren Rales because you are getting ready to do something and based on past experience, you are going to be finding all sorts of trouble, and there is no way you are going to make it without me watching you."

Hawk laughed. "You are sounding pretty tough for someone who is strapped to monitors in a hospital room."

"I'm fine." In horror Hawk watched as she proceeded to start unhooking the heart monitors leads she had under her hospital gown. The alarm and sudden flat line readout was jarring.

"No, no, no!" Hawk was trying to catch the flying lead wires that had been tossed, he plucked them out of mid-air. The woman who had seemed to have been gobbled up by the bed was now fighting back and about to escape. She seemed anything but small now. In a flurry of arms flailing and legs kicking back sheets, she was on the verge of a hospital break out.

The nurse came running into the room from the observation station and then suddenly there was a stream of medical personnel that all poured into the room simultaneously. As Hawk stepped away from the bed, he also noticed two armed police officers standing behind Juliette and Jon.

A doctor took the leads from Hawk and proceeded to scold Jillian. Hawk heard something along the lines of "Ms. Batterson, you have to relax. I know you want to get out of here, but we have to monitor you to make sure the poison is out of your system and the anti-venom is working correctly. You are not leaving right now or anytime today. Got it?"

Hawk stepped back and found a space at the bedside. Once the medical staff realized there was no real emergency beyond a bull-headed patient, they receded from the room as quickly as they had arrived. In a slightly less than gentle fashion, they had managed to settle her back into her bed.

"She's got it." Hawk glared at her. "Don't you Jillian?"

He saw her eyes flash anger and then something else, a twinge of fear as her eyes widened ever so slightly.

"Yes," she turned her head away from the door and looked toward the window as the nurse was resetting the monitor. "I've got it."

The doctor looked up at Hawk and then toward Jon and Juliette as they approached the bed closer. "Tomorrow, if she behaves and continues to react well."

"We will have guards outside her door overnight," Juliette informed the doctor.

"For?" The doctor looked up from his work.

"Well, originally they were here to keep unwanted guests out, but they can also make sure that she stays in." Jon offered, he sounded like he was kidding but Hawk knew that he might be serious.

Juliette reached over the rail, patted Jillian and said softly, "Tomorrow."

Jillian nodded, scrunched up her nose and said back. "Thanks for getting me here."

At this point of the conversation, the attending physician disappeared from the room as well. Hawk could see him pause and begin speaking to the nurse outside and one of the police officers.

"You are very fortunate," Jon reminded her. "Having Dr. Redfield show up was brilliant and I'm so glad he was at the resort."

"Yes, me too." Jillian said as she now rolled her eyes back toward Hawk. "Well, you have any wise words for me?"

Hawk grinned. He knew she hated the fact that they were right, the doctors were right, and she was wrong and was going to have to stay the night in the hospital. Personally he was relieved because he wanted to make sure she was going to be better quickly.

"They told me that you shot the snake. A tiger snake and killed it." Hawk said as a statement of fact.

"I did. Got it in one shot after the beast bit me on the leg when I stepped out of the shower. I about stepped right on it. It was all reared up, head was flattened out like a cobra and it struck." Jillian described what happened. "It hurt and set my leg on fire instantly."

"So you shot it?" Hawk asked for clarity.

"Are you having a hard time keeping up the story Disney Dude? Yes… I shot it."

"Where did the gun come from? You were in the shower. Do you keep a loaded gun with you in the shower? I'm just trying to figure out how that happens or what that looks like." Hawk was half smiling as he said it.

"Oh, I just bet you would." Jillian playfully shook her head. "That is personal and none of your business. Now get out of here. I need to rest." She smiled and closed her eyes.

Hawk realized the conversation and explanations were over. He again grabbed her hand, bent over the bed, kissed her on the cheek and as he pulled away heard her whisper.

"Stay out of trouble until I get out of here." He felt her fingers tighten their grip on his hand. They no longer felt tired, they were strong and determined. Hawk knew she was going to be OK.

Found It

Chapter Twenty-Nine

Day Two - Night

Suddenly he was eight feet off the ground. The creature below him had a constricting grip with one hand on his throat and the other hand encircled his leg. The movement and effort to find himself in this position had been effortless. Shep found himself stunned but not believing his own eyes. He glared down the hairy arm that was choking him while holding him in place. The massive shoulders below him were roped with muscle that would cause the thick hair on the creature to ripple as his outstretched arms hoisted Shep into the air. Spinning slightly, Shep felt the creature bend his arms and was hoping that he was about to be released. However, he feared that release would come from being thrown.

In the next instant, the flight he had anticipated occurred. The creature had heaved his body forward and now he was spiraling through the air out of control. His arms and legs jostled like they were disconnected from his frame as he fell to the ground of the forest with a jarring crash.

Shep had reentered the woodlands to once again search for this elusive creature. It was twilight and he was hoping that creature might be moving in the cool of the evening. Was it a Bigfoot he wondered? The march into the dense wall of trees had been routine, as it had been the day before. That had all changed as the sound of snapping limbs came crackling from behind him. As he spun, he surveyed what seemed like a wall of thick brown fur racing directly toward him from out of the breaking branches. Shep thought he felt the ground shake with each heavy step the creature made as it covered the distance from the break in the trees to where he was standing in only three steps. As his brain told him to run, he had barely had time to turn when he felt the massive paw of the beast grab him around the throat and lift him from behind. While his feet left the earth below, the hairy beast had managed to get another massive paw on his leg and hoist him catawampus up into the air over his head. The rapid movement had been dizzying but that was nothing compared to the feeling of defying gravity and flying through the air. Really he had no clue as to how far he flew. His brain was registering this attack in slow motion but he had a sudden concern about the pain he was going to feel as he hit the ground.

Yep, that was it. Searing pain rippled through him as he tumbled upon impact and rolled into a heap next to a tree. Blinking away the dark spots that threatened to cover his consciousness he focused on the large creature that had tossed him so easily through the air. It was moving toward him, unconcerned it appeared that he would try to get away. Shep raised up on one elbow in a feeble attempt to get up, but sapped of strength, his muscles would not comply. He fell back into the floor of the forest, his cheek sagged into the dirt. An unanticipated thought crawled across his brain – *Hawk really had seen a Bigfoot and now he had too. No one is going to believe it.*

The Sasquatch now stood over him and prodded him with a massive oversized foot. Maybe he should lay there and play dead. Maybe then the creature would turn and leave. Shep remained still, not really because he believed it was the best course of action, but that his body was completely uncooperative. Stabs of pain punched through him and every little movement seemingly found another place for the pain to find him. The creature grabbed Shep by the hair jostling him across the ground and then boosted him upward once again. Shep knew that being picked up by his hair should hurt but the pain ripped through him in so many other places, being lifted this way didn't seem quite so bad.

Now the creature, still holding him in one hand slammed him back down into the ground again. This blow caused Shep to feel bones break as his ribcage caved inward releasing another excruciating blast of pain. He was vaguely aware that the creature was raising him upward again and this time he felt his ribs crumble as he was placed over the ropey shoulder of the brown creature. Shep managed a groan. He wanted to say more, wanted to fight back, but the fight was gone. As darkness closed in around him, he could feel himself slipping away but it was not peaceful. The pain constricted around him, swallowing him, and then there was nothing-only blackness.

Kungaloosh

CHAPTER THIRTY

Day Three – 12:01 a.m.

Drawing in a deep breath and slowly exhaling, Hawk tried to clear his mind and focus. The fear he battled when Jillian had been attacked, had yielded to worry, and then relief as she was now was recovering. He had wanted to remain at the hospital with her but with a sense of urgency he knew that he must begin to unravel whatever mystery had put her there and the new one that Farren Rales had given him. Conflicted yet confident, his flashlight cut through the darkened restaurant. Choosing to leave the lights off had been a calculated decision based upon concern that someone, although he had no idea who, might be watching him. The beam of light traced its way across the Jungle Navigation Co. LTD. Skipper Canteen in the Magic Kingdom. Most called it the Skipper Canteen. This was the fictional dining outlet of the Jungle Navigation Company, which in the world of Disney storytelling was the company that managed the Jungle Cruise attraction. The founder of the Jungle Navigation Company was Dr. Albert Falls, the famous discover of Schweitzer Falls in the Jungle Cruise attraction and the notorious back side of water joke. Hawk loved the detail that here within the walls of the canteen was a barrel marked appropriately "Backside of Water."

The main dining area, which he now stood inside was known as the Jungle Cruise Crew's Mess Hall. The smaller dining area at the back of the Mess Hall is the Falls

Family Parlor, since in the storyline the entire company is run by Albert Fall's granddaughter. She has carried on the family business. The place he was looking for specifically was the S.E.A Room, the former meeting place for the Society of Explorers and Adventurers. He used his hand not holding the flashlight to fish the coin Farren had given him and rolled it over in his hand. Emblazed on the back were the words – Society of Explorers and Adventures, Dream it and Do it. This was the only place he could think of to start looking.

The empty restaurant felt much more cavernous minus the usual rush of people inside. The beam of the flashlight illuminated the crew's notice board on the wall to the left of the kitchen door. It is packed with notes from crew members that pay tribute to Adventureland attractions. He allowed the light to stop on the parrot talisman hanging on a thin leather strap in the left half of the crew's board. The letter behind it is addressed to Rosita from the Enchanted Tiki Room attraction. The detail that many missed was the postage stamp on the letter. It is a Susan B Anthony stamp issued in 1936, commemorating the Nineteenth Amendment to the Constitution, which granted women the right to vote. Hawk made his own mental note that if you were able to transpose the 36 in 1936 you ended up in 1963, which is the year the Tike Room originally opened in Disneyland, introduced by Walt Disney himself.

There is another note that is easily missed but not by the flashlight beam, it reads – "I'm putting the spare key for the notice board cabinet here for safekeeping" and of course, in true Jungle Cruise Skipper style, there is a key inside the locked cabinet. It was a funny detail, Hawk found himself smiling as his light continued the search of the room. Near the middle of the Mess Hall is a *Lost and Unfound* shelf hanging on the wall with several stacked up items that includes, most noticeably a box marked "J. Lindsey" with a bright yellow sticker that reads, "Warning. May Contain Live Snake." This reference is the Indiana Jones movie, Raiders of the Lost Ark. Jock Lindsey is Indy's friend, whose snake Reggie scares the lead character.

The S.E.A Room is behind a hidden wall of bookshelves. It is now permanently opened for guests to eat inside and you must travel through a short hallway lined with bookcases to enter in. The book that triggers the opening of the hidden doorway is appropriately The Jungle Book by Rudyard Kipling, a classic book and classic Disney film. The book is pulled out so the door remains open. Hawk moved toward the hallways of bookshelves when he heard a voice behind him.

"Kungaloosh," the female voice with an Indian accent came from out of the shadows.

A sudden coldness hit at his core. He thought he was alone, apparently he was wrong. Instinctively he pushed the button on the flashlight allowing the room to be covered with a blanket of darkness. Turning toward the direction the voice came from, his eyes began to adjust to the room which was dimly being illuminated from the scant light filtering in through the windows from the walkways outside.

"Who's there?" Hawk spoke into the dark.

"I said, Kungaloosh." The female voice spoke softly. It was not a whisper, but one that caused him to turn his head slightly and lean forward straining to hear. "It is incredibly rude not to return the greeting, unless you don't know what it means."

"I know what it means." Hawk wanted his eyes to adjust to the darkness so he could see who he was talking with but she remained in the shadows where the light could not reach. "It is the all-purpose greeting used by members of the Society of Explorers and Adventurers. It is like "aloha." It can be used for hello or goodbye, and depending on the inflection a variety of other things I suppose."

A soft laugh came in a gently wave out of the darkness. "I knew you would know it. How could you not?"

"I'll ask you again, who's there and what are you doing here." Hawk tried to sound serious now that he was less startled.

"I might ask you the same thing Hawk, why are you here?"

So, Hawk now knew that whoever it was in the darkness knew him. He once again turned on his flashlight letting it come to rest on the woman in the corner of the Mess Hall. She shielded her face with her hands. She turned her head to keep the light from her eyes. Her dark hair fell across her shoulders, it was long and from the glimpse Hawk got of her face. She was very pleasant looking. In a red dress, scarf wrapped stylishly around her shoulders, her outfit was accented with a leather belt around her waist and in one hand, she held a leather explorers hat.

"I'm not sure who you are but I am sure you are not supposed to be here." Hawk said.

"Turn that light off," the woman said.

A soft light now enveloped her. She was carrying a lantern of some sort, the light inside flickered like a flame. It was an effect used throughout the Magic Kingdom, but now there was light and he could see her. He complied and turned off the flashlight.

"That's better," her soft voice said.

"I've asked you twice – who are you?" Hawk blinked away the white spots of the beam of his flashlight and again his eyes adjusted to the light now causing shadows to dance across the room.

"You can call me Alberta."

"As in Alberta Falls?" Hawk knew the backstory of the Society of Explorers and Adventurers well enough to know that Alberta Falls was the granddaughter of Dr. Albert Falls. It was Alberta who in the fictional world of Disney stories now ran the Jungle Navigation Company.

"I didn't say that." She laughed.

"So you are not supposed to be Alberta Falls?"

"I didn't say that either." Her laughter brightened the room even more.

"Are you a cast member here?"

"And again, I didn't say that either."

"But yet, you are here." Hawk was confused.

"If you can see me, then yes, indeed, I am here." She offered. Alberta stepped forward gripping the lantern. "And here you are, in my place."

"Your place?"

"Yes, my place and I know why you are here," she stated.

Hawk took a step closer to her and looked closely at her. Her eyes were bright, her face was kind, but there was something that made him stop his approach.

"So tell me, Alberta… why am I here?"

"Well, it is not to eat. We used to have piranha on the menu, but we took it off. Guests said it had too much bite." She didn't smile at the line she effortlessly had just delivered before continuing. "You are here to poke around, to look for something you desperately need to find." She smiled and her voice grew even quieter. "It has been said that when you are traveling down the Nile but refuse to admit it - you are in denial. Many people who come to this edge of the jungle are here because they have no place else to go or they are seeking something. Which are you Grayson Hawkes?"

Hawk knew that in some ways, no in many ways, she was right. The coin Farren had given him emblazoned with words, led him here. He did not think it had any other meaning and he was looking for something, even though he didn't know for sure what it was. So she was right.

"So which is it?" She smiled as she asked.

"Both."

"Farren said you would tell me the truth and he was right." She seemed pleased. Noticing the surprise on Hawk's face she continued. "Yes, I know Farren Rales, very well and he told me you would be coming to my place."

"You keep calling it your place. How is it your place?" Hawk wanted to know.

"Is there some reason you think it's not?" Alberta placed the lantern on a table and stood facing him. "You storytellers at Disney are always creating stories and worlds that spring out of the imagination. Do you not think that imagination can't creep into reality?" Alberta looked toward the ground and raised her head as if a thought had just occurred. "Because you are the Chief Creative Architect of the Disney Company you somehow believe that this place is yours. You belong here, because you are in charge. Yet, you have come in here under the cover of darkness, shining your flashlight looking around. People in charge don't usually do that. And if you don't find what you are looking for, you won't be in charge much longer."

How could she possible know that? Hawk took another step toward her closing the distance once again.

"You're wondering how I know that. Simple." She stated without emotion. "I saw it on television. But then Farren asked me to come, he thought that you would need some help."

"So you came to help me?"

"Perhaps. You ask a lot of questions, don't you?"

"And you don't?"

She tilted her head to the side and laughed softly. "Fair enough."

"So how can you help me?"

"By telling you that you are starting in the right place. I suppose that means "safari" so good." Alberta pointed toward the hallway lined with bookshelves. "You must explore there for your adventure to begin. And you will need this."

In her hand, she held a folded piece of parchment. It looked very old, very fragile, very brittle. Gently she placed it in the palm of his upturned hand.

"Is this a map?" Hawk looked at the folder piece of paper.

"No, it's a folded piece of parchment. But what's on it is important." She stepped back. "If you don't go where it takes you then you will never understand what you are doing."

Hawk looked at her as she slowly began to back away from him in the direction she had come from. "Why didn't Farren give me this?"

"You'll have to ask him." She nodded toward the book shelves behind him. "You are getting off to a good start."

"But you are supposed to help me."

"I have."

"This piece of paper?" Hawk held it between his fingers.

"I've helped you more than you realize." She again smiled, sweetly this time. "But I am sure you will appreciate my help soon. Get moving, as much as I enjoy having you here, I hope you enjoy being had – find what you are looking for and then get out." She stepped back a half step and then continued. "I'm sorry if that sounded rude, please get out."

Her tone rang out just like the banter of a Jungle Cruise Skipper. Hawk glanced away and allowed his eyes search the room for a moment as if looking for some other answers. When he looked back to where she was standing, she was no longer there. He cut on his flashlight and pointed it toward the corner of the Mess Hall that she had come from. She was gone.

Alberta looked very familiar to him but he was certain he had never met her before. Turning his attention back to the delicate parchment resting in his hand, unfolding it slowly, he found not a map, but handwritten script which read *HQ 94-4-4667*. That was all it said.

Hindenburg

CHAPTER THIRTY-ONE

Day Three - Early Morning

It isn't every day you find yourself standing below the largest hand painted helium balloon in the world. With a massive diameter of nineteen feet, the balloon is loaded with over 210,000 cubic feet of helium, or it used to be until the last refurbishment. The dark haired man watched as his associate, no longer wearing his sunglasses because it was night time, navigated the guest basket of the Aero30NG, or The Aerophile as it is called at Disney Springs. Each day this ride takes twenty-nine guests along with a pilot, four hundred feet into the air. From that height, guests can see nearly ten miles across the property of the Walt Disney World Resort. The balloon is tethered, so it rises from and returns to the same spot on every trip. The eight minute ride is enjoyed by guests each day as long as it is not too windy.

The dark haired man shimmied across the railing into the basket where guests would stand on this aerial flight of fancy. Most of what he knew about the balloon itself had come from reading up on it on internet sites. Usually these tourist sites all shared the same information, nearly verbatim, along with a picture or two. That is how he knew about the balloon.

Always noticeable, the scar on the other man's check glistened with sweat as he worked to open up the silver metal box, which contained the mechanism the pilot used to fly the balloon up and down. Each man, dressed in a black suit, with a black tie, and because they were working in the dark they had been instructed to wear black shirts. The outfit was highly impractical and uncomfortable for the work they were doing, but this is what they had been told to wear and the rules were the rules.

"So why did the last refurbishment replace the helium in this balloon with hydrogen?" He asked the scarred sandy haired man working to open the box, which was mounted on the inside ring of the round basket the guests would stand in as the balloon went up and down.

"Hydrogen is cheaper, it is easier to find. There is a helium shortage. Hydrogen is actually lighter than helium so it saves money and is more practical." He answered as he continued his task.

"But," the dark haired man cleared his throat and whispered. "Isn't hydrogen explosive?"

"Yes, of course it is." The sandy haired man paused and looked at his accomplice. "But someone decided to save money because it is cheaper and we are going to use that to our advantage." The panel was now opened, revealing the electronics used in raising and lowering the balloon for guests. There was a lot of unused open space inside the panel. Jerking his head to call the dark haired man over, he waited until he got there and began opening up the backpack.

Removing a case from the backpack, he opened it revealing two long cylinders containing a bluish fluid. Gently he handed them to the sandy haired scarred man fastening a contraption to the inside of the panel. He was not feeling very good about what they were doing. It seemed to be unnecessary.

"So explain to me what is in these oversized vials again please." He watched as they snugly fit into a predesigned holder, lining them up next to each other like hotdog buns in a serving tray.

Sighing, the dark haired man continued to work, this time fastening an additional two cylinders of explosive material on either side of the vials. "They contain a genetically engineered recombinant virus made from the NPV used in pesticides, the rhinovirus, which is the common cold virus, a strain of SARS Cov 24 , a variation of the COVID-19 virus called SCARS, smallpox, and a hantavirus."

"A hantavirus?"

"Yes, it is a virus that infects you when you inhale the fecal matter of rats. In a concentrated formula it is lethal. In other words it is a biological cocktail. If it had a name it might be called Ratpox."

"But that stuff is all bad and together, it will kill people?"

"Of course it will." The sandy haired man smiled ever so slightly. "That is the idea. The virus has to be real or they will never do what we are demanding.

Relax, no one is going to get hurt, there is no way they will let this ever be released."

"What if there is an accident, what if they don't pay? What happens then?"

The sandy scarred one paused to wipe the sweat from his face with the sleeve of his black suit coat. "Then the balloon will explode, because that is what hydrogen does and the virus will become airborne in a cloud of contagion that will cover most of the Walt Disney World Resort. It will infect most of the people here. The molecules are heavy and they will fall quickly, it will be like a rain storm of viral material." He twitched his shoulder as if to loosen it up and then added. "It will be contained, but it will send a message."

"But no one is supposed to get hurt." He said, it was more of restating what he had been told instead of a question.

He watched as a small black box was then connected to the mechanism holding each of the cylinders in place. The sandy haired man pulled back on a small lever on the side of the box once it was connected. A small red light began to glow. He pushed it into place and heard it click. The man pulled back his hand, stepped back a half step to admire and visually inspect his handiwork.

"That's not up to us. We don't get to hold the switch to release this stuff. Our job is to put it into place and then it will be up to everyone else whether or not anything happens. That is why you have been paid so well – so I suggest you quit talking and help me put this panel back in place."

He reached down and lifted the panel, holding it while the scarred man reinserted the screws he had removed in dismantling it.

"If I remember, the medical bills for your family were paid, your parent's house was rescued from foreclosure, and your brother suddenly was approved for parole. That is in addition to the cash. Did I forget anything?"

He continued to hold the panel in place without answering. His silence was the answer.

"What happens now is not our concern. Today we did what needed to be done. Like always." The sandy haired one turned after the last screw had been tightened. "Are you still OK with that?"

"Yes, I'm still fine with it." His response was empty, he knew it, but the money had been spent, the needs had been met, and this was the price he had chosen to pay.

The two men retraced their steps through the empty streets of Disney Springs. Empty this time of the night, in their suits they would have appeared very out of place had anyone there been looking at them, but they were not. The dark haired man glanced back over his shoulder to the massive balloon, knowing that tomorrow, there would be guests unknowingly floating into the air with a bioweapon that had the potential of killing most of the people in the resort. And although he had been assured, it was not his concern, he was very concerned.

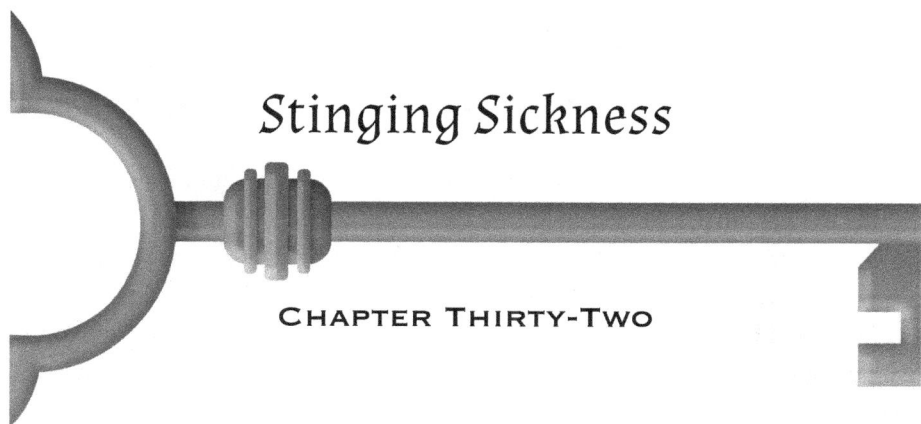

Stinging Sickness

Chapter Thirty-Two

Day Three – Early Morning

The automatic sliding doors exploded open with a thundering racket as the emergency medical team from the Orange County Fire Department burst through the opening with the first of two stretchers. Dr. Briggs Kuhn, the head of the emergency department snapped his attention to the incoming patient. He was surprised to discover the clatter of a second stretcher being shoved in behind the first one.

In a fluid series of hand motions and verbal commands, the response team in the ER rushed to meet the patients and immediately began triage as they joined in the racing procession of people, stretchers, and equipment moving down the hallway toward the emergency treatment rooms.

Glancing back, Briggs also saw that there were at least two firefighters that seemed to be in some type of distress. Turning his attention back to the first stretcher, he looked down at the patient to begin evaluating what they were dealing with. Instantly, appearing out of nowhere to the casual observer, a rolling supply cart, a metal tray covered in medical instruments, blood pressure monitor stands, and digital display screens were all wheeled into place surrounding the double emergency unfolding in the treatment room. Looking into the hideously swollen face of the first patient, Briggs had a flash of recognition, he had seen the man before, but he did not know from where.

"Talk to me." Briggs yelled to no one in particular and everyone who needed to respond.

He listened as vital signs were given for the patient in the other bed, a female, who had lost consciousness and was displaying a weak and rapid pulse. The patient on the gurney in front of him was semi-conscious, having difficulty breathing, and his skin was extremely pale. Using a tongue depressor, he pried past the man's lips and saw the man's tongue was frighteningly swollen and he immediately began to open up an airway for the patient.

"Anaphylaxis is what this looks like" Brooks said to the entire room as they quickly went about their work.

"Both patients, Doctor." The voice of one of the firefighters standing in the doorway of the room offered. "Both patients were attacked by bees."

"Attacked by bees?" Briggs glanced up quickly but then went right back to the male patient. "These patients look like they are in their pajamas. Bees swarmed their house?"

"Yes, doc." The firefighter began. "It was a scene straight out of a horror movie. We pounded on the door, got no response and broke it down. Got to the bedroom and saw the woman first, then her husband. They were in their bed. Both were covered from head to toe in a shroud of angry killer bees."

"Killer bees? The bees were trying to kill them?" Briggs asked as he allowed an associate to take over on the male patient as he slid over to attend and evaluate the female patient.

"Yes, sir. Killer bees." The firefighter stared as the team worked. "The bees were coming out of the lighting fixtures, or at least the small spaces around the edges. The lady had bees all over her eyes and nose. She screamed and they crawled into her mouth and were stinging her and almost choking her. We thought she was swallowing the bees."

Briggs again glanced back at the firefighter, whose face was also puffy. Apparently he had also been stung.

"The man was out of it. Barely responsive, bees all over his body as well. It was so horrendous. It was awful. And I felt so powerless. There was nothing to do. We didn't have time to put on our protective gear so we went in unprotected, started spraying the bees and the people with a carbon dioxide fire extinguisher, scooped them both up and ran out the door with the them into the front yard away from the bees." The firefighter took a deep breath. "I've never seen anything like it. We all got stung. I've got a couple of my team getting treatment down the hall."

"You better get down there and let them take a look at you too." Briggs said, again glancing up before the man moved away. "Good job getting them out."

"Vitals are falling." The attendant working on the man cried out to Dr. Kuhn.

Moving instantly back toward the male patient, Briggs ordered. "Give both another shot of epinephrine, to reduce the severity of the allergic reaction. Increase the oxygen and start a drip." He glanced back toward the female patient. "I want to get both patients examined closely and let's try to remove any stingers left in their bodies."

"Doctor, there must be thousands of stingers." An attendant said.

"I don't care, get them out." Briggs barked, "Also move in with some cold compression where we can. We need to get them stabilized and see if one of the firefighters brought one of the bees in with them."

"Sir?"

"We need to know what kind of bee this is." Briggs kept on working. "It doesn't matter if the bee is dead or alive, I prefer dead. And somebody ring that doctor that was in here earlier tonight with the snakebite, we might need some outside resources."

"Right away." A nurse grabbed a clipboard and headed toward the door. "Tell the guy what we are dealing with. Ask him for suggestions or better yet, tell him to drag himself back in here to take a look if we can get them stable."

Briggs felt the sweat roll down his cheek and watched as it slowly fell off his face and dripped onto the patient he was working on.

"The patients names are Sally and Jonathan Carlson, doctor." Came a voice from across the emergency treatment room.

"Carlson, Jonathan Carlson…" Briggs remembered. He had met this man and his wife a few years ago when he had treated a Disney Imagineer. He reached back for the name. Scales, no Rales was the name. He had hidden the patient at the request of the police after an assassination attempt. Jonathan Carlson was one of the old man's friends. This patient was some big time leader for the Disney Company, so how in the world did he get attacked by bees?

Rubber soled shoes squeaked across the floor as another rack of interveinal fluids were wheeled into place on a stand. The tubing was quickly unfurled and attached to the needles already inserted into the patient.

Much to the relief of Briggs he began to hear a steady pulse thumping from each of the monitors and began to see the man stabilize. He had slipped into unconsciousness, but at least he was stable. Turning swiftly, he now went back to the wife's gurney, she too began to stabilize.

Stepping back he once again gave his orders.

"As soon as they are stable, get them out of this treatment room into separate rooms down the hall. Let me know as soon as that snake doctor gets here." Briggs said.

"That would be Dr. Redfield, sir."

"OK, fine Redfield, he's the animal guy. Let me know when he gets here." Briggs strode out of the room. Over his shoulder, he said moving away. "I'm going to check on our firefighters, I need to know what else they saw and we need to make sure that no one else goes into the house where these people were found."

The Autograph

CHAPTER THIRTY-THREE

Day Three – Early Morning

The beam of the light gave him the next steps forward as he crept across the hard wooden floor toward the Society of Explorers and Adventurers Room. Hawk had safely tucked the piece of parchment Alberta had given him into his back hip pocket and moved in the direction she had pointed. In order to enter the S.E.A. Room coming from the Mess Hall, you must pass through a hallway. The hall was lined with dark brown book shelves, which previously disguised the room entrance back in its hidden days. Now, they were opened so guests could move back into the room for dining.

In the darkness, standing between the bookshelves on either side of him, he allowed the light to pass over the spines of some of the books slowly enough for him to read them. He knew that most every book on the shelf contained some sort of joke or nod to a Disney Legend or Imagineer. Another detail most would miss or never take the time to see. Some were so obscure, he was convinced he would not know what they meant.

His attention immediately went to a copy of *The Jungle Book* by Rudyard Kipling. It was pulled out and was at an angle compared to the other books on the shelf. This book is on the movable bookshelf, the one that would allow entrance into the room. It was by design, the book that members of the S.E.A. would pull to open the wall!

Of course you had to be a member of the group to know that. While the book was pulled out, the hallway remained opened.

The light continued to explore the books and the punny humor of the Jungle Cruise attraction captured in the titles of some of the books. *The Illustrated Guide to Radio Broadcasting* was composed by the Skipper behind the Voice of the Jungle you hear in the Jungle Cruise queue, Albert AWOL. The same shelf contains *Boat Evacuation Procedures* by Cap Size. The light danced quickly across other books, their titles funny to those who are well versed in the secrets of Disney. *Native Orange Birds of the Southeastern United States* is a gracious nod to the Orange Bird from Sunshine Tree Terrace. It's written by Dr. Sid Truss. The first time he had read the name of the author he missed it. Once he had said it out loud, he got the joke. *Crooning Flowers* isn't only a tribute to Walt Disney's Enchanted Tiki Room attraction, but Sherman and Sherman are the authors. The famous brothers were the creative force behind the signature song "Tiki, Tiki, Tiki, Tiki Room" and many other classic Disney songs. Prof. Boag — referencing the great Wally Boag, who voiced Jose in the Tiki Room— penned the classic *Songs of the Tiki Bird*. And *Bathing with Elephants* and *The Congo Queen* were tributes to the inspiration behind the Jungle Skipper Canteen, the Jungle Cruise ride itself.

While the search would have been entertaining on a normal day, the humor was not as appreciated as Hawk was waiting, hoping, longing for some type of clue to click in his mind as he read the book titles. Slowly, meticulously he eyed each volume on the shelf. *Great Characters of World Literature* by J. Lasseter, a reference to the former CCO of Pixar Studios. The pale green book, *Left at the Falls* with no author listed, *Meeting Royalty* by Sklar, which was a tribute to Disney Legend, Marty Sklar, and then the confusing to most, *FUZNEWI PDMWH CHF JD U* written by Albert the Monkey. Hawk knew that Albert the Monkey is one of the main characters of Hong Kong Disneyland's Mystic Manor. In the past, he had once asked about the strange title of the book and was schooled on the infinite monkey theorem. The letters on the spine that form the title are a string of random letters, "*FUZNEWI PDMWH CHF JD U*." The infinite monkey theorem states that a monkey hitting keys at random on a typewriter keyboard for an infinite amount of time will almost surely type any given text, such as the complete works of William Shakespeare. It is a goofy idea, probable but not likely. But for those with nothing better to think about, it occupied their time. But what was it that Farren had told him?

Go Left Next to the Monkey. Hawk cut his eyes to the book to the left of the title created by Albert the Monkey. The book was *Meeting Royalty* by Sklar. Marty

Sklar had been the voice of Walt Disney and the company, writing endless scripts, documents, and notes that gave Walt a voice through the written word and through his speeches. Reaching into the shelf, he drew out the book leaving a gap between the book by the monkey and the book called *Left at the Falls*. The clue, go left next to the monkey, had brought his search to this book, surely this was it. Taking it and moving into the meeting room, he placed it on a table and flipped opened the pages. Page after page were blank, which actually wasn't that big of a surprise, since it was a decoration prop. The fact that he could remove it should have surprised him because most props could not be adjusted, picked up, or played with by guests – yet this book was not secured in any way to the shelf or the books next to it.

The paper of the pages was crisp, not old or laced with a musty smell that you might expect from an older book. After all, it was a prop, but Hawk believed this book had been placed on the shelf recently. It was not aged at all. The shuffle of the flipping pages took an unexpected break as Hawk saw there was a piece of paper, folded up, and nestled between two pages. Flexing his fingers he reached in and carefully removed the small sheet of paper. Gingerly sliding the now opened book to his left, with reverence he unfolded the page until it was completely flattened and positioned on the table in front of him.

Hawk's eyes widened at what he saw. His insides vibrated as he studied the page, taking it all in, and trying to comprehend what was in front of him. He ran his hand across the paper, flattening the creases from where it had been folded. The manila page contained a note, slightly faded, handwritten in a vaguely familiar script. Hawk realized it was a handwriting that he had seen before. In a controlled, intentionally slow movement, he placed his hand on the page and turned it toward him closer.

He carefully read the words ... *"If I were a fatalist or a mystic, which I am not! It might be appropriate to say I believe in my lucky star. But I reject 'luck' – I feel every person creates his own determinism by discovering his best aptitudes and following them undeviatingly."*

Just below the note, slightly skewed to the right side was a signature. It was one he had studied, instantly recognized and had not expected to see...the signature of... *Walt Disney.*

This autograph would be worth more than those of any movie star and most American presidents. The unique curvy, loopy signature is priceless because it carries with it global recognition. The company logo of the Walt Disney Company is a stylized version of Walt's actual signature to this day. Hawk understood that Walt had taken pride in his signature and he was pleased with its design. He was always an artist. There were stories of Walt practicing signing his name in various styles early in his career. He enjoyed penning his signature and made a production out of signing his name, moving the pen in his hand in florid circles before it even touched the paper. Truly, getting an autograph from Walt was a show in and of itself. It is arguably the world's most famous signature. And now here it was, an original, below a note scribbled in Walt's distinctive script. Spinning the paper, Hawk read each line, squinting slightly as the ink seemed to have faded over the years.

Pushing himself back from the table slightly, he glanced back toward the *Meeting Royalty* book. Leaving it on the table he slowly turned the pages of it again to see if there might be anything else tucked inside or hidden. Marty Sklar had given the world so many messages from Walt Disney throughout his career and now, once again, had delivered a message for Walt from Walt himself. Fitting, Hawk thought. Then he noticed it. Something else was written on the inside back cover of the book. This was also a familiar handwriting to Hawk but it did not belong to Walt Disney, instead it belonged to Farren Rales. It read –

Did the page you found sound like anyone you know?
I sure thought it did!
You don't believe in luck
Walt Disney rejected luck
The two of you would have gotten along just fine

That means it is up to you to discover one of the most valuable things Walt Disney ever possessed. My friend Hal found it for him, we kept it safe, now you have to do the same.

I'd wish you luck
But you don't believe in it!
So let me simply say – Go find it

At the top of the crow's nest look up
The key is wrapped around the lock
Farren

Hawk allowed his eyes to go from Farren's note to the Walt designed page. First one, then the other, then the other, back and forth over and over again. He lost count of how many times his eyes made the journey. Running his fingers through his white mop of hair, he closed his eyes and forced himself to concentrate. A puzzle to unravel, more secrets, always more to figure out. His mind began to churn, cycling through a cascading cluster of ideas that all were going too fast. His head tipped back over the top of the bench he was sitting on behind the table and his noggin thudded against the wooden carvings on the wall behind him.

Ouch – he rubbed his head and opened his eyes looking up the wall. Once the ripple of annoyance of hitting the wall had passed, his eyes focused and he slowly turned his head, never breaking his upward gaze at the wall behind him. He let out a gasp of disbelief and euphoria. Could that be what he was looking for?

That Guy

Chapter Thirty-Four

Day Three – Early Morning

The glow of the screen provided the only illumination in the eerily lit room. David Walker shut his eyes, rubbed them, and then blindly reached for his coffee mug. Still with shut eyes he took a swig and his eyes popped open at the cold bitter taste. What time was it? How long had the coffee been sitting there? Glancing at his watch, his mind cleared a bit and he knew daybreak was coming soon. As often happened, he was lost in researching and looking for answers in the back-story he was working on. In this case, it was the mysterious Otto Guy, whom he was convinced now was masquerading as Dr. Redfield.

He had to be correct. The mannerisms were the same, the ticks were the same, and the face was slightly different but reasonable enough to believe it may have been surgically altered. The resemblance was definitely there. Allie Crossman had told him not to get too lost in his research before she left him sitting there in the Iron Spike Room. She had been a good sounding board and offered up a number of very reasonable explanations as to why his theory about Redfield might be incorrect. He took those arguments to heart but he believed he was right and so he was digging.

Otto Guy, prior to his disappearance certainly was nothing short of a brilliant, mad doctor. Although much of his work had been done before the invention of the internet. His research was archived and available, if you were willing to look. One fascinating and disturbing article had Guy suggesting that civilization was ripe for a radical reboot. As Otto shared in an interview with a reporter, he said a transformation in human behavior was necessary, and would take decades to achieve and would entail rebuilding the infrastructures of human existence.

It was horrifying to conceive that a doctor would think that, or so David believed. That kind of thinking could be disregarded if it did not have the potential of being so destructive. The more David read the more convinced he was that Otto Guy was a madman that concealed his despotic ambition under a mask of false modesty. He contradicted himself constantly, but demanded blind faith in his every discovery and proclamation just the same. He even seemed to take some satisfaction in being more informed and doing what was needed to others for their own good. No matter what the results.

In a phone call conversation with a source from India, David had discovered that Otto Guy had said that human beings are sacks of flesh that emit germs. He publically declared he was anti-god. The only faith worth having is in "science," which, it turns out, is ethical according to what Guy believed. This source was bothered that David had been inquiring and warned David against continuing to dig, and said he would offer no more information.

The next few phone calls he made across the globe to various sources had come up empty, so he had gone back to searching the web and diving into the darker side of cyberspace.

The more he read, the deeper he researched Otto Guy, the more bothered he became. Guy's research had involved what was questionable treatment of animals under the guise of research. There were some shady allegations of unauthorized work and human testing in third world countries. And there were snippets of information suggesting that a form of *gain to function research*, which involves a virus moving from an animal to a human with a rabid intensity, had been one of the main points of controversy in the eyes of critics. He was reported to have been intensifying his work in the regeneration of cellular structure when he suddenly disappeared in a mysterious laboratory accident.

The accident in question happened in a Soviet military research facility near the city of Sverdlovsk, Russia. Why was Otto Guy working at a research facility in Russia? David pondered. There was an event, where spores of anthrax were accidentally released resulting in approximately 100 deaths. Although the exact number of victims remains unknown. Initially the cause of the outbreak was denied by the Soviet authorities and all medical records of the victims were removed to hide serious violations of the Biological Weapons Convention that had come in effect in 1975.

Eventually researchers and investigators from the United States proved the incident was the result of an aerosolized plume of anthrax spores. The spores were genetically identical to the strain studied in a nearby laboratory. The spores had come from environmentally contaminated meat, which was the official Soviet explanation.

David shook his head, putting anthrax into an aerosol, making it an airborne super weapon was insane. The accident is sometimes referred to as biological Chernobyl according to some accounts. Yet in the following investigation, Otto Guy had mysteriously and forever it appears, disappeared. His research was never discovered, those he worked with had no information as to where he had gone, and many of the projects he was leading were deemed classified and no other information was available about them. He was simply no more. Gone, his work, his life, his research had all disappeared.

Leaning back into his chair, David stretched out his legs. He had been sitting there way too long. He wondered, is it really possible to just disappear like that without help? Someone must know something, somewhere, and if Antonio Redfield was indeed Otto Guy, where had he been and why had he come back now?

So many question and no answers – yet.

Wherever Here Is

Chapter Thirty-Five

Day Three - Morning

Shep felt cool air crawl across his skin as his consciousness ripped him back from the brink of knocked out isolation. His vision was blurred as he opened his eyes and slowly began to clear as he blinked back the cobwebs that seemed to be layering his brain. The images that registered first was a cement floor with mildew branching across it. Raising his head caused a pain to run from the base of his neck down his spine. He managed to glance toward the ceiling at the bare lone light bulb, with a pull string hanging from the fixture that threw illumination that died before it reached the corners of the space he was sitting in.

The heavy wooden chair had a high back and his arms were secured behind him and somehow, beyond his eyesight, were fastened to the chair itself. His legs were secured to the front legs of the chair with ropes and there was one double wrapped rope encircling his midsection. He was locked into place and other than his head, which seemed to be battling his neck for permission to move, nothing else had that option.

His muscles felt cramps twinging through them. He knew he must have been sitting in this position a long time. Sweat gleamed across his face and he remembered the attack in the woods. The memory caused his arms and legs to twitch against the restraints, which confirmed his inability to move. A sudden sensation of dread washed over him as he remembered the power and the strength of the creature that had attacked him.

Was it a Sasquatch? If he hadn't believed in them before he now believed in at least one of them. But could a creature like that have tied him up and placed him in here? Wherever here was. Straining into the shadows he tried to take some type of inventory of where he might be. He immediately knew he had never been here before. The windowless room depended on the solitary light bulb for whatever light he had. Surrounding the edges of his eyesight were old wooden crates, along with some boxes that appeared as if they hadn't been moved for years. There was a layer of dust, dirt, or mildew that seem to accent some of them. Against the wall he saw the shape of an old breaker box with a series of pipes running from it to someplace beyond his vision.

Pain radiated through his side and chest. There was no way to move that relieved the hurt. His mind thought about a line he heard someone say or a quote from somewhere that declared that feeling pain is a hard way to know you're still alive. If that was supposed to be encouraging, it was not. Motivational sayings did nothing to bring relief to the hurt in his body in this moment. But the pain brought him back to his question again, was it a Sasquatch?

If it were a legendary cryptozoological creature, then it was capable of more than just running around in the woods, using sticks to knock on trees, and throwing things at human beings. Because like it or not, whatever it was, had managed to find a building, electricity, and rope to incapacitate him in this wooden chair. That was not the usual behavior of a Bigfoot romping through the forest. Yet, it happened and here he was.

Lock and Key

Chapter Thirty-Six

Day Three - Morning

Hawk now was gawking at the massive work of art on the wall in front of him. A slow disbelieving shake of the head gave way to reading the imprint on the bottom left side of this artwork. Legendary Beasts of the Mediterranean was written just below the seal of the S.E.A. giving the drawing, which in actuality was a huge map, a name. It had been created by Captain Mary Oceaneer. She was an English sea-captain and celebrated treasure-hunter during the late-19th century, according to her mythical backstory. As Hawk remembered it, the Captain had launched her experimental vessel to study the ocean and excavate goods from the ocean. Ultimately, this led to her being enlisted as a member of the Society of Explorers and Adventurers. Hawk had signed off on some elements of her story being incorporated into the Typhoon Lagoon waterpark, which is probably why he could remember as much as he did.

What he had not known is that she had been given the credit for this massive map covering the wall in front of him. Specifically the spot on the map that meant the most to him. The clue had been, *At the top of the crow's nest look up - The key is wrapped around the lock.* The wooden ship he had hit his head on when he was seated featured a crow's nest that ended just below the Legendary Beasts of the Mediterranean. As he was seated there, he allowed his eyes to go straight up the picture and that is when he saw the giant squid from the Disney film, 20,000 Leagues under the Sea. Its tentacles were wrapped around the Nautilus, the famous and iconic submarine from the film.

Farren had taken a lot of time telling him about his friend the diver. The diver had found something for Walt Disney, and that had to somehow tie into the Nautilus. Deep sea diving, exploration, all of those story elements had been part of the story Farren told him. Then to top it off, just in case he wouldn't have figured it out, he gave him the "Building Walt Disney World One Story at a Time" pin, featuring the squid and the attraction, 20,000 Leagues under the Sea. So if the key is wrapped around the lock… Hawk thought to himself. Then the key is the giant squid and the Nautilus must be the lock.

He grinned slightly at his ability to figure it out, but the smile was erased as he realized that even though he understood it, he had no idea what it might mean. The attraction had opened just a few weeks after the Magic Kingdom was opened to the public. It was incredibly popular for a number of years, but as he remembered it, the wait times were slow and they could not move a large number of people through at one time. As a result the attraction, which was tricky to maintain, was closed. As far as he knew, the giant squid was not anywhere in the resort and the Nautilus submarines were no longer on property.

He reached into his pocket and pulled out the collectible pin. It had a raised golden construction hat and the pin was designed to resemble a file folder. The tab on the folder said Big Squid and when opened revealed a golden outlined Goofy, taking a wrench from the tentacle of the squid while working on the Nautilus. The squid was giving Goofy what he needed to do complete his task. Hawk bit down on another grin that reminded him that this was the same type of cryptic clue Farren Rales had been giving him for years as he had slowly unraveled and discovered the secret world of Walt Disney. This was the real Walt Disney World, the world of the man, his connections, his genius, and his importance.

Hawk had been on the attraction years ago. It was fun and as he remembered it, it entailed a ride on the Nautilus, just like in the movie. He noticed back then that it had taken up a huge piece of Fantasyland real estate. The shore featured small beaches and one had a chest of abandoned pirate treasure. He was especially intrigued by that. The words "20,000 Leagues" were spelled out in nautical code from signaling flags at the entrance to the attraction. He hadn't known that when he first saw it, it was revealed to him by a cast member and was an early Disney detail that he never forgot. He also knew that the cast members operating the attraction played the roles of Nemo's always-silent crew and even wore authentic replicas of the screen production's costumes. It was just like being part of the movie.

He gathered his discoveries from the table, took another look at the map, and then slowly retraced his steps to exit the restaurant. Pausing, he looked around to make sure he was alone and he appeared to be. Although, he reminded himself, he had thought that earlier. Allowing his eyes to explore the details of the room once again, this time he looked for some connection to the old Magic Kingdom attraction or the film itself. Nothing registered and his search concluded empty.

His mind was drifting back to the attraction of old. He recalled the attraction vehicles were not actual submarines, but instead boats in which the guests sat below water level. Still pretty cool as he remembered it. The interiors were a mix of metal paneling, rivets, and bolts, as well as Victorian styled fittings in the form of passenger seats that could flip outwards, and armrests beneath the portholes, in keeping with the concept from the film. It was very steam punk, before it was stylish to be so. Each "guest" aboard the Nautilus had his or her own seat, as well as a round porthole to look out into the watery seascape. A small button located in the porthole recess was intended for defogging the window if needed, it had never worked as he remembered it. Above the seating area was the sail where the "helmsman" stood and controlled the vehicle's operation. The "diving" effect was produced by bubble machines located throughout the attraction, as well as using the waterfalls at the entrance to the show building near the back of the lagoon, where much of the action of the attraction would take place.

There was much debate and mystery over the exact reason the ride was permanently closed. From high maintenance costs and lack of accessibility for the handicapped, to guests fainting either because the air conditioning was unreliable, or the giant squid was too scary. Hawk had been given some of the history by some long time cast members. There had been a rumor that Disney fully intended to refurbish the ride and was seeking a corporate sponsor to foot the bill. It was much more likely that Walt Disney World operations had been trying to find a reason to shut down the ride for years due to having grown fed up with the constant maintenance. In 1995, then-Disney president Michael Ovitz visited the Magic Kingdom and brought up guest complaints about the closure of the subs. Operations wanted to make sure the ride stayed closed, according to reports, they had actually lied that the attraction was in poor condition and unsafe.

Ovitz, suspicious, demanded to be taken on the ride at 7 a.m. the next day before the park opened to guests. This is where the stories all seemed to coagulate. Operations chose the submarine that was in the worst condition with speakers that barely worked and an engine that belched smoke. To make it more uncomfortable, they poured several buckets of water into the cabin to simulate a pinhole leak and finally recruited a ride operator guaranteed to give Ovitz a rough ride. Upon returning to the dock, Ovitz quickly climbed out of the mildewed interior to tell Operations that they had made the right choice in closing the attraction.

According to some historians, the event that closed the attraction was unofficially called "20,000 Leagues Ovitz the Sea," and inside the Disney inner circles, it was called "The Time We Slipped Mike Ovitz a Mickey." After being shut down for two years, much to the disappointment of park goers, the attraction was permanently closed.

Hawk pressed open the doors and strode back into the morning of Adventureland. He had a mystery to unravel. Actually more than one. There was the slip of paper that he had been given that meant something. And he had to find the Nautilus because it was some kind of lock and the giant squid was some type of key. His first steps were lost in the thoughts of what he might be searching for, when he felt a surge of edginess, and sensed he was being watched. Turning and looking toward the Magic Carpets of Aladdin, he saw a man standing beneath the golden camel, which during park hours would spit water on unsuspecting guests. If the park were open, the man was standing in one of the camel spit zones. Planting his feet firmly and squaring his shoulders to the unexpected company on the pathway, Hawk squinted slightly trying to distinguish if he knew who this person might be.

The unknown person, Hawk guessed it was a man, but maybe it was a woman, could it be Alberta? Waiting for his eyes to adjust, he could not be sure. He or she was wearing a hoodie which was pulled tightly around their face. The low light, the dark hoodie, and the protection of the early morning light did not let Hawk see clearly. Both people stood in stances that might have been more fitting in the streets of Frontierland. They looked as if they might have a shootout. It was that thought that caused Hawk to rock backward ever so slightly on his heel and wondered if that was indeed what this was. If the person in the street was armed, the Disney CCA was definitely at a disadvantage. It had happened to him before after hours in the Magic Kingdom, although most guests would never have believed it. On more than one occasion, the safe surroundings of Walt Disney World for Hawk had become a battleground to survive.

The hoodie twitched and then bolted toward the left, on a path that would take them toward the same Frontierland that Hawk had just been thinking about. Reflexively, Hawk broke into a run, giving chase without knowing who the person was, what they were doing there, and what would happen if he caught up. There was something about the person that was just off. They were out of place, they did not belong. Hawk's heightened sense of worry led him to believe that this was not a cast member or just someone working in the park after hours. The proof in the person running from him verified that. As Hawk rounded the corner past the Island Supply gift shop, he thundered across the planked walkway that transitioned Adventureland into Frontierland. It wasn't until he made the turn that he spotted the chasee for the second time. The running hoodie had taken a left at the Country Bear Jamboree and was racing toward the back exit of the park. If the direction didn't change, hoodie would move beyond Pecos Bill Tall Tale Inn and Café, across the railroad tracks, and then into a backstage area. There was no way Hawk would let them get away.

Clearing the covered wooden western frontage, Hawk now planted his foot and powerfully stepped back into the street, making the turn to follow. Out of the corner of his right eye, he saw a quick flash of light, really more like a spark that emanated from the Westward Ho food service area. What came next, tucked in right behind the spark was an eruption of sound, heat, energy and fire unleashed with a powerful rush of air which lifted Hawk off the ground and sent him spiraling backward, in the very direction he had just come from. The blast registered in his brain as an explosion while the searing heat billowing from the direction of the Westward Ho now washed across his back in a red hot wave of pain. He was face down on the wooden walkway, a ringing in his ears, and his mind screaming that something had just blown up in front of him.

Invincible

Chapter Thirty-Seven

Day Three - Morning

The whirling streaks of red and blue light that rolled across the buildings, the pathway, and the faces of the people gathered in Frontierland chased away the carefully crafted western illusion of Disney magic. Juliette's mouth was dry and her eyes flitted across the landscape of emergency vehicles, firefighters, police officers, and security people that were all involved in somehow unraveling the explosive event that had destroyed a dining area and left pock marks of damage from flying debris as far as the eye could see in the strangely lit darkness. Her conversation with Tim had centered on making sure he and the kids were safe and doing fine. Doing her best, she tried to convince them that they needed to be extra cautious without causing too much worry. Their conversation had been interrupted by the message that arrived via text and she raced over to the Magic Kingdom from her office in Bay Lake Towers. Her trip down Main Street USA had given her pause to check above the Fire Station to see if Hawk was in his apartment. He was not, and Juliette assumed that he had beaten her to the crisis. It was the cell phone call from the Reedy Creek Emergency Rescue team informing her that not only was Hawk there, but he had been the only one to see the explosion that caused her to move even faster. The report was that he was injured, but at this point, his condition was unknown.

Turning her head from side to side, then under the sign reading Frontierland Trading Post, 'Texas' John Slaughter- Trail Boss, she saw the form of Grayson Hawkes next to an EMT, just inside the gift shop. It is themed to resemble a rugged, old-fashioned western trading post and offers a variety of items for purchase fitting the western theme. The Frontier Trading Post offers a wide range of merchandise, such as clothing, toys, and souvenirs, which are related to the theme of the area as well as to the characters and stories of the American Old West. The walls and shelves are lined with cowboy hats, bandannas, sheriff badges, and toy guns. It also offers a selection of snacks, candy and collectible pins. The Frontier Trading Post is the place in the Magic Kingdom for guests to take home a piece of the Wild West. The lantern lights illuminated his face and she could see blood running down his cheek.

Pinching her skin lightly at the base of her throat, she looked over the shoulder of the EMT and said softly, "Are you alright?"

"What?" Hawk said with a confused expression.

"He is having a bit of ringing in his ears from the explosion," the EMT stated as he stopped the bleeding on the cut at the side of Hawk's temple. "You might have to say it louder."

Nodding, Juliette repeated, louder this time, "Are you alright?"

"Huh?" Hawk said as he winced at the touch of the EMT.

She faked a smile but knew if she said it again, she would be screaming. He obviously was not all right. Still, even louder she screamed. "Are you alright?"

Hawk winced again, this time looking in her direction. A look of shocked horror came across his face.

"What are you screaming about?" he said with irritation in his voice.

"I was seeing if you are OK, the EMT..." Juliette looked at the emergency worker and saw a huge grin break out across his face. "He told me to play along, I'm sorry..."

"So you can hear me?" Juliette looked back at Hawk in disbelief.

"What?" Hawk again feigned deafness.

"You jerk!" Juliette punched Hawk and then looked at the EMT and added, "You too."

"Ouch," Hawk rubbed his shoulder where she had punched him. "I've just been in an explosion and that hurt worse than the blast."

"Good," she said. "Are you OK?"

The EMT finished working and Hawk moved out the door and sat down on the porch of the trading outpost. Juliette sat down next to him.

"I'm going to be OK." Hawk said in a low voice. "But I was chasing someone and they drew me into following them, right to here, just as the explosion happened."

The two were interrupted as another EMT, this one female approached.

"Sir, we are going to transport you to the hospital now," she said with a sense of urgency.

"Why are you going to the hospital?" Juliette looked at Hawk. "I thought you said you were OK?"

"I am and I'm not going to the hospital." Hawk snorted.

"We really think it would be a good idea so we could see what might be going on in your head. You might have a concussion, some internal bleeding, we won't know…"

Hawk cut the EMT off. "There is nothing going on in my head."

"That's the truth," Juliette muttered softly.

"I will go get checked out if I have any problems, for now I am fine. I'm just going to go home and rest." Hawk shakily got to his feet. "And this kind, nice, and caring lady is going to help me get there."

"If you are sure." The EMT seemed not so confident.

Then a Disney Security officer came over to where they were now standing. "We are going to need to close this area off. The police want to search the entire park for explosive devices."

"Do it." Juliette said instantly. "Whatever it takes, as long as it takes."

Hawk turned to start moving back toward the hub. As he did, his knees buckled slightly. Juliette reached over and half caught him, half steadied him.

"Maybe you should go to the hospital," Juliette said. "We can have a staff meeting."

"What are you talking about?"

"Oh, you don't know." Juliette felt Hawk leaning against her, trying to stabilize himself. With each step he seemed to be getting his legs back under him. "Jonathan and Sally were admitted to the hospital. I tried to call but you don't have a phone right now."

"In the hospital? What?"

"They were attacked by bees. They had an allergic reaction. They are in bad shape."

"I…I don't…bees?"

"We called in Dr. Redfield again, the doctor that helped Jillian. He was able to get them a protocol to ease some of the reaction. They are serious but they are going to be OK. And now someone has tried to blow you up, after you were attacked by a Sasquatch earlier." She tightened her grip on his arm, tighter than she should have considering he had just been in an explosion. "So tell me right now, what is happening? Because there is something happening and you know more about it since we talked earlier – right?"

Hawk was quiet as they walked down Main Street USA toward the Fire Station. Juliette waited, somewhat impatiently. She had been in this situation with Hawk before. They knew the resort was under attack, but she did not know by who or why. She believed that Hawk might, she could wait a few more moments.

"Have you heard from Shep?" Hawk asked, he was walking steadier, as if the news of what had happened to Jonathan and Sally had made him sturdier.

"No, I haven't. Not since earlier when he told me about you and Bigfoot." Juliette had not thought about Shep. The relationship between Shep and the rest of them had been strained for a few years now. It was not bad just not as close as they had once been. Hawk had tried to reach back into the Shep's life more than the rest of them. But now that his name had been mentioned, Juliette knew it was odd that she nor anyone else hadn't heard from him. Immediately she allowed the unwelcomed thoughts creep in and the possibility that somehow Shep was involved in this latest problem.

"I had him searching the woods. He never checked back in with me. I thought you might have seen him." Hawk continued and they turned the corner at The Emporium to head towards the stairs on the side of the Fire Station. "Jillian, Jonathan, Sally, and now, me have all had some brush with death. Has anything happened to you?"

"No." Juliette shook her head. She was going to call Tim and warn him again as soon as she got the chance.

"Shep hasn't been in the hospital has he?"

"Not that I'm aware of."

As if on cue, Juliette's cell phone rang and she fished it out of her pocket. It was not a number she recognized.

"Yes." She answered.

"Ms. Keaton." The male voice on the phone said. "This is Sergeant William Shakespeare."

"Seriously, this is William Shakespeare?" She saw Hawk tilt his head to one side and purse his lips as he heard her half of the conversation.

"Most people call me Bill." The sergeant said. "I am with the Orange County Sheriff's Department. I am the lead on our bomb squad and you are my contact if we find anything else in the resort."

"Yes, Sergeant Shakespeare. Is something else wrong?"

"Ma'am we have found another explosive device in the resort."

She swallowed hard. "Where?"

"In your office." The sergeant replied. "We are emptying out the Bay Lake Towers and The Contemporary Resort as we speak."

"Where are you evacuating people to?" She stopped walking and looked at Hawk with a mixture of disbelief and panic.

"Out of the buildings. I suppose where they go is up to you."

"I'm on my way." She ended the call.

"What?" Hawk grimaced slightly with confusion.

"They found another bomb, in my office."

"So they have tried to get all of us." Hawk now picked up the pace toward his apartment. "We need to see if Shep is OK."

Juliette felt a pang of guilt since her default had been that Shep might be involved, not that he might be attacked or hurt. She slowed and felt Hawk change his pace to match hers.

"I have to go." Juliette said. "We have to move guests out of the Tower and The Contemporary."

Hawk did not respond. Juliette saw his gaze drift off toward something else. He was looking up the stairs of the Fire Station.

"Do you see that?"

Juliette looked up the stairs but saw nothing. She stretched her gaze into the landing and surrounding railing and then, the door. There was something on the door. Hawk pulled away from her and pushed toward the stairs, he stumbled slightly as he tried to rush up them. Deliberately, he gathered himself and pushed through what was obviously some pain. He really should have gone to the hospital she thought. Hawk made his way to the top of the landing and then removed a piece of paper that had been stuck to the door with a sharp object, something that looked like the tip of a spear. Jerking it out of the door, Hawk pulled the note into his hand. Juliette arrived and stood next to him and silently read the words on the page along with him as they stepped inside his apartment.

You have found out that none of your friends are safe.
I can get to them all and you cannot stop me.
If you want to prevent any additional pain, then you need to bring me the spear

If you do not comply – then I will be forced to unleash devastation on Walt Disney World
Many will die and it will be because of you.

Place the item on the Eastern Star at Midnight tomorrow
Or – the end of the world will happen

"So someone wants to get your attention, they attack all of us just to prove that they can?" Juliette summarized. "And then they put their demands on your door with a spear so you can give them that spear that Farren Rales told you about?"

Juliette didn't remember the name of it. Hawk had explained to both her and Jonathan his conversation with Rales as they rode in an elevator at Celebration Hospital.

"The Spear of Destin,." Hawk told her.

"Right, and what is that exactly?"

"Not really sure yet, but I have been working on it."

"And you know where it is?"

"Not yet."

Juliette sighed deeply. "Hawk, I've got to get over to The Contemporary and solve another crisis. We are still under attack here. We need a plan."

"I know, go…I'm working on a plan." Hawk smiled reassuringly.

She didn't believe him.

"Are you sure you are alright?"

"What?" he smirked.

"Stop it!" she moved to the door.

"I'm fine." He waved her to move along as she turned the handle.

Glancing over her shoulder she saw him smiling at her. She doubted he was fine. Hawk had the ability to appear calm, nonchalant, and very much in control when the world was in chaos around him. That gift, if you would call it that, had worked well for him as a leader because it kept people calm in crisis. This time for her, it helped a little bit.

He was hurt, she just didn't know how badly and he was not about to let her know. He was scared because he was always protective of those he loved and they all seemed to be vulnerable and he didn't know how to stop it. But she did know, if anyone could figure it out, Hawk could and would. That belief did reassure her. She stuck her head back in the door before closing it. One more question.

"You can find the Spear of Destiny, right?"

"He who holds the spear is invincible," Hawk said, his face growing serious. "He who loses the spear loses his life…. Or so goes the legend."

"So who holds the spear right now?" Juliette said with an eyebrow raised.

"I suppose, I do…sort of…it is hidden here, I think, somewhere in Walt Disney World."

"Then find it fast – and be invincible!" Juliette closed the door behind her and raced down the steps to solve the latest catastrophic event of the week at Walt Disney World.

Please Move to the Exit

CHAPTER THIRTY-EIGHT

Day Three - Morning

People streamed out of the doors of The Contemporary Resort in pajamas, night shirts, t-shirts, and various styles of sleepwear. The puffy eyed tourists who had been roused from their sleep by an alarm and a more alarming security detail moving floor by floor through the resort hotel making sure rooms were empty and the guests were herded outside. David Walker had been caught in the herd, but he hadn't been asleep. He left his workspace at The Wilderness Lodge and had migrated to The Contemporary in search of stronger coffee and the prospect of an early breakfast. David's contacts across the globe had been working on his digital archaeological expedition into the life of the now missing Otto Guy trying to tie his disappearance into the emergence of Antonio Redfield.

Snapping his laptop shut, he rubbed his eyes and then drained his last swig of coffee from the white paper cup swaddled in a clutch. The clutch was not necessary now, the once hot drink had grown cold and tasted bitter on his taste buds. Definitely not good to the last drop. That was when the alarm had sounded. The fire alarm followed by the semi-calm voice activated alert system instructing everyone in the building to leave. A Disney cast member came out from an office somewhere behind the front desk and with frantic arm motions was telling him to exit through the glass doors. Initially startled but insatiably curious, he moved to the front desk instead to see if he could get more information.

Moments later the lobby had begun to fill with people and he lingered along the edges of the crowd as it pushed out the doors into the early hours of the morning. It was surprising orderly and although irritated, there was not as of yet, any great resistance to the interruption. Confusion and tiredness lined the faces of the people moving through the entrance area past the couches, chairs, and kiosks. David managed to eavesdrop and catch snippets of what he thought was taking place. This was a security evacuation, he had heard the words bomb threat used, there was some type of floor by floor search taking place and the guests would wait outside until the sheriff's department could verify that it was all clear to reenter. From his vantage point he could see that people were coming down escalators and moving through exits in both the front and rear of the building. The elevator doors were open and they were not moving or being used. Eventually, security managed to get him to the door and shoved outside. He moved through the families seated along the massive paved entrance, beside the reflecting pool, beyond the flag poles, behind hastily placed barricades, which he wondered were adequate if there was indeed some sort of explosion.

His cell phone rang and he answered it to hear Allie's voice on the other end of the call.

"David, are you awake?"

"I am now." He smiled.

"I'm sorry. I just got an alert that something was happening at The Contemporary Resort. Meet me in the lobby," Allie said. David heard her moving about the room, he assumed she was getting ready to exit.

"I was just in the lobby."

"Great, it is late, I mean early..." she seemed to be trying to figure out what he was doing up at this hour. "I'm on my way."

David knew that she had assumed he was at The Wilderness Lodge lobby, since that is where they were staying and where they had been the last time he had seen her. He wanted to correct her before she started looking for him.

"I'm at The Contemporary."

"How did you get there so quick? I just got the notification that something was up. What's going on?" Allie was now awake.

"Some kind of bomb scare or threat from what I have picked up." David looked around at the sea of people. "It is pretty surreal, all of the guests are outside. If you want to send a camera over, we could get some shots. This is something you don't see every day."

"Great, on it!"

"But Allie...." David waited for her response.

"Yes."

"Most importantly, I need you to get me an audience with Grayson Hawkes. I've found some stuff that I think he needs to know about. Or at least, he should be a good source to help me understand what I am finding."

"Stuff?" Allie asked.

David could hear her door shutting behind her and she was now moving. Her voice reflected she was walking at a pretty healthy clip.

"I've been doing some more digging on Otto Guy."

There was silence on the line for a moment, then Allie responded.

"You've been up digging up stuff about your theory that Guy is Redfield? All night, you've been digging this stuff up?"

There was a sense of urgency in David's voice when he answered.

"You will not believe all that I have uncovered. I've had my sources at work. This is, well...to use a bad word at the wrong time...explosive." As David spoke he became aware he was pacing back and forth among the people seated on the concrete in front of the main entrance of the resort. "I've been digging. Before Redfield became head of the IIH, the doctor – Otto Guy wasn't just involved in questionable research, the man was out of his mind."

"Out of his mind?"

"Crazy, strange, weird, loco...pick a word. This guy was a full bubble off."

"Are you sure about this?"

"Would I mention it if I weren't?" David inhaled deeply as he began to ponder the magnitude of the information he had unearthed.

"I'm on my way to the resort and I'll see if I can get you an audience with Hawk."

"Thanks." David ended the call.

There was a burning inside his chest that was not indigestion. It was the fire he felt when he was getting ready to challenge some powerful people or expose some hidden secret that he believed had been hidden too long. His attention turned toward the front entrance as he saw the line of fire trucks and rescue vehicles in the driveway along the main entrance to the resort. Glancing around at the people scattered everywhere across the front of the resort, into the parking areas, and any place else they could find to go, he knew this would become a story that they would repeat about their vacation to Walt Disney World for years to come.

Out of Here

Chapter Thirty-Nine

Day Three – Late Morning

Enough was enough!

Jillian stretched her legs and swung them over the side of her extremely uncomfortable hospital bed. She had been here long enough. Glancing to her left at the array of medical monitoring devices, most of which she was no longer tethered to, she pulled off the oxygen monitor and flung it back over her shoulder. It was satisfyingly defiant. She was checking herself out of the hospital. She had been here long enough and the images dancing across the television screen in her room were making her feel worse than when she checked in.

Every news channel was covering the unfolding events in the Walt Disney World Resort. There had been an explosion inside of the Magic Kingdom. Reports were very sketchy but it was being rumored that the company Chief Creative Officer, Dr. Grayson Hawkes had been injured. Jillian had tried reaching him on his phone and as usual, it was not with him, missing, stolen, not working, or neglected which always translated to he was unavailable and that meant he was in some kind of trouble. Over the past few hours she had been watching the reports and the latest was the footage of The Contemporary Resort being evacuated. The press was having a field day running with every bit of rumor, gossip, and speculation they could create. To make matters even more disgusting, Mr. Mark Gross, the president of the executive board of the company was continuing his monologue of trash babble about the leadership of the company, the failure of Grayson Hawkes, the poor culture, and the current crisis the company was in. That guy loved to find a camera, any camera, he was available for every news channel. She was sure he was on every internet news service and was probably making appearances at birthday parties, graduations, and weddings if someone was dumb enough to give him a microphone.

Jillian had been allowed to go back to wearing her own clothes, which was a much needed upgrade from the open backed hospital gown of previous days. Now in a pair of stretch pants, sports running top, and in a moment, her tennis shoes she was checking herself out. Pulling the probes off her chest and flinging them to the bed with the same flourish as the oxygen counter, the resulting alarm and flat line reading on the monitor was once again, satisfying.

A nurse burst into the room. His name was Elmer. She had been calling him El.

"And where do you think you are going?" El surveyed the room and could figure out what was happening.

"I'm going home and back to work." Jillian now was on her feet, moving to rescue her socks from the drawer, and then slumped into the recliner at the side of her former resting place to put them on, followed by her shoes.

"You can't check yourself out. You have not been discharged yet."

"El, let me explain something to you." She pointed at the television set as the second sock slid into place. "You see what is happening in Mickey Mouse land up there? That is where I work. That is my job. My job is to help keep it safe and sane. Does that look safe and sane to you?"

The footage showed guests pushing their way out of the futuristic resort and then a drone shot showed the massive assembly of people on the front entrance to the hotel.

"No, but you are in no condition…"

"Come on, I heard the doctors earlier, I am in great condition. They said I was a good patient, I was lucky… if you believe in luck… that there was a doctor who knew how to treat the snake bite. And so at the end of the day. I am better, the snake is dead. Extremely dead. And I am needed elsewhere."

"I have to advise you that you are failing to adhere to the prescribed discharge process. It'a a bad decision we are not responsible for and it can have serious implications for your long term health and recovery."

"Got it, thanks." Jillian was now up trying to gather her belongings that were scattered about the room.

"Your healthcare professionals need to equip you with your appropriate after care procedures and this is against our best judgment in managing your health." El said as he followed Jillian from station to station in the hospital room. He paused as she entered the small bathroom and closed the door.

"I'm going to be fine." Jillian looked in the mirror and began gathering her toiletry items that had been placed on the silver shelf below the mirror.

"I really do advise against this. We want to be sure the poison is completely out of your system," El's muffled voice came through the bathroom door.

"Are you still out there?" Jillian shook her head at her own reflection the mirror.

Shoving the door and nearly hitting El with it, she was on a mission, a mission to leave the hospital and get back to whatever was happening in the not so magical world she called home.

"Take care of my friends Jon and Sally. They are still recovering from their reaction to the bee stings." Jillian smiled, "I have to get to Disney."

Seeing the police officer rise from his station outside of her room where he was guarding the door, she pointed at him with an intensity that caused him to pause, mouth opened, getting ready to speak.

"I don't care what Hawk told you. I am leaving this hospital. You can either take me back to the theme parks or I will get an Uber – if you plan on trying to keep protecting me then you will need to keep up and stay out of my way."

Leaving the Station

CHAPTER FORTY

Day Three - Noon

The red bricked pathway that winds along the edge of the Magic Kingdom stretches from The Contemporary, which now had guests returning to their rooms, past the bus loading area to the Main Gates of the Magic Kingdom. The foliage that provided the break in the sight lines between the loading areas and the attractions of the theme park caused the path to be darker than David Walker had expected. He was doing his best to walk alongside Juliette Keaton, who was taking a brief respite from problem solving to take him towards his requested meeting for a conversation with Grayson Hawkes. David knew that Juliette had her hands full and a public relations catastrophe on her hands. To the casual observer, thanks to some of the media coverage, the Walt Disney Company, in particular Walt Disney World, seemed to be in a total meltdown with anything that could possibly be going wrong, going wrong.

"You are dealing with a firestorm right now, thank for doing this," David said to Juliette.

"It gives me a break from the madness for a moment."

"I know that Disney is taking a beating right now in the news, but that is because what is happening here is so chaotic and out of control."

"You're telling me." She didn't smile as she said it, brushing a loose strand of hair from across her face.

"I've known you too many years to think it is chaos." David sincerely told her. "I have to believe there is something bigger going on here." Then the reporter in him couldn't resist adding, "Let me tell the story."

"David, Allie called and asked if I could get you a meeting with Hawk. She assured me that you had something that might be extremely helpful for him and us right now. I assume, based upon her assurance and yours that is accurate." Juliette slowed her walk as they cleared the bus loading area which was strangely vacant at this time of day. "If that is not true, I can promise you, we will never give you a story or insider information ever again."

"Message received," Walker continued moving, throwing his hands up in a mocked surrender. "I promise, I have something that I think is important or I wouldn't have asked."

Juliette stopped as they reached the entrance area where the green coverings over the gates and turnstiles were located. She pointed as she spoke and instructed David where to go next.

"You will be able to go through the turnstile on the far left end of the gates. That is the one that our cast who has to work nights will access. There is no one on the streets working however, the area in Frontierland is still a crime scene and all of our focus is on putting it back together. We aren't opening the park today." Juliette sighed. "I've got to get back to The Contemporary so we can get everyone settled back inside. Hawk is expecting you. Go through the train station, past City Hall and when you get to Station 71, the fire station, take the stairs on the right hand side of the building. They aren't marked, the door at the top is Hawk's apartment. He should be there, he is expecting you."

"Thanks, Juliette." David said as he moved away from her toward the gate. He walked through the opened turnstile, which let him through just as she had said it would. He chose the tunnel on the right to enter the train station. He had heard that Main Street Train station had been modeled after the old Saratoga Springs Railway Station, which no longer exists, making the design of this station both classic and historic. The tunnel opened to his left which is an area where strollers could be rented for a day of fun in the parks. The counter was closed as expected and the station underneath was minimally lighted. As David moved through he stopped for a moment and thought he heard what could best be described as a roar. The roar was out of place. Clearly it did not sound like a train but more like an engine of some type of machine, no a vehicle, getting louder and echoing off the walls of this space beneath the station itself.

The walls were suddenly illuminated with a jerky set of spotlights that danced across the space around him and the roar became recognizable the moment he saw the source. Two motorcycles entered the station from the Town Square opening and buzzed on either side of him. The riders were wearing helmets with dark visors and their clothing was black. The rider to the right struck David with a fist as he passed causing him to lose his balance from the unexpected blow. Slightly stunned, more surprised than hurt, he turned to see the riders disappear around the corner from where he had just been only to reappear, on foot, no longer on their bikes.

His mind registered that their arrival had not been an accident and his brain told him to run. His first steps were sluggish but he broke into a run that carried him out of the station. He sensed the presence of at least one of the riders behind him but his own footsteps were all he could hear. Moving to his left he saw the ramp that was used for wheelchairs and those with disabilities to move up toward the loading area of the train station. That is the direction he headed. He raced across the concrete to the first landing and then turned to his left to ascend the second level. It was there that the other rider cut off his path, David reasoned that he must have circled around the other direction and now he was trapped between the two men who had appeared from the shadows.

One of them threw another fist toward David. He ducked as the second assailant grabbed him from behind, pinning his arms to his side. This allowed the first attacker to throw yet another punch, this one cracking David across the jaw. His head snapped to the side as he twisted and turned, trying to extract himself from the grip of the assailant so he could fend off the attack. Finally he was able to break an arm free as he forced the man holding him back against the wall It gave him just enough room for him to move his right arm. He raised it in front of his face to fend off another blow that was aimed at his head. The attacker facing him followed with another punch, this one finding its mark on the opposite side of David's face. The reporter felt his knees buckle and darkness began to close in from the corner of his vision. Whoever this was had surprised him, attacked him and beaten him, and he had no idea why. He was trying to stay consciousness but felt his clarity begin to fade. As he slumped toward the ground a sudden gust of what seemed like wind blew across the landing.

A figure, in a whirl of motion appeared. Light and darkness combined in a blur that brushed past him out of nowhere. David watched as the mysterious stranger threw a flurry of punches toward the rider who had hit him in the head. Each punch drove the man backward. David wondered how he could be hitting him so precisely with uppercuts able to connect from below the helmet covering. The first attacker fell to the ground and rolled down the ramp. He felt the man behind him let go as he battled the darkness to see the man trying to run away.

The mysterious rescuer moved with precision, his movement fluid and calculated with no wasted motion. He caught the second man and dropped to one knee and executed a sliding leg sweep that tripped the second biker into the air. It was almost funny the way he flipped with both legs no longer on the ground and he thudded to the concrete with a crash. David crawled, lost his balance and pitched forward. As he turned his head toward the battle on the ramp, he watched as his rescuer grabbed the man from behind, and to a semi-conscious mind seemed to defy the law of physics and threw him over the railing into the popcorn stand on other side of the retaining wall. He could hear the breaking of glass and the twisting of metal. The first attacker, disoriented and defeated got to his feet but should not have. The rescuer hit him with a lunging attack, catching him at the waist, lifting him off the ground, and using his body as a projectile battering ram drove him back, his helmet hitting the wall with a loud crack.

David once again tried to regain his balance and get to his feet. The dark clouds crawling through his brain kept progressing and his vision grew darker. He felt a mixture of gratitude, awe, and curiosity and intended to say "thank you." The words never made it from his brain to his lips, the darkness enveloped him and his last coherent thought was wondering why he had been attacked.

The Fallen

CHAPTER FORTY-ONE

Day Three – Early Afternoon

The reporter stirred and tried to sit up. He was stretched out on a couch in the Hawk's Nest, as Jillian, fresh from being a patient herself, held an icepack on the side of his head. David Walker regained his bearings and looked at her, before reaching up and taking the ice pack away from his face.

"There you are." Hawk was sitting in a chair facing him, leaning forward trying to survey the damage. "I wasn't sure if you were going to bounce back or not for a minute there. You took a couple of shots to the head."

"Were you the one?" David's voice was hollow and faint.

"Do you know who attacked you?" Jillian helped ease him into a sitting position. "Take it slow, you are going to need to go to a hospital and get checked out."

David looked back toward Hawk once he was stabilized on the sofa. Hawk could tell he was trying to focus his vision on him so he waited. Again, David asked, "Was it you who helped me?"

"Yes," Hawk smiled. "Glad I showed up when I did, you were in a world of hurt. I'm sure you could have eventually taken those guys, but thanks for letting me help."

"You were phenomenal." David closed his eyes remembering. "You destroyed those guys."

"Over the years, I've been in a few…dust ups." Hawk looked toward Jillian and winked. "I came down when I heard the motorcycles. I thought I was the only one with a motorcycle on Main Street."

"Did you get them?" David croaked, his voice was slowly coming back to him.

"No, I actually got you out of there. Brought you up here about the same time Jillian got here. By the time I got back downstairs, they were gone. I heard the bikes crank up, so I wasn't surprised."

"You never got a look at their face?" Jillian was talking to David. She then turned to Hawk and nodded, it was the same question for him.

"Nope, I was busy." Hawk said. "David, I'm sorry you got hurt. We have called our medical team and they are on the way. You probably need to get checked out. You have a nasty bump or two on the noggin."

"I will, but I needed to see you." David pushed back the ice pack that Jillian had once again planted upside his head, then leaned back against the couch cushion. "I've got something to tell you that is interesting and bothersome."

"The EMTs will not be here for a few minutes, go ahead if I can listen in." Jillian said as she moved to the window, her work as a nurse done, to glance outside.

Hawk looked at her, he was still worried about her checking herself out of the hospital, but she was tough and resilient. She seemed to be fine. The sunlight glimmering off Main Street USA cast a soft shadow across her face as she looked outside. He liked the look. The day had been tough, he was still nursing a dull headache from being blown up and his tussle with the two motorcycle riders hadn't helped his head. He had heard the bikes thundering down the street and looked out the window as they moved below the train station. Putting two and two together, he realized that the reporter who was coming to see him had to be there. So, he had gone down to help.

"Before you say anything, I read the email you sent me about Dr. Antonio Redfield not being who he says he is." Hawk informed him.

A few hours earlier, Hawk had received an email from David Walker with an extensive amount of information, documentation, and reasons why he believed he was the former Otto Guy. Hawk had shared some of it with Jillian as they were waiting for David to regain consciousness. The struggle they were having was that if he was indeed Otto Guy, why had he been willing to help Jillian, Jon, and Sally at the hospital? He had also been willing to talk with Juliette and even do a press conference to help them understand the animal behavior from earlier at Animal Kingdom. He was a prestigious and well respected member of the medical community, it seemed a stretch that he wasn't who he said he was. Yet, Hawk had seen enough to know and believe that sometimes conspiracy theories are only conspiratorial because they haven't been proven yet and usually it was in the best interest of someone else for people not to believe them. Calling them conspiracies was an easy way to dismiss the truth if it needed to be hidden. Over his years at Disney, most things did not surprise him.

"Otto Guy was a bad man." David said. "His research was not just questionable, it was diabolical, and he was weaponizing diseases and viruses. He disappeared just before he was about to be caught, probably charged with murder or attempted murder, and crimes against humanity."

"I read some of what you sent me." Hawk leaned back. "It seems far-fetched, but I am not going to disagree with you. You did your research, you found evidence, you may be right."

"Is that why you were attacked?" Jillian asked as she continued to keep a cautious eye out the window toward the street below.

"I have no idea." David shrugged. "It is just information. But there is more, more that I didn't send you."

"Really?" Hawk raised an eyebrow slightly and slid his chair closer to the couch.

Hawk followed the reporter's gaze and could tell his head was clearing. Walker was now taking in his surroundings, making notes it seemed with his eyes. Hawk watched him do so. He saw his glance lingering on an area right off of the kitchen in the apartment. It was Hawk's command center. It was a desk actually with a couple of computers, stacks of papers, maps of the Disney property, and a collection of what most would consider junk. For Hawk, the place is where he often worked out the complex puzzles of life. At this moment, the desk was loaded with scribbled notes, pages off a printer, and pictures of the Spear of Destiny, one of the pressing mysteries of the moment.

"Listen, what I am going to tell you sounds like some crackpot conspiracy garbage. I know it does, but I promise you, from what I have been able to find out so far, I can verify some of this from my sources." David rubbed his chin. "This Otto Guy is a member of a secret society group that call themselves the B'nai ha Nephilim."

"The what?" Jillian returned from the window and plopped onto the sofa next to David.

"The B'nai ha Nephilim, it means the Sons of the Fallen." David answered.

"That helped." Jillian shot Hawk a look of skepticism.

"The Sons of the Fallen are disciples of Lucifer." David continued.

"You mean, Lucifer, as in the devil?" Jillian clarified, again looking with disbelief at Hawk.

Hawk gently lifted his right hand slightly, a soft hand signal to let David continue to talk without interruption or expressed disbelief.

"Right, I mean the devil." David looked at Jillian. "I know, I know, it sounds crazy." He now looked toward Hawk, clearing his throat. "You have to understand what that means. They believe that the God of the Bible is evil and that Lucifer is good."

"That is not the way I have heard Hawk talk about the Bible. God is not the bad one in the story." Jillian offered her theological assessment.

"Let him talk." Hawk felt as if time was slowing down, which usually happened when he was getting ready for a battle or to solve a crisis.

Just a little earlier, Hawk had stepped into the street to help David Walker and as he moved into the area, he could see the events unfolding in what could best be described as slow motion, allowing him to plot his strategy and counterattack. It was a gift that he had for years and for some reason, as he was listening to David Walker that sense of an epic battle washed over him. He nodded toward David to continue.

"So this is a good versus evil thing. According to what I have been told, the Sons of the Fallen believe that when the Temple is rebuilt in Jerusalem..."

"That is an End Times event." Jillian smiled and nodded at Hawk knowing she was correct.

"Yes, it is." Hawk confirmed her statement and her smile grew bigger.

"Once the Temple is rebuilt in Jerusalem, then they will send their handpicked leader into the Holy of Holies, he will shed his own blood on the altar and then proclaim himself to be the messiah. The Sons of the Fallen will follow him and they intend to rule the planet."

"That is intense." Hawk exhaled.

"Otto Guy is one of the leaders, which means Redfield is a leader and dangerous. So all of that research, all of that sketchy unethical work he has done, in his mind is a quest, some type of holy horror quest in my opinion." David shook his head. "It is messed up, I know... but even now, the Sons of the Fallen have people working to make this happen, to rebuild the temple, they are looking for religious artifacts like Hitler did, and they are going to put their plan into motion."

"They're nut jobs," Jillian summarized.

"Yes, without a doubt. But these people exist and are active." David turned to her.

"Tell me more about the religious artifacts you mentioned." Hawk asked.

David waved his hands as he spoke. "I left out that part. There is a relic they have to use to spill blood on the mercy seat altar in the Holy of Holies. It is called a destiny spear."

Hawk swallowed hard. "You mean the Spear of Destiny?"

"That's it!" David pointed at Hawk as if they were playing charades. "The Spear of Destiny is the weapon they have to use to spill the blood on the altar."

The knock on the door startled all three of them as the paramedics announced their arrival.

The Devil Boys

Chapter Forty-Two

Day Three - Afternoon

Closing the door behind her, Jillian strode across the room to the table where Hawk sat lost in thought, looking through the window toward Main Street USA. The morning sun was chasing away the shadows outside and she followed Hawk's gaze as the paramedics loaded David Walker into an ambulance for a ride to the hospital.

"We're going to have remember to write thank you notes to the hospital staff after all of this." She tried to sound nonchalant, but she was bothered, worried, trying to figure out what was going on.

Hawk slid a folded piece of paper across the table as she took a seat. She unfolded it and read the handwritten letters and numbers… *HQ 94-4-4667,* then glanced up at him.

"Where did you get this?" she asked.

Hawk pushed his sleeves up on each arm. "It was given to me by a stranger in the Skipper's Canteen. Why? Do you know what it is?"

Twisting the paper on the table, she hummed. "Maybe…it looks like the way they categorize FBI files."

"FBI?"

"I can't be sure, but it does look like it." She folded the paper back up. "I can check. Is it important right now?"

"I think it is. But I'm not real clear on why right now."

"So what is the Spear of Destiny?" she reached over and placed her hand on his. "That means something to you, right? It has something to do with what is going on around here – right?"

"Yes." Hawk raised his chin slightly, exposing a tension in his neck. "The Spear of Destiny may be history's most sacred relic."

"I've never heard of it, until a few minutes ago."

"There are some who believe that it holds mystical powers." Hawk looked her in the eyes.

"And that is why the devil boys need it in the new temple in Jerusalem one day?"

"Exactly. It has been pursued and maybe even possessed by Napoleon, Hitler, and even Patton."

"Huh?"

"The spear is mentioned in the Bible one time in John 19:34, it says – "*But one of the soldiers pierced His side with a spear, and immediately blood and water came out.*" Those eighteen words are at the heart of the story."

"The Spear of Destiny is the spear that pierced the side of Jesus during the crucifixion?" she tightened her grip on his hand.

"That is the spear. It is believed that over time that whoever was the keeper of the spear had unlimited power and was invincible." Hawk was very still. "Those who held the spear had replicas made so the real one could not be stolen. It was sought after, fought over, and protected at all costs. It is said that Hitler saw it on display in a museum in Vienna as a young man and was consumed with one day having it so he could conquer the world. Some have even suggested that Hitler's ruthless rise to power, the entire creation of the Nazi Party, and the actual beginning of World War II was all about getting the spear. Nothing else mattered to Hitler except having the spear in his possession."

"Hold on, that sounds crazy," Jillian sat back in her chair.

"I know it does, I didn't say I believed it." Hawk looked back out the window.

"Did the Nazis get the spear?"

"It is believed they did." Hawk looked back at her, his voice was firm. "After the Nazis had it, that is when the replicas started showing up, so there was always some doubt as to where the real spear was."

"But Hitler had it, didn't he…the real one?"

"I think so." Hawk nodded. "As the war was about to end, the spear and all sorts of other relics were hidden and transported to Antarctica so eventually there would be a resurgence of the Fourth German Reich."

"The spear is that powerful?"

"So some think." Hawk paused before continuing. "Those that believe the spear has supernatural power believe that the spear will make you more than a ruler, they believe it will make you a god."

"Ah, now we are back to the devil boys wanting it." Jillian was beginning to put together the pieces of the important backstory.

"See, it doesn't matter whether the spear really has any power or not. The scary thing is that some people believe it has that kind of power and will do whatever it takes, with no regard or concern for others, to have that power for themselves. They will fight for it and they will die trying to attain it. That makes them very dangerous zealots."

Hawk stood and walked over to his command center. With a wave of his hand, he indicated the pile of paper strewn about. "This is what I have been researching. When David mentioned it, that is when I began to understand."

"I get it. The spear is important. Very important. But why? Where does all the power come from?"

"Remember what the Spear of Destiny is," Hawk began.

"It is the spear that was used on Jesus," Jillian pursed her lips.

"Yes, and so what might the spear contain?" Hawk asked and waited for her answer.

Jillian thought, her mind went back to the ancient city of Jerusalem, she blurred through the story of the crucifixion and the aftermath, then it hit her.

"There is blood on the spear!" She stood.

"Exactly." Hawk was thrilled she figured it out. "It is believed that there will be remnants, DNA of the blood of Jesus on the spear that pierced his side. A researcher doing gain to function research, cross mixing DNA, and creating genetic variations, might like to have the unique blood of God Himself to work with."

"You've got to be kidding me!" Jillian heard her own voice rise just a bit. "Redfield wants to use the blood of Jesus in his experiments!"

"So goes my theory to this moment." Hawk came back to where she was standing. "The legend says that he who holds the spear is invincible and he who loses the spear loses his life."

"But what does that have to do with you, with us, with Walt Disney World?"

"It is what Farren Rales was trying to point me toward. Apparently, the spear went to the bottom of the ocean on its way to Antarctica. For years it was on the bottom of the ocean off the coast of Florida. Walt Disney had a friend, Werner von Braun, who had disclosed what he believed was in that submarine and how important it was. And that story has more credibility because at one time, he was working with the Nazis." Hawk put his arms around her waist.

"So this is another mystery of Walt Disney himself." She wrapped her arms around the back of his neck. "Walt Disney found the Spear of Destiny."

"He found it, had it recovered and kept it hidden because of the power that so many believed it could give them. And it is now mine."

She suddenly released her grip and took a half step back.

"You have the spear?"

"No." Hawk shook off her question. "I don't even know where it is. I have to find it. It is hidden here somewhere at the resort. But someone wants it and I have to give it up before midnight or the end of the world is going to happen."

They stared at each other for what seemed like a very long time. Her eyes could see the worry in the lines of his face. She was amazed that he was so calm, so confident, and there was not the slightest hint of fear. What she saw was a man whose chest was thrust out assertively and he looked as if he were ready to go to war.

"So, what do I need to do to help?" she asked.

"Start by seeing if you can find out what that number on the paper is. It is supposed to be helpful somehow."

"And what are you getting ready to do?"

Hawk leaned in and gave her a kiss on the cheek. "I have to find the Nautilus."

Up and Away

Chapter Forty-Three

Day Three – Late Afternoon

Juliette heard her name and turned on her heel to see Dr. Antonio Redfield coming across the lobby of the Bay Lake Towers. Finally able to move all of the guests back into The Contemporary Resort, Juliette was headed back to her office and was walking across the gleaming lobby of the resort. She waited by one of the towering silver pillars which gave the Bay Lake Towers a minimalist futuristic look. Juliette had explained to Hawk it was sleek yet simplistic, he had agreed, and that had been the day they decided to set up their offices in the building away from the other administrative hubs throughout the resort.

"My dear, Juliette Keaton," the doctor said as he approached with a mound of papers messily stacked in his left hand. "I have the final reports you asked for right here. I just finished them, so I rushed them right over. It took longer than I thought with my trips back and forth to the hospital."

Juliette reached out for the paperwork. "Doctor, you were a life saver. You saved the lives of Jillian, Jon, and Sally. I don't know how ever to repay you."

"There is no need for that, my dear." Redfield looked his usual rumpled self. "I was just glad I could help." He adjusted his glasses as he said it. "How are the patients?"

"Doing well. Jon and Sally are still recovering." Juliette paused then added. "And I have been told that Jillian is doing so well she is no longer in the hospital."

"Amazing!" the doctor pressed his palms to his cheeks. "That is so quickly. Ms. Batterson must possess incredible recuperative powers, she should not be up and moving so quickly. By doing so, she has defied the odds."

"Can you give me a summary?" Juliette glanced down at the mess of papers.

"Certainly." Redfield adjusted his glasses once again. "I found a slight variation of the virus in the gorilla that I found in the tiger. Very strange indeed. Not unheard of, not usual however. That was the cause of the aggressive behaviors. Sadly we may never be able to trace how they contacted the viruses, but we will continue to do our research."

"I thought you said at the press conference that the gorilla did not have the same virus."

"I did not believe at the time there was any evidence of that. However, being a man of science, I am always willing to be wrong if the science proves me so – in this case it did."

The sound of latex balloons bashing into one another with a thunk was heard across the lobby. Two cast members were carrying huge clumps of helium filled balloons with the iconic mouse ears inflated, surrounded by a clear balloon exterior. Between the two staff members they were maneuvering over one hundred balloons into the lobby. It was not a quiet process coming through the entrance.

Juliette felt the need to explain. "We are giving complimentary balloons to all of our guests here in the tower. We had a bomb scare last night and had to evacuate the building. It was very inconvenient. We will do a variety of things to help plus their stay due to the disruption."

"A bomb scare?" the doctor exclaimed in disbelief. "That is unfortunate."

"Actually, it was fortunate."

"Explain please?" The doctor widened his eyes.

"Fortunate that it was just a scare." Juliette smiled. "There was no explosions here."

One of the cast members let out a cry of frustration. Redfield and Juliette turned just in time to see three balloons get away from clutches of the struggling cast member. Despite some rather impressive gyrations and heroic attempts to catch them, the balloons floated off toward the interior roof of the lobby area, well out of reach of the cast member who had done their best to corral them before they left the lobby's atmosphere.

"Ah, such a pity." Redfield said as he watched the balloon float away. "As a child when I lost a balloon and it floated away I cried like it was the end of the world."

"Yes, when you are young, balloons floating away can be devastating and feel like the end of the world. By the time we reach adulthood those kind of things are just frustrating."

"Don't be so sure, it could be the end of the world…" Redfield let the statement drift off and away much like the balloon.

"What was that?" Juliette asked.

Then turning back to her, Redfield said, "I have bothered you enough, you have to get back to work."

With that, the doctor turned and ambled his way back across the lobby. Something he said as he left bothered her. She looked back up at the balloon now firmly being blown about by the air vents as it floated in the air. A floating balloon could be the end of the world? Juliette straightened the papers and made her way to the elevator, still pondering what the doctor had said.

That Hurt

CHAPTER FORTY-FOUR

Day Three – Early Evening

The pings, rings, and bleeps of equipment bounced across the tiled floor of the hospital as Allie Crossman entered the room. The rake of rings against metal clanged as the curtain was slid open revealing David Walker sitting up in his hospital bed. His face had an assortment of bruises still in the process of blossoming in the aftermath of his being attacked in the Magic Kingdom.

"How are you feeling, David?" Allie smiled softly as she asked. David could see she was taking in his condition and winced ever so slightly as he answered.

"Allie, don't worry, I am great." He pushed himself up higher in the bed. It hurt. "OK, I've been better, but I am going to be great again soon."

"I can't believe that you were attacked." Allie leaned closer. "Did you see who did this to you?"

"I've been replaying the event over and over, trying to remember anything that might be helpful, but I never really got a good look at them."

"Them?"

"Yes, there were two." David swallowed hard and slowly stretched his neck from side to side in an attempt to loosen the still stiffening muscles.

"What you went through is unimaginable. I'm glad you got away alive."

"I wouldn't have if I hadn't been rescued by Hawk. He appeared out of nowhere. He was fast, he was effective, he was almost otherworldly, or so it seemed."

"I'll be sure to thank him for rescuing you." Allie took inventory of all the monitors and tubes running across his bed. She could see that most were disconnected. "Are you sure you're going to be fine?"

"No doubt." David motioned to the paraphernalia of patient care around him. "They are getting ready to kick me out."

"So are you going to tell me?" Allie was now staring him directly in the eyes. "Why did this happen?"

"It has to be because of what I have been digging into."

"You mean, your conspiracy theory mystery is the reason you had two people attack you?" Her voice was tinted with disbelief.

"It has to be. I was going to tell Hawk what I found and then this happened."

Allie pushed a few stray hairs off of David's face gently and smiled. "Had you told anyone else what you had been looking for? I mean, how would they know what you were up to or thinking?"

David frowned. She was right. How could they have known? There is no way that anyone could have known what he was thinking or researching.

"What about Hawk?" She interrupted his thinking. "Did he have anything to add to your research?"

"Some," David now rubbed his shoulder trying to loosen that group of muscles. Man, his body was hurting. He was going to feel awful for the next few days. "Hawk is up to something. Don't know what, you know he is not always real forthcoming. But there is something bigger than we first thought happening here. I was right and Hawk pretty much confirmed it, not by what he told me but by what he didn't tell me."

With a groan he swung his legs over the side of the bed. Allie helped to steady him. Another groan provided the soundtrack for his slide out of the bed to get his feet on the floor. Straightening up to his full height was aided by another moan of pain.

"You sure you're ready to leave here?" Allie watched and smiled slightly. "You sound awful."

"Help me find my stuff. I'm ready to leave." David began making his way to the lavatory. "After I get dressed I can fill you in on what Hawk and I talked about on the way back to the media tent."

Elvis, Nixon, and Nemo

Chapter Forty-Five

Day Three - Evening

Yellow crime scene tape encased the area damaged by the explosion in Frontierland. Flapping and spinning loosely in the breeze it had been stretched and was barely holding its place around the blast area. Over what seemed like an endless number of hours, the sheriff's department and Disney Security had combed the area looking for clues and anything that might give them a lead on the person who placed the bomb. Hawk was skeptical that any evidence would be found. As he walked with Jillian, she was telling him what she had discovered about the mysterious combination of letters and numbers Hawk had asked her to check out.

As they walked through the street in the old west along the wooden planked porches next to storefronts, Hawk noticed the massive truck parked on the walkway where normally guests would move in and out of Frontierland. The truck bed was flat and it was designed to be used to tow massive objects. It could be slid backward, the end dropped to the ground, and whatever item needed to be lifted raised upon the platform through the use of a winch. Right now, the platform formed what looked like a massive ramp aimed toward the sky above the Rivers of America. It looked ridiculously out of place and caused Hawk to feel the pressure of getting the Magic Kingdom reopened quickly. Work trucks like this one reminded him how easily the perfect illusion of a magical kingdom could be ruined by one detail out of place.

"HQ 94-4-4667 was an FBI file." Jillian looked at her phone where she had placed the information in her notes. "It was a file on Walt Disney himself."

"I don't think I knew Walt Disney had an FBI file," Hawk said as he walked and then suddenly realized he was walking alone. He turned to see Jillian standing behind him, mouth opened, feigning amazement. Hawk rolled his eyes.

"What?"

"There is something about Walt Disney that Grayson Hawkes does not know? I am not really wanting to share it with you now. It makes me feel superior." She smirked as she quickly stepped up beside him. "If you didn't know that, then I also am sure you didn't know that Walt Disney was a SAC."

"A what?"

"SAC – Special Agent in Charge. It means that Mr. Disney had been granted special status by the FBI. In some cases these were just honorary recognitions of someone who offered some important service to the FBI and other times they were more than that." Jillian was now referring to her notes again.

"Kind of like Elvis and Nixon?" Hawk asked.

She looked at him and connected to the reference he was making. "That was a random bit of trivia to pull out of your hat." But Hawk could tell she was impressed by her satisfied smile at the thought of then President Richard Nixon making Elvis Presley a special government agent.

"Most people would think that Walt's title was honorary like Elvis," she admitted. "But there is more than that in his file. Amazingly enough, there is a lot redacted and not available to the public."

"But you could see it."

"Yes," Jillian nodded. "My contact is good and I could see what was in the file, the complete file. Apparently Walt was an acquaintance of J. Edgar Hoover himself and did some consulting work for the bureau. He was especially useful in finding out and reporting information about communist activity here in the states."

"Walt testified before Congress." Hawk remembered.

"More than once," Jillian continued. "But he frequently talked with or corresponded with Hoover. Walt also hosted leaders from around the globe at Disneyland, he traveled abroad, and there were times that his meetings were less helpful to the studio than they were to diplomacy for the government. And… here is the best part. There is a reference, a bit obscure, to an ancient relic that Walt Disney had reportedly acquired that the FBI was extremely interested in."

"You mean the spear?" Hawk stopped.

The old west had now been absorbed inside Colonial America. The Liberty Tree and the Liberty Bell were just feet away. This was the Magic Kingdom's hub dedicated to freedom. Hawk often feared that people did not respect and revere the cost of freedom.

"It doesn't call it that specifically. But the reference refers to an item of great archaeological and political value that was acquired through Disney resources with information provided by some contact of the filmmaker. Whatever the item was reported to be was being held by the entertainer."

"So the FBI knew about the Spear of Destiny?" Hawk asked as they walked below the dining area of the Columbia Harbor House heading into Fantasyland. Rounding the pathway, Peter Pan's Flight was to their right and the Small World attraction was on their left.

"It appears they did. And you are taking me to it now, right?"

"Yes, but I don't know where we are going...yet." Hawk shook his head. "I have to figure it out." He reached into his pocket and pulled out the collectible pin that resembled a file folder that said Big Squid. Flipping it open he showed it to Jillian.

"20,000 Leagues under the Sea?" Jillian said as she studied the pen. Flipping it open with a fingernail and then closing it, she handed it back to Hawk.

"You ever see the movie?" Hawk asked as Juliette nodded yes. "In the movie, there is a lot of sub-story taking place."

"The movie is about a submarine." Juliette said nonchalantly.

Hawk didn't know if she was kidding or not, so he continued. "I mean subplots in the film."

"I know what you meant." She sounded disappointed that he didn't seem as amused as she was by her comment.

"The live action film was state of the art and loaded with visual effects. It tackled a complicated story and Walt pulled together a big name cast for it. None of that history would have been lost on Farren Rales as he made sure that the Spear of Destiny was safe. The spear was dangerous and powerful as well as historical and valuable. The Nautilus was the submarine but in some ways it was a character in the film. Elegant, beautiful, and full of wonders but with a razor sharp prow on her back that was used as an instrument of destruction."

"Kind of the way that some would want to use the Spear of Destiny?"

"No doubt." Hawk continued, "And even though no one knows where the spear is – yet. If Otto Guy is who David Walker thinks he is, he is a lot like Captain Nemo. Brilliant, powerful, creative and yet – bored and fed up with the world and the way it operates. He is callused enough to believe that he has a better plan and that at any cost, his work will revolutionize the world around him. Nothing, even life itself can get in the way."

"That makes him a monster," Jillian concluded. "And that monster now looks like Antonio Redfield."

"A very smart and dangerous monster," Hawk added. "And he wants the Spear of Destiny."

"If you are going to find the spear, then you have to find the Nautilus?"

The pair now had come to a stop at the carousel. Looking into the new Fantasyland expansion from years before, Hawk pointed toward the roller coaster track that could be easily seen from where they stood.

"That is where 20,000 Leagues under the Sea used to be located," Hawk pointed like a tour guide pointing out sites. "It took up a massive footprint, but over time the attraction lagoon was filled in and things were built where the submarines once carried guests. It is now the home of the expanded Fantasyland."

"So where is the Nautilus then?" Jillian followed his pointing tour.

"Gone," Hawk sighed. "For the most part. There are a couple of tributes hidden in the park remembering the attraction. That's where I figured we should start."

Hope Dwindles

Chapter Forty-Six

Day Three - Evening

Fading in and out of the space between sleep and being fully aware, Shep felt his head bob jarring him back into the present. Time was now irrelevant to him, he had no idea how long he had been there and what had happened to him in his lapses into unconsciousness. As he searched the forest he had been trying to unravel whatever it was that Hawk had seen. Each piece of evidence and Hawk's credibility had led him to believe that there was indeed something prowling the woods. He had been oblivious to the imminent encounter that had been waiting for him.

His mind remembered the shadowy darkness of the aged trees and then he vaguely remembered sensing a peculiar presence lurking in the shadows. Now, he wondered if the Sasquatch had been tracking him, watching his every move, waiting for the right moment to attack him for venturing into his domain. There was some remote part of his brain screaming at him that Bigfoot was not real. It was all a hoax and that the creature did not exist. Trepidation and dread surged through his aching limbs and he hoped that he had been missed by someone.

Perhaps there were people out looking for him right now. They might be very close and he might be moments away from freedom. That hope leaked away as once again he remembered that no one had known exactly where he was. It could be another day or even days before anyone realized that he had been missing and might be in trouble.

Shep had experienced moments in his life before of dread, but this time, the isolation and the overwhelming sense of being all alone was more terrifying than he could have ever imagined. Sweat ran in thin streams down his neck below his hairline, he could feel his resolve to stay awake and think lucidly begin to fade away again. His eyes were heavy, his head drooped. For a moment, he thought he heard someone or something outside of the door. But the darkness drew him back into the pit of nothingness again and he slipped away into unconsciousness.

A Tribute or Two

CHAPTER FORTY-SEVEN

Day Three - Evening

She loved the intrigue. Jillian watched as Hawk explored looking for the elusive tributes to 20,000 Leagues under the Sea that remained in Fantasyland. Allowing her hair to fall slightly across her face in the hot Florida breeze, she realized again that it was the mystery and complexity that she found wrapped inside the person of Grayson Hawkes that made him that much more attractive to her. In so many ways he was a mixture of daring and danger and his fearless confidence had probably been what caused her to decide to build a life here in this magical world that Disney created.

"What?" Hawk suddenly shattered her thoughts.

"Hmm?"

"What are you looking at?" he smiled at her.

"I was just thinking," she replied.

"About where to find the Nautilus?"

"Sort of." She felt her face grow slightly warmer. "I was thinking about you finding the Nautilus."

"OK, I'll keep looking, you keep thinking," Hawk said with a grin and motioned for her to follow him across the streets of Fantasyland.

They walked towards The Many Adventures of Winnie the Pooh attraction. Inquisitiveness drew her head to a tilt as they got closer to the entrance.

"So we are going to find the Nautilus at the Winnie the Pooh ride?" She asked pausing near the front of the queue line.

"Yes, where else?" Hawk pointed toward the attraction. "It is immersive, family-friendly and scenes from the movie come to life in the form of a larger-than-life storybook. Surely we can find the Nautilus in the Hundred-Acre Wood or Rabbit's garden."

"Sure, and maybe it is blown around by blustery gusts with the Heffalumps and Woozles." She almost cut off her own sentence as she knew what was coming next.

Hawk stared at her slack jawed. He shook his head from side to side. She closed her eyes waiting for him to kid her.

"Heffalumps and Woozles? Even a reference to a blustery day! I had no idea you were a Winnie the Pooh expert," Hawk smiled.

She knew he was genuinely surprised. She felt truly embarrassed at calling up this memory from her childhood.

"I've seen the movies," she pointed back to the attraction to get him looking again.

"The movies?" Hawk did not let it go. "All of them?"

"Yes, all of them." She grabbed his arm and whirled him back to the task at hand, whatever that had to do with the attraction.

"This used to be Mr. Toad's Wild Ride. It had a very dedicated following. When the company made the decision to derail the rail ride in 1998 it was controversial one. But it was a good call, the attraction based on the animated stories of Pooh has been very popular. And you are a fan. I never knew." Hawk grinned as if he now was the keeper of some sort of secret.

"You never knew because I never told you." Jillian rolled her eyes as they searched the area. "I knew it was too much information for you to handle. After all, you are the keeper of all the secrets of Walt Disney, I think Winnie the Pooh is a little advanced for you."

"Fair enough." Hawk changed subjects slightly. "The wait is always so long that the Imagineers designed an interactive queue for kids to play to help them wait. When they did, they moved a tree into it that used to be across the pathway in a playground where the old submarine attraction used to be."

Hawk grabbed Jillian's hand and walked her to the front of a faux tree. It was a playhouse, a very big playhouse. Hawk dropped to his knees and crawled inside. Not knowing where he was going or what he was doing, she did the same and followed him in. Once inside, she briefly imagined how much fun she would have had inside as a little girl. She let that memory go quickly and was again struck at how Hawk had the ability to stir up fond memories and fun moments within her.

"There," he pointed to a design above the door. "Do you see it? That is the Nautilus."

Jillian leaned in and saw the engraved outline of the famous submarine from the film.

"It's nice. A good tribute. Cute, but how does this help us?" She traced the outline of the submarine with her finger.

Breathing deeply Hawk replied, "I don't know." He glanced around the interior of the playhouse. "This is the Nautilus that came to mind when I knew I had to find one."

"Maybe there is something hidden inside the playhouse." Jillian wrinkled her nose slightly. "But hiding a spear inside a playhouse doesn't seem like that great of an idea."

Over the next fifteen minutes, she worked next to Hawk exploring, poking, and looking for any type of hidden opening inside the treehouse that might be helpful. There was nothing. She leaned back against the wall and crossed her arms.

"I think this is a waste of time," she said.

"Agreed" Hawk ran his fingers through the mop of hair on his head as he sat against the wall next to her. "Let me think."

"There has to be something else."

Silence settled across the treehouse and then she noticed that Hawk puffed out his chest subtly.

"There is something else." He now moved to his knees to crawl out of the treehouse.

Just like she followed him in, she now followed him out and together they stood on the streets of Fantasyland once again. He was pointed across the pathway to what looked like a miniature mountain of rocks forming the exterior of a cave system.

"There is where the actual submarine attraction used to be. Something that most people have no idea of is when 20,000 Leagues under the Sea was shut down, the cast bottled water from the attraction before it was drained, labeled it, and kept it safely stored for eighteen years. At the opening ceremony for Under the Sea – the Journey of the Little Mermaid, the water was then poured into the water at the attraction."

"Amazingly cool!" Jillian nodded impressed. "So that is where we are going?"

"It has to be." Hawk quickened his pace. "I just remembered another nod to the Nautilus."

"Besides the stored bottled water?"

"Yes," he glanced at her and continued moving quickly to the entrance of the attraction.

They moved into the queue line area, which would carry guests along a narrow walkway with rocks on either side.

"The Imagineers outdid themselves here and created a Hidden Mickey that you can only see at noon on Mickey Mouse's birthday. On November 18th at noon, once a year, the sun is in just the right position for the light to reveal a Hidden Mickey on the path in the ride queue for the attraction." Hawk said.

Jillian looked and saw some boat wreckage, a figure with its hand on its chest. Hawk stopped and pointed out rock formations that looked like they formed part of a Mickey head at the top.

"That is where you see the Hidden Mickey on the path when the sun shines through the rocks. It is awesome!" Hawk kept moving however.

"That is interesting, but…"

"And the Imagineers also added a tribute to the Nautilus in the rocks. Look there."

She immediately saw it, the imprint of the Nautilus submarine in one of the rock formations. Tucked away in the ride queue as you wind through to board the attraction, most, including herself never had seen it. It was bigger than she might have expected and as always amazed at how things were hidden in plain sight. Thinking, she turned back to Hawk and reminded him.

"The clue you told me about said, "look at the top of the crow's nest and look up. The key is wrapped around the lock" You explained the Nautilus, but if the giant squid was wrapped around the sub, like it was in the picture and in the collectors pin, then this might be the lock."

"But we need a key." Hawk closed his eyes in thought.

"Right, we need a key." Then for good measure she stated the obvious. "A giant squid."

Hawk paced a short distance in the line and she waited for him. He was whispering and talking to himself. She could make out some of what he said. He repeated the phrase the key is wrapped around the lock and the words giant squid. Silently, he breezed past her and made his way back out in the pathways of Fantasyland.

Their surroundings were very much themed to reflect the story of the Little Mermaid. The design, at least to her, looked like a tiny fishing village, she figured it must be something under the rule of the prince in the story. Hawk was now walking but looking up, like he was searching the skyline for something.

"What are you after?" she trailed behind him.

"That!" He pointed upward after stopping in front of the cartographer shop. "There is another tribute to the old attraction."

Jillian looked up and saw what he was looking at. She felt a sudden burst of energy and nearly bounced in place. She gazed at a weather vane. But this was not just any weather vane. While it offered the required directional markings of North, South,

East and West, what made this weather vane special was the squid that was wrapped around a harpoon with a rounded tip. The squid was gripping it, the head of the sea creature pointing south, the tentacles extending north, but it was clearly intended to represent the giant squid from the movie.

"That must be the key." A wide smile crossed her face.

"And we have to go up there and get it," Hawk triumphantly said as he moved toward the wall of the shop and firmly gripped the trellis next to the window of the building. She saw his grip tighten on it, then reach for another ledge, and he pulled himself up toward the roof of the building.

Don't Be So Sure

Chapter Forty-Eight

Day Three - Night

"If you want to have a future here, I would suggest you tell me where he is." Mark Gross thundered across the desk from Juliette Keaton. "And you should tell me now."

Juliette felt herself bristle at the obnoxious and very loud president of the executive board.

"I assure you, I will be happy to let Dr. Hawkes know you are looking for him the next time I see him." Juliette smiled and tried to hold her composure.

Her desk had become a cluttered pile of papers, booklets, reports, and those had spilled over to her usually extremely organized work space where she normally could line up the pressing projects on any given day. On this day, right now, everything seemed to be pressing and she really didn't have time for this conversation.

"Hawkes was supposed to give me his resignation," Gross continued on. "But instead we have the worldwide press in our parking lot, we have bombs going off in our theme parks, we have to evacuate our resorts, and I have to answer questions as to why."

"Actually sir, with all due respect. You don't have to answer why." Juliette felt her face redden as she spoke. "I am the one that is expected to give an answer. The people who want to know really want to hear it from Hawk. But as far as you are concerned, unless you tell them who you are, no one really knows about you, what you think your role is here, and what you want to happen."

"What does that mean?" Gross rose to his feet.

Juliette rose to her feet as well. In heels she was taller than Gross and tilted her head down slightly as she spoke.

"It means exactly what I said. I don't work for you. You have absolutely nothing to offer the media. By your own admission you don't have any clue what is going on here nor do you seem to care about this company except for getting Hawk's resignation. Which just in case you don't understand yet," she now leaned forward with her hands balled in fists on top of two stacks of papers on her desk. "You are not going to get."

Gross flushed with anger that bordered on rage and she knew it.

Pressing her advantage, "So you could do us all a favor and stay out of the way and let us do our job. You are making yourself look foolish, you are missing what is really happening here, and to be very honest with you – I think you like being on camera. You have decided that there is a battle taking place for this company. Right now, I am working as hard as I can to keep this company going and not spinning off the rails. You are standing against me, you are in the way, and you, with all due respect – are my enemy."

Gathering himself, Gross said as calmly as he could muster. "You use that phrase 'with all due respect' but you don't seem to understand what it means."

"Don't be so sure about that - I do sir, I really do." Juliette now stood upright once again. "I have given you more than the respect you are do because you have done nothing to earn my respect. Is there anything else I can do for you?"

Without another word, Mark Gross, the president of the executive board spun and exited the room. Juliette thought she heard an audible huff coming from him as he crossed paths with Sergeant Bill Shakespeare coming into her office. They did an awkward dance for space as they exchanged places. Gross was outside, Bill was now inside.

Juliette raised her eyebrows and waved slightly, sure that the sheriff's officer had heard the last part of their exchange.

"All clear on our end ma'am," Bill said. "Is there anything else you need?"

As he said it, he nodded his head toward the open door where Gross had left.

"Could you let me borrow your taser?" She smiled.

"It's against policy, but I suppose I could make an exception." He did not crack a smile.

"Not necessary, thanks for asking. We're fine here. Thanks for all your help. You made this much better than it could have been."

"We are about done over in the Magic Kingdom as well. Just so you know, the explosion there was actually caused by dynamite. Just like the old west. Someone has a very sick, twisted sense of humor it appears." Bill turned to leave.

"Dynamite?" Juliette was surprised.

"Yes, dynamite." Bill was now walking out the door. He stopped in the doorway and said in a low voice. "And ma'am, I am not sure what all is going on, but you are anything but fine here."

And with those words, he was gone.

Juliette slumped back at her desk. She felt as if she disappeared behind and was engulfed by a sea of paper piled up all around her. Each one jammed with a challenging problem that as of this moment she had little or no clarity about. The battlefield of documents, messages, and memos all contained tid-bits of a complex puzzle that was clamoring for her to somehow make sense of. There was the tiger attack and the gorilla attack in Animal Kingdom. There were the malfunctioning attractions. Those reports were stacked to her left. As she gently pushed the pile of paperwork it precariously threatened to avalanche further adding to the chaos of her desktop. There were explosions and bomb scares, there were hundreds of reporters and news services in the parking lot and those were the easy problems. The real ones, the most serious ones had to do with the injuries and threats to those she cared about. Jonathan and Sally, Jillian, she had no idea where Shep was. Hawk was facing the pressure of some deep mysterious mystery, there was the threat of impending doom looming over the resort, not to mention the executive board that threatened to steal the company away. And beyond that there was the attack on David Walker, the injury to Elliot Drayton, and the troublesome Antonio Redfield.

There was no doubt they had been attacked. The attack was viral, it was a DOT viral attack. She had not been familiar with the term until someone explained it to her but now she really understood what it meant. The D meant disease, there was a virus that as of yet they did not completely understand. The O recognized the optics. The things that people could see and they were bad and hard to explain. Explosions, animal attacks, serious injury, malfunctions, and even the footage of Hawk flying like a super hero in Dinosaur had all gone viral in the reports and accounts of the events. The T was the technological. They had lost control of the park. What worked, what didn't, who got in, where they went, anything and everything that could go wrong had been attacked and hacked. A true DOT viral attack.

Sighing deeply, she steadied herself and determined that before she went back out to face the press once again, she would begin to gradually unravel the intricacies of the problems and then dissect them with methodological precision to craft solutions and a strategy to move through and beyond them. Opening up the first report, she saw it was the one that Redfield had given her earlier in the lobby. She stared at his signature at the bottom of the report.

Antonio Redfield, he had acted a bit off in the lobby earlier. Why was a researcher like him at Disney World? It had to be more than just to be working in the lab at Animal Kingdom. There was just something suspicious, wrong, and almost menacing about him. And then her mind went to a balloon that was bouncing across the ceiling in the lobby. His words, what he said, it meant something far deeper than the way it sounded.

"Don't be so sure...it could be the end of the world." He had said and then did not want to repeat it.

A floating balloon could be the end of the world. The sound of her own heartbeat began to thrash in her ears. She bolted upright, as she did, the pages toppled the order of the mountainous stacks. She moved toward the door, never hearing the avalanche of the many pages as they flittered across the floor.

Stepping Toward the Future

Chapter Forty-Nine

Day Three - Night

In reality, it is a Disney Vacation Club booth, across the walkway from the Little Mermaid attraction that features a striking sign with several hidden details. Hawk stretched himself across the roof of this building after using those hidden details as a set of gymnastic bars to pull himself upward. For those that took the time to notice, the globe, sun, and moon create a Hidden Mickey. The sign reading "H. Goff Cartography" pays tribute to Imagineer Harper Goff. Goff was deeply involved in the set design for 20,000 Leagues Under the Sea. He also was a heavy contributor of concept art for both Disneyland and Walt Disney World.

For Hawk the base of the Cartography sign had been his first handhold, allowing him to pull himself upward. This then allowed him to stretch out another hand toward the base of the globe itself. Once he was securely hanging there, he swung up his legs until they hooked themselves to another support on the Cartography sign. At this point, he had very little time to keep moving upward or he would have quickly fallen since all of his body weight was now stretched out over the concrete below. Releasing his right hand he grabbed for the globe itself and once he gripped it, his left hand stretched out and grabbed the orb above it, which was actually Mickey's left ear. Now able to pull his entire body upward, his foot came to rest on top of the orb, which was Mickey's right ear giving him a chance to leap toward the roofline. He did and gripping the edge of the roof with both hands, again had to pull himself upward and fling his body toward the side to catch a foot on the ledge and then shimmy the rest of the way up.

His shoulder felt the burning of overuse as he now crawled across the roof, moving up the pitch toward the weather vane that featured the Giant Squid on a harpoon. Taking it with both hands he used it to steady and pull himself up to the very top of the roof line. Glancing below he could see Jillian looking up at him, he tried to measure the look on her face. If he had to name it, he would have called it a blend of concern and part amusement...concernment...if he had to call it something.

"Hurry up," Jillian instructed from the ground.

"There is no way to hurry up, up here," Hawk tossed back, he had no idea if she could hear him or not.

Now he was standing, balancing himself across the top of the roofline with a firm grip on the weathervane. He pulled upward on it and it gave only a little. He reasoned, a little give was better than none at all, so he pulled on it again, this time stretching his body upward trying to put some weight behind extracting the harpoon from the roofline. It worked! Hawk felt himself fall backward, land on his backside, and with the harpoon and squid still in his hand began to slide backward toward the edge of the roofline.

"Whoa!" Hawk yelled as he tried to turn his body, slow his slide, and find something to grab hold of.

"Careful," Jillian offered from the ground.

Hawk twisted back to his belly and reached out for the edge of the roof. He grabbed it with one hand just as his body slid over the edge. Keeping a tight grip on the harpooned squid, he tightened his grip and waited for the sudden shift in weight to plunge him downward. Hawk was hoping to slow his fall. His foot came to rest on top of one of the Mickey ears, and all of the sudden he was able to steady himself. Smiling he looked over his shoulder toward a bemused Jillian keeping an eye on his progress.

"This is just how I planned it," he offered, then added "Here catch."

He tossed the harpoon toward her in such a way that it fell sideways giving her multiple places to get her hands wrapped around it. She did.

"Hey, this thing is heavier than I thought it would be," she said with surprise.

"It almost pulled me off the roof." Hawk now reversed his climb from before to make his descent.

"No, it did not pull you off the roof, you were falling off the roof all on your own."

She waited for him to touch down and then handed the harpoon back to him.

"What now?" Jillian said.

"We use the key."

"This is the key?"

"Sure is, let me show you." Hawk wasted no time in moving back into the attraction queue area and then stepped across the rocks, into the water that formed a reflective decorative pool for those waiting to look at and moved toward the Nautilus. In the center of the submarine carved into the rock, near the bottom there was a round hole. Hawk had guessed that the end of the harpoon, which was rounded instead of forming a sharp point, would fit inside and was the key. Jillian watched him as he moved to the side so she could see him lining up the harpoon or the key with what he believed was the lock. It fit perfectly. Pushing the key in he felt it click into place and then heard the sound of the water stirring around his feet. Watching the Nautilus now with a harpoon and a Giant Squid sticking out of the sub's side, he saw it disappear into the rock itself. The water swirling below him was from the change in pressure as the Nautilus was released and the ship itself disappeared from view leaving Hawk holding the end of the weather vane as the harpoon it was attached to was now out of sight. The squid now rested at the opening and Hawk leaned over to look inside.

"See anything?" Jillian was leaning across the rocks for a better look.

Hawk reached inside and found something wrapped in some type of cloth. He pulled it out and carefully navigated it through the Nautilus shaped opening and the squid to free it from the hiding place. He moved slowly taking great care, the package nestled in both hands, and he felt his hands trembling slightly. The wrapped item was close to eighteen inches long if he were to guess and was wrapped in thick strips of cloth that had been woven into a protective layer covering what lay underneath it like some type of mummy. He reached the queue line once again and handed it to Jillian.

"This is a very short spear." She exclaimed as she took it carefully out of his hands.

Hawk turned and went back to the rock face, the place where the lock and key were now interlocked and opened. He gripped the end of the weather vane and pulled it firmly back toward him. He once again heard the water swirl at his feet and watched the Nautilus rock submarine reappear and slide back into place. Twisting the harpoon key ever so gently, he felt it release and he removed the key. Taking a half step back, it looked just as it had been before he disturbed it. A solid rock wall, a hidden Nautilus carved into the rock for a clever guest to observe and discover. He made another trip, through the water and this time climbed back into the queue line where Jillian had laid the package on the rock wall beside them.

"What now?" Jillian was staring, forgetting to blink.

"We open it." Hawk began to fumble for an edge of the wrappings.

"It is shorter than I thought." Jillian admitted. "When we were talking about a spear, I was thinking a spear ... you know?"

"Think of it as the tip of the spear. The rod of the spear would have been long gone. But in ancient Rome, the head of the spear would have been made out of metal, designed to be perfectly weighted, and then attached to the end of a treated and finished wooden rod that made the spear complete." Hawk now was unwrapping the package.

"If this is what we are looking for it is one of the most sought after relics in all of human history."

"The spear that killed Jesus."

"Sort of, Jesus was already dead according to the Bible when the spear was thrust into him. It was for verification, to make sure the job was done."

"But the blood of Jesus?"

"In theory, would be on the spear."

Hawk continued to unwrap the package. Each layer gave way to another wrapped layer and then the wrappings changed directions. In the unwinding it seemed like a puzzle in and of itself.

"There are four different spears that people believe are the REAL spear. The Austrian Spear of Destiny is considered to be the most likely to be genuine, but the possibility has always existed that the spear was located somewhere else." Hawk said as sweat dripped off the edge of his nose.

"People had no idea that Walt Disney possessed it."

"No, and you remember that whoever controls the spear is invincible?"

"Yes."

"Well that is just part of the story. It is said that mere possession of the spear is not enough. One must also know the secrets of how to use the spear to be victorious in battle. If Hitler was not successful and some of his predecessors like Constantine and Charlemagne were, it merely suggests that Hitler did not know how to use the Spear of Destiny. Or so goes the theory." The last of the wrappings revealed the spear.

Hawk reached down and reverently picked it up, holding it between Jillian and himself. She hesitantly reached out and touched it. Old tarnished metal, the connection point of where the spear would attach to the rod was wired in some silver hard wire. The middle of the spear was wrapped in a golden metal.

"Is that real gold?" Jillian asked.

"I'm not sure, but it is not there for decoration. According to legend, the spear was cracked, maybe even broken, so a golden wrap was placed around it to hold the item together and keep it in one piece." Hawk turned it over in his hand.

"Now that you have it, what are you going to do with it?" Jillian placed her hand on his shoulder.

"I'm supposed to give it to whoever left me the note at midnight on the Eastern Star." Hawk shrugged.

"And you are not going to do that, right?"

"What am I going to do with an old spear?"

"This is priceless, it is a relic, if it is the real thing you are not going to let anyone do DNA testing on it and try to take the blood of Christ off of it." Jillian sounded indignant.

"Of course not." Hawk laughed. "But I do have to go to the Eastern Star and try to get a handle on who is involved and what their threat was all about."

Jillian began rewrapping the spear. Hawk looked around to make sure there were not any spying eyes looking their way. Satisfied that there were not, he watched Jillian wrap the spear back up. Once her task was complete she stretched out the spear for him to take. He waved her off.

"You carry it." He placed a hand on her back and began the journey back through Fantasyland toward Cinderella Castle. "You can be invincible, you have the spear."

Hawk kept his head on a swivel, wanting to make sure there was no one following or watching. As Jillian carried the spear it allowed him to keep his hands free and he kept looking back where they had come from to make sure they were alone. As they moved, he became aware that she was staring at him as they walked.

"Yes?" he said as he continued to look around.

"What if this spear does contain some sort of power?"

"You mean, what if it can make you invincible?" Hawk slowed his pace.

"I guess," Jillian kept her eyes on him. "You have always carried yourself like you are invincible."

Hawk laughed softly. He felt anything except invincible. His body always seemed to ache and the more often he was on adventures like the one they were on now, the older he felt.

"I am anything but invincible."

"I don't know about that, you seem to have an uncanny way of defying the odds over and over again." Jillian held the spear in one hand at her side and used her fingers to count in the air. "You have been blown up, shot at, punched, thrown off a monorail, fallen off buildings, been trapped, chased, years ago you walked away from a car wreck, and if I remember correctly – which I do, when you got shot you did die."

Hawk took in a breath, she knew he had been through a lot.

Jillian reached up and placed her hand on his arm. "I'm sorry, I didn't mean to mention the wreck, I know you don't like to talk about it."

He nodded. "You're right, I don't."

"As a matter of clarity, we have never talked about it." she whispered, almost to the point where he could not hear her.

They moved in silence as they entered Cinderella Castle. The giant mosaic was to their right as they walked inside the dimly lit interior. The low light glistened against the finely cut glass pieces that told the story of Walt Disney's classic animated film. Hawk let his vision move across the colors and as they shimmered allowed his mind to travel back through time. The years ripped him through a tunnel, to the memory of a roadside on a dark night, a car crash, and the bone jarring reality that his life would never be the same. He felt a pain in his chest. He sighed deeply.

"No, I'm sorry." he began. "You're right I don't talk about it much."

"Ever?" She leaned her head on his shoulder.

"Ever." He agreed. "It happened so long ago, but it still hurts. I lost my family in that wreck. I have relived it over and over. How could I have done something differently? In some ways, I can't even remember what put us into those trees along the interstate. I just know I spent a long time trying to heal." He turned toward her feeling a stinging in his eyes.

"I'm sorry." Jillian was watching him closely. "To have lost your wife and kids. Did you ever wonder why God did that to you?"

Hawk pondered this for less than a heartbeat. He knew what she was asking and he knew the answer. He just wanted to make sure he said it correctly.

"You know, when people ask why, there is nothing wrong with that as long as they ask it the right way," he said softly.

"What do you mean?"

"When bad things happen, when people lose a loved one, or get sick, or there is a crisis they tend to look toward God and ask why did this happen to me?"

"Of course they do." She squeezed his arm as if to tell him it was fine.

He felt his arm tense up. She felt it to and stopped sensing she had said something wrong.

"Jillian, people ask why for the wrong reasons." He stopped and faced her. "Instead of asking God why did this happen to me, I asked God why I had been so blessed to have the years I had with my wife and kids. I didn't deserve it, I didn't do anything to earn it. I was the one that was blessed and God chose to do that for me. I could never be mad at God that they were gone, I could never get frustrated that life was unfair. My life was better because God let them be a part of it."

He could see she was thinking and could see a tear form in the corner of her eye. Tilting her head she spoke. "So, you never asked God why did it happen to you?"

"Nope. Never did. Couldn't..." Hawk turned and began to move to the exit of the castle into the hub. "I just asked why God had chosen to bless me so much. I still ask him that about my life, every day."

"And that's how you handled the grief?" She was now walking close to him again.

"You never get over losing people you love or things that are hard. You never get closure. Instead, if you ask for it, God gives you enclosure."

"I've heard you say that, I don't really understand."

"It means you enclose those moments and memories in your heart. You keep them there, you keep them safe. You let Jesus do the healing and from time to time, you open up your heart and remember and relive some things, then you close it back up. It makes you stronger, it makes you trust deeper, and you learn, you grow, it makes you better. People spend so much time looking for closure in life they never figure out what they need is enclosure." He paused. "Sorry, I didn't mean to preach at you."

"I didn't mean for you to have to open up your heart and relive the moments. You can enclose them again." She smiled. "I told you... you are invincible, you just helped to explain it to me better. Grayson Hawkes, you are not like other people."

"And just so you know." He said to her. "I thank God every day for blessing me again by letting me be with you. If it all were to come to an end... And I don't want it to." He grinned. "I could never thank Him enough for blessing me with the opportunity to know you."

They grew quiet again as they walked past the statue of Walt Disney and Mickey Mouse. The Partners statue pointed toward the future. In some ways, it may have been pointing toward their future.

"Hawk?"

"Yes."

"That was very romantic, what you just said... do you say things like that to all the girls?" She was smiling, trying to lighten the moment just a bit.

"Only when they're carrying a spear," Hawk responded.

Evel Knievel Jacket

Chapter Fifty

Day Three - Night

"Hawk, I'm telling you he messed up." Juliette tried to control her breathing. "Redfield or whoever he is, had a moment, and he slipped up."

She felt an adrenaline induced migraine starting to vibrate in her temples, but she would have to worry about that later. Now that she had been told about the connection to the mysterious Otto Guy, she knew her suspicions had been right.

"And he said a floating balloon could be the end of the world?" Hawk was seated at the small table overlooking Town Square. The Spear of Destiny was on the table in front of him.

Juliette had arrived in the Magic Kingdom meeting Jillian and Hawk as they made their way down Main Street USA after finding the spear. As always, she had been impressed as Hawk explained the process he went through to find it. She was even more impressed that once again there was so much more to the world of Walt Disney than she could ever imagine. It had been a number of years now, but just when she believed that there was nothing else left to surprise them, there were more surprises.

"Not exactly, but that is what he was saying." Juliette looked from Hawk to Jillian.

"The note we found said, many will die and it will be because of you. Place the item on the Eastern Star at midnight tomorrow or the end of the world will happen."

Jillian was explaining out loud what they were all thinking. "So we have to figure out how a balloon can be used to cause the end of the world when it floats."

"Yes, I think that is what it means," Juliette was pacing.

Rubbing her temples trying to massage away the pain she moved to the table and gently picked up the spear.

"Be careful with that, legend says if you have it you are invincible." Hawk said nonchalantly, he was thinking about what she had shared.

"The spear has a supernatural power." Jillian added. "If you believe that kind of stuff."

Juliette turned it over in her hand and surveyed it. It was almost unimaginable that she was holding what many believed to be a holy relic. Blinking, she suddenly realized her oncoming headache had receded. That is weird, she thought. Scrunching up her nose she considered the possibility that the spear might contain some sort of miraculous power but quickly discarding the thought handed it back to Hawk.

"And you are going to take this to the Eastern Star?" Juliette asked.

"No, not really." Hawk got up from the table and went into his bedroom, speaking loudly through the doorway as he went. "I'm going to let you guys hold onto the spear. I'm going to take a backpack and see who picks it up."

"What about the devastation that will be unleashed according to the note. You remember the death and destruction?" Jillian moved to the table to retrieve and rewrap the spear.

"I'm going to let you figure out the whole balloon riddle." Hawk said emerging from his bedroom. "I can't imagine that anyone is going to get destroyed until whoever gets the Spear of Destiny."

Juliette almost laughed as Hawk zipped up the deep blue leather jacket he had put on. It had a white V down the front that started at the shoulders and came together at the waist line. In the wide leather V there were red and blue stars forming a line down the center of the strip. It was not what she had expected

"You trying to keep a low profile and not be seen?" Juliette pointed at his jacket as she asked.

"Truth be told, I am trying to make a statement. I want them to see me coming. This is my Evel Knievel motorcycle jacket, thank you very much. Not everyone has one of these."

"Most people don't want one," Jillian shook her head.

"Maybe it makes me feel invincible." Hawk slung a backpack over his shoulder. "Can you give me a ride, please?"

"If I remember right, Evel Knievel wasn't so invincible. He broke every bone in his body, right?" Jillian followed him toward the door, motioning for Juliette to join.

"No, that's an urban legend. He didn't break every bone in his body."

"But he broke a lot of them," Juliette injected. "And isn't he dead? That is not so invincible."

Hawk paused. "I didn't say he was invincible, I said maybe it makes *me* feel invincible. Remind me never to ask you guys for fashion advice."

"Maybe you should." Juliette followed them to the door but was curious. "Where are we giving you a ride to?"

"I have to give up the Spear of Destiny."

"And you need a ride?"

"Yes, he hid his motorcycle earlier today getting ready for this." Jillian moved past him and headed down the stairs. "We're taking your car." Her voice crawled back up as she moved away.

"So you do have a plan?" Juliette felt a bit steadier than she had a moment ago, hope does that she determined.

"I have the beginning of a plan." Hawk waited for her to exit his apartment and closed the door. "But I need you to figure out this whole balloon thing. Maybe David Walker and Allie Crossman might help. There may be some insight into the Antonio Redfield – Otto Guy guy that might help you."

"Hawk," Juliette began before he cut her off.

"If you are going to tell me to be careful again, don't bother – you already know I don't know how."

The Eastern Star

CHAPTER FIFTY-ONE

Day Four - Midnight

The Eastern Star Railway borders the town of Harambe and the Harambe Wildlife Reserve. Any guest that would seriously study the Harambe Wildlife Reserve map could see the route the train takes entering and departing the area. Each day at Disney's Animal Kingdom people can board the Eastern Star line that transports them to Rafiki's Planet Watch and Conservation Station. Upon closer inspection, there is an ominous unease around Harambe Station where hints of other stops along the railway, and an answer to why those station are currently closed.

It is common practice for railway stations, like interstate rest areas, or even airports to post delays or closings. The closures along the Eastern Star Railway are decided by the railway and the Harambe Town Council whenever they feel a situation requires caution or there is a reason to believe a station could be dangerous. The information available in the Harambe Station, informs guest that the Bwanga station is closed in addition to the line to Shabi. The reasons are noted. In Bwanga, the station has been closed due to erosion of the tracks. In Shabi, the situation is more of a precaution, as the area has been stricken by an outbreak of Kipindupindu. Hawk had no idea what this was for a number of years, but discovered as often in the details at Disney the world meant something. In Swahili, Kipindupindu is cholera, an intestinal disease which can be fatal to those who contract it.

The Eastern Star Railway and the Harambe Town Council state that, "It is the right of railway travelers to receive the highest level of facilitation at this station." This is a statement they take seriously. The Eastern Star, Hawk had instantly recognized as a mythical African railroad company which ran the railway that connected Lusaka to Nairobi, Kisangani and the port of Harambe. The train passed through the Harambe Wildlife Reserve. What he realized is that the warnings in the Harambe Station now needed to be taken far more seriously as the fear of disease, research, and bio labs might be real at Disney's Animal Kingdom. If David Walker's suspicions were correct, and Hawk now believed they were, Otto Guy had opened up a biological research lab right here in Animal Kingdom.

The Eastern Star was the transport to get to that conservation station. Hawk noticed the train was ready to move as midnight approached. The trains at Disney's Animal Kingdom feature beat up smoke stacks, dented domes, and a rusty paint scheme that bring to life the illusion that these trains are barely still chugging on an African Railway. Despite the builder's plate on the side of the locomotives that state they were manufactured in 1926 by the Beyer, Peacock, & Company, a British railway manufacturer, they weren't actually built until 1998. Why are the locomotives based on a British steam locomotive when they are supposed to be pulling trains through Africa? Hawk knew this as well, his mind tended to dig out the details he had learned when he was feeling pressure. The majority of the real steam locomotives that pulled trains through Africa back in the day were actually manufactured by British railway manufacturers.

Glancing at his watch, it was now midnight. He stepped on board the train and slid the backpack to the ground beside him. A high-pitched train whistle signified the departure from Harambe Station. The train rumbled down the track and Hawk looked out into the darkness as they traversed through the lush vegetation, shadowy hideaways for anyone to be watching. Hawk knew the train would pass through several railroad crossings before viewing the behind the scenes areas for some of the wildlife that call Disney's Animal Kingdom home. Once arriving at Rafiki's Planet Watch station, passengers can choose to depart and explore Conservation Station or stay on the train and return to Harambe Station. The complete circle of the tour is a little over 1 mile long.

Hawk knew someone had to be the engineer on the train as they didn't run by themselves. Whoever this was had managed to stay out of sight until Hawk got on board. They clearly did not want to be seen. Who else might be out there, Hawk had no idea. While all of this went through his mind, he felt the passenger car he was in slow and then squeak to a stop at the Conservation Station, standing there all alone in the station was Dr. Antonio Redfield. Hawk stared as the doctor waited for the train to come to a complete stop. Motioning at Hawk with a outstretched palm he indicated he needed to stay in his seat. The doctor stepped aboard the train and walked to where Hawk was seated, reached down, and picked up the backpack and placed it on his shoulder.

"I know this was not easy for you, Dr. Hawkes," Redfield nodded. "But you did the right thing. Now no one else will be hurt." Redfield reached up, pulled back his glasses, placed some pressure on the bridge of his nose and allowed the glasses to slide back into place.

"Why?" Hawk watched him closely and then glanced out to see if anyone one else was in the area.

"That is not difficult. The spear makes whoever can harness it's power a god."

"And you want to be god?"

"No, Hawk, my interest is much nobler. I just want to create the ultimate bio-organism. One that is capable of bringing life and destruction. One that can save the planet and help us survive into the future," Redfield said as he stepped off the train. "Thank you, Hawk. You have done the right thing."

Hawk felt the train shift and it slowly began to move away from the station. Still watching Redfield, he saw the man set the bag down and open the zippered pouch. Hawk had not seen anyone else, although he expected there had to be someone out there watching him. He also knew that the engineer would now be concentrating on the return trip to the station and due to the side view seating could not tell what was taking place on the train itself.

Hawk slid down his seat as he saw Redfield pull out the item and slowly begin to unwrap it. That was his signal to move. Hawk ran toward the researcher kneeling on the platform. He saw him unwrap the item, study it, and then instantly recognize that he had been duped. Hawk had wrapped up his Star Wars collectible lightsaber. It was valuable to be sure but no Spear of Destiny. A look of horror crossed Redfield's face and he turned toward Hawk just as Hawk had finished closing the distance between them and had launched himself airborne to collide with the doctor.

The collision was hard. The doctor fell to his side and Hawk landed on top of him, leaned to the side and with one motion, stuffed the lightsaber and the cloth wrapping back in the bag. Glancing back, the train continued to move away, the engineer could not have heard and now it was Hawk alone with Redfield. The doctor was on the ground, lying on his back, with a big smile on his face.

"Well done, Dr. Hawkes," Redfield said. "I thought you gave up the spear far too easily. I feared you would try to trick me and you did. Well played. For a minute I thought it was mine."

Hawk grabbed the doctor by his coat and drug him across the pavement toward him.

"Tell me what you have done, Dr. Redfield."

"Call me by my real name please, by now you know it. I know you know it, I am Otto Guy."

"What have you done?" Hawk repeated.

"I did what I had to do. I did research and was given permission to work and create weapons of incredible power." Dr. Guy seßemed to have trouble breathing.

"Permission? Permission by who?"

"Oh my," Guy coughed. "You are not as smart as I thought. You think I was in charge of this project? I was not. I was merely the hired help."

Hawk watched as a foam oozed out the side of Otto Guy's mouth. Guy seemed to fade and then rally. Hawk held his grip on the doctor's coat.

"You are too late. They were always going to try out my latest virus. Once they don't hear from me, they will know you did not play nice."

Otto Guy convulsed, more foam rolled down his cheek and his back arched for a moment and he was gone. Hawk felt his mouth go dry and a sudden heaviness settled across his shoulders. The ping of a bullet hitting a steel handrail behind him caused him to turn toward the Conservation Station. As he had suspected, there were eyes upon him, and now he had to escape. Shoving himself up off the ground, he began to run toward the railroad tracks. Jumping off the landing of the station, he touched down on the gravel below and jetted off into the woods. Pushing through the trees and into a clearing, he knew there was at least one person pursuing him. As he had planned, he would make that more difficult. Stumbling slightly after tripping on a tree root, he entered the clearing and there was his motorcycle. Sliding his arm through the open loop on the backpack, he swung one leg over the bike, then shifting his weight, stomped down on the pedal to fire up the engine.

Waiting and Worry

CHAPTER FIFTY-TWO

Day Four – Early Morning

"Hawk is giving Otto Guy the Spear of Destiny?" Allie Crossman ran her thumb over the tips of her fingers back and forth.

David, Allie, Juliette and Jillian were all seated in the GNN broadcast tent. There were a few people lingering in the other tents, but most news services were now replaying their prime time programming unless there was something breaking to report. Her neck was stiff and she was wondering what was happening with Hawk. She regretted letting him go alone but he had been insistent and stubborn as usual. She had thrown herself into doing what he asked, trying to figure out the mysterious comment made by Guy to Juliette. So they had called David and asked him to meet them here at the GNN tent.

"Not exactly." Jillian responded to Allie.

"He is giving him something but not the real spear. We have that," Juliette added.

"What will happen when he realizes he doesn't have the spear?" Allie asked.

"Mayhem, confusion, madness, and chaos I assume," Jillian stated. Then she added, "Hawk calls mayhem, confusion, madness, and chaos a vacation."

David smirked at the summary and internally agreed.

"David, you have done the digging into Otto Guy. What do you make of his balloon and the end of the world comment? Is there something there? Are we just chasing the wrong thing?" Juliette asked.

"Didn't sound to me like a real threat," Allie said with a shrug.

"Ah, but it could have been. In my research, Otto Guy was designing all sorts of nasty delivery systems for viruses and airborne pathogens. It seemed outlandish and crazy at a quick read, but he was even trying to figure out ways to spread filth with aerosol weaponry, bombs, poisoned water systems, so I am sure that there is something that he could do with a balloon...I guess." David scratched his head.

Jillian tapped her foot, she was trying to image what Hawk was doing and what might have happened when he gave Guy the fake spear. Did he have time to get away? Could he get to his hidden Harley? What was going to happen next? Her internal questions were stopped by Juliette clearing her throat. She turned and noticed that worry had etched itself into the corners of her eyes.

"I think I know what he is going to do," Juliette said.

David leaned forward and glanced at Allie before looking back toward Juliette.

"What?" Allie inquired.

Sirens blared and instantly they saw a number of law enforcement vehicles blowing out of the parking lot of the Magic Kingdom. As if a switch and been turned, they all had come to life and immediately turned on their lights and sirens and were screaming away from the media area and the perimeter they had set up. In a matter of moments, there were just a handful of officers left to watch over the media. Everyone else was gone, chasing an emergency.

"I wonder what that is all about." David asked curiously.

Juliette turned and caught Jillian's eye, Jillian nodded slightly at her.

"I can promise you – all of that was for whatever Hawk has done," Jillian said, she turned on her heels and started toward her car which was parked on the other side of the blocked off restricted area. Juliette followed her and as they opened their car doors spoke across the roof of the vehicle.

"We need to let Hawk take care of himself. I think I know what is going to happen. We need to check it out." They slid into the car and the motor came to life.

That Is Going to Hurt

Chapter Fifty-Three

Day Four – Early Morning

The Harley Davidson was a gleaming rocket as it raced through the streets of the Walt Disney World Resort. Once Hawk had emerged from the forest at Animal Kingdom, he had found himself being chased by two motorcycles. The revving of their engines had happened almost instantly after he thundered onto the empty streets of Harambe. The sudden death of Otto Guy had surprised him but he was more surprised at the revealing that Guy was not the mastermind of what was happening. Hawk had been convinced that it had to be the doctor, but the fact that Guy was dead and he was being chased gave proof to the reality that the crisis was not over yet.

As the motorcycle banked around the corner, Hawk veered it into a series of roadways that were off limits to most guests. These service roads provided the network of connection points that were necessary to keep the resort running. Many of them were unmarked, most would lead back to main thoroughfares and he was hoping that he might lose his pursuers along the way. He glanced down at the speedometer and saw he was moving in excess of seventy miles per hour, far too fast for this stretch of road, but he was determined not to slow down.

The chase was seen by others and the rumble of racing motorcycles had been drawing attention every place they passed. The road bent toward the main entrance of the Magic Kingdom and Hawk blew through the entrance beneath the marquee feeling a rush of adrenaline as the bike moved past the booths where guests would normally pay to park. The path he chose would take him toward The Contemporary Resort, traveling underneath the water bridge, and then he would ride through the turnstiles onto Main Street USA.

Stealing a glance over his shoulder, he could see that there were two pursuers still close enough to see him. Twisting the throttle, he asked the Harley for more speed, and the bike gave it to him. Going slightly airborne as he jumped the cycle onto the sidewalk, the normally used walkway was now a raceway with the destination of the Magic Kingdom. Hitting the brakes and feeling the bike slide underneath him, he placed a foot on the ground and twisted the handlebars to the right. The motorcycle swung around below him and once again with a twist on the throttle, he maneuvered the cycle skillfully through the maze of obstacles including the entrance turnstiles.

With a precision path he made it into the park, through the tunnels and then blasted beneath the train station onto Main Street USA. Normally he would cut through the Car Barn, park and go to his apartment, but not this time. The ambiance of the lights of Main Street became a blur as he took the cycle into the hub and then cut across the bridge heading into Tomorrowland. Again, glancing over his shoulder he could see his two pursuers and then something else that he hadn't seen before, two additional motorcycles, sheriff department officers that had managed to join in the chase. Hawk did not intend to stop and let the police sort this out. He had no idea how it would end, but he was determined to get away from the riders chasing him.

Taking the bike around the corner, he passed Space Mountain and the Tomorrowland Speedway. He considered going to the right but instead headed to the Mad Tea Party, zooming past the now still spinning teacups, back into the streets of Fantasyland. As he often did when he was under pressure, Hawk began to compartmentalize a strategy to escape. He would need to get away cleanly and then find a way to turn the tables on his pursuers so he could get more answers.

Peter Pan's Flight flew away behind him and the Haunted Mansion loomed to his right. It was then that a thought began to fill his mind. More speed rolled the tires as Hawk pushed the motorcycle forward,into the Old West, which was still under renovation. Past the lift truck with the ramp and then twisting the bike again, he banked around the turn toward Adventureland. As he moved into Caribbean Plaza he could see that he had put additional space between himself and the men chasing him. He could no longer see the policemen. This was the moment and the space he needed. If the plan he had been visualizing was going to work, he had to get the twists and turns just right, or he would probably end up being hurt.

Splitting the opening between the Enchanted Tiki Room and The Magic Carpets of Aladdin, he aimed the Harley back toward where the explosion had happened earlier in Frontierland. The tires resisted the sudden change in surface as the bike moved off the concrete onto the wooden walkway transitioning the two lands. Then with a jolt the bike was back on concrete and whined as it worked to give Hawk more speed.

In front of him, Hawk could see the elevated ramp on the back of the towing vehicle. With one end on the ground and another rising up into the air, he envisioned it as the perfect, or almost perfect motorcycle jump ramp. After all, he was wearing an Evel Knievel jacket. He gulped as he shifted his weight back slightly onto the seat. His plan was to keep accelerating up the ramp and just as he reached the end of it, straighten his legs on the pegs of the bike. Lifting the handlebars and causing the front end to rise up into the air. Before he could plan any further, he was on the ramp, in less than a second he had reached the top and the Harley was now airborne.

Lifting the motorcycle into the air, Hawk now felt himself flying with steel beneath him. At the peak of his flight, he could look through his helmet and see that he was going to be descending toward Tom Sawyer's Island, but his distance was going to be short. He was going to land not on the shore but in the very shallow Rivers of America. The river rose to meet him as the cycle fell out of the sky. As it hit the shallow water, the rear tire sunk into the mucky bottom and the front tire slammed into the muddy water with a splash. Hawk let loose of the handlebars and was launched over them. The thought dawned on him that he would actually make it to the island and it was going to hurt when he landed. It did.

Sprawling out onto the ground he looked back to see a second motorcycle airborne. He could not believe it, one of the pursuers had tried the same move but with much less style. His bike was descending at an awkward front tire first fall into the river. The bike and the rider momentarily disappeared beneath the surface and then the rider bobbed back up. The flashing of lights let Hawk know that the law enforcement officers were at the ramp, hopefully capturing the second pursuer. Hawk plunged into the water and made his way out to the floating semi-conscious motorcycle rider. Reaching him with a splash, Hawk wrapped his arm around his neck and with sidestrokes headed back to the island. The man was waking up and Hawk was bracing for a fight. He was about to push the man under the water thinking he was about to be attacked when he heard the man whisper.

"Thanks."

Hawk pulled him ashore and opened the visor on the rescued man's helmet.

"Who are you?" Hawk looked down at him keeping a firm grip on the man's shoulders.

"Kevin," he gasped. "Kevin Grey."

"Who do you work for?"

"You."

Hawk eased his grip. "What?"

"I work..." Grey gasped. "At Animal Kingdom."

"Then why are you chasing me?"

"I needed extra money for my family, but this has gone too far. They are going to hurt a lot of people if you don't do something. They are going to release some kind of virus. It has a long name but I was told to call it Ratpox or something like that."

Hawk looked back toward the makeshift jump ramp he had used to escape. Two officers were looking over the railing toward them, shining a flashlight and shouting some instructions. Hawk didn't take the time to listen to what they were saying.

"How? How are they going to release it?" Hawk asked.

The man seemed to be losing consciousness again and Hawk jerked him upward. Placing an ear down near the man's face, he listened as the man barely whispered the answer. Looking back toward where he had jumped from, he could still see the officers and made a decision. Letting Kevin Grey go, the one time pursuer slumped with his head on the shore, the rest of his body still in the water. Hawk forced himself up to his feet and made his way up the pathway. He knew he was now invisible to the men on the other shore. He had no idea what had happened over there, if the other man had been caught. But he knew what he had to do before it was too late.

Oh, That Balloon

Chapter Fifty-Four

Day Four - Early Morning

Jogging through the streets of Disney Springs as they passed The Edison, Juliette looked up and felt a shakiness run through her arms. In the sky, now visible above the buildings was The Aerophile.

"Oh no!" She cried catching Jillian's attention.

Juliette had figured out the meaning of what Otto Guy Antonio Redfield had meant about a balloon being the end of the world. The helium balloon that had floated off and bounced along the ceiling had momentarily caused him to reveal the evil plan he had put into place. As the massive blue balloon hung in the sky, they rounded the corner to see that it was tethered to the ground, anchored as it was supposed to be as guests would be taken up and then brought back for the price of admission each day.

"That's the balloon he was talking about?" Jillian allowed her mouth to gape open at the sight of the huge object in the sky.

"The Aerophile is the largest tethered helium balloon in the world. So when Redfield saw the helium balloon, he was thinking about this one. This is how they are going to release whatever they are going to spread over Walt Disney World, and people might die." Juliette had horrific images of what could be flashing in her mind.

"So the distribution system is in the balloon." Jillian slowed and began to size up their surroundings and what to do next. "All we need to do is get the balloon down and then we can figure out what they are going to spread."

"You don't understand, the balloon is stored down on the loading dock. It has already been deployed and it only has one tether connected to it. The safety protocols and redundancy is not connected anymore. This has been placed there on purpose. Whatever they were planning is happening, right now."

Both women stood below the balloon. It spanned nineteen feet in diameter and Juliette knew it contained over 200,000 cubic feet of helium. It was indeed a giant helium balloon that might very well be the end of the world or at least Walt Disney World.

Jillian made her way to where the tethered mechanism was connected.

"Let me ask you something," Jillian looked at her, eyes wide but focused. "If we were able to release it and let it go, the helium inside would just keep carrying it up and away. If it got high enough before it released whatever junk is on board, then it might be so high we could keep everyone safe. Right?"

"Or it could cause whatever is in it to spread even farther." Juliette pushed her hair back over her ears as she looked upward.

She was battling back fear, even though she was afraid time was short. She didn't want to make a bad decision by jumping past all of the other options, even though she could not think of any options. The picturesque landscape provided a startling contrast to what Juliette knew was a weapon of destruction that gently swayed in the breeze, pulling on the tether that anchored it to Disney Springs.

"Juliette, we have to do something." Jillian was gripping the tether cable in her hand. "Which is it?"

The tug of war between courage and fear slung her back and forth before she heard herself saying to Jillian. "Release it, we will take our chances with trying to get it far enough away where it will do the least amount of damage."

"I agree." Jillian's hand tightened on the tether. Her knuckles turned white as she gripped it with all her strength, now all she had to do was figure out how to release it.

Suddenly her back pocket began to vibrate as her phone began to ring. Reaching behind to retrieve it, she looked at the name on the screen. She smiled and held it up for Juliette to see. The name read HAWK.

Air Lift

Chapter Fifty-Five

Day Four – Early Morning

The Flying Mouse lifted of the ground and the roaring sound of the helicopter's blades drowned out the world around him. Hawk's heart was pounding valuing every second that he needed to save Walt Disney's kingdom. Glancing at the control panel, it was illuminated with various indicators that he was trying to understand as he was now airborne. Kirkus had been reluctant when he had told him to prepare the helicopter for flight. As always, the good captain was ready to take Hawk any place he needed to go, but this time, Hawk knew it was best for him to fly solo. After a quick refresher on what to do, Kirkus reluctantly had stepped away from the airship.

"Hawk, I don't know what you are up to. I think it is crazy." Kirkus had said.

"I know Cap, it probably is." Hawk had tried to be as reassuring as possible.

"Hang on, Hawk." Kirkus reached into the pocket of his flight jacket and pulled out Hawk's cell phone. "Here, you dropped this somewhere in the conference room in the back. I found it on the floor. I had planned on getting it back to you."

"Hey, there it is. I wondered where it was hiding. Thanks!"

The helicopter was ready and so was Hawk.

"Hawk, please be careful." Kirkus said.

"I always am." Hawk watched as he was getting ready to close the door. "Thanks for everything Vince."

That had caused Kirkus to not close the door. An ashen look of concern crossed his face.

"You called me Vince." Kirkus said over the noise. "You never call me that. What are doing?"

"I've got to go." Hawk grinned and reached over snatching the door from Kirkus and closing it.

He refocused his attention and lifted off. Now that he was in the air, he was trying to recall and refresh his mental checklist on what it took to make this flying bunch of parts stay in the air. The weather was clear, so he did not have to worry too much about gusting winds buffeting the aircraft. Hawk understood his piloting skills were limited, but he hoped they would be good enough. Looking at the floor next to the pilot's seat he made sure he had brought everything he needed. Satisfied, he banked the stick and turned toward Disney Springs. Kevin Grey had whispered to him where the explosives and the virus were located. The Aerophile at Disney Springs. The Flying Mouse was equipped with advanced navigation tools, searchlights, and a powerful winch that he planned on using in just a few moments. Steadying the craft, he then gripped his cell phone, scrolled through the favorites, and pressed "call" to reach Jillian. Plugging the phone into the copter's audio system, he now could talk and have the use of his hands to attempt to fly. He was feeling energized and had a sensation of buoyancy as the aircraft cut a path through the nighttime sky over Walt Disney World.

"Hello, Hawk?" Jillian's voice was clear in the cabin.

"Hey there." Hawk was glad she answered. "How are you and where are you?"

"I'm at Disney Springs with Juliette." She replied. "Where are you?"

"I'm on my way to Disney Springs as well."

"We are at the big helium balloon, this is the balloon that could be the end of the world," Jillian said.

"That is why I am headed that way," Hawk said to her. "I have a plan and I'm going to need your help."

As Hawk closed in on the Disney Springs area he could see the giant blue balloon was already in the air. That surprised him, it was usually stored tethered to the ground.

"You aren't in the balloon are you?" he asked Jillian.

"No, do you see the balloon?" Jillian paused. "Where are you? What is that noise?"

"I am above you. I'm in The Flying Mouse," Hawk said. "We are going to use the winch to attach the balloon and pull it away from the resort."

"Does Kirkus know how to do that?" Jillian asked.

"I'm not sure." Hawk hesitated and then closed his eyes as he said, "He is not with me."

Silence followed and for a minute Hawk thought the connection had been lost. Then that idea quickly disappeared as he heard Jillian speak.

"YOU are flying the helicopter?"

"Yes, look up. I am coming in right above you." Hawk looked out of the window and began to circle the balloon, being careful not to get to close to it.

He looked across the control panel. Finding the control for the winch that Kirkus had shown him, he steeled himself and flipped it beginning the process of guiding it down.

"What is that?" Jillian yelled into her phone as she was now trying to speak over the steady beating of the air from the chopper above.

"I am sending you a cable. I will drop it and give you enough slack to connect the guide cable of the balloon to it."

"We don't know how to release the tether down here."

Hawk tried to remember how the balloon was anchored. He had seen it many times but had rarely paid attention to it. His gaze fell across the black starry sky as he tried to remember what was down below.

"Jillian, there is a check in stand where guests enter. Look in the cabinet below and see what is there. I think there is a massive wrench like tool.It is designed to give you a quick release to the tether line. You can use that once you have the cable."

Hawk could see Juliette making her way to where the winch had dropped the cable from the helicopter, he was holding his position as she took hold of it. He didn't want to hurt her, wanted to make sure she had enough slack to get it to the tether, and didn't want to get any closer to the balloon than he was so it would also stay in place.

"Hawk, I can't get into the cabinet. It is locked," Jillian said.

"Shoot the lock open. You have your gun, right?" Hawk asked.

"I don't usually discharge it in the resort."

"Fire away."

Hawk could hear the shot fire. It only took one and he knew the cabinet was open. Looking down he could see Jillian lugging the big wrench across the landing platform for the balloon and attaching it to some mechanism that he could not see details of from his height. He watched as she struggled with it, then slowly it looked like she got it to move.

"Got it."

"Fantastic." Hawk admired their tenacity and was quickly calculating what was going to happen next. "Attach the hook on the winch cable to the tether line and then twist the locking mechanism into place so it does not come loose."

Both women, worked the cables into place and then he watched as they attached them together.

"You are attached," Jillian's voice filled the cabin.

"You guys did real good." Hawk was still watching from his perch way above them. "Now move away so I can pull this balloon away from you and then get it away from the resort. I don't trust how smooth this is going to be once I start toting the weight of the balloon. I am thinking it is going to be a rough ride."

"Which is why you should have brought Kirkus with you," Jillian reprimanded.

"That is one more body than I needed on this trip," Hawk smiled a half smile.

Hovering in place, he slowly eased the chopper forward and the cables pulled taut. He felt the tension and a slight jerk as he realized he now had the full weight of the balloon in tow behind him. Moving with more speed, the helicopter lurched forward as the balloon was now fighting a light breeze, battling against the wind of the rotors, and being drug to the side instead of floating upward. Hawk knew that somewhere on that balloon, he assumed it was in the cage at the bottom, there were explosives and a virus that was waiting to be detonated and dispersed. He was determined to battle the balloon in the air to get it away.

Increasing his speed he began to pull the balloon away in the nighttime sky. As he increased speed he also increased altitude. He was calculating that he had an object in tow that would naturally have lift since it was loaded with hydrogen instead of helium. Grey had told him this unexpected news. He realized he was towing a miniature version of the Hindenberg. Hawk hoped with speed and forward motion he could keep the cable pulled tight between him and the balloon and get clear of the resort.

He was hyper-focused and his mind was churning through a constant cycle of checking gauges, calculating, glancing back to see the balloon, and praying. Leaning forward as if willing the helicopter to give him more speed, he noticed an ever so slight tremble in the responsiveness of the controls. Since he had no idea what it might mean, much less what to do about it, he pushed forward even harder trying to coax every last bit of metal muscle from the flying beast in his control. Suddenly, he was aware of his name being called out over and over again.

"Hawk – Hawk – can you hear me?" Jillian's voice called out to him through the darkness.

The Kiss Goodnight

Chapter Fifty-Six

Day Four - Daybreak

"Hawk, Hawk – can you hear me?" Jillian was practically screaming into the phone as she and Juliette looked into the nighttime sky as the helicopter towing a balloon disappeared in the distance.

"Sorry, I was distracted," Hawk finally answered. With a laugh he added, "I am a little bit busy right now."

"So what is your plan?" Jillian positioned herself along the dock next to where the balloon had been tethered. Juliette continued to look toward the now empty sky where the balloon had disappeared from sight.

"I'm getting the Hindenburg away from Walt Disney World," Hawk said calmly.

"But how do you release it?" Jillian asked.

There was no answer. She looked back at Juliette. Juliette allowed her head to droop and her shoulders hunched forward slightly. Jillian suddenly found it difficult to swallow and momentarily could not speak. Fighting back and trying to ignore a tingling in her chest she gathered herself.

"How are you going to release it, Hawk?" She asked a second time.

"I'm making this up as I go," Hawk's voice sounded eerily calm.

As far as she was concerned it was too calm. Her ribs felt as if they were suddenly too tight in her own body.

"You better have a plan." Jillian felt her hand shaking as she held the phone tightly. "You have an idea of what to do, right?"

There was a pause before Hawk answered.

"I have a plan." His voice was clear and still calm. "I think it will work. I don't think you are going to like it, but trust me, it is going to be OK."

Juliette was shaking her head side to side, she had been able to hear both sides of the conversation. Jillian realized that she had the phone on speaker from when they were connecting the cables earlier. Juliette reached up and took the phone from her and held it flat in her palm between them.

"Hawk," Juliette said.

"Hi Jules," Hawk answered.

"You have to figure something out. This is not a suicide mission for you. There has to be a way for you to get rid of the balloon before it explodes." Juliette leaned in as she spoke.

"Well, you guys cinched it up. I am open for suggestions." Hawk laughed. "I told you I am making it up as I go and well, my concern was getting it away from the resort. Now I have to find a place where it is going to be safe."

"Where are you going?" Jillian asked, her mind was trying to figure out a way for him to release the cable. "You have to be able to disconnect the cable from the balloon."

"Jillian, I don't have enough hands to do that."

"Then you should have taken me with you." She felt herself sob as she said it.

Quickly brushing tears back from the corners of her eyes she looked up and saw Juliette's eyes were filling with tears.

"Grayson Hawkes, you figure out a way to get your annoying self-back here." Juliette tried to sound strong but her voice cracked.

"Listen, I appreciate you wanting to see my smiling face, but this was the only way I could figure to get rid of this monster," Hawk explained. "I think this is probably a one way trip. It is the only way to be sure that it is going to be safe."

Jillian looked at Juliette and watched as she sadly shook her head. They were both staring at the phone in Juliette's palm with the word HAWK emblazoned on the screen.

"Please listen to me." Hawk's voice was strong. "This thing is not over yet. Otto Guy was not running the show. He was not in charge. He was working for someone else."

"The police captured both of the men who were chasing you on motorcycles. The one who went off the ramp after you that you fished out of the Rivers of America was Kevin Grey. The other one that bailed off his bike at the last second, his name was

Reese Bolin. Both were cast members. Neither one has given up who was really calling the shots, if they even know." Jillian tried to check her emotions for a moment.

"They knew enough to chase you to get the spear after you left Otto Guy," Juliette added.

"You both need to figure out who is pulling the strings here because we are just managing to take away the biggest weapon in their arsenal, but they will keep trying." Hawk said.

"Any ideas?" Juliette asked him.

"A few, but not anything solid."

"Care to share?" Jillian bit her lip as she asked.

"No, I think you will figure it out," Hawk said. "But there is more. You have to find Shep. Something has happened to him, I know it. He was helping me trying to track down whatever walloped me in the woods. He doesn't do well when he is left alone."

"When you get back you can find him," Jillian responded defiantly.

"Jillian, you know how this is going to end," Hawk stated.

Over the phone they could hear the sound of the helicopter. It seemed to have changed pitch just a bit. The silence between them somehow deadened the noise.

"There is far more inside of both of you than you can ever imagine," Hawk said slowly. His voice had grown heavy. "Juliette, don't let the Board of Directors steal our company. Today what we are doing is important. Tomorrow is the most important day to come next. Every single day is a gift. Every day I have had knowing both of you has been a gift. I love you both but you've got stuff to do."

"No..." Jillian's voice broke.

"I love you Hawk, you have made my life so much better," Juliette's voice was breaking as she choked back tears.

"I love you right back. Tell Jon and Shep how much I love them...OK?"

"I will," Juliette pushed the button on the screen and turned off the speaker. She handed the phone to Jillian and walked away sobbing.

Holding the phone to her ear, Jillian said softly, "Hawk, please don't do this." The phone felt so heavy now.

"I have to do this. You know that. You'd do the same."

"I lost you once, I don't want to lose you again." Jillian let her tears flow.

"Hey Jillian, I want you to know that I am so thankful for every single moment that I have gotten to be with you. I have no idea why I have been so blessed to be able to know you and be a part of your life. I am so so so thankful. I left something for you in my apartment."

"Hawk..."

"Jillian, I love you." Hawk whispered.

Tears and a wave of emotion that she didn't know was within her drove her to her knees. She sobbed into the phone.

"I love you too..." she managed to say.

"I've gotta go – you are amazing."

The signal went dead. The connection ended. Hawk had stopped the conversation and now there was nothing. The world momentarily slowed down around her and stopped. A pain from deep inside cut through her and she felt her heart breaking. She covered her mouth with her hand as if trying to silence the cries that were coming from within her. Looking up, she could see Juliette seated on a bench, head in her hands, body convulsing in grief.

She had a dream that this magical place, the secrets it contained, would give her all the joy she had ever hoped for. Now it had turned into a nightmare.

A New Day

Epilogue

One Week Later - Daybreak

The pontoon boat glided across the surface of the serene and quiet lake. The air was clear, cool, and refreshing. There was a slight chill in the early morning gentle breeze that did nothing to disturb the glassy water. The soft creaking of the wooden boards beneath her feet mingled with the sounds of waking birds, allowed the tranquil scene stretching out before her to become a symphony of a new day. Today what she was doing was important and every day is a gift.

The water sparkled with the first rays of sunlight that created a magical golden path across the surface of the water that she used to guide the vessel. The trees along the shore mirrored their beauty in their reflection on the water's edge. It was peaceful and to be honest, there had not been that many moments of peace as of late. The boundaries between her grief and reality had somehow become seamlessly blended together and this trip was a welcomed relief from life as it had been.

Jillian stood behind the wheel of the boat. She was the skipper although she didn't really look the part. Dressed in a pair of sandals, running shorts, running top, and wearing a red, white, and blue Evel Knievel jacket, she looked like anything but a boat captain.

"Nice jacket," The soft gentle voice came from the man seated behind her.

As the boat moved at a leisurely pace, the lapping of the water against the pontoon created a soothing rhythm and she closed her eyes trying to absorb the serenity of the moment.

"Where are we going?" The soft voice came once again from behind her.

"I don't really know," she sighed.

A family of ducks glided by, the fluffy ducklings trailing behind like a miniature flotilla. A heron guarded the edge of the shoreline, craning it's head on a search for breakfast. This morning boat ride was an unexpected chance to escape the bustle of everyday life for a moment and immerse herself in the simplicity and harmony of nature. She was not in a hurry, she knew this moment, like most good moments, never last – but for right now, she would cherish it.

"If you don't know where we are going, how will you know when we get there?" A laugh came from her passenger. The comment was not confrontational simply conversational, which added to the pleasantness of the moment.

"I have a set of coordinates, so I'll know when we get there."

"Of course you do," another laugh.

She was smiling now and turned to her passenger. The frail old man sitting on the bench seat behind her was staring at her. His eyes had a twinkle to them, almost magical she thought.

"I know you didn't pick out that jacket yourself." Farren Rales pointed at her.

She zipped the jacked up tighter almost like she wanted to disappear inside of it.

"No, it was his," she laughed. "The man had no style. Always wanted to wear jeans, hated to dress up, and collected everything, including this jacket."

"Yes."

"You know he jumped a motorcycle across the Rivers of America in this jacket?"

"So, I hear," Farren said.

The calm soothing conversation added to the enchantment of this moment. Farren Rales was heartbroken when he heard of the events that had happened. This was the first chance that she had to talk with him in person. She had to unpack some painful memories, take them out of their enclosure as Hawk would have said. The problem was that she hadn't time to think through them all yet.

"He managed to pull that huge balloon with the helicopter away from Walt Disney World. According to the reports, he made it as far as Lake Kissimmee before the explosion took place. The virus was disbursed but wasn't designed to carry long distances or survive for too long after it was airborne."

"Thank goodness," Farren said.

"The lake is huge, it is in the middle of nothing. No one else was... hurt... except," a tear leaked out of the corner of her eye. She brushed it back with a finger. "They are still pulling parts of the balloon and the helicopter from the water and surrounding area. The explosion was massive." She shook her head ever so slightly. "Apparently the balloon was filled with hydrogen instead of helium, it was less expensive and more explosive."

"And?"

"No survivors. No body found." Breathing deeply and looking at the colors of the morning sun she swallowed hard and continued. "Probably not enough to find according to what they told us."

"I'm sorry." Farren stood up on wobbly legs and stood next to her.

He placed an arm around her and she buried her head into his shoulder. This old Imagineer was one of Hawk's dearest friends and having him with her now meant so much.

"I am so sorry, I love Hawk so much," Farren said very softly.

"I loved him too, nothing will ever be the same." She sobbed again, that is all she had done for the past week and she had no desire to stop. The pain was overwhelming. "Nothing will ever be the same."

The moment seemed to hang in the air and could have lasted a minute or an hour, she didn't know but she did see the blink of the navigation system notifying her that they had arrived.

"We're here?" Farren looked about as they floated out on Lake Fairview, very close to his home in College Park. "What now?"

"According to the note he left me pinned to this leather jacket that for some reason, I want to wear all the time now, you are supposed to sit down next to me at the front of the boat and wait." She guided him toward the bench in the front of the boat.

Glancing at her watch, she said. "Any minute now."

KA-BOOM with a splash a geyser of water blew skyward out of the lake. The water formed a huge floom that shot skyward and then fell back to the surface of the water with a small series of splashes. Farren laughed and then started to laugh even harder. He coughed and had some trouble breathing he was laughing so hard. As Jillian sat next to him arm in arm she looked over and saw a tear run down his cheek.

"I don't mean to ruin a moment here, but what is this?" she asked.

"A gift." Farren said. "A gift to an old man from a dear friend. I told Hawk about a geyser that had been in this lake once. It was a mistake but it became a bit of tourist attraction. I told him I would have loved to have seen it. And he made it happen."

"From what Juliette told me, he had a team of Imagineers out here in the middle of the night working on something but no one knew what," Jillian said.

KA-SPLASH the geyser fired off into the sky again. This time the water seemed to dance even longer on the glistening surface of the water.

"Thank you for bringing me here." Farren pulled her closer and gave her a kiss on her head.

"Oh and I almost forgot," She turned to him smiling. "After it happened, and it didn't know what it was, but I guess this is it. I am supposed to look at you and say Abracadabra!"

With a flourish she raised both hands in the air.

Farren laughed. "It was indeed magical. Thank you."

"You are welcome!" Jillian turned and looked back out at the water. "You know, Hawk scribbled the note for me and pinned it on the jacket the night of the explosion. He was in such a hurry he misspelled it."

"He what?" Farren raised an eyebrow.

"He misspelled it."

"What?"

"Abracadabra," she made a face as she wrinkled up her nose. "He spelled it AbracadaBar… but like I said he was in a hurry."

"Are you sure?" Farren sat up straighter.

"Yes," Jillian felt her thoughts freeze as she mentally saw the note and the way the word had been spelled. "It said AbracadaBar."

Farren stood and walked back to where Jillian had been piloting the boat.

"What are you doing?" she asked him.

"We have to get back to shore – NOW!"

KA-SLOOSH another blast of water pierced the sky and danced across the water as the pontoon boat churned the water up into a frenzy of splashes as they made their way back across Lake Fairview.

Bibliography

The following resources were invaluable in understanding the background, history, operation, and attractions within Walt Disney World.

Broggie, Michael. *Walt Disney's Railroad Story.* Virginia Beach, Virginia: Donning Company Publishers, 2012.

Canemaker, John. *Walt Disney's Nine Old Men & the Art of Animation.* New York: Hyperion, 2001.

Crawford, Michael. *The Progress City Primer*. Orlando : Progress City Press, 2015

Emerson, Chad Denver (editor). *Four Decades of Magic: Celebrating the First Forty Years of Disney World.* United States of America: Ayefour Publishing, 2011.

Gabler, Neal. Walt Disney: *Triumph of the American Imagination.* New York: Knopf, 2006.

Ghez, Didier. *Disney's Grand Tour.* United States of America: Theme Park Press, 2013.

Ghez, Didier editor. Brightman, Homer: *Life in the House of the Mouse.* United States of America: Theme Park Press, 2014.

Gordan, Bruce and Jeff Kurtti. *Walt Disney World: Then, Now and Forever.* New York: Disney Editions, 2008.

Green, Katherine and Richard. *The Man Behind the Magic: The Story of Walt Disney.* New York: Viking, 1991.

Hench, John. *Designing Disney: Imagineering and the Art of the Show.* New York: Disney Editions, 2003.

Imagineers. *Walt Disney Imagineering: A Behind the Dreams Look at Making the Magic.* New York: Hyperion, 1996.

Imagineers. *The Imagineering Field Guide to the Magic Kingdom at Walt Disney World.* New York: Disney Editions, 2005.

Korkis, Jim. *The Vault of Walt.* United States of America: Ayefour Publishing, 2010.

———. *The Vault of Walt Volume 5.* United States of America: Theme Park Press, 2016.

Kurtti, Jeff. *Imagineering Legends and the Genesis of the Disney Theme Park.* New York: Disney Editions, 2008.

Marling, Karal Ann. *Designing Disney's Theme Parks.* New York: Flammarion, 1997.

Miller, Diane Disney and Pete Martin. *The Story of Walt Disney.* New York: Holt, 1957.

Moran, Christian. *Great Big Beautiful Tomorrow – Walt Disney and Technology.* United States of America : Theme Park Press, 2015.

Neary, Kevin and David Smith. *The Ultimate Disney Trivia Book.* New York: Hyperion, 1992.

———. *The Ultimate Disney Trivia Book 2.* New York: Hyperion, 1994.

———. *The Ultimate Disney Trivia Book 3.* New York: Hyperion, 1997.

———. *The Ultimate Disney Trivia Book 4.* New York: Disney Editions, 2000.

Pedersen, R. A. *The Epcot Explorer's Encyclopedia.* Florida, USA: Encyclopedia Press, 2011.

Pierce, Todd James. *Three Years in Wonderland – The Disney Brothers, CV Wood, and the Making of the Great American Theme Park.* Jackson, Mississippi: University of Mississippi Press, 2016.

Ridgeway, Charles. *Spinning Disney's World: Memories of a Magic Kingdom Press Agent.* Branford, CT: Intrepid Traveler, 2007.

Smith, Dave. *Disney Trivia from the Vault.* New York: Disney Editions, 2013.

———. *Disney Facts Revealed.* New York: Disney Editions, 2016.

———. *Disney A to Z: the Official Encyclopedia.* New York: Hyperion, 1996; updated 1998, 2006.

Smith, Dave and Steven Clark. Disney: *The First 100 Years.* New York: Hyperion, 1999; Disney Editions, updated 2002.

Thomas, Bob. *The Art of Animation.* New York: Simon & Schuster, 1958.

———. *Walt Disney: An American Original.* New York: Simon & Schuster, 1976.

———. *Building a Company; Roy O. Disney and the Creation of an Entertainment Empire.* New York: Hyperion, 1998.

Thomas, Frank and Ollie Johnston. *The Illusion of Life: Disney Animation.* New York: Hyperion, 1995.

Vennes, Susan. *The Hidden Magic of Walt Disney World: Over 600 secrets of the Magic Kingdom, Epcot, Disney's Hollywood Studios, and Animal Kingdom.* Avon, MA: Adams Media, 2009.

Walt Disney World Explorer CD-ROM. Burbank, CA: Disney Interactive, 1996.

About the Author

Jeff Dixon is one of the rare people that can call themselves an Orlando native. He had a chance to spend time in Walt Disney's Magic Kingdom before it opened to the general public and was instantly captivated and in awe of the Disney magic. Jeff would later become a cast member and over the course of his lifetime created many memorable moments in the Walt Disney World resort. He has earned degrees in Sociology and Theology. His study and experiences at Walt Disney World have made him a collector of Theme-Parkology. His calling as a Transformational Architect has made him an expert in Story-Telling Methodology… and he has blended those ***ologies*** together to create a unique view of the world of Disney. His desire is to see each and every individual become the best version of themselves and he believes that life is not only a precious gift but a compelling adventure waiting to be lived.

Jeff lives in Orlando with his family and pastors an amazing church family in Winter Springs, Florida.

Printed in the USA
CPSIA information can be obtained
at www.ICGtesting.com
CBHW030432111024
15506CB00002B/8

9 781636 984957